THE LOYAL TRAITOR

The Loyal Traitor

Truth Is a Weapon

By Charles M. Wayne

Dragonfly Associates LLC
Publisher
New York | North Myrtle Beach
2026

Table of Contents

Dragonfly Associates LLC
Independent Publishers
publisher@dragonfly.associates

ISBN (Paperback Edition): 979-8-9936193-5-4

PUBLISHER'S NOTE

This is a work of fiction. Names, characters, places, and incidents are either the product of the author's imagination or are used fictitiously, and any resemblance to actual persons, living or dead, business establishments, events, or locales is entirely coincidental.

GSAFD: Spy stories. Classification: LCC PS3559.G54 Q36 2025
Wayne, Charles M.
Published in the United States 2026
10 9 8 7 6 5 4 3 2 1

Book Industry Study Group
FIC006000 FICTION / Thrillers / Espionage
https://www.bisg.org/fiction

For Louis W. Maier III—"Billy"

Fifty-five years of friendship.

Over twenty years as partners.

A lifetime of trust.

We built everything on a handshake. No contracts. No disputes. Not one argument that mattered. Just quiet understanding, year after year. In a world that demands contracts and proof, we had something better—we had belief in each other.

The man at the center of this novel is meant to represent integrity, loyalty, and strength of character. But the truth is, fiction has its limits. Will Morgan has nothing on Bill Maier.

I've seen the way Billy shows up for people—without hesitation, without expectation. He didn't just help when it was easy. He helped when it mattered. Lending money when others couldn't. Supporting family when they needed more than words. Giving someone a second chance—not just with advice, but by putting them back on their feet and believing in them when no one else would.

He never made a show of it. That's the part that stays with you. The quiet way he carried people. The way he stood beside you, steady as ever, whether things were going well or falling apart.

Trustworthy. Honest. Dependable. Loyal.

Not just words—but a way of living.

And through it all, he never lost his sense of humor. Even in the hard moments, he could find the light in things—and somehow make it easier for everyone else to breathe.

If you're lucky, you get a friend like Billy once in your life.

I was lucky enough to get him for all of mine.

—Thanks, Partner

INTRODUCTION TO THE WATCHTOWER SERIES

Most espionage thrillers focus on the CIA. The Watchtower Series explores a different battlefield—modern army counterintelligence.

At the center of these novels is Team Watchtower, an elite fictional unit within the U.S. Army Counterintelligence Command (ACIC), headquartered at Fort George G. Meade, Maryland. Led by Major Will Morgan and his investigators—known inside the Command as Morgan's Mustangs—the team hunts sleeper agents, insider threats, cyber-espionage networks, technology thieves, and covert foreign operations hidden within America's defense and intelligence infrastructure.

In the world of Watchtower, the National Defense Authorization Act of 2025 transformed ACIC into a hybrid counterintelligence and law-enforcement command with expanded global authority. Today, ACIC stands as the only counterintelligence organization with both foreign and domestic jurisdiction—and the legal authority to investigate, detain, arrest, and prosecute espionage within and beyond U.S. borders where national defense is involved.

Positioned beside the NSA, U.S. Cyber Command, and other intelligence agencies at Fort Meade, Watchtower operates at the intersection of espionage investigations, cyber warfare, digital forensics, and emerging technology.

The battlefield in these novels extends far beyond alleys and dead drops. Wars are fought through stolen algorithms, compromised supply chains, weaponized artificial intelligence, hacked infrastructure, and invisible cyber intrusions capable of crippling nations without firing a shot. The enemies are not merely spies but also hostile intelligence services, criminal syndicates, oligarchic networks, and private actors operating in the shadows between governments and corporations.

Many of the technologies and investigative methods depicted throughout this series are inspired by real-world intelligence capabilities. Readers familiar with the NSA's Tailored Access Operations (TAO) unit and the leaked Advanced Network Technology (ANT) catalog will recognize the influence of real cyber-espionage tools, firmware exploits, covert hardware implants, and supply-chain compromises that once sounded like science fiction but are now part of modern intelligence reality.

In the Watchtower Series, the most dangerous weapon is rarely a gun.

It is information.

Who controls it. Who steals it. And who is willing to betray everything to protect it.

Thank you for stepping into the world of Team Watchtower.

—Charles M. Wayne

Dramatis Personae

ACIC—Watchtower Operations

Will Morgan (Sentinel)—Major, ACIC team lead. Keeps his heart behind armor, then gives it once and never asks for it back. Commands as if every second of indecision costs a life, because it usually does. Quietly funded Gussie's treatment and would deny it if asked.

Sara Brandt (Vesper)—Senior field officer. Will's closest operational partner. Sees the disaster forming three moves out and can't always resist saying so. The calmer she sounds, the worse it has gotten.

Grace Roberts ("Gracie," Eagle)—Quantum physicist and intelligence analyst. The mind behind the science and the person who reads Will when no one else can. Protected under Operation Radiant Sentry. She waited for him because she knew what kind of man he was.

Derek Wilshire (Resonant)—Pattern-recognition specialist. Finds the forty-five-degree angle no one else noticed and won't let it go. Counts coins for calm and reads a room one signal at a time.

Rick Huang (Vector)—Cyber analyst. Loud, fast, and improvisational at a keyboard. Card counter and former Wall Street hand, which explains how comfortable he is reading other people's odds.

Cecil Brandon (Nomad)—Field operative. One of the few Will trusts without a second thought. Steady under fire, the kind of man you want at the bottom of the stairs first.

Gussie Brindisi (Monarch)—Team member. Watchtower, which means family. Her health pulled her off the field; the team brought her back on her feet for one bright, unguarded moment.

Cathy Wang (Echo)—Junior analyst. Sharp at the terminal and quietly observant. Her private doubt about Chrysalis-7 doesn't stay private for long.

Ed Perry—General, Will's superior. Carries rank lightly and plays his part when the team needs cover. Trusts Will enough to follow a thin excuse into a dark conference room.

Thomas Carrone (Glass)—Team member. Reliable hands, easy to move on a look. Close enough to the inner circle to be trusted with what Will won't say out loud.

Karen Bolanowski (Phoenix)—Embedded liaison turned operator. Grew from a desk role into the person holding the door. Stood as Nusquam's ground defense commander when the SVR came, and held the line.

SYBIL—Systemic Yield-Based Intelligence Liaison. A heuristic, adaptive learning system built for ACIC under a joint directive with the NSA. Her neural lattice linked every major open-source, law-enforcement, and classified database—everything from Census Bureau data to non-FISA NSA intercept repositories. Technically, she was a machine-learning construct. Practically, she was something closer to a silent partner.

Nusquam—he Vermont Facility

Genevieve Larsson (Sable, Gayle Persson, Gloria Jansson) Quantum physicist, former double agent. A ghost who learned to disappear in plain sight: floppy hat, halfway shades, a face

the satellites never caught. Protected at Nusquam, hunted by Moscow.

Shen Ke (Andrew Chan, Nemo) Quantum computing lead. Went underground through a prison swap that should not have worked, and tells the story like it cost him nothing. Drawn to Genevieve, careful about saying so.

Marie-Claire Pellitier (née Bouchard) General store owner. Knows who comes and goes on the back roads near the LaVoie farm. An informal asset who notices the deliveries no one is supposed to notice.

Allied Intelligence

Adrian Keller (Pythagoras) — Intelligence strategist. Thinks in puzzles and self-selection. The mind that proposed letting an adversary recruit a machine instead of a person.

Helena Quinn — DARPA strategist. Works the seam between the lab and the politics, and stays in the room when the fallout lands.

Joanna Lisik — Secret Service agent. Stands between Grace and the world without ever looking like she's standing there.

Judd Lockwood — Senior intelligence officer. Moves clean and fast when an asset's life is on the table. Trusts no channel that might leak back to Moscow.

Adversaries

Kir Smirnov (Cobalt)—SVR primary antagonist. Patient to the point of cruelty and not hunting secrets so much as closure. His brother Sergei died in a 1993 cover-up; the man who buried that thread died in his bed, and Kir was left with only Vermont.

Li Shun — PLA Strategic Support Force. The other hand reaching for the same prize, working the quantum theft from the far side of the board.

Jacob "Jax" Miller (Shutter) — SVR non-official cover officer. American on paper and in accent, built over years of layered fraud. Found Sable through a country store, a long lens, and a classified ad for a dog.

Mirov — SVR field controller. Takes Smirnov's orders and the Sable file without flinching. The hand that carries out the clean, deniable work.

In Memoriam and Off-Stage

Yasha Moravec — Deceased asset, architect of EIDOLON. Left a map instead of a manifesto, a string of coordinates pointing toward a box in the Alps.

Sergei Mikhailovich Smirnov — Kir's older brother. Died in 1993 trying to stop a transfer he believed was wrong. The accident no one was prosecuted for, and the wound that drives his brother still.

In this world, loyalty is variable. Trust is a liability. And everyone is running two operations at once.

CHAPTER ONE

Supermax

"Sometimes truth was what it needed to be. Sometimes only deception endured."

Florence, Colorado - ADX Supermax Transfer Bay - 0110 Hours Tango

Steel gates screech open as a blacked-out U.S. Marshals van rolled into the secure underground intake. An alert sounded across the internal security system: INMATE CATILINE - LEVEL 6 - SAM RESTRICTED.

Shen Ke, still wearing Bureau-issued restraints and black hood, was escorted by a heavily armed five-man Convict Movement Team (CMT). A supervisor from the Federal Bureau of Prisons confirmed the identity with biometrics. There were no verbal exchanges permitted—Shen's SAM protocol had already begun.

Admissions And Orientation Holding Area

The intake room was white. One Officer read from a script without looking up.

He was strip-searched under full-body scanner. Tattoos were scanned and logged. DNA sample verified against the DOJ's covert detainee database.

His few personal items—a cheap pen, one notepad with thermochromic ink, a pair of prison-issue glasses were bagged, documented, and later shredded under the Special Evidence Disposal Order.

H-Unit Secure Corridor

The H-Unit was the deepest tier, built to house terrorists and traitors, Codename: CATILINE was assigned to Shen's cell block—a nod to the Roman figure who waged clandestine war against the republic.

As the biometric door opened, dual overhead motion sensors activated. Shen was taken through a series of four sally ports, each required two independent operators to authorize passage.

All steps were recorded, logged, and timestamped.

Shen was locked in a sound-dampened cell. He stared at the 4-inch-thick plexiglass over steel bars.

A wall-mounted camera recorded every breath. Audio monitored 24/7 by a dual team from DOJ and FBI Behavioral Threat Assessment Unit.

Cell 42 - 0317 Hours Tango

The corridor was silent..

Camera feeds looped a thirty-second buffer of empty hallway. Cell 42-A was designated for "routine inspection." But nothing was routine tonight.

The man inside the cell sat silently on the edge of the concrete bed, dressed in the standard khaki jumpsuit, his thin fingers resting on his knees.

The lights droned overhead.

On the inside of his left wrist, four small characters in ballpoint ink, still sharp: 月是故鄉明. He'd written them at intake, in the seven seconds between the strip search and the jumpsuit, while the officer's back was turned to log his tattoos. The moon is brightest over the home village. Du Fu, eighth century, written from exile during a war that outlived him. Shen had memorized the poem at twelve, reciting it to a grandfather who corrected his tones with a chopstick laid flat across the table. The grandfather had been dead for nineteen years. The village was gone. The line was the only piece of either he could carry into what came next.

He blinked briefly, as if emerging from a long fog.

He didn't stand when the outer door clacked.

The hatch opened.

Two men entered without speaking. Their uniforms were generic black—no rank, no insignia. One carried a biometric override panel. The other, a tightly sealed duffel.

The first guard scanned a palm print, followed by a retinal check on the prisoner. A pause. A chirp. Green light. The cell door disengaged.

"Mr. Ke," one of them said.

He looked up slowly. "It's time?"

"Yes. You'll be pronounced dead at 08:14 from a brain aneurysm. Autopsy will be sealed. Body will be cremated."

He nodded once. The charade had been expected. Every man in his position knew death was the only way out.

They moved quickly. Clothes were swapped: civilian layers over a black thermal base. Beard trimmed. Contacts in. A minor prosthetic applied to break the facial profile.

Down the hall, two orderlies wheeled a covered stretcher. They passed two checkpoints, flashing fabricated incident reports and medical memos from a fake Bureau of Prisons physician.

The body under the sheet wasn't Shen. Swapped under executive authorization.

It was a nameless man from ADX's morgue, a lifer with no living family, no visitors, and a matching blood type. The kind of man who disappeared without questions.

Shen Ke followed his escort to the service elevator. No cameras on this shaft. It was designed for food delivery and body disposal—either worked, in this case.

Below, a tunnel. Sealed during construction. Denied in records. The air had the scent of rust, water, old copper. It led beneath the bluff to an unmarked service garage where a white utility van waited. No logos. Wyoming plates. Winter-dirty.

Inside waited a woman. Compact frame, gray field jacket, clipboard. She did not introduce herself.

"You're in the system as dead. Chinese surveillance chatter has already picked up the autopsy report. The leak was intentional. They're mourning a hero."

The van rolled out moments before shift change. No spotlight tracked it. No drone followed. No one on duty would remember it ever arrived.

He didn't speak. He watched the bluff disappear in the side mirror until the road bent and took it from him.

——

Three Months Later — Rural Vermont

The plan was simple in structure, complex in execution. A farmhouse tucked in the folds of misty pines. No neighbors for miles. A single phone line. Satellite uplink buried beneath a fresh dusting of snow. An unremarkable facility on the outside, spare and rural. A mini Area 51 hidden in plain sight. Inside: Nusquam. A quantum computer lab, designed and programmed by Shen, dedicated solely to military applications.

Inside, Shen Ke — now "Andrew Chan" — sat near a fire, reading a worn paperback in Cantonese.

In Beijing, a brass memorial. In Washington, his name struck from every file. In Vermont, a man no one was looking for.

Outside, the first snow of the season fell soundless on the pines.

Granville VT Route 100

The car sat alone at the edge of the small gravel lot, engine off, headlights dark, positioned so it looked like nothing more than an early arrival waiting for the day to begin. Frost clung to the edges of the windshield. The mountains were still silhouettes. Eight and a half miles away, Nusquam slept.

Inside the vehicle, he waited without fidgeting, hands resting lightly on the steering wheel, breath slow and measured. Anyone passing would have seen a man killing time before the post office opened, nothing more.

He reached into his jacket and produced a small, palm-sized device, matte black, unmarked. His thumb pressed a recessed button. There was no sound, no vibration. After a brief pause, a single green light appeared. Live. He watched it for a heartbeat longer than necessary, powered it down and slipped it back into an inner pocket.

Next came the briefcase. It clicked open on his lap. From it he removed a device no larger than a cigar box, heavier than it looked. He set it on the passenger seat and switched it on. Five amber lights came alive, rotating in a precise sequence-one, two, three, four, five, cycling again and again. He did not stare at them; he glanced, checked the rhythm, the timing, the absence of deviation. After roughly a minute, satisfied, he shut it down, returned it to the case, and closed the latch.

Stillness again.

When the post office lights flickered on and the door unlocked, he stepped out and returned to the role without seam. Inside, he moved with unhurried purpose. A single envelope to an address in Glilot, Tel Aviv-Yafo, Israel appeared from his coat. He chose the out-of-town slot set into the wall, angling his body enough so the security camera caught only the side of his head, never his face. The letter slid in. No pause. No correction.

Moments later, he was gone.

The car pulled out smoothly, tires crunching on gravel, merging onto the road without haste. Within seconds it blended into the Vermont morning, leaving behind nothing but an ordinary errand completed—and no reason at all to remember who had done it.

CHAPTER TWO

Echo Reef

Arlington, VA -DARPA Headquarters 0930 Hours R

The room was already hot with disagreement when Helena Quinn stopped pacing and let the silence stretch.

The Director of the Defense Advanced Research Projects Agency—"the Pentagon's brain"—took the floor. Across from her sat Major General Owen Edwards, commander of the Army Intelligence and Security Command (INSCOM), and Brigadier General Ed Perry, commander of the Army Counterintelligence Command (ACIC). At Perry's side was Major Will Morgan, his presence unusual for such a senior gathering. He had just gotten back from his presidential-mandated month of leave and Helena had pulled him in before he could even check in at Fort Meade. Helena had insisted. She didn't want her message filtered through ranks or watered down in a memo. Morgan's team Watchtower would inherit Nusquam; their commander needed the unvarnished truth.

Helena carried authority like a tailored suit—unassuming, but impossible to miss. Her words were precise, each pause intentional, the kind that made even generals lean forward.

"Nusquam exists," she said finally. "And if we mishandle it, we won't get a second chance."

General Edwards leaned back in his chair, arms folded, jaw tight. "That's the problem, Director Quinn. Everyone in this room has been told it's operational. We've also been told it's revolutionary, transformational, and existentially important. But every time we ask what it actually does — what it delivers in practical, defensible terms — we get metaphors."

A few heads nodded around the table.

Helena met his gaze. "Because the underlying science doesn't map cleanly to twentieth-century acquisition language."

"That's not an answer," Owen shot back. "That's a warning sign. We're being asked to protect facilities we can't fully explain, fund programs we can't benchmark, and prioritize threats we can't quantify. Every black project in this building claims it's the hinge point of the future."

She stepped closer to the table, palms flat on the polished wood. "Nusquam is different."

"You say that about all your new programs," Owen replied evenly. "Until the next one."

"Here's the part we can explain," she said. "Nusquam changes the confidence level of everything upstream — sensors, prediction models, command decisions. It doesn't give you a weapon. It gives you truth density. A satellite photo where every decoy tank is circled in red before you even know to look for them."

Owen exhaled through his nose. "Truth density isn't a line item."

"No," Helena agreed. "But survivability is. Decision advantage is. Strategic surprise, or the lack of it is."

He leaned forward now. "And how do we defend that in a budget hearing? When a senator asks why Nusquam gets priority over missile defense, cyber, hypersonics? When they ask why a farm in Vermont needs more protection than a carrier group?"

Helena didn't hesitate. "Because Nusquam is the thing that tells you whether the missile warning is real, whether the cyber intrusion is noise or preparation, whether the hypersonic launch is a bluff or a first strike."

The room went quiet again — this time heavier.

Owen tapped his pen once against the table. "You're asking us to fund an oracle."

"I'm asking you to fund the protection of epistemic advantage," she said.

"And if it fails?" someone down the table asked.

Helena turned. "We lose money."

Owen sat back again, quieter now. "You understand the bind you're putting us in."

"I do," she said. "But obscurity doesn't make Nusquam less real. It makes it easier to kill with spreadsheets."

The chair at the end of the table creaked as someone shifted.

Owen nodded once, reluctantly. "We need a new priority framework."

Helena allowed herself a thin smile. "That's why you're here."

She let the moment hold, then turned toward Perry and Morgan.

"It's time Army Intelligence — especially Counterintelligence — comes fully inside the loop on Operation Echo Reef."

Her voice was calm, but the weight of her words pressed on the room.

The lights dimmed until the room was little more than silhouettes. The soft, surgical hum of the smart-wall powered up. The first slide glowed to life: Quantum Defense Applications.

"Generals," she said, "this morning I'm not here to explain quantum computing. I'm here to show you what it can do on its best days."

Perry's eyes narrowed slightly. "Best days?"

"Yes." Helena's tone didn't shift. "Before I show you anything, you need to know what you're looking at. ECHORITHM is still experimental. Its coherence times are short, its error-correction layers, frankly, are held together with duct tape and prayer." A thin, humorless smile. "What you're about to see represents the runs that worked. The lucky collapses of the wavefunction. For every result I'm about to put on that wall, there are nine I can't show you because the machine produced noise."

She let the room absorb that.

"I'm not selling you a finished weapon. I'm selling you a head start on physics that's coming whether we fund it or not. Watch what it does when it works. You decide what it's worth to be the country that gets there first."

She clicked the remote.

The wall behind her erupted into a lattice of swirling interference patterns.

"This is the Nusquam prototype—ECHORITHM. Nemo's machine. Fragile, temperamental, and powerful in ways classical computation can't imitate."

She tapped the control. The lattice collapsed into a 64-digit encrypted key, glowing in icy blue.

"First demonstration. Watch closely."

She divided the wall into two halves:

Left: a standard Army-grade brute-force cracking simulation.

Right: ECHORITHM quantum factoring module.

"General Edwards," Helena said, "how long would INSCOM estimate to break a key of this size with classical resources?"

General Edwards grunted. "Decades. Maybe longer. Could require a cluster the size of Fort Meade."

"Correct."

The left simulation began churning, slowly, painfully, counters climbing toward infinity.

"Now, quantum."

The right side pulsed. Blinked and burst on the screen:

KEY FACTORED — 0.0042 SECONDS

General Edwards sat back slowly. "And this is one of the runs that worked."

"This is one of the runs that worked," Helena confirmed.

Perry's jaw tightened. "How many didn't?"

"On a key of that size, this week? Eleven failures before this one. Some produced wrong factors. Most produced nothing at all."

Will didn't move, but his stillness was sharper now—like a knife laid flat.

Helena turned back to the room. "This is not a faster crowbar. When it works, it's a master key. The problem is knowing, in the moment, whether you're holding the key or the noise."

She didn't let the silence settle. "Second demonstration."

The screen went blank except for a live feed: a swirling chaos of propaganda posts, synthetic media, fake accounts, all harvested from an adversary botnet during the last six hours.

Helena tapped again. A second stream appeared beside it — the same data, quantum-analyzed.

In the blink of an eye, the fog cleared.

Bots glowed red. Synthetic video signatures pulsed violet. GAN faces detached from their background vectors. Russian, Chinese, and proxy narratives braided into visible strands of manipulation.

The room went quiet.

Helena stepped aside so they could see the two screens fully—chaos on one side, clarity on the other.

"A flashlight versus sunlight," she said. "We've been walking through fog for twenty years. Quantum turns the fog into glass."

General Edwards' eyes hadn't left the right-hand screen. "And the runs that don't work? On a dataset like that?"

"Phase errors collapse the analysis. The fog comes back. Sometimes the machine tells us bots are humans and humans are bots. The cost of a confident wrong answer in this domain is higher than the cost of no answer at all. That's part of what makes the stabilization problem urgent."

Perry leaned forward. "Show me something offensive, Helena."

She studied him for a heartbeat, before she obliged. The screen shifted to a satellite map over the South China Sea. Shipping lanes. Buoys. AIS beacons. Military patrol paths.

"This is real-time quantum signal inference. The prototype can detect spoofed satellite positions, naval ghost routes, and hidden vessels by analyzing electrical noise patterns that classical sensors treat as background static."

She highlighted a section of open water. A moment later, a submerged submarine silhouette appeared, one not listed in any U.S. or allied database.

General Edwards stiffened. "We didn't know that was there."

"No," Helena said. "But ECHORITHM did. On the third attempt this morning. The first two attempts placed it forty kilometers off."

"And if an adversary gets there first?" Perry asked.

Helena's expression hardened.

"We become visible. Every classified briefing, every nuclear command handshake, every operation you've ever buried under three layers of clearance." Whoever stabilizes coherence first doesn't only win a race. They rewrite the physics of intelligence. And everyone else plays catch-up for the next fifty years."

Will was looking at the dark patch of ocean where the submarine had been a moment before. He had spent the past month on a beach in North Carolina trying not to think about his job. He had read three novels and learned how to make a passable coq au vin and gone running every morning until his knee started to complain. He had not been ready to come back. He was not ready now. But he understood what was happening in this room, and he understood that Watchtower was about to become the agency standing between a machine that was right one time in ten and the people who would kill for a working version of it. He thought, briefly and uselessly, of Grace — of what it would cost to tell her any version of this that didn't terrify her, and of how quickly she would see through whatever version he chose. She would know before he finished the sentence. That was the worst part. She would already know.

He pulled himself back to the room.

Perry was absorbing the full weight of what Helena had said. General Edwards clasped his hands, eyes narrowed. "So Echo Reef is only our head start."

"It is," Helena said. "Our first, fragile foothold on the second floor of the ocean."

As the meeting broke up, Helena lifted a hand toward Perry and Morgan. "Stay a moment."

The others filed out. The door clicked shut behind General Edwards.

Helena turned to Will. "Everyone in this building gets a version of what you just heard. You get the unfiltered version because Watchtower inherits this.

The successes and the failures. The keys and the noise. The machine that can save the country and the machine that can collapse every secret we have, sometimes in the same week."

Will met her gaze. His face gave nothing away.

"Understood."

Helena studied him and then nodded once. "Welcome back from leave, Major."

——

I-95 North — 1120 Hours

Ed Perry and Will Morgan rode in silence in the back of the General's Escalade, the red plate with its two white stars gliding north at a steady, unhurried pace. The sun dropping low, turning the highway copper.

Perry closed the folder on his lap.

"You're thinking what I'm thinking."

"That if we can hunt their moles with quantum, they can hunt ours."

Perry nodded once. "And we've got more seams. One weak clearance chain, one sloppy compartment—and quantum cuts through it like glass."

Will leaned back. "The real problem isn't building Echo Reef. It's keeping it contained, from them and from ourselves."

"That's why POTUS locked it down," Perry said. "No CIA. No DIA. No FBI. Only us and your people."

Perry watched him for a beat. "Sometimes the enemy isn't foreign."

Silence settled again, broken only by the tires and the hum of the road.

"Nusquam can't afford a misstep," Will said.

Perry reached into his jacket and handed him a photo. Snow. A fencepost. A slender metallic device half-buried in shadow.

"NSA found it three hundred meters outside the perimeter," Perry said. "Passive. No transmission. Designed for physical recovery."

Will studied it. "Whoever planted it knew our envelopes."

"They told Nemo," Perry said. "Didn't tell the lab. Didn't tell DARPA. And Nemo asked for you—specifically."

Will looked up. "He's scared."

"That's what concerns me."

Will handed the photo back. "I'll send Sara and Genevieve ahead. Quiet sweep. Perimeter, ingress points, wildlife cams. And I want Genevieve in the lab before I get there."

"Good," Perry said. "Brandt sees people. Larsson sees the math."

Perry hesitated, “Helena doesn’t want Nusquam hardened.” He said.

Will didn’t blink. “She wants it ordinary.”

“A farm that never changes,” Perry said. “No fences. No growth. No signal it’s worth watching.”

Will considered that as the car rolled past an exit sign. “That’s not naïve. That’s camouflage.”

“Or a gamble.”

“Continuity is the best disguise there is,” Will said. “People stop watching what never changes.”

Perry looked down at the photo again. “Someone still came looking.”

“And that means it worked long enough to matter,” Will replied. “Now we watch the road. Who drives it. Who doesn’t.”

Perry studied him, then nodded. “All right. Nusquam stays plain.”

“And watched,” Will said. “In the right ways.”

Perry studied Will for a long moment. “You know why this job breaks people?”

Will didn’t hesitate. “Because success looks like nothing happened.”

A small smile tugged at the corner of Perry’s mouth. “And failure looks like history.”

The Escalade continued north, unremarkable among hundreds of other cars, just another vehicle on the road.

CHAPTER THREE

Operation Nemo

Granville, VT - Route 100

Marie-Claire Pelletier drove the same stretch of road every morning, out of habit more than necessity.

Route 100 curved gently north out of Granville, the trees leaning inward as if listening. In winter, the road narrowed under snowbanks; in summer it opened up, green and forgiving. She knew every bend, every frost heave, every place where the fog liked to settle low and thick in the early hours.

She passed the old farm a short ways after the third curve.

She didn't look at it directly. That would feel rude. Instead, she let it sit in her peripheral vision, the way you do with something familiar that's changed enough to unsettle you.

The place had belonged to Arthur Lavoie once. Arthur with his bad knees and quiet laugh, Arthur who'd insisted on shoveling his own steps until the winter finally beat him. Marie-Claire had brought him soup on Thursdays and listened to the radio with him when the power went out. She still expected to see his old pickup parked crooked by the barn.

Instead, there were trucks.

Not today—not right now—but there had been. Plenty of them. Over the past year. White vans mostly. A few dark ones. Out-of-state plates. They came early and left late and never stayed long enough to feel like they belonged.

What struck her wasn't the traffic. It was what didn't follow.

No dumpsters.

No lumber piles.

No half-finished siding or plastic sheeting flapping in the wind.

No chatter at the store about delays or contractors or permits.

Work without mess. Motion without result.

Except—and this she noticed only later, in passing—there had been a window of activity. Sustained, intense, and deliberately hidden. She'd seen it around the turn of the seasons, autumn bleeding into early winter, when the work had shifted from daytime to something else entirely.

She couldn't see behind the barn where the construction was actually happening. The angle of the road didn't permit it. But she could hear. Heavy equipment arriving at night—always at night—hydraulic sounds, the beep of backing vehicles, the low thrum of machinery working in darkness. The activity seemed endless: midnight sometimes, once she'd heard it at three in the morning, the sound carrying on the cold still air.

Trucks arrived after dark. Swarms of utility-clad workers, visible briefly in headlights, toiled in the winter cold with a sense of hurried necessity. The work was relentless—not the steady rhythm of normal construction, but urgent, driven, as if against a deadline.

As suddenly as it had come, the activity ceased.

A short time after that, a new power substation was built a short ways down the road. She thought it strange because the only new facility in the area was whatever had been so rapidly built at the LaVoie farm. The timing was precise—the substation erected right after the construction behind the barn had finished. The crew that arrived was efficient, professional, moving through the work with the kind of coordination that suggested this had been planned months in advance. Utility-clad workers in the winter cold, long hours, high pressure.

For all the activity, there was not much additional traffic at the general store. The same early morning regulars, coffee, and buns—and nothing else. It was as if everyone involved had been instructed not to talk, or perhaps they simply understood that some things didn't warrant conversation.

What remained was silence. And the small, certain knowledge that something significant had been built in the dark, on purpose, in a hurry.

Marie-Claire signaled left at the junction and continued on toward Hancock, the heater lowly humming. She opened the market and breathed in the familiar smells of coffee and bread.

By seven-thirty the regulars began to arrive. Marie-Claire greeted them all the same way, warm and attentive without pressing.

That was the skill her parents had taught her behind the counter at Bouchard's Country Store:

Listen, but don't lean.

Remember, but don't repeat.

Around ten, someone mentioned the farm.

Not by name, a comment, tossed casually.

"Must be some operation they're running up there," the man said, nodding vaguely north. "All those vehicles."

Marie-Claire smiled politely and slid his receipt across the counter.

"People come and go," she said. "Always have."

Which was mostly true.

After lunch, when the store quieted, she stood by the window with her coffee and watched the road. A dark SUV passed—too clean for the season, moving at a speed just shy of careless. She noted it without judgment. Not because she suspected anything. Because she noticed.

On the drive home that evening, the light was fading. The farm came into view again, the house sitting back from the road. No porch light yet. No sign of life.

And yet—

A brief flicker. Something inside like a reflection off glass.

Marie-Claire slowed without realizing she had.

She thought of Arthur. Of the way he'd once said, "You know when something doesn't want to be seen, Marie-Claire? It's not hiding. It's holding still."

She drove on.

At home, she made dinner with her husband, listened to his stories. Later, she spoke to one of her sons on the phone—Boston noise in the background, a life moving too fast for Granville.

That night, as she locked her door and turned off the lights, she looked toward the darkened road beyond her window.

But some part of her, the part that knew what belonged had begun taking notes.

She looked once more toward the road.

CHAPTER FOUR

Tasking

Fort Meade - ACIC Headquarters - Ernie Pyle Street

The McDonough Building sat on Ernie Pyle Street, tucked well inside the secure perimeter of Fort Meade. From the outside, it looked like any other government structure. Unremarkable. That was the point.

Access started on the first floor, the only part of the facility above ground. You checked in with a receptionist who worked from a clean, uncluttered desk. No small talk. Your name was verified against the visitor manifest.

A retinal scan. A brief pause. A green light. You were issued a temporary badge that never left your line of sight. Most visitors never went any further.

Beyond reception sat a conference room positioned outside the first sally port. It was designed for those who didn't need access to Watchtower itself. A controlled space. Because once you went past that point, everything changed.

Watchtower lived below ground. Two subterranean levels, each protected by its own sally port. To enter, you didn't move alone. A Marine escort met you at the threshold.

In the elevator he keyed in the access codes himself, his body angled deliberately to shield the pad. You understood immediately. Even the act of entry was classified.

The doors opened with a muted mechanical release. Inside, the first operations floor came alive all at once. A low, constant energy filled the space.

Directly ahead and slightly to the left sat the bullpen, the operational heart of Watchtower. A dozen workstations formed a tight grid. Each station carried three in line monitors, glowing with data streams and live feeds. Analysts moved between them with quiet urgency.

To the right, a single office stood near the entrance, beyond it a passage leading into the expansion area. That space opened up into a ring of six offices surrounding four additional workstations. The same configuration. Three screens per station. Everything mirrored. Everything scalable. It was clear this place had grown, and was built to grow further.

Will Morgan's office sat just to the left of the entrance. Deliberate positioning. From his desk, he could see the bullpen. He could see the door. Nothing happened in Watchtower without crossing his line of sight.

A wide interior window looked out over the bullpen, giving him a clear, uninterrupted view. With a single click, the glass could turn opaque, sealing him off when needed. Most of the time, it stayed clear. He preferred to see everything. To his left, a secure conference room connected directly to his office. It allowed him to move from observation to decision without ever stepping into the open.

A large display screen hung on the exterior wall of that room, mirrored by an identical screen inside. Briefings could shift from open floor to sealed compartment in seconds.

The rest of the offices formed a quiet perimeter around the bullpen, smaller and efficient. Every inch of Watchtower had a purpose.

And once you were inside, you understood something immediately. It was a control node.

——

Fort Meade - Watchtower Ops - 1400 Hours R

Will entered Watchtower Ops for the first time in a month.

The space felt different today. More alive. More aligned.

Watchtower had returned from the enforced month-long break with the same unspoken cohesion that had carried them through Radiant Sentry, but there was something else layered beneath it, a sense of readiness that hummed just below the surface.

He took it in silence.

His deputy Sara Brandt's eyes sharpened when she saw him.

The month away had been restorative, long runs, lots of tennis, long overdue sleep, brunches with friends who still didn't understand what she did for a living. but her brain had never powered down.

Patterns still whispered to her even when she tried to ignore them.

She stood there watching people moving with purpose, and the ambient hum of servers. A smile tugged at her lips.

"Back where you belong," she murmured.

Break or not, Sara had missed the pressure. Missed Will's spare, quiet sentences that somehow cut straight to the heart of a problem.

She tugged her hair into a ponytail and headed toward her office.

A new case was coming. She could feel it.

Genevieve Larsson was now a part of the team as much for her own protection as for utility stepped through the biometric door and paused, letting Watchtower's familiar atmosphere settle over her. After a month away, splitting time between a seldom used ACIC training range and a quiet apartment where she'd forced herself to rest. The return felt like slipping back into a well-cut suit.

Breaks were odd for her, necessary, but odd. Stillness sharpened her more than it softened her.

She scanned the corridor automatically, Nothing out of place. But something in the air felt... coiled. As if Meade itself had inhaled and not yet exhaled.

Genevieve loved that sensation. It meant a new case was coming.

——

"Sara...Gene," Will said waving them into his office.

Like his epigrammatic speech, the office reflected the man. Efficient. Revealing absolutely nothing.

Only two personal objects broke the disciplined austerity.

On the credenza behind the desk stood an aged 6×9 portrait of a beautiful woman in a pensive pose, graceful, timeless. Everyone assumed she was his mother. No one ever asked twice.

Beside it rested a small, meticulously crafted model of an ancient Greek trireme. The ship was the real mystery. When someone finally worked up the courage to ask about it, Will only smiled—an expression so brief it might have been a trick of the light—and said, "It's a question I'm still answering."

The desk itself was a monument to precision.

One file sat centered on the desk, its spine aligned perfectly parallel to the edge. A right-hand return held two large monitors, a slim keyboard, and a small black remote. One click of the remote and the room's floor-to-ceiling windows shifted from crystal clear to fully opaque, sealing conversations from even the idea of outside observation.

A small meeting table surrounded by three chairs. A glass door led to an adjoining eight-seat conference room outfitted with a wall-mounted Vibe screen, usually scrolling with live threat maps or secured briefings.

The chairs were neutral, uninviting, designed to make visitors state their purpose and leave.

Over the years Will Morgan had acquired something like a mythical persona. A man whose quiet demeanor made him a disquieting mystery to those outside Team Watchtower.

No one at the ACIC Training Directorate had ever officially met Major Will Morgan, but everyone knew who he was. Or thought they did.

Some were absolutely convinced he was a myth given human shape.

Others whispered stories, reverent, exaggerated, darkly funny and full of the kind of half-truths that make legends durable.

No one understood how or why he had assembled such an eclectic cadre of rejects, and irreverent rascals.

Ed Perry once tried to explain it to a room full of department heads.

"They're not show ponies," he'd said, tapping his pen thoughtfully. "They're sure-footed mustangs."

Someone in the meeting muttered, "Morgan's Mustangs."

Ed adopted it instantly.

"I hope you're both well rested because this next assignment is as important as it is strange," he said as he handed them files marked top-secret eyes only,

The room settled into a taut, almost reverent quiet as Sara and Genevieve leaned over the thick Nusquam files. LED light washed across the pages and their faces—white, clinical, unforgiving—showing every flicker of reaction with merciless clarity.

At first, there was curiosity.

Sara's brows drew together in that analytical crease she got whenever something didn't immediately map to any known doctrine. Beside her, Genevieve tilted her head a fraction to the left. It was her tell when she encountered a piece of intelligence that didn't behave as expected.

A few pages deeper, bewilderment took hold.

Sara blinked twice, the way she did when processing an equation she suspected was engineered to insult her. Genevieve's lips parted, just slightly, as if the words on the page had momentarily stolen her concept of the possible.

Concern followed like a cold draft through the office. Sara's shoulders tightened, rising half an inch as she skimmed a page describing one of Nemo's early prototypes and the classified fallout around it. Genevieve leaned back the smallest degree, her eyes narrowing with the dawning recognition that whatever this was, it was outside normal physics. Outside normal anything.

Finally, disbelief.

A shared, silent disbelief that needed no words.

Sara's jaw set, the muscle feathering in slow, incredulous acceptance that, yes, this was real, and Will had been sitting on it. Genevieve's gaze froze on a paragraph describing the earliest echoes of Echo Reef. She looked as though she had just read the first lines of a secret history of the universe—one written in someone's handwriting she almost recognized.

Neither woman spoke. They just stood there, the files open, and their expressions shifting in four unmistakable stages that told Will everything he needed to know:

Will didn't ask what they thought. He didn't need to—their expressions had already given him the entire spectrum. So he simply folded his hands in his lap and laid out the orders in a quiet, even tone that cut through the stunned air of the room.

"You'll both depart for Nusquam first thing in the morning," he said. "A charter flight to Burlington is wheels up at zero-seven-hundred. Once you land, you'll run a preliminary security assessment of the facility and get an updated read on Nemo's condition. You'll remain on-site until we know what we're dealing with."

He didn't raise his voice. He didn't soften it either. It was the same tone he used when a mission had already begun.

"Cecil will join you in a couple of days," he added. "I want his eyes on the perimeter and on Nemo himself."

He let the words settle. No follow-up questions. Just the operational truth, delivered cleanly.

Sara pushed herself deeper into the chair, her movements slow and almost mechanical. The open file still lay in front of her, and she stared at it as if it might rearrange into something more reasonable if she looked long enough.

Beside her, Genevieve sank into the second chair. She placed one hand flat against her thigh, grounding herself, her eyes unfocused in that way she fell into after reading intelligence that rewrote an entire map of reality. Her jaw worked once—an aborted effort to speak— she simply went still.

Neither woman spoke. They just sat there in Will's sparse, immaculate office, the hum of the overhead air duct suddenly too loud, the files lying between them.

For a long, heavy moment, the only sound was the quiet, steady turn of Will Morgan's breathing giving them space to absorb the fact that by morning, their lives would be different. And nothing in the Nusquam file suggested the change would be gentle.

——

Fort Meade - Watchtower Ops

SYBIL was the Command's edge. An artificial intelligence built from NSA collection systems, DARPA research, and years of classified counterintelligence data. She operated inside Fort Meade's most secure networks, buried behind layers of compartmented access. Most people in the building did not know she existed.

She processed intercepted calls, financial records, encrypted traffic, surveillance feeds, travel manifests, and public data at the same time. A human analyst might follow three or four active threads before fatigue set in. SYBIL tracked thousands without losing continuity.

To Will Morgan's team, SYBIL felt less like software and more like another analyst in the room. She never slept. Never lost focus. Never cared about office politics or careers.

Her official name was Systemic Yield-Based Intelligence Liaison. The title had been chosen carefully. The people who designed her understood that analysts worked better with systems they could talk to naturally. So they gave her a name people would use in conversation.

"SYBIL, rerun the anomaly filter."

"Yes, Major."

The voice was female, calm, and controlled. No emotion. No hesitation. Some analysts still swore they heard attitude in the pauses.

SYBIL began as an NSA research program. Over time, the Command expanded her access and trained her on real investigations. Her reach covered military databases, financial crime records, travel systems, law enforcement reporting, open-source material, and intelligence holdings that did not require a FISA warrant.

That limit mattered.

SYBIL could not touch protected domestic collection without human authorization. A request required legal review, documentation, and a signature trail. Will enforced that rule hard. He knew what happened when people convinced themselves the mission justified everything.

Technically, SYBIL was a machine-learning platform. In practice, she acted more like a senior case analyst with unlimited memory.

Her strongest capability came from the behavioral modeling layer built into her architecture. She tracked speech patterns, timing shifts, spending changes, travel deviations, contact frequency, and stress indicators buried inside ordinary conversations. A subject who suddenly called home every night after years of silence meant something. A contractor who changed gym locations twice in a month meant something. Most signals were harmless alone. Together they formed patterns.

SYBIL assigned probability scores, threat rankings, and predictive estimates. She could flag a likely recruitment attempt before the target realized they were being cultivated.

She also built long-term behavioral baselines. The longer she observed someone, the more accurate her projections became. That included the Watchtower team itself. She learned cadence, habits, preferred wording, and silence patterns during interviews.

Will kept his distance from the mythology growing around the system.

“SYBIL finds correlations,” he reminded the team more than once. “She doesn’t understand loyalty. She doesn’t understand fear. Data tells you what happened. It doesn’t always tell you why.”

He trusted the system because he understood its limits.

“Use SYBIL for pattern recognition. Then use your own judgment. A machine can flag a liar. It still takes a human being to decide what the lie means.”

CHAPTER FIVE

Nusquam

Burlington International Airport 0950 Hours R

The UC-35B Citation Encore cut through the morning haze and touched down with practiced grace at Patrick Leahy Burlington International Airport, Vermont's largest and most discreetly watched airfield. The hour-and-forty-minute flight from Davison Army Airfield at Fort Belvoir was uneventful—on paper, a routine civilian charter. The passenger manifest listed only two names: Sandra Bowman and Gayle Persson, aliases for Sara Brandt, Counterintelligence Agent, and Genevieve Larsson, Senior Scientific Analyst for ACIC.

As the sleek low-winged, twin-engine jet taxied across the tarmac, it passed under the weathered but resolute "Green Mountain Boys" banner—an original Revolutionary-era flag now proudly replicated on the hangar of the Vermont Army National Guard Aviation Facility.

There was nothing theatrical about the arrival. That was the point.

In intelligence work, blending in was survival—and while both women had trained for low visibility, the truth was: you can't always mute presence. Even in black parkas and ball caps, even with civilian posture and neutral makeup, Sara's poised intensity and Genevieve's cool, exacting calm stood out like anomaly vectors in a SIGINT graph.

The National Guard soldiers were happy to give them a lift to the car rental counter inside the terminal—though a few clearly lingered longer than necessary, smiling a little too wide. Sara slid her Sandra Bowman license and credit card across the counter with the same confidence she used when handing off a burner to a source. The clerk didn't blink. They had a Hyundai Palisade waiting in economy silver, Vermont plates.

They didn't waste time.

Once on Route 100 South, cutting through wind-worn forest and sleepy hamlets, the atmosphere in the car shifted from idle to focused.

Their secret service detail ordered by President Stratton from Essex Junction followed in a trace car.

"Granville?" Genevieve asked, half-checking her iPad GPS. "Middle of nowhere. Population 303."

"Exactly," Sara said, eyes on the road. "Three hundred people, 127 households, 5.8 humans per square mile. Perfect place to go extinct."

Genevieve smirked. "Nemo."

Sara nodded.

"Andrew Chan. Chosen by Witness Protection (WITSEC). 'Chan' for being one of the most common Chinese surnames in the West. 'Andrew' because it ranks in the top twenty first names Chinese parents pick for assimilation."

Genevieve flipped through her encrypted briefing notes.

"And Nemo... Latin for 'no one.' Literary ghost. Man without a country."

"Or a spy without a side." Sara glanced over. "Perfect fit."

The hour and twenty-minute drive took them through long stretches of barren pasture and iced-over streams. Occasionally, a post-and-beam barn would rise in the distance, framed in the washed-out amber of winter light. Every once in a while, the landscape would flash a memory—some Cold War safehouse or SIGINT relay—then fade.

They were headed toward Chan's new identity, buried at the edge of Granville's south ridge. A remote farmhouse reborn as a classified sanctuary, ringed in silent layers of surveillance, fencing, and federal airspace controls.

The Secret Service had detailed three agents for physical protection—though technically, ACIC held jurisdiction under a joint directive with DOJ and the Defense Threat Reduction Agency (DTRA). Their objective was two-fold: assess existing physical and digital security protocols, and determine how stable "Nemo" truly was after two decades of walking the double line.

There was the persistent rumor.

"They really built a lab in the barn?" Genevieve asked, side-eying her screen. "Quantum-class?"

Sara shrugged.

"That's what the bill says. DHS and DOE shell accounts authorized almost six million for 'rural renovation and applied materials integration.' No one calls it a quantum computer outright—but the wiring diagram's thick enough to power a research center."

"Doesn't make sense. Energy draw alone would blow every substation within ten miles."

"Unless it's not built yet," Sara added. "Or it's not for computing."

"Well, there it is," Said Genevieve reading her tablet, "They actually built a new substation for him."

They rounded the bend off a narrow gravel shoulder—cell service dropped to a single bar. The final mile was paved in silence, broken only by the faint hiss of the tires on wet stone and the distant, rhythmic thrum of high-tension lines.

As the old farmhouse came into view—roofline modernized, the barn's upper window sealed with high-grade ballistic glass—Sara slowed the SUV.

The place looked... still.

But it wasn't.

Inside those walls was a man named Shen Ke, now called Andrew Chan, codename Nemo, who had played the Chinese Ministry of State Security (MSS) like a violin for over fifteen years.

And now, all he had left was secrecy, surveillance, and the hope the wrong people never found out he wasn't really dead.

——

The Farmhouse – Codename Nusquam

The driveway crunched under the weight of the Palisade as Sara pulled in and brought the SUV to a deliberate stop outside the barn-turned-laboratory codenamed Nusquam - Latin for nowhere. The structure had been gutted and rebuilt beneath the original frame—an architect's homage to rural camouflage. The siding was preserved, but the foundation was reinforced, window angles adjusted for optimal coverage, and heat signatures vented through a buried coil system.

Three men stepped out of the main house's side entrance.

Standard issue cold-weather jackets, dark jeans, earpieces. Secret Service agents, clean-cut, posture squared, but bored—the way men get when danger is theoretical.

Sara rolled down the window.

"Sandra Bowman, ACIC. That's Gayle Persson."

The lead agent nodded, stepping forward. His eyes took in everything: the rental plate, the tread on their boots, the way Genevieve's coat was zipped up too precisely.

"You're clear. He's expecting you. Barn."

They parked.

The inside of the barn smelled faintly of ozone and cedar. A fresh coat of insulating stain covered the walls, and warm air rolled from a recessed HVAC system. There were two floors: the upper mostly empty, the lower converted into a climate-stabilized chamber with fiber-coupled workstations, biometric locks, and a Faraday-shielded server rack humming in a corner.

And seated at the center of it all, in a gray wool sweater and quiet slacks, was Andrew Chan - Nemo .

He was older than his last intelligence file. Not aged, but tempered. Sara had read enough of his file to know he was built to disappear. But now, in the quiet of isolation and resurrection, there was something else behind the eyes. A watchfulness. Not the kind born of fear—but of habit. Of knowing he could never afford to stop calculating.

He didn't rise when they entered. He simply looked at them for a long moment before speaking.

"Which one of you is ACIC?"

Sara stepped forward. Genevieve held back, as they'd planned.

"I'm Sandra Bowman, officially. Sara Brandt, if it matters more to you."

He studied her, and offered a dry smile.

"You look younger than I expected. But your file didn't mention arrogance, so that's a good sign."

Sara said, "I keep it off the file. People get nervous when they see it documented."

Nemo smiled.

"This your work?" she asked.

"Some of it. Some of it's legacy Defense Threat Reduction Agency junk they thought I wouldn't notice. The cabinet labeled 'calibration tools' has a surveillance tap hardwired into the back panel. If that's your team's idea of secure installation, you've got a mole or an idiot."

Genevieve stepped up, now interested.

"Where's the tap connected?"

"Outbound signal. Standard compression, but the handshake's off-pattern—probably satellite-bounced. Not domestic."

Sara's expression didn't shift. But her mind moved fast.

"You think it's Chinese?"

"I think you've made a lot of people nervous, bringing me back from the dead. And not all of them are on the other side."

He stood now, slowly.

"You want to assess security? Here's your assessment: the perimeter's soft on the west line—thermal blind spot behind the woodpile. Your agents rotate posts too predictably. And someone in supply chain either got bribed or got lazy, because I've counted three RFID components in here that were never in my specs. And, oh yes, you already know about the device the NSA found outside the perimeter."

Genevieve jotted a note, her face hardening.

Sara looked at him.

"You weren't supposed to notice any of that."

——

As they walked out of the barn, Sara said, "Fifteen years running double. You don't survive that by handing people your full assessment in the first five minutes."

Genevieve was quiet and then said. "Unless the assessment is the message."

Sara glanced at her.

"He's not reporting vulnerabilities," Genevieve said. "He's demonstrating that he found them before we did. That's not a security briefing. That's an audition."

"For what?"

"To not be managed." Genevieve tucked the tablet under her arm. "He wants us to know the equation only balances if he's treated as an asset, not a subject."

Sara looked back once toward the barn. "Or he's telling us something's already wrong and he needs us sharp."

Neither of them said anything for a few seconds.

"I'll call Will," Sara said.

——

Farmhouse Perimeter, Granville, VT

The cold hit hard the moment they stepped outside. Not only wind-chill, but the kind of cold that crept beneath layers and numbed trigger fingers. Vermont in January was merciless. Sara zipped up her coat, popped her collar, and glanced once over her shoulder toward the barn.

"Fifteen years running double and he's still spotting our RFID tags. Our supply chain has the security posture of a county fair." she muttered. "West perimeter first."

Genevieve was already pulling up the thermal overlay on her tablet. "We need a tighter security ring. He's right about the blind spot. Heat wash from the woodpile masks drone-mounted Light Detection and Ranging system (LIDAR). Our sensors are reading it as background noise."

They rounded the barn's southeast corner and moved quickly across packed snow toward the edge of the treeline. To anyone watching from above, they might have looked like two women out for a brisk walk—until one of them dropped to a knee behind a stump and pulled out a multispectrum field wand.

"Let's test it," Sara said, crouching beside her. "Any RF anomalies?"

Genevieve activated the scanner. The wand pulsed in her glove, LEDs ticking from green to yellow.

"There. Weak burst, 1.3 GHz, low-duty cycle. Could be a buried sensor or a passive relay node."

Sara pulled out a compact handheld transceiver—encrypted military band—and thumbed a private channel keyed to ACIC liaison command.

"Vesper to Nest, priority sweep. Possible passive repeater near west property line. Check manifests for embedded devices in the construction shipments. I want eyes on every logistics contractor who touched this build."

A pause. The reply was low and clipped.

"Copy, Vesper. Spooling satellite pass in six minutes. Eyes in orbit will confirm."

Sara clicked off and rose.

"We're going to need to bring in a SIGINT team. Discreet. No NSA prints."

Genevieve nodded, scanning the horizon. "This wasn't built for isolation. It was built for observation."

They walked another forty meters until the woods swallowed the property line. Deer tracks crossed the fresh snow, but Sara wasn't fooled. She knelt again and ran her gloved hand over the frozen ground. Smooth indentations. Patterned.

"Pressure pads," she said. "Old school. Wired into the power line maybe. No radio burst—hardwired to something local."

"This is turning into a surveillance honeypot," Genevieve said. Her tone was cool, but her posture was tense now. "Someone built this place either to keep Nemo alive—or to keep him under control."

Sara straightened and looked back toward the farmhouse, now framed against a steel-gray sky.

"Or both."

She said, almost to herself:

"He didn't just see the trap. He knew it was already closed."

——

Granville, VT-Nusquam 1400 Hours R

The main house was warmer than expected, but not inviting. A wood stove crackled in the corner like a polite lie. Thick rugs deadened footsteps, and the air smelled faintly of varnish and diesel—remnants of recent upgrades no one had bothered to make livable.

The lead Secret Service agent, SA George Oastler, sat at the dining room table sipping weak coffee from a Vermont state park mug. The kind of man who could be charming in a fundraiser room but didn't miss a single detail in a kill box. He looked up as Sara and Genevieve entered, unzipping their coats and tracking snow across the wide pine boards.

"Ladies." His tone was neutral. "You finish your walk?"

Sara didn't smile.

"Let's talk about the barn."

Oastler's jaw flexed once, then relaxed. He took another sip. "You found something."

Genevieve stepped forward, tablet in hand.

"RF anomaly on the western perimeter. We traced it to a low-profile repeater node embedded under a gravel patch behind the woodpile. Not on your site diagram. Want to explain?"

Oastler didn't blink.

"We didn't plant it."

"Who did?" Sara asked.

He set the mug down and folded his hands, elbows on the table.

"This is your op. You brought him in. We're here for physical protection—exterior only. Everything inside the barn and house falls under ACIC's purview. If someone compromised the build, they did it before our team ever deployed."

"You're saying your agents didn't sweep the structure?"

"We swept for conventional threats: explosives, weapons, broadcast beacons. Not embedded fiber, not passive traps. That's not our protocol."

Genevieve cut in. "That's not good enough."

Silence.

Oastler leaned back slightly.

"With respect, Agent Larsson, if you wanted NSA-grade counter-surveillance, maybe you should've asked for more than three guys with sidearms and a thermal drone."

Sara's eyes narrowed.

"One of those 'three guys' is assigned to post rotation that walks right past the anomaly every eight hours. He didn't see anything?"

Oastler hesitated. It was enough.

“He’s getting pulled,” Sara said, already reaching for her phone. “Your entire detail gets re-screened starting tonight. DCIS will fly in a Technical Surveillance Countermeasures team. Until they arrive, no one enters the lab except me and Larsson. Nemo stays cold.”

Oastler rose. His expression was tight now.

“You’re overreacting. The signal’s cold. If it was active, we’d have seen telemetry spikes.”

"You can always tell who's never been shot at.” said Sara, “they use phrases like 'overreacting.'"

Genevieve stepped closer, voice low.

“It doesn’t need to transmit. It only needs to store. Someone’s planning a physical retrieval. Maybe soon.”

Sara’s voice was colder than the air outside.

“And if they come, Agent Oastler, you won’t see them coming.”

A tense beat passed. Finally, Oastler nodded once—tight, professional.

“Understood.”

He stepped aside. The tension stayed.

Sara and Genevieve exited through the back door toward the barn, wind pulling at their coats.

Observation Post, 1.8 Miles West

A nondescript SUV sat parked off a service road under canopy cover. Inside, a laptop screen lit up. A still image: Sara kneeling near the gravel pit. A timestamp. A heat signature.

The system blinked twice.

> AUTOMATED TAG: PRIMARY OBJECT — COMPROMISE IMMINENT ESCROW PROTOCOL STANDBY [Y/N]?

Cursor blinking.

No answer.

Yet.

——

Team Watchtower Conference Room, Fort Meade

The walls of the ACIC Ops Center were a steel-gray blur of status panels, encrypted data flows, and live intelligence feeds scrolling faster than most minds could process. But Will Morgan (Sentinel) wasn’t most minds.

He stood with arms crossed at the center of the command floor, facing a central screen divided into three sections:

— Thermal overlay from the Granville property

— Sensor data logs from the barn perimeter

— Live video of Genevieve's field wand readings and Sara's voice clipped through a low-latency feed

Sara Brandt (Vesper) and Genevieve Larsson (Verity) remoting in from Nusquam, cool and focused, tablet in their laps. Cecil Brandon (Nomad), their surveillance expert, checked his notes. Giuseppa "Gussie" Brindisi (Monarch) had two notebooks open—one physical, one digital. At the far end, Rick Huang (Vector), computer scientist, laptop open.

Will opened without ceremony.

"Where are we?"

Sara. "We're pulling the Secret Service detail. Verity found a passive node embedded west of the barn. It's buried—hardwired—no transmission, passive storage. Someone's planning to collect it physically."

Will's jaw tightened.

Behind him, Gussie, the thirty-year veteran analyst, muttered, "Someone wired the grave before we finished digging it."

Will turned. "Who vetted the construction contractors?"

"Joint team from Department of Homeland Security, Defense Threat Reduction Agency and private subconsultants out of Denver. But you want my opinion?" Gussie handed him a printed profile sheet. "Subcontractor two layers deep. Dead drop op in 2020. Chinese signature."

Will skimmed it—Qilin Industrial Services, registered in New Mexico, DBA through Zhang Modular Systems, a shell company dissolved six weeks ago.

"Of course."

"We flagged them three months ago in the Calyx sweep," Gussie added. "But they resurfaced under new paperwork."

Will turned back to the screen. Sara was visible now, sweeping her glove across a frozen trail. The way she moved, steady, precise—told him everything he needed to know about her mental state. Controlled, but reading escalation.

He keyed into the encrypted uplink.

"Vesper, this is Sentinel. Full lockout authority confirmed. You have discretion to isolate the site and remove all friendly assets not under ACIC credential. Anything leaves that barn without your sign-off, it burns."

A beat. Sara's voice again—firm, low.

"Acknowledged. We're already sealing internal systems. Verity's isolating the server rack—air-gapped and sealed under double-authentication. Nemo's not rattled."

Will's eyes flicked toward a fourth screen, tracking SIGINT intercept alerts from Northeast Quadrant. Still clean—for now.

Behind him, Ed Perry, Commander of ACIC, stepped into the room in a black wool coat, hands in his pockets, his eyes already locked on the screen.

"How bad?"

Will didn't hesitate.

"Bad enough that whoever placed the node wasn't in a rush. They expected it to stay in place long enough to finish the collection cycle."

Perry exhaled slowly. "And Chan? He spot it first?"

Will nodded once.

"Of course he did."

"That makes him valuable."

Will looked at Perry.

"That makes him hunted."

Perry nodded silently, looked back at the screen as a drone pass fed in. A thermal pickup of a coyote, but no human figures yet.

"You think MSS is watching in real time?"

Will's reply was quiet. Measured.

"I think they're waiting. And I think we may have rung their bell."

——

"We're not asking if someone's watching Granville. They are. We confirmed that with the RF leak, the west pad anomaly, and the relay handoff we traced to Quebec. The question is what do they think they're watching."

He pointed to the satellite image—an overhead of the farmhouse and the lab-modified barn.

"So, do they know Nemo's alive? Or do they just see a million-dollar rural build, high encryption signatures, and the unmistakable whiff of something black-budget buried in a ski town?"

Rick answered first.

"They're probing for signature, not identity. If they knew it was Shen Ke, we'd have seen more chatter on their diplomatic link and more aggressive posture—surveillance drones, tradecraft layers, indirect deniables. Right now, they're watching. Waiting. Not acting."

Sara nodded slowly. "They're not in exfiltration mode. They're in calibration mode."

Will raised an eyebrow. "Define it."

"They see heat where there shouldn't be heat. A six-million-dollar retrofit in a town without a supermarket. Fiber optics running to a barn in a field with no academic affiliation. Power load suggests quantum-class architecture. So they calibrate—slow, passive, pattern-match. If they guess wrong, they waste an asset. If they guess right, they confirm a new operation or worse, a ghost's heartbeat."

Gussie added, flipping through her yellow legal pad.

"Precisely. They're hunting a project, not a person. There's still chatter around the old Spindle and Vortex programs—if they think someone resurrected part of that tech and moved it off-grid, they'd want to confirm before risking interference. MSS likes certainty."

Genevieve tilted her head. "Unless... someone in their orbit suspects. Not the upper echelon. Someone mid-level. Field side. They don't have a name—they have a pattern. A feeling."

Will looked at her. "Why do you say that?"

"Because they're acting like we do when we think someone faked their death. Controlled patience. Passive channel triggers. Layered surveillance waiting for an anomaly to reveal a truth they want to believe but can't prove yet."

Cecil chimed in. "So what? They're fishing for an echo."

Sara added, "And if we're not careful, we give them one."

Will paced once.

"Here's the truth. If they knew Nemo was alive, there'd be a cruise missile in that barn or a 'missing hiker' report by now. Instead, we've got a live tap. Hidden. Cold. Passive collection. That's insurance. That's doubt."

He stopped pacing.

"And that means we still have a window to pull the teeth out of this thing before they decide they've seen enough."

The room was quiet for a beat.

Will looked to Rick.

"Tear apart every component in that lab. If there's one node, there could be ten. Assume physical collection is scheduled within a week."

He turned to Sara. "You and Larsson stay close to Nemo. See if he's talking to anyone off record. I don't care if it's a thermal gesture through a window or a scratched message into a toolbox. If he has a leak, I want it corked before it spreads."

And finally, to the room, "Until proved otherwise, we operate under this assumption: the MSS suspects. They do not know. Our job is to keep it that way."

CHAPTER SIX

Ground Truth

General Store — Hancock, VT — Early October

Marie-Claire was restocking the cooler when the bell over the door rang.

She straightened and glanced up out of habit.

The woman who stepped inside paused just long enough to take in the space—small, clean, functional. Not lost, orienting. Early thirties, maybe. Practical coat. Boots that had seen real weather. Hair pulled back without fuss.

"Morning," Marie-Claire said.

"Morning," the woman replied, smiling easily. "Do you have half-and-half? Not the sweetened kind."

Second shelf. Back left. Marie-Claire pointed. "That one sells faster than the milk."

"Figures," the woman said, amused.

She moved through the store unhurriedly, selecting a few items—coffee beans, bread, apples. Nothing extraneous. At the counter, she set them down neatly.

"Passing through?" Marie-Claire asked, conversational, as she rang them up.

"Sort of," the woman said. "I'm staying a little ways up the road."

Marie-Claire nodded. She didn't ask where. The road narrowed possibilities on its own.

"Quiet place," she said instead.

"That's why I like it."

The register chimed. Marie-Claire glanced at the woman again—noted the faint tiredness around the eyes, the kind that came from thinking too much rather than sleeping too little.

"You're not from around here," Marie-Claire said gently. Not a challenge. Just a fact.

The woman smiled. "Is it that obvious?"

"Only to people who aren't trying to be noticed," Marie-Claire said, and immediately softened it with a small shrug. "No offense."

"None taken," the woman said. "I'm Gayle."

"Marie-Claire."

She slid the bag across the counter.

Genevieve using her cover name of Gayle said, "I drive by your place often. You're always open early."

"Someone has to be," Marie-Claire said. "Road doesn't wait."

She laughed at that. She paid—cash, exact change—and picked up the bag.

As she turned to leave, Marie-Claire said, almost as an afterthought, "If you're here a while, winter comes fast. People think they're ready. They usually aren't."

She paused, considering that.

"I'll keep it in mind," she said.

The bell rang again as she left.

Marie-Claire watched through the window as Gayle/Genevieve walked to her car—an older model, clean but unremarkable—and drove north.

Only when the car disappeared around the bend did Marie-Claire allow herself a small, thoughtful frown.

Not suspicion.

Recognition.

The woman hadn't asked questions.

She hadn't looked around like a tourist.

And she hadn't lingered.

Marie-Claire wiped the counter, returned to her work, and thought no more about it—at least, not in any way that would show.

Some people came to Granville to be seen.

Others came because it was a good place not to be.

— —

Nusquam — The Following Spring

The trucks stopped coming in the spring.

Marie-Claire noticed the absence the way one notices a clock has stopped ticking—not immediately, but with a faint sense that something familiar was missing. March and April passed. The road settled back into its old rhythm: pickups, delivery vans, the occasional lost tourist braking too late for the curve.

Normal.

And yet, not.

Because now, when she drove past the farm, it no longer felt empty.

She didn't see movement. No vehicles. No men in reflective vests or heavy coats. No equipment staged too close to the road.

But the place had weight.

It sat differently on the land, as if it had decided what it was and no longer needed to announce itself.

One morning, late April, she slowed without meaning to. The trees were beginning to leaf now, the road greening and alive. Through a narrow break in the branches, she caught a glimpse of the house—unchanged, modest, unremarkable. The big red barn immediately behind it.

And behind the barn—

Nothing.

That was the strange part.

Not a sound. Not a bird lifting off. Not the small, incidental noises that usually followed a car passing. The quiet held, tight and deliberate, like breath being managed.

Marie-Claire's hands tightened on the steering wheel.

She drove on.

At the market, she found herself thinking back through the year, unspooling it in reverse.

The early arrivals.

The winter work crews that never complained about the cold.

The way some vehicles had left before dusk, others after dark.

The fact that no one ever asked her for directions.

She realized that she could place them all—roughly—by season, by light, by snow depth.

Not because she'd tried.

Because she'd lived there.

Later that afternoon, Gayle/Genevieve came in again. Not often—just enough to be familiar. She looked less tired now. More settled. Like someone who had stopped waiting for the ground to shift beneath her.

"Busy today?" She asked.

"Always," Marie-Claire said. "In different ways."

Genevieve smiled at that, and hesitated. "Have you noticed how quiet it's been up the road?"

Marie-Claire met her eyes.

"Quiet comes in phases," she said carefully. "Sometimes it means something ended. Sometimes it means it finally started."

She studied her for longer than politeness required, and said, “I should get back.”

“Yes,” Marie-Claire agreed. “You should.”

That evening, at home, Marie-Claire sat on the porch as the light faded. She listened to the frogs begin their evening chorus, the sound rippling across the fields.

Normal sounds.

Comforting sounds.

And yet, layered beneath them now was something else—a sense of order, of intent. The road still carried people. The farm still stood.

But whatever had passed through there had left a shape behind.

Marie-Claire didn’t name it. She didn’t speculate. That wasn’t her way.

She simply accepted that some changes announce themselves loudly.

Others leave only a before and an after.

And if someone ever asked her—truly asked—she knew she could tell them when the line between the two had been crossed.

Not to the hour.

Not to the day.

But close enough to matter.

She went inside, locked the door, and turned out the lights.

Tomorrow, she would drive the road again.

And she would notice what remained.

——

Hancock, VT - General Store

They came on a Tuesday.

Not together. Not in a way that suggested coordination. Two people, an hour apart, asking questions that sounded like curiosity more than purpose.

The first was a woman—late thirties, maybe—who bought coffee and a paper map she clearly didn’t need. She lingered by the window while Marie-Claire rang her up.

“Do you mind if I ask you something?” the woman said, smiling the way people do when they want to seem harmless.

“Of course not.”

“I’m helping with a regional transportation study. We’re trying to understand seasonal traffic patterns. Especially winter ones.”

Marie-Claire nodded. That, at least, made sense.

"Do you remember when heavier vehicles tend to pass through?" the woman asked. "Plow trucks, contractors, deliveries—things like that."

Marie-Claire thought. "Depends what kind. Logging trucks are early. Always early. Contractors change with daylight."

"Daylight?" the woman asked, pen poised.

"Yes," Marie-Claire said. "In winter, people who know the road avoid mornings. Ice holds longer in the shadows. Afternoon's safer."

The woman wrote that down, thanked her, and left with her coffee.

Marie-Claire didn't think much of it.

The second visitor arrived closer to closing.

A man this time. Older. Polite in a practiced, unassuming way. He bought batteries and a candy bar and waited until Marie-Claire handed him his change.

"Mind if I ask—how long you've lived around here?" he said.

"All my life."

He smiled. "I guess you'd know when things feel... different."

She shrugged lightly. "Different comes and goes."

"Sure," he said. "But you'd remember when it started."

Marie-Claire considered that.

"I remember winters more than years," she said finally. "Easier that way."

He nodded as if that answered what he needed.

"Last question," he said. "Do you recall when traffic on the way to Granville picked up?"

Marie-Claire didn't hesitate. "It picked up twice."

He blinked. "Twice?"

"Once when it started," she said. "Once when it changed."

He thanked her, genuinely, and left.

Marie-Claire locked the door behind him, turned off the lights, and drove home thinking no more about it than she would about the weather.

——

Rochester, VT-General Store

They hadn't meant it to be an interview.

Will had been clear about that. A courtesy visit. A few clarifying questions. A chance to confirm dates already "pretty well nailed down" by telemetry, traffic cameras, and SYBIL's reconstructed model.

Marie-Claire sat at the small table in the back of the Hancock market, hands wrapped around a paper cup of coffee she hadn't asked for. She looked comfortable—present.

Cecil Brandon flipped open his notebook. "We're trying to confirm when activity at the old Lavoie farm slowed down," he said. "Our data suggests late March. Possibly earlier April."

Marie-Claire tilted her head slightly.

"No," she said.

The word was gentle. Almost apologetic.

Rick glanced up from his tablet. "No?"

She smiled faintly. "It didn't slow down. It changed."

The room went still—not tense, attentive.

"How so?" Sara asked.

Marie-Claire thought, eyes drifting toward the front windows, as if the road itself might answer.

"March is when the trucks stopped coming every day," she said. "But that's not when things quieted. That was earlier. Mid-February, maybe a little before. That's when they stopped coming in the morning."

Cecil frowned. "Our records show—"

"I know," Marie-Claire said, nodding. "They started coming later. After dark sometimes. Not often. But enough."

Will hadn't spoken yet. He was watching her carefully now.

Rick scrolled rapidly. "Hold on... if arrivals shifted to post-dusk, our traffic cameras wouldn't—"

"And winter makes sound carry," Marie-Claire added, still mild. "You hear engines farther when the air's cold. I remember thinking it was strange I wasn't hearing them anymore."

Silence.

SYBIL's soft tone filled the room.

"Recalibrating temporal activity model."

The display on Rick's screen changed—dates sliding backward, clusters reshaping.

Cecil stared. "That moves the internal activation window up by almost three weeks."

Marie-Claire blinked. "Oh. Does it?"

Will finally spoke. "Yes. It does."

She looked at him, a little embarrassed now. "I'm sorry. I didn't mean to contradict anyone."

"You didn't," Will said. "You corrected us."

She smiled politely, unconvinced it mattered.

"Well," she said, standing and gathering her cup, "winter's funny that way. Makes patterns clearer if you're used to listening."

She excused herself to tend to a customer at the register, leaving the team behind her.

Rick exhaled slowly. "She invalidated half our working assumptions."

Sara nodded. "With one sentence."

Cecil closed his notebook. "She didn't even realize she did it."

Will watched Marie-Claire greet the customer, her manner unchanged, unremarkable.

"That's because," he said, "she wasn't trying to be right."

He turned back to the team.

"She was telling us when normal stopped."

And in the recalculated timeline glowing on the screen, the truth finally settled into place—earlier, quieter, and far more deliberate than any of them had assumed.

All because someone who lived there had noticed when the road went silent.

——

Fort Meade-Watchtower Ops

Sara Brandt set her pen down slowly.

"That's it," she said. "That's our confirmation."

Cecil exhaled. "She didn't speculate. Didn't editorialize. Didn't even realize she was correcting us."

Will said nothing, eyes on the transcript.

Finally, he spoke.

"She didn't give us intelligence," he said.

"She gave us ground truth."

SYBIL's voice followed, neutral and precise.

"Civilian observation verified. Confidence level: high."

Will leaned back.

"She never once asked who we were," Sara noted.

Will allowed himself the faintest smile.

"She'll never know how important she was."

——

Fort Meade - ACIC Cafeteria - 2010 Hours R

Rick Huang jabbed the B7 button harder than necessary.

The vending machine hummed, considered his request, and did nothing.

Rick stared at it. "I saw the chips drop last time. Don't play dumb."

The machine responded with a low, smug whirr.

"Oh, come on," he muttered, leaning in. "You have one job. Dispense sodium and regret."

He pressed B7 again. The spiral twitched—enough to tease—then stopped. The bag of chips remained lodged at a forty-five-degree angle, perfectly balanced between freedom and betrayal.

Rick folded his arms. "This is a mechanical failure, not a negotiation."

He rocked the machine gently. A red warning light blinked on.

"Don't threaten me," Rick said flatly. "I've reverse-engineered Russian malware older than you."

The vending machine beeped. The chips did not move.

Rick exhaled, dug into his pocket, and hit C4 instead.

The chips fell instantly.

Rick stared at the machine for a long moment, then nodded once.

"Fine," he said. "You win. But this isn't over.

——

Late that afternoon Sara walked past Rick in the bullpen and said, "I heard you lost a fight with a vending machine."

"Tactical withdrawal."

"Mm. Interesting."

CHAPTER SEVEN

Logic

Fort Meade - Derek's Apartment

How quickly everything had changed. Not long ago, Derek Wilshire had lived inside a world measured only by equations and noise. His life had been a sequence of patterns—predictable, repetitive, comfortable in its solitude. Loneliness was simply the absence of interruption.

Now there were people in that quiet. Real people.

He looked around his small Fort Meade apartment—half lab, half living space. On the far wall hung a framed letter embossed with the Presidential seal, his commendation for distinguished service. It still felt like a misprint. He'd checked it three times for errors before hanging it up.

Across from it, the soft blue glow of his aquarium filled the room with shifting light. Two clownfish drifted lazily through the coral—a gift from Will, who had helped install the tank himself. Derek had named the brighter one Nemo, which amused everyone except Will, who had only muttered, "Figures," and smiled anyway.

He crouched to feed them, watching the tiny flakes swirl downward like slow-motion snow.

"Some company," he murmured.

On the shelf below the aquarium sat a different kind of collection. Coins, arranged in careful sequence, ancient Roman denarii in labeled sleeves, medieval silver groats organized by country and century, modern circulating pieces graded and cataloged by mint mark. Derek had been collecting for twelve years, each acquisition carefully vetted for weight, metallurgical composition, die variations, strike quality. Most people saw it as hoarding; Derek saw it as taxonomy. Each coin told a story crystallized in metal.

He picked up a 1922 Peace Dollar, examining it under the desk lamp. The wear patterns on Lady Liberty's cheek told him exactly how many hands had held this coin, how much circulation it had seen. The microns of loss encoded a readable history.

This was where his mind lived when there was no work. Pattern, sequence, order. The satisfaction of knowing where each piece belonged.

He thought of Watchtower—the laughter spilling from Sara's office, Grace sketching waveforms on a napkin, Genevieve's sharp wit over morning coffee. Even Will, who spoke more with his eyes than his words, had become a kind of anchor. They didn't treat him like a curiosity or a tool. They treated him like... one of them.

A friend.

He still wasn't used to the word.

His gaze drifted to the adjoining wall—the one that connected his apartment to the Secret Service command post. A faint hum came through, the sound of quiet voices and equipment on standby. His detail, as they called it. He didn't fully understand why he needed one, but Will had insisted. "Out of an abundance of caution," he'd said, which usually meant something was being hidden for his own good.

He didn't mind, though. It was nice, in a way. Having people nearby. Knowing someone cared enough to guard his safety even when he barely noticed danger himself.

He sat back on the edge of his couch, letting the rhythmic pulse of the tank lights wash over him.

For the first time in his life, he wasn't the outsider.

He was part of something larger, something that mattered.

And if Will Morgan was overprotective, well, so was everyone in Watchtower.

He smiled faintly to himself.

——

Fort Meade-ACIC Headquarters Commander Perry's Office

Gussie Brindisi hadn't been her indestructible, tireless self for weeks. The woman who once ran on caffeine and sheer will was now moving slower, taking private days—which she never did—and coming in on weekends to make up the time. Will had once caught her asleep in her office, head resting on a file folder like she'd simply run out of fuel. It was as if she were storing up strength for the trip home each night.

He remembered, with quiet fondness, the day Ed Perry had come into his office, closed the door, and said, "Need a favor. Gussie's new boss doesn't want her. Make some room for her in Watchtower?"

They both knew Will would say yes. But as it turned out, it was Will who got the favor.

Two days later, Ed stopped by to check in. Before he could speak, Will said, half in jest, "No, you can't have her back—she stays. Anything else?"

Ed had laughed, winked, and said simply, "Told you so."

She'd become the team's quiet center, the den mother no one realized they needed until she was there. A firm hand in a velvet glove. Will often wondered how he'd ever managed without her.

Now, seated across from Ed in the dim office, he finally asked the question that had lingered for months.

"Whatever happened to Gussie?" Will said. "She was your deputy back in the early days. Tough as nails."

Ed's expression softened, the faintest smile cutting through the fatigue. "Gussie," he echoed. "Yeah, she was a fighter. Stayed with me through some rough years." His eyes clouded slightly. "She got sick—Hep C. This was before they screened the blood supply. She thought it was exhaustion, turned out to be something much worse."

He paused, folding his hands. "They didn't have antivirals at that time. Only Interferon, and that stuff was poison. Clinical trial in New York. She survived it, but it stripped her immune system clean. She wasn't lucky."

Will was silent, letting the words settle.

Later that night, back in his quarters, he searched the disease out of quiet respect. Hepatitis C: often symptomless until too late. A silent predator. Damage accumulating cell by cell until the body gives up its fight.

He shut the laptop and sat there for a while, thinking about the quiet endurance of people like Gussie—who fought unseen wars long before anyone noticed.

He was concerned about her.

——

Fort Meade - Gussie's Office

The corridors of Fort Meade were empty, the hum of ventilation the only sound. Will stopped outside Gussie's office. The light was still on, as he'd known it would be.

She was there at her desk, a single lamp casting a pale circle over scattered papers. She looked up when he knocked lightly on the frame.

“Everyone else went home hours ago,” he said gently. “That includes you.”

“I needed to finish a few things,” she murmured, her voice thin.

Will stepped inside, closing the door behind him. “Gussie... I know something’s wrong. And I want to help.”

She held his gaze as if deciding whether to deny it. Her composure cracked. Shoulders trembled. Hands covered her face. crossed the room, dropped to one knee beside her chair, and put his arms around her. He didn’t care about HR or protocol—this was family.

When she finally steadied, he said softly, “Come on. I’m driving you home.”

“You don’t need to—”

“It’s not out of my way,” he lied. It was.

He got her to the car, made sure she was buckled in, and when they reached her apartment, he said, “I’ll pick you up in the morning.”

The next day, and the next after that, he did just that—sometimes Sara took a turn, sometimes he did. Between them, they became what he jokingly called “the ACIC Uber.”

Not long after, the truth came out. Stage Three liver disease. One step from transplant.

He’d seen enough brave people break before—but never anyone so strong fight in such silence.

——

Fort Meade-Kimbrough Ambulatory Care Center, phlebotomy bay 0920 Hours R

The chair was a beige vinyl recliner with a wear pattern in the headrest from ten thousand other heads. Gussie had memorized the wear pattern. Three sessions ago it had been a single faded oval. Now it was an oval inside a wider halo, the vinyl gone slightly tacky where the foam had given up.

"Mrs. Brindisi? Ready when you are."

The specialist was new. Twenty-two, maybe twenty-three, the OCP-pattern ACU’s sleeves rolled just past the elbow the way the regs allowed. The name tape on his chest read NGUYEN. The rank tab above it: SPC. He laid out his tray the way they were taught at Fort Sam — alcohol prep, tourniquet, butterfly, gauze, tape — left to right, evenly spaced. The good ones eventually stopped doing that. They reached for what they needed.

"Small veins," Gussie said. "Rollers, too. Left arm's better than the right."

"Yes, ma'am. I see the note."

He extended her left arm on the rest and snugged the tourniquet. His thumb worked the inside of her elbow, pressing, lifting, pressing again. There was a vein there. There was almost a vein there. Gussie knew the geography of her own arm the way she used to know the layout of a Cold War station chief's office. Every entrance, every blind spot, every place where something could go wrong fast.

"Little stick, ma'am."

The needle went in. The vein moved.

"Sorry, ma'am. Let me just—"

The needle adjusted under the skin. Gussie kept her eyes on the wear pattern in the recliner across the bay, the one nobody was sitting in. Three sessions ago that one had been the cleanest in the row.

"Got it, ma'am. Sorry about that."

"It's fine, Specialist."

The bag began to fill. Dark and slow. They took a pint every week now. A pint was what you donated when you were healthy and felt good about yourself afterward.

She turned her face toward the window. Through the half-shut blinds she could see the corner of the parking lot, and past it, the access road that led back toward the main gate at Fort Meade. Somewhere down that road was her office. The two notebooks. The pile of subcontractor profiles she had not finished reviewing. Will would be in the conference room by now. Sara would be making coffee that no one would drink.

The bag kept filling.

"Doing great, ma'am."

Gussie did not answer. She was watching a sergeant cross the parking lot with a coffee in each hand, walking carefully so as not to spill. It was something to do.

Each session left her paler, slower to rise.

The woman who once commanded a room with a look now needed an arm to steady her step.

When she finally became too weak to come in, Ed made the call himself. "Set her up to work remote," he told IT. "I don't care what it takes—make it easy."

No one in Watchtower cared how much she actually managed to do. That wasn't the point. They wanted her to know she still mattered—that she was still one of them.

Even from her quiet corner at home, her name still came up in the office almost every day. And every time it did, the tone was the same—a mixture of affection, respect, and something that sounded a lot like love.

Sara found Will in his office, staring at a stack of case reports that hadn't moved in an hour. She closed the door behind her and sat down without being asked.

"There's something you should know about Gussie," she said .

Will looked up. "Go on."

"There's a new liver drug—early results are promising. In some cases, it's actually reversing the damage."

Will leaned forward. "That's wonderful."

Sara's expression didn't change. "Yes... and no. Insurance companies still label it experimental. Ninety-six thousand dollars a year. She can't afford it. Her old medical bills already buried her."

Will exhaled, rubbing his temples. "Damn."

"She's looking into a trial," Sara continued. "Macrophage immune therapy. They take the patient's own stem cells, reprogram them to promote tissue repair. It's not FDA approved yet—and the side effects can be brutal. She doesn't even know if she'll qualify."

The silence hung between them. Will said, "She deserves better than this."

Sara nodded. "She does. But this is the fight she's got left.

——

Odenton - Gussie's House

Derek Wilshire sat in the passenger seat, watching the houses slide past, hands fidgeting with the strap of his watch. The Secret Service agent behind the wheel glanced over. "You sure she's up for visitors?"

Derek nodded. "She'll say she isn't. But she'll mean the opposite."

Gussie's house was small and warm-looking, a tidy three-bedroom she'd once shared with her husband of twenty-five years. Now the driveway was full—two cars tight to the garage, another at the curb.

When Derek knocked, he expected silence. Instead, the door swung open and Cathy Wang stood there, smiling like she'd been caught raiding a cookie jar.

"Hey," she said. "You're late."

The sound hit them first—laughter, the murmur of a game on TV. The family room looked like a Super Bowl party. Z and Rick were parked on the sofa, mock-arguing over the remote.

And there was Gussie—frail, yes, but glowing with that quiet steel of hers—settled into her recliner with a blanket over her knees.

She looked up, saw Derek, and her whole face lit. "Well, if it isn't my favorite numbers man."

He grinned back. "You must be mistaken, Gussie. I'm everyone's least favorite numbers man."

She laughed—a thin sound, but genuine. "Not mine."

They'd always had that strange, easy connection. He could almost finish her thoughts; she often finished his out loud. Now, standing in that room full of warmth and noise, Derek realized what everyone in Watchtower already knew: Gussie was the heart of the place.

——

Fort Meade-Watchtower Ops

Two weeks later, Sara found Will by the coffee station, staring into a mug he hadn't touched. She waited until he looked up.

"It's about Gussie," she said.

Will's posture straightened instantly. "What happened?"

Sara smiled faintly. "Something good, for once. Her doctor found a research fund willing to cover the cost of that new liver drug - Rezdiffra. She started the treatment yesterday."

Will blinked, almost not believing it. "You're serious?"

"Dead serious," Sara said. "It's not a cure, but it's hope. They won't know if it's working for a couple of months, but she's... different. You can hear it in her voice."

Will nodded slowly, his expression softening. "Good. She deserves a break."

Sara smiled, seeing the rare ease in his eyes. "Yeah," she said. "She really does."

CHAPTER EIGHT

The Primer

Do you really believe the moon only exists when you are looking at it?" — Albert Einstein

University of Maryland – Lecture Hall 2A

Laptops flickered awake. Coffee lids snapped. Grace Roberts, PhD, strode to the front—navy blazer, sleeves rolled, hair pinned back. She didn't need to call the class to order; her presence did that.

In the back row, Joanna Lisik scanned the room. The clear acoustic tube in her ear carried the faint hiss of comms—Secret Service chatter. One of three agents assigned to Grace since Radiant Sentry. She looked like a grad student. Her eyes said otherwise.

Grace tapped the whiteboard once.

"Entanglement," she said. "Einstein hated it. Bell proved it. Today, you'll learn why it still bothers everyone else."

Click.

The projector came alive: two drifting photons bound by a faint, luminous thread.

"Quantum entanglement is real. It's been tested and confirmed, and now useful. It breaks a sacred law of classical physics: locality."

Another click—Einstein's words appeared:

'Spooky action at a distance.'

A ripple of laughter.

"He meant it," Grace said. "He thought nature shouldn't play favorites faster than light."

She drew two dots—A and B—on the board.

"Einstein believed hidden variables explained this trick. But Bell showed no local theory could reproduce these correlations. Reality doesn't care what makes sense to us."

Silence. Then a hand rose near the front.

"Wait," the student said. "Doesn't this violate relativity? Nothing can travel faster than the speed of light. That's... foundational."

A few heads nodded. This wasn't confusion, it was resistance.

Grace smiled slightly. Not dismissive. Interested.

"Good," she said. "That objection is exactly why this took decades to accept."

She turned back to the board, drawing a line between A and B.

"It looks like information is traveling faster than light. One particle is measured, the other 'responds' instantly. But here's the problem—"

She paused, letting it settle.

"—you can't use it to send a message."

A beat.

"If I measure particle A, I get a result. But I can't control what that result is. And the observer at B can't tell whether anything happened at A without comparing notes—through a classical channel, limited by the speed of light."

A low murmur moved through the room.

"What does travel," she continued, "is correlation. Structure. A shared state that exists outside our classical intuition of space and time."

She tapped the board.

"So, no usable information travels faster than light. Relativity survives. Barely."

She clicked again.

Both appeared:

'Those who are not shocked by quantum theory cannot possibly have understood it.'

Grace folded her arms.

"Entanglement isn't theory anymore. It's infrastructure. And in five years, it may decide who wins the next war."

"You're not here to memorize. You're here to be bothered. That's how you know you're learning."

The bell rang.

No one moved.

Outside, Joanna touched her earpiece, eyes tracking Grace through the dispersing crowd.

"Lambda moving."

Outside the Lecture Hall – Dusk

Students spilled out into the autumn light. Grace walked toward the faculty lot, tote bag over her shoulder, the day's applause already fading behind her.

From a shaded column near the steps, Joanna Lisik tracked her progress—hand on her earpiece, the picture of casual.

"Lambda moving. No tails. North approach clear."

She fell in behind Grace at a polite distance. Another pedestrian, phone in hand.

Grace unlocked her own phone, thumb moving fast.

The draft sat unsent.

"Lambda stationary. Thirty seconds. Moving again."

She hit send. No signature, no trace.

Have an idea I would like to share. When can I see you to discuss?

The answer came back immediately.

Can you drive down today?

She answered simply — K.

Above her, the sky deepened to violet.

——

Fort Meade - Morgan's Office 1730 Hours R

Grace Roberts had learned to wait until the room was quiet.

Not the superficial quiet of people pausing between conversations—but the deeper one, when Will Morgan's mind had shifted out of operational triage and into pattern recognition. That was when ideas landed.

She stood near the edge of his desk, tablet in hand, eyes bright in a way that had nothing to do with nerves.

"I know I'm not field," she said, almost apologetically. "But I've been thinking about Nusquam."

"Gussie and Sara have seen it. They said to bring it to you."

Will looked up. "That's usually how it starts."

Will set down a report that was in his hand. Not dramatically — just set it down.

She smiled and tapped her tablet. The wall screen behind his desk came alive—not with equations or simulations, but with boxes. Names. Dates. Corporate trees.

"What if we don't hide Nusquam," Grace said. "What if we bury it inside a maze?"

Will leaned back slightly, studying the structure.

"A labyrinth of false research sites," she continued. "Manufactured targets. Plausible enough to attract attention. We don't block the adversary—we invite them. And we watch who bites."

She handed him the tablet.

"Read it," she said.

Will did.

"Dormant LLCs," he read aloud, voice steady.

"Staggered organization dates. Synthetic bios pulled from expired clearance rosters. No active names. No HR flags."

He paused before he continued.

"Six shell companies. Plausible on paper. Deniable in practice."

"DARPA issues subgrants. Black-budget routing through cover line items. No paper trail in public appropriations."

Will looked up at her now, something sharpening behind his eyes.

Grace met his gaze. "Make it look operational. But when they dig in—"

"We make sure every road leads nowhere," Will finished.

She nodded. Encouraged now.

"Give them something shiny to chase," she said. "Let them exhaust themselves while we build the real thing in silence."

In an extremely rare visit Helena Quinn stood at his door. She had been listening from the threshold, arms folded, expression unreadable in the way that meant she was impressed.

"We log every probe," Helena said. "Every ping is metadata. Every probe tells us who's watching—and how they move."

The room settled into that dangerous stillness again.

Will exhaled slowly. "We've done variations of this before," he said. "Decoys. Mirrors. Noise farms."

He looked back at Grace. "But not like this."

He handed the tablet back, a small smile pulling at the corner of his mouth.

"You're spending too much time with Sara," he said. "You're getting dangerous."

Grace smiled—not flattered.

Validated.

"Maybe that's a good thing," said Helena with a devilish smile.

Fort Meade - Officers Club - 1800 Hours R

The Officers Club was nearly empty—late enough that the dinner rush had thinned to murmurs and the clink of silverware. The light was warm, restrained. Civilian comfortable, military precise.

Grace had rambled on about False Constellation over the first course. Will had listened without interruption, fork resting untouched, eyes steady. When she finished, he didn't rush to respond.

"It's an excellent plan," he said at last.

She believed him immediately. Will Morgan didn't waste words on false flattery. When he approved something, it was because it deserved approval.

They ate for a few minutes in companionable silence before she spoke again, quieter this time—careful, as if testing the edge of something delicate.

"Can I ask you about the Trireme?"

He looked up. No surprise. No deflection.

"Sure."

"I always thought it represented something from your childhood," Grace said. "Something you lost."

His expression didn't change, but something behind his eyes did—a minute recalibration, like an internal compass adjusting to an unexpected magnetic pull.

She continued gently, sensing the shift.

"People hold onto symbols like that when they're trying to preserve something fragile. Or honor someone. I thought maybe it was... your father. Or your mother. A connection you were afraid might disappear if you didn't keep at least one piece of it intact."

Will was silent long enough that she nearly apologized.

Finally, he said, "It's not a memorial."

Her shoulders dipped, barely perceptible. "Oh. I'm sorry. I didn't mean to make assumptions."

"It's all right." He paused, considering the ship as if seeing it through her eyes for the first time. "But your guess wasn't wrong. Not exactly."

Grace looked at him, attentive, patient. She didn't press.

Will spoke too softly for anyone else in the room to hear.

"It's less about losing something... and more about understanding what stays."

Her breath caught. The words brushed something unguarded in her chest, something she hadn't realized was exposed.

She nodded once, accepting the boundary he kept. yet feeling, unmistakably, the door behind it.

Will added, almost reluctantly, "But it isn't a symbol of grief."

Grace offered a small, thoughtful smile. "Maybe it's a symbol of hope."

He didn't agree.

Not out loud.

But he didn't disagree either.

And that was enough.

——

Helena had In-Q-Tel the CIA's venture capital arm, set up as a non-profit spin up seven corporate legends—fully fabricated identities—stories good enough to make Chinese intelligence chase ghosts.

Within two weeks the first three were stood up physically as well - Orono—cryo assembly. Schroon Lake—QKD testing. Plattsburgh—superconductors. Real-sounding, geographically believable. Enough to trigger interest, not enough to be proof."

——

Odenton, MD - Thomas Carrone'e House

If anyone could read Will, really read him, it was Thomas Carrone. Sara came close, maybe closer than anyone else on the team. But Thomas... Thomas had history with him. Years of it. The quiet kind of understanding that didn't need explaining.

He was one of Will's few real friends. Not just colleagues. Not just people who respected him. A friend.

Whenever something got stuck in Will's head, something he couldn't quite shake, Thomas was where he went.

Thomas lived not far from him, in Odenton. Same quiet rhythm of life, a few streets over. He and his wife, Margerie, had built something steady there. Twenty-six years of marriage. Margerie wrote novels, the kind that actually got published and read. She understood Thomas's work in that unspoken way. Knew what not to ask. Knew when to let things sit.

Their kids were grown now. Both nearby, doing their own thing in D.C. Close, but not hovering. The house had that feeling of something lived in, not passed through.

Will couldn't quite shake that dinner with Gracie. It lingered. The way she'd looked at him, like she could see around corners he didn't even know were there. And the trireme... how she'd landed so close to something he hadn't even put words to.

Thomas picked up on it almost immediately. He always did. Not big, obvious changes. Small ones. A pause. A shift in tone. A look that lasted half a second too long.

"Margerie's heading out tomorrow," Thomas said casually. "Book signing. Supporting a friend."

He let that hang there for a beat, before adding, "Feels like you could use a proper meal. Wine. Conversation."

Will gave a quiet laugh. Shook his head a little. "I really can't hide from you, can I?"

"Not even a little," Thomas said. "Tomorrow. Seven?"

"Done."

The next night, Thomas cooked like he always did when it mattered. Nothing flashy. The kind of meal that made you slow down without realizing it.

Afterward, they moved into the family room. Comfortable chairs. Soft light. The UCONN pennant on the wall, a little faded now. Margerie's Kenyon one beside it. Photos over the fireplace. Years of moments, all lined up without trying too hard.

Thomas waited. Let the silence do its work.

Finally, he said, "What's going on in that inscrutable mind of yours?"

Will leaned back slightly. Exhaled. "Something Gracie said. The other night."

Thomas nodded once. "The trireme."

"Yeah." Will paused. "She said people hold onto symbols like that when they're trying to preserve something fragile. Or honor someone."

"Sounds like her," Thomas said. "She sees things."

Will stared at nothing for a second. "She thought maybe it was my father. Or my mother. Like... if I don't keep some piece of it intact, it just disappears."

Thomas didn't rush in. Just let it sit. "That tracks."

Will nodded slowly. "She said it could be hope." He let out a quiet breath. "I never thought of it that way."

Thomas smiled a little. "That's Gracie. Finds the light even when no one's looking for it."

"Yeah," Will said. "I'm not used to that."

A small silence settled in again. Not awkward. Just... full.

Thomas said, "What was it Gussie called her?"

Will's mouth curved, slightly. "Empath."

"Right," Thomas said. "Fits."

Will nodded. “It does.”

Thomas leaned forward a bit, resting his forearms on his knees. Looked at him more directly now.

“Will,” he said gently, “she’s a keeper.”

Will didn’t answer right away.

But he didn’t disagree either.

——

Fort Meade-Watchtower Ops Annex

Derek Wilshire sat in the bullpen at Fort Meade, waiting for SYBIL to finish a batch process. Bored, he'd pulled up a paper he'd been noodling with for months, something about Euler's totient function. Not classified. Not operationally relevant. Just... beautiful.

The totient of a number n, written φ(n), counts the positive integers up to n that are relatively prime to n. For a prime number p, it was simple: φ(p) = p - 1. But highly totient numbers—those rare integers where φ(n) had an unusually high value, those fascinated him.

He sketched on a notepad: 120 has φ(120) = 32. But 5040 has φ(5040) = 576. The ratio was... elegant. Wasteful in an orderly way.

"Still playing with math toys?" Sara asked, passing by his desk.

Derek didn't look up. "Euler's totient function. Most people think it's useless outside number theory."

"And you think?"

"I think," Derek said slowly, "that patterns which seem useless in one context sometimes solve problems in another. That's the whole point of mathematics—it finds the hidden skeleton in noise."

Sara smiled. "Well, when you solve the world's problems with your skeleton hunt, let me know."

Derek returned to his puzzle, already halfway forgotten by the time Sara reached the coffee station.

CHAPTER NINE

Echo Reef

"Physics is becoming too difficult for the physicists."

Nusquam Dinner Table 1900 Hours R

The fire crackled low in the stone hearth, casting gentle amber light across the long table at Nusquam. The others had stepped away for dessert, leaving only Genevieve and Nemo at the far end, still nursing their wine.

She leaned in slightly, her fork idle.

"So, Nemo," she said, with a knowing smile, "what are you working on now?"

He hesitated. Not because of secrecy, but because of habit. His eyes flicked toward the door.

She noticed. "It's okay," she added, with quiet confidence. "I have code name clearance for ECHO REEF."

He looked at her a moment, almost amused. "I know," he said, and set his glass down. "I wasn't sure you'd want to hear it."

"I do."

He leaned back, exhaled once. The cautious mathematician in him briefly warred with the delighted physicist.

"All right. Based on initial work by scientists at the U. S. Department of Energy Ames National Laboratory we began looking at "quantum echoes."

Our work began as a noise anomaly in niobium samples—leftover from the Radiant Sentry shielding, ironically enough. We were testing superconducting phases when we started seeing... signatures that shouldn't persist. Faint, recursive waveforms—like echoes—but not in the acoustic or electromagnetic sense. Quantum echoes."

She tilted her head. "From what exactly?"

"From Higgs modes. Vibrational patterns in superconductors that occur during phase transitions. Normally, they vanish so quickly they're nearly impossible to observe. But in our case, something strange happened. Using high-resolution terahertz spectroscopy that sits in that middle ground between microwaves and infrared we picked up what we're calling Higgs echoes—residual patterns that linger and reveal hidden quantum dynamics inside the material."

Genevieve blinked. "So... echoes not of sound, but of symmetry breaking?"

"Exactly," he said, and his eyes sparked now with genuine excitement. "The Higgs modes interact with quasiparticles—quasi-electrons, really—that emerge when superconductivity partially breaks down. That interaction creates a kind of feedback loop, which under the right THz pulse, causes an echo to reverberate back out. But not just as a diagnostic tool—these echoes remember pathways. They reveal hidden coherence structures buried in the material."

She smiled. "Quantum memory."

"Better," Nemo said. "Quantum recall. We found we could manipulate the pulses—control the timing—and actually use the echoes to encode, store, and retrieve information. The material responds like it has a second language, hidden behind the first."

"And all in niobium?" she asked.

"Niobium's the sweet spot," he said. "Stable enough for circuits, reactive enough for phase coupling. The same stuff they used in the Sentry shield turns out to be a mirror—one that reflects the ghost of a quantum state long after it's supposed to be gone."

Genevieve's expression shifted slightly—curiosity giving way to something more serious.

"You're not just looking at information storage, are you?"

Nemo's voice lowered. "No. We're probing coherence itself. Control it... and you've got the skeleton key to fault-tolerant quantum memory, advanced sensing, even counter-surveillance tech. Imagine detecting tampering not from a breach—but from an echo of one."

We're not entirely there yet. Much left to do," said Nemo, "but we're on the right track."

She stared at him. "ECHO REEF isn't just a physics project."

"No," he said. "It's a map to how quantum information remembers itself."

Genevieve set her glass down carefully, her voice quiet but direct.

"Aren't you going to need a lot of help?" she asked. "Lab assistants, physicists, some poor postdocs to run the cryostat overnight?"

Nemo smiled, as if she'd said something quaint.

"I have help," he said. "But not too much. Most of the setup is automated. The data gets compressed and pushed to an air-gapped archive where I process it manually."

She raised an eyebrow. "You don't trust your own lab?"

"I trust the laws of thermodynamics," he said. "Everyone else has a clearance ceiling—and some of them don't know they're even working on quantum echo models. It's all partitioned. It has to be."

"Because of what ECHO REEF could lead to?"

"Because of who's already looking for it," he said. "SVR chatter picked up an encrypted reference to 'ghost harmonics in cryo arrays.' That was six weeks ago. We were still running calibration tests."

Genevieve sat back slightly. "And you didn't shut it down?"

"No," he said. "Because it works. The phenomenon is real. And if we're fast—and very careful—we can stay ahead of whoever's watching. But this isn't something you spread across a university lab floor. This is something you lock down so tightly, you start to wonder if you're paranoid... or not paranoid enough."

She studied him for a long moment.

"You're doing all of this alone?"

Nemo didn't answer immediately. Then said, "I'm doing enough to keep it alive."

Genevieve glanced toward the hallway where the others had disappeared. The sounds of laughter drifted faintly from the adjoining room. This place—Nusquam—was meant to be a refuge. But she could see it in Nemo's face: the burden of knowing too much, too soon.

"You should let me help," she said, gently. "At least with the modeling. Coherence mapping is in my wheelhouse."

He hesitated. Not because he doubted her, but because saying yes might change everything.

"You're cleared for it," he admitted. "And I could use someone who understands the math."

Genevieve smiled. "Send me the problem set."

Nemo leaned forward again, the spark of camaraderie flickering in his eyes.

"Okay," he said. "But don't blame me when you can't stop thinking about it at three in the morning."

She raised her glass. "You say that like it's a bad thing."

Later that night - Cold Room

Nemo stood under the hum of the chillers, reading a line of code until the numbers blurred.

Genevieve leaned in the doorway, a mug steamed in her hands.

"You should drink that before it goes into cryo," she said.

He smiled without looking away from the screen. "You'd accuse me of marrying my work."

She set the mug on the console and, for a heartbeat, their hands brushed over the keyboard.

Neither pulled back. The contact was electric and absurdly ordinary.

— —

Much Later that night

The others were long asleep. Outside, Nusquam was silent—thick with stars and alpine chill. The only sounds came from Genevieve's room: the soft hum of her tablet fan, the occasional scratch of her pen, and the whispered cadence of someone thinking too fast to stop.

A datapad lay open beside her bed, a secure transmission from Nemo with a single header:

ECHO REEF – Working Model (ver. 2.4) – Clearance Required

She'd entered her credentials. The file decrypted with a dull click. No introduction. No footnotes. Raw equations—layered, recursive, annotated only in terse shorthand. She recognized pieces—Bogoliubov transformations, terahertz pulse sequencing, low-temperature decoherence matrices. But stitched together in this way, it felt alien. Like someone had taken known physics and pulled it halfway into another dimension.

She sat cross-legged on the bed in flannel pants and a worn Michigan Wolverine sweatshirt, her hair tied up hastily, a half-drunk cup of black tea forgotten on the nightstand.

She scribbled across a notepad:

Higgs echo = $\int \psi(x,t)\, G(q,t')\, dq \rightarrow t' = t - \Delta t(\mathrm{THz})$

She frowned. That minus sign again.

Nemo wasn't modeling just a memory effect. He was modeling backflow. The echoes didn't just store information—they pulled coherence forward and backward across boundaries of time. She ran a simulation on her pad, hands moving with unconscious precision. The result came back with the signature curve—two spikes mirrored around a nonlinear center.

"Jesus," she whispered.

The pulses didn't reflect off the quasiparticles—they bent around them, reconstituting part of the pre-collapse state. As if the system remembered the possibility of what it could have been and sang it back in a buried harmonic.

She sat still for a long moment, absorbing it.

This wasn't only quantum storage. This was temporal encoding. Echoes from unobserved futures. And Nemo had barely scratched the surface.

Her eyes were wide now, tired but electric. The kind of tired that couldn't sleep.

She opened a fresh notebook and scrawled at the top of the page: Nonlocal forensic potential?

Outside, the mountain wind stirred faintly across the treetops. In the silence, Genevieve tapped her stylus once, twice, her mind spinning through interference patterns and second-order topologies.

She reached for her encrypted tablet and opened a blank message to Nemo.

Subject: Re: Echo backflow – temporal interference

Message: You didn't tell me about the folding interval. —G.

She hit send. A minute passed. Her screen blinked. One line reply:

Nemo: I wanted to see if you'd find it.

She exhaled, somewhere between awe and exhaustion.

She turned the page.

CHAPTER TEN

Team Watchtower

Nusquam 0700 Hours R

The secure Zoom.gov line made its distinctive alert on Will's monitor. He was surprised to see Nemo already in the Nusquam SCIF eating a hardboiled egg, cereal, juice, and coffee.

"Good morning, Major—"

"Will, please."

"Will, early riser or a tough night?" asked Nemo, smiling.

"The bad guys have been up for some time. It's 1 p.m. in Moscow and 6 p.m. in Beijing," answered Will.

"So, Watchtower is my Praetorian Guard?"

Will shrugged his shoulders and furrowed his brow in friendly acquiescence.

"Are you, my Sempronius Densus?"

Will paused.

"Semp...who?" "Oh, right," he said with a faint exhale, "the Roman who bought everyone else thirty seconds with his life."

He added, "I can see why you thought of me. I'm hoping my version comes with better odds."

"I hope so because I'm impressed by your people.

"Who the hell are they anyway—this team you sent? They sure as hell aren't your average everyday agents."

Will gave a low chuckle.

"You noticed."

"Your lead agent—Sara? She watches everything and says nothing unless she wants to rattle your spine. Your physicist, Genevieve—hadn't realized she was such an accomplished physicist. "

Will's voice sharpened slightly.

“Sara’s the one I trust when trust is dangerous. Genevieve was Deputy Director for Radiant Sentry. You’ve probably read her math without realizing it.”

Nemo was quiet before he said, “Well, you’ve got it. Whatever they are, they’re not normal. And I mean that in the most respectful, vaguely terrifying way.”

Nemo paused, then said, “Thanks for pulling me out when you did.”

Will’s voice softened a fraction.

“Don’t thank me yet. The storm hasn’t started.”

"I've been briefed on Echo Reef by Director Quinn," said Will. "I kept thinking about the man who built it."

Nemo smiled.

“We’ll take custody. We’ll run the front line, quiet and tight we’ll protect you and the op. Everybody wants this—Russians, Chinese, non-state actors—everybody. We’ll need guarantees—technical and political—that this doesn’t leak into a thousand hands.

“That’s why Stratton wanted this in-house with DARPA and the Army. No CIA. No DIA. No FBI. They’d lose their minds knowing it exists. Not even everybody in Watchtower is fully briefed either, need to know basis—that’s it.

“I want your read on security.”

“You’re the first to ask..”

Nemo set down his coffee. "Your biggest problem isn't code. Code you can harden."

"Hardware," Will said.

"Hardware. The cryogenics alone has three vendors, two of them with Chinese supply relationships. You can't audit your way out of that. You either manufacture domestically under black contract, or you accept residual risk and watch for anomalies."

"And if we miss one?"

Nemo looked at him steadily. "You've handed them the master key. And they won't tell you."

——

Espionage is the world's second oldest profession

Fort Meade Watchtower Conference Room 1145 Hours R

Thomas had never carried a weapon. Will had always found that interesting. Thirty years in this world, and the man had never needed one. His dissertation was on long-term embedded agents — how someone rewires themselves to live two lives without cracking. Will had read it once, years ago, and hadn't mentioned it. Some things you don't admit to.

The lights dimmed and a chart bloomed on the wall. Rick leaned in. Sara and Genevieve listened from the Nusquam SCIF. Genevieve crossed her arms. Will stayed quiet as Thomas Carrone cut to the chase.

"The part that matters," Thomas said, "is how they compete."

He advanced the slide. "The Joint Staff Intelligence Bureau does HUMINT—old-school spying. Internal counterintelligence lives in the Political Work Department's Liaison Division—ruthless, no appeals. And outside the PLA, the Ministry of State Security competes and cooperates with them depending on the prize."

Will glanced at Ed. "Who's on Nemo?"

Ed didn't hesitate. "SSF cycled him first; if MSS smells he's alive, they'll move fast—and ugly."

Sara leaned in. "So we pit them against each other."

Will nodded slowly. "Yes. Let them bleed each other trying to find a ghost."

Rick pulled up the False Constellation overlay. "Grace's shell architecture is holding. MSS is still chasing the Plattsburgh node."

Will nodded once. Said nothing.

Thomas watched him. Not the screen. Him.

It wasn't much. A half-second where Will's expression didn't quite stay where he'd put it. There and gone. Anyone else in the room would have missed it.

Thomas didn't miss things.

He didn't say anything. He waited until the briefing broke up and the room emptied, he closed his notebook and looked at Will with the particular patience of someone who had spent thirty years understanding why people don't say what they mean.

"She's good at this," Thomas said. Neutral. Giving Will nothing to push against.

Will gathered his file. "She is."

"The False Constellation design was elegant. Structurally sound. Better than most professionals I've seen."

"Yes."

Thomas let the silence sit. "That all you've got?"

Will looked at him. Brief. Unreadable to most people. "That's all I've got, Thomas."

Thomas nodded slowly, the way he did when someone told him the truth in the wrong words.

"Right," he said.

He picked up his coffee. Said nothing else. Will was almost at the door when Thomas spoke again, without looking up. "She doesn't know."

Will stopped. Didn't turn around.

"No," he said.

"You going to do anything about that?"

A beat. Long enough to mean something. "Probably not."

Thomas nodded to himself. "That tracks," he said.

And Will left.

CHAPTER ELEVEN

Nusquam Security

Fort Meade— Team Watchtower Conference Room

The lights were low. Screens lined the far wall — an encrypted video feed window active. Will Morgan, Ed Perry, Rick Huang, and Cecil Brandon sat at the table.

On screen: Sara Brandt, face calm but sharp from a secure uplink at Burlington National Guard hangar. Beside her, Genevieve Larsson, composed as ever, stylus tapping a tablet just out of view.

Codename: NUSQUAM

Status: Elevated risk, internal breach unlikely, external surveillance suspected.

Ed Perry opened with a sentence like a scalpel.

"The party's over. ACIC is flying in a full TSCM unit by 0800. They'll sweep the entire Granville perimeter — house, lab, fiber conduits, power mains, the relay barn, even the damned compost bin."

Genevieve said, "The cleanup's easy. Continuity isn't. We need eyes there, twenty-four seven. Someone who blends."

Ed Perry looked to Will Morgan. "Candidate?"

Will shook his head. "Not one I like. Sara and Genevieve are already split."

Sara smirked. "Appreciated."

Genevieve's tone stayed flat. "If Shen Ke feels watched, he'll shut down. We need someone who doesn't smell like surveillance."

Cecil flipped a dossier. "Who's left?"

"Karen Bolanowski or Cathy Wang. Maybe Z, but he's tasked at the moment."

"Cathy's sharp," Sara said. "But she has zero field time."

"Karen's raw but instinctive," Cecil countered.

Ed leaned forward. "Fine. Vet Karen. Tier-3 clearance, burn-in protocol. Any wobble, she's out."

Will nodded. "Karen's learned fast. Street smarts are always worth betting on. Prep packet by midnight. She's airborne in forty-eight."

Genevieve added, "Make sure she knows who to call when things start humming at one a.m."

——

Fort Meade – Will Morgan's Office

Karen entered, stiff with uncertainty and Will waved her into a seat as he joined her at the table in front of his desk, something he rarely, if ever did,

Will slid a sealed envelope across the table. "You're being reassigned."

"I didn't know I was assigned."

"You are now."

Inside: a burner ID, coordinates, and a title page—

NUSQUAM: Embedded Field Liaison / Security Analyst (Provisional)
Granville, Vermont – Subject: CHAN, ANDREW (WITSEC)

Karen looked up. "A witness-protection science op?"

Will: "The subject's a former double agent. Fed Beijing poisoned fruit. Now he's in deep cover—and quiet's getting to him."

"You think he's breaking?"

"Or being watched. Either way, we need someone who can see without being seen."

"When do I leave?"

"Twenty-two hours. Pack for winter."

She hesitated. "Why me?"

Will's answer was quiet. "You're still curious. And curiosity's the one trait Nemo respects."

She glanced past him at the mysterious Greek trireme on his credenza.

Will smiled and said, "No, you may not ask."

——

As she left Will's office Karen Bolanowski thought about the path that had brought her here—and how absurdly narrow it had been.

Pure luck, she told herself.

If Diane Watson hadn't trusted her gut.

If Will Morgan hadn't backed that instinct without qualification, without hedging, without asking for guarantees—there was no telling where she would have ended up.

Probably somewhere familiar. Somewhere that tolerated her, but never claimed her.

She leaned back in her chair and let the thought settle.

For the first time in her life, she didn't feel like she was borrowing space.

Everywhere else, the story had followed her eventually—the dumpster baby legend, dragged out like a joke, or worse, like proof that she didn't quite belong anywhere decent. It surfaced in sideways comments, in cruel humor, in the quiet recalculations people made once they thought they knew what she came from.

Here?

Here they shrugged.

No one cared.

Not because they were kind—though many of them were—but because it simply wasn't relevant. At Watchtower, origin stories didn't outweigh outcomes. Background didn't excuse failure, but it didn't predefine it either.

What mattered was what you did when it counted. Whether, when things went bad—and they always did—you were the person they wanted beside them in a foxhole.

If they wanted you there, you were one of them.

That was it.

You belonged.

Karen closed her eyes.

I can't let Watchtower down. I can't let Diane down.

The thought wasn't dramatic. It wasn't desperate.

It was steady. Anchored. Certain.

I won't.

And for the first time, the promise wasn't made out of fear of losing a place.

It was made out of loyalty to one she had finally earned.

——

Nusquam, Vermont - Winter

Snow swept the ridgeline as the black SUV crawled toward the farmhouse.

Sara Brandt checked the perimeter. "Rule one: don't treat him like a subject. He's his own gravity well."

Karen managed a grin. "Don't interrogate the sun. Got it."

Sara smiled back. "Close enough."

They stepped inside the renovated barn. Warm air, humming power, fiber conduits, quantum arrays.

At the far table stood Nemo—Andrew Chan, once Shen Ke—gray hair, MIT sweatshirt, hands steady over a sealed chamber.

Without looking up: "You're early."

"Andrew," Sara said, "this is Karen Bolanowski. She'll be around."

He turned, studying Karen. "Another handler?"

"No," Sara said. "Information pathways. Perimeter security."

"They send new minds when they expect trouble."

Karen met his eyes. "Only when there's something worth protecting."

A flicker—almost a smile. "Don't get underfoot."

"I won't."

He turned back to his work. Sara leaned close. "Good start. He didn't dismiss you."

Karen's voice low. "He didn't accept me, either."

Sara: "He might never. Doesn't matter. Your job's balance."

"Between what I see and what I let him think I don't?"

Sara nodded. "Exactly."

Snow rattled the barn roof. The hum deepened. Nusquam had a new heartbeat.

——

Nusquam 0800 Hours R

The morning mist clung low over the pines as three jet-black Suburbans turned off the gravel road and eased up the long drive toward the Granville property. The quiet was broken by the muted crunch of tires and the low hum of equipment warming in the back.

A full ACIC Technical Surveillance Countermeasures Team (TSCM)—had arrived. Twelve operators in gray field jackets, each with the unhurried precision of people who had done this too many times to count.

Within minutes, the air filled with the faint chorus of handheld spectrum analyzers, RF detectors, and ultrasonic scanners. They moved in pairs: house, lab, relay barn. One team traced the fiber conduits to the main feed; another pulled the cover plates off electrical panels, working by headlamp even in daylight.

The team leader, a wiry warrant officer with a coffee thermos in one hand and a broadband sniffer in the other, gave a dry grin as he passed Nemo on the steps.

"Commander Perry says to sweep everything—" he gestured toward the compost heap by the fence, "—even the damn compost bin."

Nemo smirked faintly. "You'll find more worms than wires out there."

"Orders are orders," the warrant replied, and kept walking.

Inside, Genevieve Larsson stood by the kitchen window, arms folded. Her reflection hovered against the glass, pale and still, while the yard beyond teemed with motion.

"They're not taking chances," she said.

Sara Brandt leaned against the door frame, badge clipped to her belt, watching an operator run a wand along the baseboard. "After last week's intercept at Fort Meade? No one's in the mood to gamble."

One of the TSCM techs crouched near the floor vent, running a fiber optic camera into the duct. The monitor on his wrist flashed a faint green. Clear.

From the lab, a muffled voice came over the encrypted channel:

"Control, Lab-1. Negative for active transmitters. Proceeding to Phase Two."

Nemo exhaled slowly, feeling the knot between his shoulders ease—but not by much.

He knew that if anyone had managed to slip a passive device inside Nusquam's walls, it wouldn't be something a handheld wand could catch.

"Do they really need to check the compost bin?" Genevieve asked without looking away from the window.

Sara gave a half-shrug. "If it makes Perry sleep better tonight, I'll let them dig to bedrock."

Outside, the warrant officer knelt by the heap, running a magnetic flux probe through layers of damp soil and leaves. "Nothing but earthworms and coffee grounds," he said into his mic, deadpan.

The channel crackled back: "Copy that. Move to the relay barn."

By 0930, every outlet, junction box, and conduit had been logged, scanned, and resealed. The team packed up as efficiently as they'd arrived, engines idling in the drive.

Sara stepped out to sign the clearance report.

"All clean?" she asked.

"We found everything that was on your report," the warrant officer said, flipping his tablet to face her, "and everything Commander Perry had installed. No surprises there. Nemo has already found some of them. "

He hesitated long enough to matter.

"But we also found a passive collection device—no transmission capability—mounted about fifteen feet up in the big red maple next to the main house. Hardwired cache only. Someone planned to come back for it.

"If you've got ghosts, ma'am, they're staying off the air."

Granville, VT-Route 100 0600 Hours R

Marie-Claire Pelletier was already thinking about dinner when she reached the bend in the road—the last gentle curve before Nusquam disappeared behind the trees.

That was when the SUVs appeared.

One black Suburban, another, and a third, noses lifting as they pulled cleanly onto Highway 100 from the Nusquam access road. The timing was too precise, the spacing too deliberate. They accelerated smoothly, unhurried, settling into formation as they headed in the opposite direction.

As they passed, Marie-Claire glanced instinctively into the windows.

Four occupants in each vehicle. Twelve faces, all dressed alike in slate-gray field jackets—no logos, no insignia, no color variation. Not construction. Not utility crews. Not tourists. Their posture was wrong for that. Upright. Alert. Eyes forward. No one looked at her.

The last SUV went by, its tinted glass reflecting only trees and sky, and they were gone, swallowed by the road.

Marie-Claire slowed without quite meaning to.

That's strange, she thought.

Nusquam rarely saw strangers—certainly not convoys, certainly not men dressed like that. Whatever they were doing there, they were finished now. And whatever it was, it hadn't been meant for her to see.

——

Nusquam -Secure Line to Commander Perry 0952 Hours R

The last of the Suburbans rolled through the gate and vanished down the road. The quiet that followed felt heavier than before, an acoustic void that made every sound inside the house sharper, more intimate.

Sara's secure phone buzzed once on the table. No ringtone. Only the vibration.

She checked the ID: PERRY / SCIF LINE 3.

As she answered, she created distance from Nemo who was standing near by.

"Granville perimeter sweep is complete," Sara said. "They found one thing that wasn't ours."

Ed Perry didn't speak at first. When he did, his voice was clipped, all trace of humor gone. The low hum of Fort Meade's command floor bled faintly through the line.

"Go on."

"Passive collection device," Sara continued. "No transmission capability. Hard cache only. Mounted about fifteen feet up in the red maple next to the main house. Line of sight to the lab roof and the south windows."

Another pause—longer this time.

"So the microburst wasn't coming from you," Perry said. "It was someone checking whether their gear was still alive."

"That's our assessment," Sara said. "The team believes whoever planted it planned to retrieve it later."

Perry exhaled slowly. "That tracks. NSA lit up a Burlington relay window last night—twenty-one seconds. Too clean to be accidental. We assumed remote telemetry. Now we know it was a confidence check."

Nemo had drifted closer, listening without asking.

Sara lowered her voice. "You think they know we found it?"

"No," Perry said. "Not yet. And I want to keep it that way."

She straightened. "Understood."

"SYBIL's already reconstructing the collection profile," Perry went on. "If that device was harvesting what I think it was—emanations, timing artifacts, optical leakage—we'll know what questions they were asking."

Sara's eyes flicked to Genevieve, then to Nemo. Both were very still.

"Until then," Perry said, "assume you were being watched, not listened to. That matters."

"It does," Sara agreed.

"Dark mode stays in effect," Perry added. "No open comms. No pattern changes. And Sara—good catch."

The line went dead.

Sara set the phone down, staring at the display until it dimmed.

Genevieve broke the silence. "So it wasn't paranoia."

"No," Sara said. "It was preparation."

Nemo moved to the window, his gaze settling on the red maple at the edge of the mist, its branches motionless.

"Whoever planted it," he said, "was patient."

"And careful," Sara replied.

The house settled into silence again, but now it was the kind that listened back.

CHAPTER TWELVE

Mossad

Fort Meade - Morgan's Office - 1100 Hours R

Will sat arms folded, eyes fixed on the still image of the device.

Sara, Rick, and Cecil sat at the small table in front of his desk.

"NSA says it's Israeli," he said.

Everybody understood that the main goals of the Mossad are national and operational security, with everything else being secondary and sometimes sacrificed for the sake of secrecy. Whatever else the agency considered necessary to protect its operations and mandate.

Tensions often arose over issues like the use of foreign passports for Israeli agents. Mossad spied on everything anywhere that suggested an impact on their national interests.

Cecil noted, "The Israel National Quantum Initiative (INQI) is a well-developed quantum computing research effort."

Cathy said, "I looked it up. It has a budget of about $390 million (NIS 1.25 billion). At least that's what they admit to in public."

"Israel certainly understands the existential risk of falling behind," said Rick.

Will almost smiled. "They have no idea what's going on in Vermont. But they're curious. That's enough."

No one spoke at first.

Sara broke the silence. "That's... earlier than I expected."

Rick leaned forward. "It's clean work. Military-grade fabrication. Power profile matches Israeli passive collectors we've seen before. No transmit hardware."

"So they weren't sending anything out," Cecil said. "They were waiting."

Will nodded. "Or assuming they'd be back."

Sara's brow furrowed. "Which means they had to know about Granville before it existed. Not the science—the land."

Z exhaled slowly. "DARPA cutout bought the Lavoie farm six months before any visible activity. The ownership chain goes through three LLCs, two jurisdictions, and a trust with sealed officers. On paper, it's dead, eh?"

"Dead to us," Sara said. "Not necessarily dead to them."

Will looked at her. "That's the part I don't like."

Cecil tapped the table once, decisive. "Let's say Mossad got a whiff of something. They don't know what it is yet, but they know it smells strategic. So they plant a passive listener and wait for the world to explain itself."

Rick nodded. "Bluetooth long-range variant. Line-of-sight, elevated placement. Ten klicks if the terrain cooperates."

Sara glanced at the satellite image. "So whoever collects it won't need to come onto the property."

"No," Cecil said. "They'll park somewhere boring. A turnout. A trailhead. Maybe a rental cabin with a good view and bad internet."

Will was quiet before he said. "We can't confront them."

Sara didn't argue. "And even if we did, they'd shrug and say nothing."

"Mossad doesn't apologize," Rick said. "They deny professionally."

Will allowed a thin smile.

Cecil straightened. "So, we watch."

"Physically and electronically," Will said.

Rick was already pulling up a diagram. "Wide capture net. Directional antennas, spectrum logging, mobile receivers. We'll blanket the radius. No dead zones."

"How fast?" Sara asked.

"Yesterday," Rick said.

Cecil nodded. "I'll get eyes in place. Quiet ones. Anything that loiters gets cataloged."

Will looked around the table. "We're not trying to stop them."

Sara met his gaze. "We're trying to see who comes to collect."

"And when," Rick added.

Will nodded once. "Because whoever shows up will tell us how they knew."

"And whether this was curiosity," Cecil said, "or something more."

The room fell silent again.

Will said, "Until then, the farm isn't a vulnerability."

Sara smiled faintly. "It's bait."

"Exactly," Will said. "And we don't blink."

Fort Meade-Will's Office

As the meeting broke up Rick stood up pointing to the trireme with the expression of a man who believed he had cracked a major philosophical code. That alone should've been Will's warning.

Rick waved his finger at the model "I've figured it out."

Will didn't look up from the file. "No, you haven't."

Rick ignored that. "It's a metaphor for the team."

Will closed the folder. Slowly. "Is it."

"Yeah. Look—three rows of oars." He pointed enthusiastically. "Three layers of Watchtower. Field ops, analysis, tech. Perfect symmetry. Perfect synchronization."

Will blinked once. "Rick."

"And the hull? Obviously, that's you. Holding us together. Guiding the mission. Keeping us from sinking."

Will stared at him a moment longer than usual. "Rick."

Rick pressed on, gaining speed. "Plus the fact that the ship fought the Persians? That's like us fighting hostile foreign intelligence networks."

Will exhaled through his nose, the closest he ever got to laughing during office hours. "No."

Rick's face fell. "No?"

"No."

"So it's not... a Watchtower metaphor?"

"No."

Rick pointed at it again. "Not even a little?"

Will allowed the faintest, fractional upward curve of his mouth. "The Persians were not the point."

Rick stepped back, eyes narrowing as if trying a fresh angle.

"Okay. Fine. I accept defeat. But for the record, that was a damn good theory."

Will nodded. "It was confident."

Rick frowned. "That's not praise."

"It's all you're getting."

——

Panama City, Panama - a year earlier

For years, Lavi Alon had paid a clerk inside López, Rodríguez, Morales & Castillo to alert him about information for a list of known DARPA domestic entities.

The Lavoie farm had been purchased by Aldea Grande LLC, a Panamanian Sociedad de Responsabilidad Limitada. A quick inquiry with the Registro Público de Panamá revealed the next layer: ownership traced to Granville S.A., with the Lopez law firm listed as nominee member.

The registered agent was the firm itself, the one entity legally permitted to maintain the private record of beneficial ownership. And that record—carefully shielded, deliberately mundane—pointed not to an oligarch or a shell empire, but to a DARPA-linked Delaware entity.

A Vermont farm purchased by DARPA Carefully buried offshore.

Government money.

Government intent.

That was enough.

Lavi headed to Granville.

——

General Store - Early Morning

Morning came slowly to Granville.

The early autumn air was dry and carried the sweet scent of the decomposing leaves that lined the ground and the metallic smell of the river which lay hidden behind the screen of trees. In the general store the warmth of the place hit him the moment he stepped inside - coffee fresh on the stove, the aroma of cinnamon from the muffins made early in the morning, the soothing murmur of the refrigerator in the case against the wall.

Marie-Claire had already been there for two hours.

She slid onto the worn counter the way she always did—quickly, silently, without a fidget or wasted second—her hands navigating with practiced ease the space she knew as well as her own face. Time had weathered the counter to a deep, burnished color; the steady attrition of arms laid flat on the wooden lip, of dropped change, of clumsily folded evening newspapers.

From the front window you could look right out onto the road as it stretched past the store to the post office and out to the surrounding farmland and rolling hills of Nusquam. In season mornings light streamed in through the low leveled windows in long rays of warm yellow light scattering in the suspended motes of dust as fine as snow falling downward.

Marie-Claire wiped the espresso wand with a clean cloth and put the milk pitcher away.

She listened.

A pickup truck had driven by ten minutes earlier. Old suspension, loose tailgate. A delivery van came a bit earlier. Nothing unusual. Nothing new.

The store breathed in its quiet morning rhythm until the bell over the door rang.

Marie-Claire looked up.

The man who entered did not remain in the doorway long. Long enough for the colder air to move past him, but no longer than that before the door swung shut behind him.

People did that sometimes.

But most people paused to look around.

He didn't.

He looked around the cafe with a slow, easy glance that didn't seem to find anything out of the ordinary. The refrigerator, the display case of pastries, the bulletin board above the counter that faces the window. The two tables nearest the coffee counter, both currently unoccupied.

His gaze didn't linger anywhere.

Which meant, Marie-Claire thought, that he had already seen everything.

He stepped toward the counter.

Mid-40s, maybe. Travel jacket with a bit of wear around the seams. And a neutral color that might once have been white or at least pale, but had long since faded into a muted off-shade of beige. The kind of clothes a person buys in order to blend into the scenery, to become another faceless anonymous entity among the bland facades and dusty motorways of some forgotten town, unremarkable and unremembered.

There was nothing wrong with him.

Nothing unusual.

But he moved like someone accustomed to unfamiliar rooms.

Marie-Claire had spent her whole life behind the counter. She knew the endless stream of tourists coming to Granville to see the island of Tatihou, the slenderness of the Peninsula, and the beauty of the bay. And she knew, too, the waves of escapees who came there simply to get away from the demands of their everyday lives.

He was the second kind.

"Morning," she said warmly.

"Morning."

His voice was calm, unremarkable.

He didn't study the pastry case.

"Coffee," he said. " Black. And one of those blueberry muffins."

He indicated the tray without looking closely at it.

People who didn't shop here dawdled in the produce stand—they'd peer into the display, ask what was in season, and mull their choices.

He chose instantly.

Marie-Claire nodded and turned.

She poured her coffee from the pot they had started brewing early this morning. She picked up a muffin from the table and slipped it into a paper sleeve.

"That'll be four twenty-five."

He placed the money down immediately.

A five-dollar bill and a quarter.

Close enough to exact that she didn't need to make change.

Minimal transaction. No delay.

"Road's clear this morning?" he asked casually.

Not quite a question.

Marie-Claire smiled the way she always did.

"Road is quiet at the moment. Leaves are starting to drop. Can make the corners very slippery if the frost is early."

He nodded.

"Post office open yet?"

"Another fifteen minutes."

"Good to know."

He took the coffee and muffin with a small nod of thanks.

"Have a good morning."

"You too."

He left the way he had entered—unhurried, controlled.

The bell rang again as the door closed behind him.

Marie-Claire peered out the window as he made his way across the street to the parking lot near the post office. From her view, she could see a huge black SUV idling in the lot.

Rental plates.

She returned to wiping the counter.

The store breathed again.

——

Later that morning the bell rang once more.

Cecil Brandon walked into the lounge, a draft of fresh air entering with him. He nodded in the direction of the counter.

"Morning, Marie-Claire."

"Morning, Cecil."

She poured him a coffee. He supposed she'd poured it long before he'd said anything. He'd been coming in here long enough now that she must have worked out his order.

He set a few bills on the counter.

"Well," she said pleasantly, "this is the morning for out-of-towners, I guess."

Cecil paused.

"Oh? How so?"

"You're the second one in the past hour."

He lifted an eyebrow.

"You've got some memory. Did you recognize him as well?"

Marie-Claire shook her head slightly.

"Only by his car."

"His car?"

"Yes," she said, sliding the coffee cup across the table. "I guess you notice most of the people who come through here." "Yeah, pretty near everybody who comes driving by," he agreed.

Cecil waited.

"Also saw him in the post office parking lot," she said. "I guess he was waiting for it to open."

"What kind of car?"

"Like yours," she said. " Big black SUV."

A small pause.

"Rental plates though."

Cecil nodded slowly.

"Thanks," he said as he gave her a small, easy smile.

"And have a nice day."

"You too, Cecil."

The morning air was colder now.

He stepped outside with his coffee.

Cecil gets in behind the wheel, slams the door, and reaches into his suit pants for his phone.

His thumbs moved quickly across the screen.

Watchtower Ops:

Be on the look out for new arrivals. I think Marie-Claire might have stumbled upon a pre-collection reconnaissance.

Rochester, VT

SYBIL noticed the scan before any human could have.

It was subtle—low-power, directional, disguised as commercial spectrum noise—but it was wrong. The signature brushed against a protected envelope around Nusquam's outer perimeter, a probing whisper that assumed the terrain was ignorant and the watchers asleep.

SYBIL disagreed.

SYBIL: Anomalous electromagnetic interrogation detected. Vector origin: mobile platform. Confidence: 97.4% hostile intelligence collection.

Cecil Brandon's tablet chimed once. He was already moving.

"Source?" he asked, jacket half on, voice steady.

SYBIL: Triangulating... Confirmed. Static vehicle. Coordinates match Rochester Town Garage. Intersection of River Brook Drive and Recreation Field Drive.

Cecil didn't swear. He never did. He simply tapped his earpiece.

"All units, Watchtower Actual. We have a live scanner probing protected property. No flight risk indicated, but I want clean containment. Block Beans Bridge Road anyway. Quiet and fast."

The response was immediate. Engines turned. Doors closed. The choreography unfolded the way it always did—efficient, practiced, unrehearsed only in appearance.

——

Lavi Alon sat in his car with the engine off, hands resting lightly on the steering wheel, eyes tracking reflections in the garage's concrete pillars.

He knew the scan had landed. He also knew he hadn't crossed the line far enough to justify panic.

Yet.

The first black SUV rolled in without lights or sirens, gliding to a stop nose-to-nose. The second and third arrived from opposing ramps, sealing him in from angles no civilian would ever anticipate.

Three vehicles. Simultaneous. No wasted motion.

Lavi exhaled once.

"Well," he murmured. "That was faster than expected."

Doors opened. Boots on concrete. Cecil Brandon stepped forward alone, posture relaxed, badge visible but not flaunted.

"Afternoon," Cecil said. "Mind telling me what you're doing here?"

Lavi blinked, feigning mild surprise. "Parking," he replied evenly. "Is that suddenly regulated?"

Cecil smiled thinly. "It is when your equipment pings classified federal property from a municipal garage."

Lavi's eyebrows rose enough to be convincing. "Classified? That's interesting. I wasn't aware I was anywhere near such a place."

"You were," Cecil said. "And you ran an illegal electronic collection device while you were at it. That's a felony."

Lavi studied him for a beat, nodded once, accepting the reality, not the accusation.

"I think there's been a misunderstanding."

"There usually is," Cecil replied. He gestured. "Step out of the vehicle."

Lavi complied without resistance. No sudden movements. No bravado. A professional recognizing another.

They blindfolded him gently, methodically. Not punitive. Procedural.

——

Granville VT-Nusquam Basement Holding Room

The holding room at Nusquam was spare by design—concrete, steel, no clocks, no adornment. The kind of place that denied narrative leverage.

When the blindfold came off, Lavi smiled.

"Comfortable," he said. "I assume this isn't where you keep your dangerous people."

Cecil leaned against the wall, arms crossed. "You're not dangerous," he said. "You're curious."

Lavi chuckled. "That's generous."

"You're a NOC," Cecil continued. "No diplomatic cover. No embassy safety net. If you were here officially, this conversation would be happening somewhere else."

"And yet," Lavi said calmly, "here I am."

He wasn't wrong—and he knew it.

"My government will deny any knowledge of this," Lavi went on pleasantly. "They will say I was tracking terrorist financing, or arms transfers, or something equally alarming and conveniently unverifiable. They will be offended. Loudly."

Cecil didn't respond.

"They will also insist," Lavi added, "that they had no idea this was a classified facility. After all, how would they?"

Cecil pushed off the wall and met his eyes.

"They won't be lying," he said. "About that part."

Lavi's smile widened a fraction. "We understand each other."

Later, upstairs, Cecil briefed the team.

"Device confirmed Mossad," he said. "Passive scan. Recon only. No transmission attempt."

Will Morgan listened without comment.

"They're curious," Cecil finished. "Not hostile. They'll stay curious. But they're not a threat."

Will nodded once. "We'll let them stay that way."

Cecil closed his tablet.

SYBIL logged the encounter, categorized it, and adjusted the perimeter.

And the message—delivered without words—had been received.

Cecil nodded when he released him. Lavi nodded back. Two professionals mostly on the same team neither in a hurry to share anything about this Vermont farmhouse.

But as Cecil watched the rental car pull back onto Route 100, something crystallized in his assessment. Mossad didn't waste assets on fishing expeditions. That passive scan wasn't curiosity—it was validation. Someone in Tel Aviv was already asking the same question Watchtower was asking. Which meant, by straightforward logic, that Israel and the United States had discovered at least one common adversary.

That was worth remembering.

——

Lavi Alon sat in the rental car and stared blankly at route 100 without really seeing it.

It was rare that Lavi was ever caught and even rarer still to be caught in the Americas. It was as if he was invisible to them. But Watchtower wasn't everyone and he respected that.

Lavi had long ago stopped counting operations. The numbers had no beginnings, middles, or ends. Only continuations. Long threads of continuations that he picked up in one city and dropped in another. Years later someone else would come along and tie them off, never knowing their origins.

There had been a time, once, when every mission counted for something. Meant something. He remembered the first mission; the strange way his hands had been shaking, while the rest of him felt numb. He'd assumed with time, that would change; that the shock of it all would wear off. It hadn't. It had only refined them.

He didn't have to think about it anymore. Somewhere along the line of lies told without guilt or the truths omitted without qualm, he'd given up wondering whether he had to. Not because he cared, although he did; it was that every second lost to indecision meant more people died, and morals were a luxury they couldn't afford. Still, there were moments. Brief, uninvited.

A face he could not always keep out of his mind. Occasional overtones of a voice that sounded from time to time in his room at midnight. No sense of guilt, which he recognized easily enough. Something less sharply defined, but no less disturbing—a kind of bookkeeping, or an attempt to keep books that he could not quite close, only continue. The concept of yesterday required some sort of mental adjustment. In another life, he might have been something simpler. A man who measured time in years rather than the number of operations he could perform in an hour. Someone who felt rich and powerful because he could spend years with the people he loved, rather than tallying the number of successful operations. But that life had required a different kind of faith. Lavi had chosen certainty. And certainty, he knew, always came at a cost.

Whatever was happening on that Vermont farm was apparently of some concern to someone in his office. His task was to determine what. He had failed, at least for now.

CHAPTER THIRTEEN

Psychological Profiles

Evening at Nusquam – The Fireplace Room

The fire cracked low in the hearth, shadows dancing along the stone wall behind them. A decanter of brandy glowed amber on the table, next to a tray of coffee, cups half full. Sara sat closest to the flames; legs tucked beneath her. Karen leaned into a throw pillow, eyes flickering with curiosity. Genevieve, perched on the arm of a nearby chair, held her cup but hadn't sipped in minutes. Nemo sat back, eyes soft but unreadable in the firelight.

They had moved from shop talk to stories—odd memories, things left unsaid. It was Genevieve who brought up the question they'd all danced around. "So how long were you actually in ADX?" she asked.

Nemo smiled faintly. "Oh, about five hours."

Karen blinked. "Five hours? I thought you were arrested in 2022."

"I was," Nemo said, placing his cup gently on the coaster. "But ADX was just the illusion." He glanced toward the fire, the light catching the lines around his eyes. "Standard intake. Strip search. Orientation. Paper scrubs. They moved fast. I was escorted underground, switched into a jumpsuit identical to another inmate's. He was Chinese, serving twenty-five years under a sealed conviction. Offered a deal where he takes my identity, my cell, my silence. No contact was allowed between inmates on that wing. No talking. No exercise yard. So, the swap? Easier than you'd think."

Sara raised her eyebrows. "So, you went ghost."

"I did. But the best-laid plans," Nemo said with a dry chuckle, "often go sideways. My double died of a heart attack. They had to hustle me back. I was snuck into ADX, marched to the cell for the retina scan, standard morgue verification procedure. Two guards saw me, confirmed the body. Then I vanished again."

Karen looked stunned. "You were gone for three and a half years. Where were you?"

Nemo leaned back in his chair, fingers steepled lightly in front of him. "Bay Ridge. Brooklyn." "Brooklyn?" Sara echoed in disbelief.

Nemo chuckled. "Not the first place you'd think for an off-books DARPA holding, I know. But Bay Ridge has a large Chinese population—about twenty-five percent—many of them foreign-born, speaking various dialects. I could live there and speak nothing but Cantonese without anyone questioning it. No one asked who I was as long as I kept a low profile and kept quiet.

"DARPA bought a four-story tenement on a side street near Fort Hamilton Parkway. The Secret Service controlled the first two floors—entry monitoring and staging. The upper two floors were mine. One for living. One retrofitted into a crude lab. The walls were so thick with insulation and noise baffling, you could've dropped a wrench and no one would've heard it."

Genevieve's eyes sparkled. "You felt safe there?"

"I did," Nemo said. "The anonymity of density. Fifty thousand people per square mile and Fort Hamilton a mile away, the only active military installation in the city. The perfect place to disappear."

He lifted his glass again, took a sip, and added, "But eventually, the work outgrew the space. I needed helium cycles, superconducting shielding, high-stability platforms. Hard to hide a dilution fridge in a Brooklyn walk-up."

Karen smirked. "So, you upgraded to a barn in the middle of nowhere?"

Nemo grinned. "Absolutely. We saw an opportunity to relocate somewhere with fewer eyes, fewer questions, and more room to breathe. So, when the timing aligned, we moved everything here. The cold. The isolation. The Faraday shielding. It's ideal."

Genevieve leaned forward. Her voice dropped just above a whisper. "You've been working on Quantum Echoes this whole time?"

Nemo nodded once. "In a sealed lab. Just metal, helium, and math. But eventually we couldn't risk staying there either. Too much noise. Too much visibility. So, when the opportunity came—we moved."

Sara folded her arms, studying him. "To an old man's dairy barn in Vermont."

Nemo gave a short nod. "Where better to vanish?"

The fire popped. Karen muttered, almost to herself, "This is insane."

Genevieve smiled, but her eyes were locked on Nemo. "Insane... or brilliant."

CHAPTER FOURTEEN

Inside the Barn

Nusquam Facility – Barn-Lab Conversion 0622 Hours R

The steel bay doors groaned open on hydraulic pistons as a specialty flatbed backed into the newly reinforced entryway. The driver from Massachusetts looked around the icy hills, unimpressed.

"Thought this was a barn."

Nemo stood silently in the cold, arms crossed, watching every movement of the rig. He was leaner now than he had been during his IBM days — the years of double agency had carved him down to essence.

"It is," he replied. "A barn for quantum ghosts."

The technician escorting the load — a steel-caged cryogenic assembly packed in vibration-damped foam — didn't laugh. He knew what this was. And more importantly, what it wasn't.

A dilution refrigerator: the heart of any serious quantum computing system. Nearly two tons, rated for sub-10 millikelvin operation. Delivered in components for final assembly.

The system had been sourced from two vendors under shell identities. The final plumbing and latticework had been machined off-books, with help from a semi-retired MIT cryo engineer now living "off-grid" in Maine.

Nemo turned to the local contractor supervising the winch setup.

"No power tools past the black line," he said sharply. "From here on, it's hand-lift only."

The man hesitated. "That's over 300 kilos of—"

"Adjust the lift strategy."

Karen, watching from the upper catwalk, made a note. She was still adjusting to Nemo's rhythm — monastic, cerebral.

As the team worked the cryostat crate onto the reinforced cleanroom floor, condensation plumed from the open doors. It mixed with the ambient chill in the air like a veil.

Sara Brandt entered from the south wing in a gray jacket, eyes sharp, coffee in hand.

"You really think this is going to stay invisible?" she asked.

Nemo didn't look up. He was watching the torque as the unit settled into its magnetic vibration-isolation bed.

"Not invisible," he said. "But uninteresting to anyone not already infected with obsession."

She raised an eyebrow.

"You mean the MSS?"

Now he looked at her.

"I mean... people like me."

The final component was in place. The inner vacuum canister gleamed dully under the LED strips. Inscribed in small black ink on the support ring was a phrase in Latin:

Silet universum in glacie.

"The universe is silent in the ice."

Sara saw it, read it silently, and asked:

"What's the heat load profile at full qubit fidelity?"

"Sub-10 millikelvin requires 10^-9 thermal watts. Any vibration, any EM spike, any inconsistency—and the coherence fails."

He looked up.

"That's why it matters who's around me."

From the corner window, Karen Bolanowski observed the final calibration device being uncrated. She watched Nemo—not with awe, but with uncertainty. The man was brilliant. No question. But there was something else here. A loneliness? A fracture?

Sara turned toward her.

"Karen, you're on environmental integrity now. Nothing gets powered up until we test for EMI and acoustic harmonics. Full sweep."

Karen nodded. "What if we get a spike?"

Nemo answered her himself.

"We tear it all out and start again."

Barn Lab, Lower Deck Day 5 1112 Hours R

Cold, crisp light filtering through narrow windows. The main lab was starting to resemble something out of a science fiction novel. The steel framing was in, cables coiled neatly along the walls, and a rectangular isolation chamber now sat centered beneath the overhead gantry system. Power conduits snaked out of the floor like veins searching for a heart.

Nemo, in his black hoodie and scuffed boots, crouched beside a panel, running diagnostics on a bank of precision voltage regulators. Sara, Genevieve, and Karen stood nearby, coffee cups in hand, all three watching the infrastructure take shape.

Genevieve broke the silence. "So... how much power does this thing actually need?"

She gestured toward the half-built cryogenic tower with a skeptical brow.

Nemo straightened, wiped his hands on a rag, and gave a half-smile — the kind that meant he knew the question wasn't simple.

"The quantum processor itself? Almost nothing. Microwatts. The problem isn't the chip."

He tapped the metal floor. "It's everything we have to do to keep that chip quiet."

Sara, perched on a rolling stool, took a slow sip. "How loud is the world, to a qubit?"

Nemo turned, thoughtful.

"Like a battlefield. Heat, photons, magnetic fields — even the vibration of a truck half a mile away. Any of it can decohere the system.

"So we build it a fortress. And fortresses need power."

He pointed upward toward the second floor.

"The dilution refrigerator alone pulls twenty kilowatts when running full depth. That's like powering six or seven homes to get one cubic inch of space cold enough — near absolute zero."

Karen frowned. "Wait... that tiny chamber we saw? That's where the qubits live?"

"Yes. About the size of a thimble. And the entire barn—the power, the shielding, the fiber timing, the noise cancellation, everything—exists to keep that thimble quiet."

Genevieve raised an eyebrow. "So how much total?"

Nemo shrugged, dry. "Forty kilowatts minimum. Fifty with margin. Enough to trip every breaker in Granville if we tried pulling it without our isolation grid."

Sara laughed. "No wonder they had to build a substation for you alone."

"Quite right." Nemo nodded. "Quantum computing isn't hard because the math is advanced. It's hard because nature doesn't want it to exist."

The three women were quiet, taking that in. The silence felt heavier now — the barn no longer a Vermont outpost, but something colder, more fragile. More consequential.

——

The last of the light spilling gold over the trees as the lab had gone quiet. The DCIS install team was gone for the night, the hum of active equipment replaced by a kind of alert silence — like the space itself knew it had become sensitive.

Sara, Karen, and Genevieve stood around the overhead viewing table with Nemo, who'd laid out a physical mockup of the qubit architecture in small 3D-printed modules. He rotated one piece carefully between his fingers.

Karen, notebook in hand, asked, "Why can't they you know... scale it? I mean, if someone else had the specs for this design, couldn't they build their own?"

Nemo smiled faintly — the kind of smile that signaled respect for the question, and its misunderstanding.

"Because scaling quantum systems isn't like adding more servers to a rack. It's like trying to build a thousand pianos that all have to play in perfect quantum harmony... while floating in vacuum, at a temperature colder than space."

Genevieve crossed her arms.

"You're saying it's not just the design. It's the execution."

"Precisely." Nemo nodded. "The tiniest error, a fabrication impurity, a timing jitter, thermal interference — and the entire system collapses. Coherence time dies. Entanglement decoheres. Your fancy algorithm is now just noise."

He tapped the table. "The laws of classical scaling don't apply. You can't brute-force your way to more qubits. You have to preserve their fidelity as you add complexity."

Genevieve replied, "And even if someone steals the blueprint, they still need to fabricate with error rates below 1 in 100,000 per gate."

Nemo smiled again, this time impressed. "Correct. At those tolerances it stops being engineering. Quantum architecture is origami made of probability. Fold it wrong once and it never folds right again."

Karen blinked and said, "Then we're guarding craftsmanship, not hardware."

Nemo looked at her, pleased she understood.

"Craftsmanship, materials, calibration tolerances, even my intuition for how the system breathes. No two of these machines will ever behave identically. That's what makes replication almost impossible."

He paused. "Which is why they want me, not the machine."

A long silence after which Sara, said, “And if they get you, they get a fifteen-year head start.”

Nemo didn’t answer. No need to.

——

Night Walk, The Ridge

Later, after Sara and Karen had turned in, Nemo and Genevieve walked the perimeter, jackets zipped, breath a string of white. Above the treeline a faint constellation of airborne telemetry blinked like a second sky... Genevieve stopped and pointed at an odd alignment. Nemo leaned in close, shoulder touching shoulder, and explained the anomaly in a low voice. The explanation was technical; the closeness felt like confession. When he finished, she dropped her arm across his back in a gesture meant to be practical and instead entirely intimate.

CHAPTER FIFTEEN

Hardening

Arlington, VA -DARPA Headquarters Day 4, 10:37 AM

Helena Quinn, Director of DARPA, paced around her glass-walled office, a blur of black slacks, navy silk, and fury barely contained.

On the secure line, the Director of the U.S. Secret Service, a man too seasoned to flinch easily, listened with hands steepled in front of him.

"We handed you one of the most significant covert installations in North America, and your people treated it like they were babysitting an IRS witness with a gambling problem."

She didn't pause.

"That site houses tech that hasn't even been briefed to half the National Security Council.

"One of those 'three guys' you assigned to post rotation failed to map low-profile repeater node embedded under a gravel patch behind the woodpile and walked right past it every eight hours. He didn't see anything."

The Secret Service Director finally responded, calm and clipped.

"We'll rotate the team. Today. The next unit will report directly to ACIC field lead on site."

"See that they do. I have eyes up there and if I get another report like this, I'm leaking their names to the Post myself."

Click.

——

The secure call lit up all at once, names blinking into place across the screens. Different rooms, same gravity. You could feel it before anyone spoke.

Helena Quinn started.

"Let's begin. I had a very uncomfortable call with the Director of the Secret Service this morning. They finally read their own field report. New team rotated into Vermont at 0800."

Helen Crowder muttered, "Numb nuts."

A couple of smiles flickered. Ed Perry leaned forward.

"ACIC already moved. Full TSCM package is in place. EMP sweeps, scrubbers, hardened shielding. We own the perimeter now."

General Edwards cut in from D.C.

"Good. But perimeter isn't the problem. What's Nemo's internal staffing look like?"

Helen brought up the file.

"He's thinking long term now. Says he'll need a small team. Five, maybe six. Techs, an admin, and someone who can bridge the science and the people."

Helena said it plainly. "He needs Genevieve."

Will didn't hesitate. "She's not rotating. If she goes, it's permanent."

That landed. A few glances across screens.

Helena studied him for a second. "All right. Let's say it clearly. Genevieve Larsson is reassigned to Nusquam. Permanent."

Will leaned in, voice steady. "She stays tethered to Watchtower. Direct access. Direct recall. If this doesn't work out, I get her back. No one else does."

No pushback. Just a beat while everyone absorbed the terms.

Owen nodded first.

"That's reasonable."

Thomas spoke up, almost lightly, but not really.

"She's already the bridge Nemo needs. This just makes it official."

Helen Crowder crossed her arms and gave a small nod.

"I fought you on her, Will. I was wrong. She belongs where she can do the most damage."

Will exhaled. Not relief. Just acceptance.

"We do it clean. She gets read in before Nemo does. Sara comes back once security locks. Karen stays for continuity."

Helena folded her hands.

"We built this project in pieces. Now it has to hold together. Nemo has the science, but he can't carry it alone."

Will didn't move.

"There's one more thing," he said. "Nemo needs the full truth. Genevieve's background. We're putting two former double agents in the same location. That's not just unusual. That's dangerous."

Thomas blinked.

"Oh. Right."

Helena gave a small nod.

"You tell him."

The call ended a moment later. Screens went dark one by one.

Will stayed where he was for a second.

"Damn it."

Thomas smiled.

"You hate it when they're right."

Will shook his head.

"I hate it more when they agree."

——

Later, in the Nusquam lab SCIF, the air felt controlled. Quiet in a way that didn't exist anywhere else.

Nemo picked up the secure handset.

"Nemo."

"I'm here."

"You're getting Genevieve. Permanent assignment."

A pause. Quick recalculation.

"Good," Nemo said. "She understands the system."

"She's also staying tied to Watchtower," Will added. "Direct line back to me. If this doesn't work, I pull her. That's not negotiable."

Nemo absorbed that.

"Understood."

"There's something else you need to know about her."

"I already do."

"No," Will said. "You don't."

A beat.

"She was a double agent for us. Over two years. Did to the Russians what you did to the Chinese. "She helped dismantle the network. It nearly broke her."

Nemo didn't move.

"And now I'm sending her to you," Will said. "To a place that already has one former double agent."

That landed.

Nemo looked toward the dark glass.

"I see."

"What you see," Will said, "is two ghosts—two targets in one place."

A beat.

"This is unprecedented."
Nemo thought about it.
Then, almost to himself, "At least we'll understand each other."
A pause.
"Yes," Will said. "That's what I'm counting on."
"It feels like karma," Nemo said.
Will took that in. "Karma cuts both ways."
"I know. But I trust her. I trust you. And I trust the work."
That hung there.
When Will spoke again, there was weight behind it. "Take care of her. It cost her more than she'll ever say."
"I already see that," Nemo replied.
Another pause.
"If either of you feels unsafe, you call me. Direct. No chain."
"Understood."
The line clicked off. Nemo set the handset down and looked out into the Vermont night. Permanent. Two former double agents. Same roof.
He let it sit. Then, said, "Karma." And he went back to work.

——

Fort Meade – Morgan's Office - 1610 Hours R

Morgan called Genevieve on a secure line. He spoke in his level, deliberate tone.
"You're being reassigned. Temporary rotation. Nusquam."
Genevieve paused her typing. Turned slightly in her chair, brows raised.
"Seriously?"
Will nodded once.
"Helena lobbied. Crowder backed it. I resisted. Before I remembered what I tell people when they question why you're on my team."
Genevieve tilted her head, half-amused.
"Which is?"
Will folded his arms.
"You see what's not said. And you do the work most people haven't even thought about yet."
A flicker of something, surprise, maybe pride, crossed her face.
"And you're okay with this?"
"Nemo trusts you. I trust Nemo. But you're still tethered to Watchtower. No one else gets to claim you. Not DARPA. Not DCSA."
She leaned back, blinking. "That's... generous. For you."

Will gave the ghost of a smile.

"Don't get used to it."

"We want a dog."

"What?"

"Nemo and I want a dog."

"A dog!"

"Read the message," said Genevieve.

Click

Morgan's phone bleeps a notice of a What's App message.

He leaned back in his chair, eyes scanning the email on his secured tablet.

Subject Line: Unorthodox perimeter enhancement request – G. Larsson

The embedded link redirected to the Craigslist ad. He read it twice.

Then a third time.

> Craigslist Ad – Burlington, Vermont – Posted Under: "Pets → Community"
>
> Title: Loyal Retired Army Dog Seeks Quiet, Loving Home (Granville/Burlingt
>
> Meet Runa—a 7-year-old Belgian Malinois with a sharp mind, gentle heart, a soldier's soul.
>
> Runa served honorably as a military working dog (MWD) and was adopted her handler after discharge. When he passed, we—his parents—promised care for her. We love her deeply. But age and health have made it too difficu
>
> She is spayed, up to date on all vaccinations, and in excellent health. She ha known aggression history but remains extremely alert and responsive to unusual behavior. Not recommended for homes with other pets or small children unless you have MWD or working dog experience.
>
> Runa loves long walks, quiet rooms, early mornings, and people who know to lead without shouting. She is crate-trained, understands both verbal and hand signals, and still responds to her command set from service.
>
> We are not asking for money. We are asking for the right home.
> You must meet her in person, provide references, and be willing to give her structure and purpose she's used to.
>
> Thank you for considering this extraordinary girl. —John & Eleanor (Granvil

He tapped his stylus against his jaw.

From across the desk, Cecil Brandon passed by and paused, noticing the contemplative look.

"Bad news?"

Will shook his head, dryly.

"Genevieve wants to adopt a Belgian Malinois."

Cecil raised an eyebrow.

"Security risk?"

"Depends who's sneaking up on who."

He tilted the screen for Cecil to read the ad.

Cecil gave a low whistle.

"Seven years old. Crate-trained. Knows military signals. Doesn't like kids. I think Runa means secret. She's perfect."

Will smiled faintly.

"She already cleared it with Nemo. He apparently 'welcomes' additional surveillance.'"

Cecil grinned.

"Of course he does. You think she's asking or telling?"

Will clicked the "Reply" icon and typed one line:

"Approved. Tell Runa she's on duty."

He hit Send.

"At this rate," he muttered, "Nusquam's going to have a better rotation than Langley."

——

Granville, VT-Nusquam 1925 Hours R

The last light of the day painted the edges of the sky in burnt gold. Genevieve stood by her car, watching the horizon, lost in thought. The door behind her clicked open.

Sara Brandt stepped out, coffee in hand, leaned against the hood without a word.

Genevieve didn't turn.

"You knew before I did."

Sara sipped.

"Of course."

"You okay with it?"

Sara shrugged slightly.

"You're ready. You've been ready. He asked for you, Gene. Nemo. That means something."

"It scares me a little," Genevieve admitted. "What if I let him down?"

Sara glanced sideways.

"You won't. And if you do, we're still your net."

"And you?"
Sara finished her coffee. Tossed the cup in the bin.
"I'm proud of you."
Genevieve blinked at that.
"You've never said that to me."
Sara smiled faintly, stepping away.
"I don't say things unless I mean them."
She left Genevieve standing in the dusk, a quiet certainty settling in her chest.

CHAPTER SIXTEEN

False Constellation

Beijing, China - MSS - Analysis Room

Zhao Wenli was a senior MSS analytical officer in his early forties—precise, reserved, and intellectually rigorous to the point of obsession. Trained as a systems analyst rather than a traditional case officer, Zhao built his reputation on pattern recognition across noisy datasets: satellite tasking, academic publishing trails, shell-company genealogies, and Western defense procurement anomalies. He believes deeply in structural coherence—the idea that true intelligence, when properly understood, must eventually converge toward a single, stable explanation. Physically unremarkable by design.

He had stopped trusting the maps.

That realization unsettled Zhao more than any missing data point ever had.

The screens in Analysis Room 3 glowed with their usual order: satellite overlays, procurement trails, academic citations, shell-company genealogies. New England lay dissected into grids and nodes, every rural town annotated with probabilities and confidence bands. Six laboratories—no, at least six—flickered amber, then green, then amber again as new inputs arrived.

The system should have been converging.

Instead, it was breathing.

Zhao leaned closer, fingers hovering above the glass, watching as a quantum optics startup in New Hampshire lost credibility while a photonics lab in Maine suddenly gained it. Venture capital flows adjusted. Publication citations spiked—then decayed. DARPA cutout signatures appeared too clean, like footprints placed carefully in fresh snow.

He replayed the timeline for the third time that night.

Each site made sense on its own.

Each had credible principals.

Each had technical depth just shy of breakthrough.

Each attracted enough attention from Western oversight bodies to be believable.

Together, they formed something else.

A constellation.

And constellations, Zhao knew, were stories humans imposed on stars to make randomness tolerable.

His colleague across the room whispered, "Which one is real?"

Zhao did not answer.

Because the question itself had begun to feel wrong.

The algorithms were now flagging mutual exclusivity conflicts—signals that suggested the labs could not all be genuine, yet offered no guidance on which were false. Worse, tasking one site for deeper collection degraded confidence in another, as if the act of observing collapsed the field in the wrong direction.

He had never seen intelligence behave like this.

The Party demanded answers, not doubts. His superiors wanted prioritization matrices and budget recommendations. MSS leadership wanted reassurance that the Americans were hiding something specific, something graspable.

Zhao felt sweat gather at the base of his neck. What if the deception was not about hiding a lab? What if it was about breaking the idea that there was a single lab?

He minimized the display and stared at the reflection of his own face in the darkened glass. For the first time in his career, he wondered whether the enemy's true weapon was not secrecy—but abundance. Too many truths, too many lies, arranged so precisely that distinguishing between them exhausted the mind itself.

Behind him, another alert chimed. Another promising lead. Another plausible target. Another choice.

Zhao looked up.

If this continued, someone in Beijing would decide he was the weak link, not because he lacked information, but because he could no longer say, with confidence, what reality was supposed to look like. And that, he realized with a quiet chill, might be what the Americans intended.

——

Zhao Wenli sat alone in his office, long after everyone else had gone. The building was quiet in that heavy way, like even the walls were listening. He leaned back in his chair and stared at the ceiling, turning it over again and again in his head.

He was sure of it now. The American operation didn't feel real. It was too clean. Too convenient. Like something designed to be seen.

A deception.

But knowing that and saying it out loud were two very different things.

The Party wanted answers. Clear ones. Confident ones. The kind that fit neatly into a briefing and made everyone else look in control. What they did not want was doubt. They definitely did not want hesitation.

And Zhao had both.

If he pushed back, if he told them this was all a fabrication, he would be standing alone. No proof they would accept. No allies willing to risk standing beside him. That kind of move didn't stall a career. It ended it.

But if he gave them what they wanted, if he signed his name to a conclusion he didn't believe, that was its own kind of danger. Because if he was right, if this really was a deception, sooner or later it would unravel.

And when it did, someone would have to take the fall.

He could already see how that story would be written. How his name would be used.

Zhao rubbed his eyes and let out a slow breath. There was no safe path here. Just different ways of losing.

He felt something close to fear. Not panicked. Just quiet and steady.

The kind that stays with you.

CHAPTER SEVENTEEN

Runa

Granville, VT – John & Eleanor's Farmhouse 0900 Hours R

The gravel driveway was uneven, winding through still-barren trees. Genevieve Larsson pulled up slowly in the rental, engine humming low as the mountains settled into quiet behind her.

On the porch, John stood with a thermos in one hand, worn work gloves in the other. He didn't wave. He waited. Eleanor, thinner than the email suggested, emerged behind him holding a leash that wasn't taut—just gently guided.

Runa stepped forward, alert but composed, scanning Genevieve before she even opened the car door.

Genevieve got out slowly, instinctively, as if meeting a fellow professional.

"Afternoon," she said.

John nodded once.

"You Larsson?"

"I am."

Eleanor stepped down the first two steps, Runa pausing obediently beside her.

"She knows something's up," Eleanor said. Her voice wasn't shaking, but there was grief baked into every vowel. "She's been sitting by the front door every morning since the funeral."

Genevieve crouched down—not low, not submissive, just level—and offered the back of her hand.

Runa sniffed, held her posture for three seconds, licked once and sat.

John's jaw tightened. He looked away toward the field.

"That means she's picked you," Eleanor said.

They sat on the porch a few minutes later—no pressure, no sales pitch. Three people and a dog who had already made the decision.

Genevieve didn't say much. She listened.

Eleanor pulled a faded photo from a pocket folder. It showed a tall man in Army fatigues crouched beside Runa, both of them squinting into the Afghan sun. Dust everywhere. Pride everywhere.

"That was Lance," she said. "He used to say she could sense a threat ten seconds before anyone else. Said he never once went through a door without her beside him."

Genevieve held the photo with careful hands.

"I know that feeling."

John finally spoke again, voice low.

"We're not asking you to be him. Only to know what she meant to him."

Genevieve looked at Runa, who now lay curled at her feet—still alert, but calm. Accepted.

"I can't replace him," Genevieve said. "But I can promise she won't be forgotten. She'll have purpose. And people who value that."

Eleanor nodded, eyes shining.

John stood abruptly, going inside. When he returned, he held out a folded dog vest with faded camo, Velcro patched with the word "VIGIL".

"He said she always worked better with it on. Even at home."

Genevieve accepted it like a ceremonial passing of arms.

"She'll wear it when it matters."

Runa stood as Genevieve rose. No command given. Just readiness.

As Genevieve clipped the leash to her collar, Eleanor placed a hand on Runa's head, whispered something, and stepped back.

No goodbyes. Just the silent handover of loyalty from one family to another.

"We are less than ten miles away and you are most welcome to stop by anytime. I'm sure she would love to see you now and again," offered Genevieve.

"Thank you, we were hoping you might say that." Said Eleanor.

Genevieve opened the car door and Runa popped in the back seat as if she owned it.

Arrival at Nusquam

Granville, VT-Nusquam Compound 1110 Hours R

The gravel drive crunched under slow-moving tires. Genevieve eased the SUV through the gate. No one greeted her. They didn't need to. The cameras had already logged her arrival, the surveillance system noting the precise weight shift in the vehicle—a few pounds heavier than her last run.

Runa stood in the backseat, silent, eyes forward. Her breathing was calm but deliberate. No panting. No bark. She was already tracking the landscape.

As Genevieve opened the door, Runa stepped out without hesitation. No leash, no command.

And in a flash—no ceremony—she was gone.

She didn't bolt. She patrolled.

First clockwise, tracing the barn's concrete apron. She paused by the generator shed. Circled the side path that led to the satellite relay. Stopped at the drainage culvert and sniffed once, deeply. Her movements were precise, as if checking off a mental checklist left behind by the man she once followed into combat.

From the barn's second floor stairwell, Nemo stood watching.

No lab coat today. Just boots, black hoodie, and a quiet detachment in his eyes.

He didn't speak as she moved.

Didn't call down.

Didn't shift his stance.

Only when Runa made her final pass along the northern treeline did he murmur to no one in particular:

"She clocks better than most humans."

Karen, beside him, looked up from the tablet she was monitoring.

"She knows she's not here to play fetch."

Nemo half-smiled.

"I wouldn't know what to do with something that was."

As Runa finished her loop, she returned to Genevieve and sat beside her—not at heel, not submissive. Aligned.

Genevieve looked up toward the barn stairs, locking eyes with Nemo.

He gave a short nod.

"She stays."

No further discussion.

> From the roof-mounted cameras, SYBIL's perimeter thread updated automatically:
> ASSET REGISTERED: Runa (K9)
> Perimeter Awareness Index: 94.6%

Disposition: Cooperative / Autonomous
Clearance Recommendation: Shadow Protocol Tier 2

Inside the barn, the hum of the dilution unit continued as if nothing had changed.

But outside, Nusquam had a new sentry.

And she missed nothing.

CHAPTER EIGHTEEN

Life at Nusquam

Nusquam – Second Floor Observation Loft – Late Evening

The Vermont sky had dipped into deep blue. The barn's second-floor observation loft, once packed with dust and nesting sparrows, now buzzed with quiet purpose: screens flickered, diagnostic data ticked by on glowing strips, and cooling fans whispered in steady rhythm.

Genevieve sat cross-legged in one of the reupholstered window seats, laptop on her knees, reviewing calibration outputs from the new dilution refrigeration cycle. Her glasses were slightly askew. Her hair was loose, like she'd forgotten herself for once.

Across the room, Nemo stood at a whiteboard, one hand tapping a marker against his thigh, the other gripping a ceramic mug. Cold coffee. Forgotten.

But he wasn't looking at the equations.

He was watching her.

Subtle. Still. Focused in that way only a man trained for decades to bury emotion could manage — but it was there.

The way he stood a little longer than needed near where she'd been working earlier. The way he ran a fingertip once across the thermos she'd left behind. The way his eyes flicked to her every time she laughed under her breath at something on-screen.

From the staircase, Sara leaned on the rail, chewing a piece of licorice taking it all in.

Genevieve didn't notice. But Nemo's gaze caught Sara's from across the loft.

Sara raised one brow a little.

Oh?

Nemo blinked, looked away. Took an unnecessary sip of cold coffee.

Sara smirked. "You know," she said casually, "when I told Gene you were brilliant, I didn't say shy was part of the deal."

Nemo didn't respond immediately. Just murmured,

"I'm not shy. I'm… precise."

Sara stepped closer, tossing the candy wrapper into the bin. "You're trying not to spook her. You think she doesn't know."

"I think she has more important things to think about," he said, staring at the window.

"That's where you're wrong." Sara's voice lowered. "People like her—people like you—don't miss things. You just both pretend to. Because pretending feels safer than wanting something."

He finally looked at her, tight-lipped but not defensive.

Sara smiled kindly. "She's not glass, Nemo. And neither are you."

Without another word, she walked away.

Back at the window seat, Genevieve looked up, sensing the room shift.

Nemo turned, eyes softening just slightly, and said:

"You left your output log open. Line 37—try adjusting the harmonic suppression factor. You were right."

Genevieve smiled, grateful but caught off guard.

"Thanks. I wasn't sure."

"You should be."

He walked away before he could say more. But this time, his coffee stayed forgotten.

And Runa, lying near the server bay, lifted her head and watched him go—ears tilted, as if she understood everything.

Nusquam Rooftop – Midnight

The attic of the barn wasn't designed for lounging, but Sara had thrown an old wool Army blanket across the wooden surface anyway. A thermos of mint tea steamed between her and Genevieve, both sitting side by side beneath a spill of stars sharp and cold above the Vermont hills.

Runa lay silently at the base of the hatch, paws crossed, eyes closed but ears twitching at every night sound.

Genevieve sipped slowly, chin tilted to the stars. "I forgot how quiet it can be. Like the whole world's holding its breath."

Sara didn't look at her. She replied, "It's the kind of quiet that makes you hear yourself again. Dangerous stuff."

Genevieve smiled faintly, knowing what she meant.

They sat in the quiet a little longer. Then Sara added casually, "He watches you when you're not looking."

Genevieve's eyes shifted sideways, not startled—more like she'd been waiting for someone to say it out loud.

"I know."

Sara nodded once. "You watch him too."

Genevieve wrapped her fingers around the cup.

"I've spent most of my adult life trying to be useful, not... visible. This place, this team, Nemo—it feels different. Like being useful doesn't mean being invisible anymore."

Sara studied her and said. "He's a good man. Odd as hell, broken in quiet ways. But he listens. He respects you. And I think... he needs someone who reminds him that genius doesn't have to be lonely."

Genevieve looked down, her voice barely a whisper. "He still has walls."

"So do you."

Genevieve smiled at that. It wasn't sad—it was something else. Something starting.

Sara bumped her shoulder gently. "No rush. Just... don't pretend you don't feel it. That kind of connection doesn't come around often. And out here?" She gestured at the dark forest around them. "It counts even more."

Genevieve turned her face back to the stars.

Downstairs, inside the barn, Nemo was still awake—reading, calculating, thinking.

But now and again, his eyes flicked to the ceiling, like he could feel something above him shifting. And maybe, for once, it didn't make him nervous.

Nusquam – Evening Routine

The wind off the Vermont ridgeline had quieted for the night. Inside the house glowed with soft amber light—fire crackling warming the living room and filling it with the smell of charcoal.

Nemo sat in his favorite armchair, a cup of unsweetened tea at his side. In his lap: a hardcover copy of Tuesday Takes Me There: The Healing Journey of a Veteran and His Service Dog. A yellow ribbon bookmark poked from halfway through. A second book, The Complete Military Working Dog Manual, lay open beside him, annotated in pencil.

At his feet, Runa curled with practiced loyalty, head resting lightly on the arch of his boot. Her breathing was steady, but her eyes followed every movement. Not anxious—just attuned.

Runa had made her decision days ago.

She had sensed it in his silences. In the way he fed her without words, walked her not out of routine but with quiet purpose. He was not her old handler—she didn't need him to be. She needed him to care. And he did.

Nemo had a new guardian.

Runa had a new partner.

He turned a page, thumb brushing a passage where the veteran described the moment his dog refused to leave his hospital bedside. Nemo's gaze lingered, then shifted to Runa.

"You would've done the same," he murmured.

From the side loft, Genevieve stood unnoticed, barefoot in thick socks, holding her laptop against her chest. She hadn't meant to stop, but the sight of them caught her.

Firelight moved across Nemo's face. He hadn't noticed her in the doorway. The book on his knee wasn't research — it was Runa's breed history, the temperament chapter dog-eared twice.

She stepped forward.

"You're on chapter six," she noted, nodding toward the dog-eared cover.

Nemo looked up, startled, then... not.

"The chapter about the hospital."

"That one made me cry," Genevieve said, kneeling to scratch behind Runa's ears. The dog leaned into her hand without lifting her head. "You two look good together."

"She's teaching me things," Nemo said.

He said it like an admission. Not self-deprecating, honest.

"That's what a good partner does," Genevieve said.

They looked at each other for a breath too long. Not awkward. Just... real.

Genevieve stood, patting her thigh to signal Runa, who stayed right where she was.

"She's off duty," Nemo said with the faintest smile. "Fire means safe."

"Smart girl," Genevieve replied, but her eyes were still on him.

As she walked off to the server console, Runa stirred only slightly.

Behind her, Nemo turned another page — but now the book was warmer in his hands.

Nusquam-Data Loft 0134 Hours R

The rest of Nusquam was dark. Even the cameras had shifted to thermal standby.

But in the data loft, the glow from a single monitor cast pale blue shadows across Genevieve's face. She sat alone, hair pulled up in a loose knot, a half-drunk cup of tea gone cold beside her keyboard. Runa lay dozing under the desk, tail twitching lightly in sleep.

On-screen, SYBIL's interface hummed, pulsing with live system health and behavioral telemetry.

Genevieve entered the root clearance protocol, and clicked into the Asset Registry Matrix.

SYBIL's voice, low and neutral, whispered through her earpiece:

"Standing by. Do you wish to modify or append asset tier data?"

Genevieve didn't speak. She typed.

ASSET: Runa

CLASSIFICATION: Biological / Canine

ROLE: Security / Environmental Monitoring

DISPOSITION: Cooperative / Independent

BEHAVIORAL INDEX: 94.6% (Autonomous Readiness Tier)

REQUESTED TIER CHANGE: PROVISIONAL → PERMANENT

ASSIGNED TIER: Tier 2

AUTHORIZING AGENT: Larsson. G

She hovered her cursor over the "Confirm" key.

Then clicked it.

SYBIL's voice returned, gentler than usual:

"Asset Runa now recognized as permanent Tier 2 auxiliary. Behavior telemetry and perimeter sync will be retained continuously. Welcome, Runa."

Genevieve leaned back in her chair, eyes resting on the black screen for a long moment.

Almost absently, she whispered:

"Good girl."

Below her desk, Runa gave a soft snort in her sleep—as if she'd heard it.

Genevieve reached down, gently resting her hand on Runa's flank.

She didn't say anything else.

SYBIL dimmed to night mode.

Fort Meade-Will's Office, 0307 Hours R

The hallways of Fort Meade's ACIC wing were silent, the kind of silence only found in buildings that know too many secrets. Most lights were motion-triggered and off.

But Will Morgan's office still glowed with desk-lamp amber. He sat in shirtsleeves, reviewing end-of-cycle intelligence feeds, wrist aching slightly from too much time on the stylus.

He tapped open SYBIL's latest sync packet from Nusquam.

Most of it was routine:

> Night perimeter logs — all green.
>
> Updated air quality metrics.
>
> Thermal variance in the comms shed — minor.
>
> Noise anomaly at 22:46 — squirrel.

A small footnote at the end of the security report caught his eye.

> ASSET TIER MODIFICATION – APPROVED
>
> Asset Name: Runa
> Previous Tier: Provisional
> New Tier: Tier 2 (Permanent)
> Authorized By: Larsson. G
> Behavioral Sync: 94.6% average
> Role: Autonomous Sentinel / Companion Entity

Will leaned back.

No blinking. No furrowed brow, a slow, private smile—the kind he almost never showed to anyone. He tapped the stylus against the desk once, and murmured, "Of course you did."

He toggled SYBIL's command line and added a single annotation of his own beneath the update.

> *Director Override Comment: Confirmed. Solid call.*
>
> *W. Morgan*

Then he minimized the screen, rubbed the bridge of his nose, and stared out the window into the dark Maryland trees.

> *"Good instincts, Gene."*

A quiet beat.

"Better than most field agents I've seen in ten years."

Then he stood. Shut the system.

Let it rest.

For now, the perimeter was in good hands. Four legs and all.

That Evening – Workshop, Near Dusk

Nemo was tightening the magnetic shielding around the dilution unit when Genevieve walked in holding a thermos of coffee in one hand and a slip of paper in the other.

Runa followed behind, padding to her usual spot by Nemo's feet.

Genevieve handed the paper to him wordlessly.

He read the line:

Director Override Comment: Confirmed. Solid call. — W. Morgan

He blinked, surprised.

"That from Will?"

Genevieve nodded.

"He doesn't waste compliments."

Nemo looked at the slip again, then at her.

"That meant something to you."

"Yeah," she admitted, casually. "It did."

She turned to head back toward the loft—but paused in the doorway, looking over her shoulder.

"You don't need permission to trust your instincts either, Nemo."

And with that, she disappeared up the stairs.

Nemo stared after her, the slip of paper still in hand.

At his feet, Runa shifted her weight and gave a low, pleased huff—the kind dogs give when they know something's moving in the right direction.

Nusquam – Early Morning

The new Sensitive Compartmented Information Facility (SCIF)—behind the barn—was still faintly smelling of fresh wiring and paint-sealed steel. A thick door hissed shut behind Sara as she stepped inside, sealing the space in perfect, acoustically dead silence.

She pulled off her ballcap and ran a hand through her hair before tapping the secure call interface.

A few rings.

Will's voice filtered through, low and clear:

"You alone?"

"Just me. New SCIF's tighter than Fort Meade's. Couldn't hear a drone land on the roof."

"Good."

Sara dropped into the metal chair at the console, feet up, comfortable. Familiar. Will rarely asked for this kind of call unless something mattered.

He got to it.

"How's Genevieve?"

Sara's expression softened.

"You mean professionally? Personally? Or psychospiritual?"

"Yes," Will replied dryly.

She smirked, leaned back, and answered seriously.

"She's good, boss. Better than good. She's... in her element out here. The kind of physics she's doing with Nemo? It's top-tier. Pure problem-solving. No politics. No bureaucracy. Just equations and impossible tech. Her brain is lit up."

Will nodded slowly on his end.

"And Nemo?"

Sara raised an eyebrow even though he couldn't see it.

"Professional. Respectful. Kindred spirit, honestly. They're cut from similar cloth—hyper-logical, focused, understated. They get each other without needing to translate."

Will's voice was quiet, but direct.

"Any friction? Vulnerabilities? I'm not worried, I just need to be sure."

Sara shook her head.

"She's not fragile, Will. Remote or not, she's adapting. She's even got a dog now, that retired MWD, Runa. The whole compound is part lab, part monastery, part animal sanctuary now."

A beat.

Then, more gently, "Honestly? You should know something."

"Go ahead."

"She may never want to leave."

Will didn't respond right away.

Sara watched the secure line flicker as he processed. "She's that steady?"

"Steady, stimulated, surrounded by people who value what she brings. And Nemo? He's not just a project. He's a mission. She's invested, not just as a physicist. As a person."

Will exhaled slowly. "That's what I hoped for. I just needed to hear it from you."

"You did the right thing, Will. She's exactly where she should be."

He hesitated again, just a second too long. "Let me know if anything changes."

"Of course. But if I were you..." she added with a smirk, "I'd start budgeting for spring. Because when the barn expands, she's gonna want her name on a plaque."

Will chuckled, a rare, quiet sound. "Thanks, Sara. Stay sharp."

"Always."

The line cut.

Sara sat in the silence of the SCIF, smiling to herself. She rose, straightened her cap, and headed out into the cold air and toward a morning that already felt more grounded.

Inside the barn, Genevieve was bent over a whiteboard beside Nemo. Runa sat nearby, alert, and relaxed.

——

Nusquam — Dusk

Karen walked the gravel path that cut between the trees, Runa padding beside her, the dog's breath steady and rhythmic in the cool air. The sky had turned that deep violet that comes moments before full dark, when the last light lingers on the tips of the pines.

Then she heard it.

A sharp, rattling hiss from somewhere above.

She froze. The sound came again—longer this time, sharper, like a dry exhale through teeth.

Runa halted mid-step. Her ears snapped upright, muscles taut, a low rumble building in her chest.

Karen scanned the treetops. Nothing moved. The forest was still—too still.

Footsteps crunched behind her.

Nemo and Genevieve emerged from the shadows, both quiet, both listening.

"You hear that?" Karen whispered.

Nemo gave a small nod and unclipped the flashlight from his belt. He always carried one on his evening walks, a habit Genevieve teased him about. He clicked it on, beam aimed low at first, a thin cone of white cutting across the path.

He swept it slowly toward the trees. The sound came again—closer this time.

Nemo lifted the light. The beam found a pair of yellow eyes glinting from a branch. A small, compact shape.

The creature moved—swiveling its head in a full, impossible circle.

A foot-tall burrowing owl stared into the light, feathers puffed, and let out an ear-splitting screech. Its wings flared wide, nearly two feet across, and it vanished upward into the dark like a phantom.

Karen jumped. So did Genevieve. Even Runa barked once, startled.

Then silence—broken by a ripple of nervous laughter.

Karen managed a shaky smile. "Next time," she said, "I'm walking before sunset."

CHAPTER NINETEEN

Chrysalis

Berlin VT-Supercenter Parking Lot 2348 Hours R

Karen shut the trunk with a quiet thunk. The grocery run had taken longer than expected—restocking for seven people and a working dog always did—but she wasn't worried. The Supercenter lot was nearly deserted. A handful of cars sat scattered in the yellow sodium glow of the overhead lights. Cold air moved through the silence in little gusts.

She slid her keys into her jacket pocket and turned toward the driver's door.

That's when she felt the pressure—an arm looping suddenly around her neck, another locking tight across her waist. The man was fast, strong, and dressed in black from boots to balaclava.

But he made one mistake.

He assumed she'd panic.

Will Morgan didn't tolerate passengers on his team. Everyone trained in Krav Maga the practical self-defense system developed by the Israeli army. Everyone drilled. And everyone learned to fight like their life—and someone else's—depended on it.

Karen's body reacted before her brain could even name the threat.

She dropped her weight instantly, driving her heel into the man's shin. His grip faltered enough for her to thrust her elbow backward into his ribs. As he exhaled in surprise, she twisted and jammed her thumb knuckle into his eye socket. No hesitation. No pause.

He let go.

She spun, closed the space, and sent a rising knee into his groin—hard.

He crumpled.

She moved behind him, yanked his wrist back against the joint, and snapped her weight down with practiced precision. His face hit the asphalt. The balaclava muffled his cry. With her knee on his spine and both arms locked, he wasn't going anywhere.

Karen's heart pounded. Her breath fogged in the cold.

She scanned the lot. No witnesses. No backup.

She leaned in close, voice flat. "Big mistake."

She reached for her phone.

It was strange, honestly. In the middle of all that noise and movement, she felt… steady. Like everything had snapped into place.

She caught herself thinking, almost amused, this is it? This is what he meant.

Will had been right. The training didn't ask for permission. It just took over. Every motion, every decision, already there before she could second-guess it.

She almost laughed. Morgan's Mustang.

The thought hit her harder than the gunfire. And for just a second, right there in the middle of it all, she smiled to herself.

Karen kept her knee pinned against his spine as she reached into her coat for the tactical flashlight. The man under her groaned, a low, muffled sound more of frustration than pain.

He wasn't some random junkie or carjacker. Too precise. Too clean.

"Don't move," she ordered, even though she knew he wouldn't. His wrists were hyperextended and locked. Any shift would feel like a knife slicing his tendons.

With her free hand, she yanked the balaclava back halfway—enough to expose his neck and the side of his face.

He was young. Maybe thirty. No scars, one tattoo. A small inked symbol just below his right ear. Karen narrowed the flashlight beam. It was a simple cicada. Stylized. Geometric. And unmistakably intentional.

Her pulse quickened. Not from fear—from recognition. She'd seen that symbol once before. In a quiet briefing room at Fort Meade. Like a synthetic evolution of Cicada 3301—weaponized.

She rolled him onto his side and checked his pockets. No phone. No wallet. No keys. Just a single RFID-shielded sleeve with a blank NFC card inside—wiped clean.

Professionals didn't always carry identification. But this one wasn't expecting to lose. She stood, keeping her Glock drawn, eyes scanning the lot again. Still empty. Still quiet. Karen dialed the encrypted line to Nusquam.

Three rings. Sara answered. "Talk."

"I have a situation," she said calmly. "Unidentified male. Attempted abduction. I have him restrained."

There was a pause. "Alive?"

"For now."

Another pause. Sara's voice shifted—measured, colder. "Is he marked?"

Karen's eyes never left the cicada tattoo. "Yeah. Chrysalis."

Another pause. "We're coming. Burn the receipt. Don't let local law get involved. Do not turn him over. Hold position. Larsson and I are en route. We will bring one of the detail."

Click.

She exhaled slowly and looked down at the attacker. "You picked the wrong grocery run."

Karen stood beside the subdued attacker, now zip-tied at the ankles and wrists with one of the heavy-duty plastic restraint sets she kept stashed in the cargo well. He was unconscious—briefly—after a second failed attempt to twist free. The cicada tattoo behind his right ear remained visible, stark in the sweep of her flashlight.

Headlights cut across the far end of the parking lot. A black Chevy Suburban slowed, engine idling with low growl. No sirens. No lights. Just quiet arrival.

Karen didn't move.

The rear door opened first. Sara Brandt stepped out, already pulling on nitrile gloves as she crossed the blacktop. She wore a dark field jacket, hair tied back, eyes sharp and scanning. Behind her came Genevieve Larsson, bundled in a navy wool coat, moving briskly, her expression unreadable—until she saw Karen.

"You alright?" Genevieve asked.

"Better than him," Karen said, nodding toward the restrained man.

The driver's door opened. A tall man in a gray tactical overcoat stepped out next. He moved with practiced caution, one hand always near his jacket zipper. Special Agent Nate Hensley, U.S. Secret Service. Forty-three. Former Counter-Assault Team. Boston accent clipped by years of whisper training. Permanent notch of calm behind his eyes. Will Morgan had handpicked him to supervise external perimeter security after the initial Nusquam debacle. Helena Quinn made it happen.

"Perimeter's quiet," Nate said. "I swept the west edge and ran thermal—no secondary."

Sara crouched beside the attacker and peeled back one eyelid with clinical detachment. "Vasovagal collapse," she muttered. "Nice work, Karen. Controlled aggression?"

"Level three Krav," Karen said flatly. "Will's favorite."

Genevieve knelt opposite her. “Confirmed cicada mark. He’s Chrysalis, no doubt. And the NFC sleeve was wiped—clean keycard.”

Nate looked down, gave a low whistle. “So this is real.”

Genevieve nodded once. “It’s real.”

Sara stood and turned toward the vehicle. “Let’s get him in. We’ll go dark and route through secondary backroads. I don’t want his comms tagged even passively.”

“I’ll drive,” Nate said, already moving.

Karen exhaled slowly and looked to Genevieve. “What the hell is Chrysalis?”

Genevieve met her gaze. “Something we were supposed to forget.”

——

Fort Meade – Project Chrysalis Briefing

The lights were low, the temperature steady at sixty-eight. A single screen glowed in the NSA’s secure conference room. Twelve cleared personnel. No phones. No notes.

At the front stood Dr. Anya Greer, cryptanalysis specialist from IARPA—blazer rumpled, voice exact.

She tapped the remote. On the screen: a white cicada symbol.

“Project Chrysalis began as a postmortem of the Cicada 3301 phenomenon,” she said.

"What had looked like an internet riddle turned out to be a recruitment engine — an autonomous talent filter. No portal, no invitation. Only the self-selected ever made it through."

Another click. Red pins dotted a world map—Paris, Seoul, Warsaw, Dallas, Moscow.

"By 2013 the operation had gone surgical — cryptography paired with steganography, layered with behavioral engineering. Then silence."

Cathy asked, “steganography?”

“It’s the art of concealing messages or data within other, innocuous files—such as images, audio, or text—to avoid detection,” answered Greer.

Greer turned.

“We studied it. Modeled it. Then built our own.”

The next slide read:

PROJECT CHRYSALIS

Iterative Evolution Through Signal.

“Chrysalis identifies operatives who don’t need orders—only opportunity. Every mission appears self-generated. Every contact is deniable.”

A voice from the back: “That’s insane.”

“That’s the point,” Greer replied.

She brought up a grainy image: a man in a hoodie leaving a cyber-café in Kraków.

“He solved four tiers of Chrysalis, rewrote one, then vanished. We never recruited him—we never controlled him. By design.”

Another analyst leaned forward. “You’re saying we lost control of our own tool?”

“We never had it,” Greer said.

The final frame zoomed on a drone photo from rural Laos—extraction in progress, the same cicada tattooed at the target’s neck.

“They’re not agents,” she said. “They’re vectors. And someone’s re-activating the architecture.”

Silence.

Will Morgan frowned. “Maybe I’m dense, Anya, but try that again.”

Sara Brandt smirked. “Yeah, use the small-words version.”

Greer smiled thinly. She was used to them.

“It’s a recursive trap,” she said. “A loop that makes subjects believe they’re choosing freely while steering them toward a single control system.”

“Every puzzle, every ‘choice,’ reinforces loyalty. The deeper they go, the narrower the path becomes until every action feeds the same design. It’s self-reinforcing—psychological pattern-lock.”

“So the question isn’t who they work for anymore.”

She advanced the final slide: a pulsating signal trace moving east across the Pacific.

Will said nothing, he just stared at the pulsing signal trace.

“It’s who’s signaling them now.”

The cicada symbol flickered once, then dissolved into static.

CHAPTER TWENTY

Every 13 Days

Nusquam Command Center – 0130 hours

The barn was silent except for the low hum of servers.

Genevieve sat alone at the workstation in the back corner—hoodie draped over her shoulders, eyes locked to the monitor, her brow furrowed.

Karen's attacker had been transferred to a holding site, but the tattoo had haunted her. The cicada wasn't just a mark—it was a signal. She knew it.

Using SYBIL's secure dev instance, Genevieve began backtracing fragments of steganographic challenges posted on obscure forums—dead Reddit threads, outdated TOR mirrors, even a long-abandoned GitHub repo marked "p03tic-s3mant1cs."

She fed the data into SYBIL's pattern parser.

At first, nothing.

Then—SYBIL flared.

MATCH DETECTED:

+Temporal sequencing correlation between Chrysalis Layer-3 dead drops and recent encrypted image posts (2025–2026).

Her fingers froze. She isolated the overlay SYBIL identified. It was a countdown.

A signal cadence emerging every 13 days, timed with lunar phase changes and embedded into unrelated datasets: weather radar noise, abandoned academic PDFs, .flac audio spectrograms.

She stared at the reconstructed signal's header.

"COALESCE://VECTOR/ACTIVATE-RECURSION"

She whispered aloud, "They're coming online."

Behind her, Runa, the Malinois, stirred from her bed.

Genevieve tapped the encrypted line to Will.

He answered immediately.

Project Chrysalis

Will's face appeared on the monitor, shadowed by the blue light of the SCIF. His jaw was tense, his shirt sleeves rolled to the elbows. Behind him, a live SIGINT feed scrolled silently across a secondary screen.

"Talk to me," he said.

Genevieve sat at Nusquam's long workbench, lit only by the backlight of the data wall and a soft-glow desk lamp. Her expression was focused, voice clipped.

"I started with the cicada tattoo," she began. "But the real breakthrough came when I ran archived Chrysalis challenges through SYBIL's newer compression-matching module. There's a recurring cadence—buried signal, consistent with third-layer activation triggers."

Will leaned forward. "When did the signal resume?"

"Thirteen weeks ago. Every thirteen days since. Embedded in white-noise data from unrelated sources—academic journals, DNS logs, .flac audio headers, and even FAA radar snapshots from remote nodes. It's multi-channel—global. Someone's waking them up."

Will's eyes narrowed. "Vectors?"

She nodded. "The signal header said COALESCE://VECTOR/ACTIVATE-RECURSION. SYBIL confirmed it as a known call-response structure from Layer 3. It's an ignition sequence."

"Targets?"

"Unknown. But it's not scattershot. It's measured. Cohesive. Someone rebuilt the network and learned how to push activation without direct contact."

Will ran a hand down his face. "Where the hell are they getting the keys? Those layers were supposed to be air-gapped and rotted."

"I don't think they're reusing the old tree," Genevieve said. "I think they've rebuilt it. New root. New branches. But the same architecture. Inspired by Chrysalis—maybe even improved. Like a forked codebase."

He sat back. "How many are active?"

"Unclear. But the pattern density implies dozens. Possibly more. Distributed. Independent. And that attacker Karen dropped—he wasn't probing. He was prepped for abduction."

Will's eyes flashed. "Which means someone knows about Nusquam."

Genevieve nodded grimly.

There was a pause. Both understood the implication.

Will broke the silence. "Can SYBIL track the next signal drop?"

"I've already got it watching for phase-timed emissions. Next spike is in eleven days, zero-four-hundred UTC. I'll have triangulation prep ready before then."

"Good," Will said. Then softer, "Nice work, Gene."

She didn't respond immediately. Then said, "This doesn't feel like a reactivation."

He looked up.

"This feels like Phase Two," she said. "Like we were never meant to catch the first wave."

Will stared at her, the glow of threat mapping flickering behind his eyes.

"We don't catch it," he said. "We kill it before it takes shape."

Interrogation Attempt

Nusquam –Basement Holding Room 1411 R

The holding cell at Nusquam wasn't designed for comfort—it was designed for control. Reinforced steel, embedded sound masking, dual surveillance angles. Genevieve called it The Box. Will called it temporary. But for now, it held a ghost.

The attacker sat shackled at the table—no name, no ID, and no signs of distress. Just stillness. Barely blinked. Breathing slow. Like he had trained for silence.

Sara, Genevieve, and Karen stood behind the glass, watching through the polarized observation window.

"He's not medicated, but his pain response is suppressed," Sara said. "No adrenaline dump. No visible tension. His baseline heart rate is lower than it should be.

"You don't get those vitals without serious neurocognitive rewiring. This isn't meditation. It's engineered detachment."

"Chrysalis protocol?" Karen asked.

Genevieve nodded. "Could be neural preconditioning. There's a theory they use auditory loops or sleep-state patterning to nullify interrogation anxiety."

"Huh," said Karen.

"He's not suppressing fear. He doesn't register it. That's sleep-looped denial training. It fractures empathy and remaps pain." Said Sara.

Sara stepped into the room. The man tracked her with his eyes—no surprise, no fear.

She sat.

"Do you know where you are?"

Silence.

She leaned in. "You tried to abduct a federal officer. We're not police. We don't arrest people like you. We study them. We find the signal you're carrying. We run you until there's nothing left."

The man smiled, slightly.

Sara narrowed her eyes. "What's the cicada for?" she asked.

Still nothing.

She shifted tone. "We know about COALESCE. We know about recursion. And we know there are more of you."

His smile dropped. A beat passed. He finally spoke. Just one sentence. "The pattern obeys itself."

Sara froze.

Then he closed his eyes—and didn't open them again.

Genevieve pushed through the door. "Vitals?"

Sara already had her fingers on his neck. "Still breathing. But he's gone inward. He's stonewalling. Hard."

Karen stepped in. "Can SYBIL predict when they break?"

Genevieve's voice was low. "SYBIL doesn't know what kind of person he is yet."

NFC Card Reconstruction

Fort Meade-Watchtower Ops Rick Huang's Office — 1539 R

Rick Huang hunched over the sandbox rig, fingers flying across the touchpad. The Near Field Communication card rested on a sterile platform beneath a microreader rig—optical, RF, and capacitive layers mapped and projected on the screen above.

Genevieve leaned against the counter, arms crossed, eyes flicking between terminal logs and SYBIL's holographic display.

"Any luck?" she asked.

Rick didn't look up. "The card's been wiped with military-grade overwrite—three-pass zeroing and randomized noise. Whoever did this was paranoid, and good."

"Can you salvage anything?"

He slid a magnified sector onto the screen. "Maybe. There's bleed-over from the parity sectors—bit decay. It's like trying to reassemble a shredded document from the shadows of ink on the other side."

Genevieve straightened. "But possible?"

"Technically." He ran a quick entropy analysis. "SYBIL's quantum modeling might give us a reconstructed fragment, if we isolate the decay fields."

He activated SYBIL's microstructure emulator and fed the partial entropy set.

Rick patted the console. "Okay, sweetheart. I need you to do something morally questionable."

Genevieve raised an eyebrow. "She likes positive reinforcement," Rick said.

After ten seconds of silence, SYBIL displayed:

RECONSTRUCTED TAG HEADER

PROTO-FRAGMENT//SEED://PRISM-THRESHOLD

Partial Key Match: Signal Family – AETHER NET [v4]

Genevieve stepped back. "That's not Chrysalis 1.0. That's a new tree."

Rick frowned. "What does PRISM THRESHOLD mean?"

She looked at him. "Nothing... unless it's a location."

Rick froze. "You're saying they're not vectors."

"I'm saying they're infrastructure."

Rick studied the result. "I'm going to need silence, three more hours, and approximately one inadvisable amount of caffeine."

Genevieve smiled. "Define inadvisable."

"I'd rather not put a number on it for legal reasons."

Middlebury State Airport-Two Days Later 1342 Hours R

The Cessna Grand Caravan EX landed without ceremony on the narrow slab of asphalt known as Middlebury State Airport (6B0)—a non-towered, lightless airstrip tucked into the hills of Addison County. No jets. No TSA. Wind, trees, and one quiet ACIC convoy waiting in the treeline.

The plane taxied to the far end of the runway and shut the engines down.

Will, Cecil, and Zbigniew Zawadzki disembarked with purpose. Will and Z to interrogate the prisoner and Cecil to survey security and plan for a major upgrade.

In the distance, temporary construction pylons marked the future footprint of a 60-foot National Guard control tower. Plans had been fast-tracked. It would soon house VTAC radar, a TCAS unit, windshear sensors, and an AWOS weather station. But for now, the airport remained off-grid and largely invisible.

That was how they liked it.

Helena Quinn had converted one of the newly acquired farms—purchased under the shell entity Aldea Grande LLC LLC—into a discreet guest house and safe house for cleared personnel rotating through Nusquam. Though the property appeared to be another aging Vermont farmhouse with weathered siding and a wraparound porch, the interior had been refitted with hardened doors, secure fiber uplinks, and biometric access points discreetly masked behind restored cabinetry and colonial charm. A SCIF camouflaged as a camper van sat next to the garage.

Rather than evict the widow of the former owner, Helena offered her a generous management contract to stay on as caretaker. For Marlene Dufresne, it meant keeping the house that had been in her husband's family for over sixty years. For Helena, it meant dependable oversight, seamless maintenance, and the kind of local goodwill money couldn't buy. With a dedicated budget for upkeep and seasonal improvements, the house became both an asset and a community bridge.

On a misty morning in late June Will, Cecil, and Z pulled in mid-morning shortly after landing. The gravel crunched under their government-plated SUV as Marlene met them with fresh coffee and a discreet nod. The house sat only three miles from Nusquam, but in terms of operational security, it was a vital buffer—close enough for access, far enough for plausible deniability. For Will, it also meant he could have eyes near the lab without putting anyone visibly on-site.

Nusquam –Basement Holding Room-Two Days Later 1411 R

The Chrysalis operative—mid-thirties, athletic, Eastern European accent suppressed but not gone—sat shackled to a composite anchor in the floor. He'd been silent for two days. No name. No reactions. No emotional tells.

Will stood across from him, arms folded, cool, professional.

"Last chance," Will said evenly. "We know what you are. We know where you were. What we don't know is how many of you were activated in the last signal burst."

The man didn't blink.

Sara leaned in. "We have authority under Title 10 and Section 812 of the Defense Authorization Act. We can hold you, charge you, or classify you as a non-state belligerent. You talk, or you disappear."

Still nothing.

Will exhaled and looked toward the glass. "Z."

The door opened.

Zbigniew Zawadzki entered without preamble—broad, calm, wearing a plain black field jacket. He pulled the chair backward, turned it, and sat with his arms on the backrest.

"Hi," Z said gently. "You're doing great, by the way. The whole silent operator thing—it's classic."

The man blinked for the first time.

Z smiled. "But the thing is... I already know your name."

No response.

Z leaned forward, elbows on the chair.

"Your gait says Romanian. But you've suppressed the back vowels. Tel Aviv trained? No. Baltic signal echo in your short consonants. Vilnius, right? Your upper canines are titanium—factory grade. Private contractor. And the skin under your jawline? Slight scarring. Burn. Surgical. Subdermal comm implant, but removed too recently."

Z nodded.

"Your name is Viktor Ardelean. Born outside Cluj. Recruited at 19 into a Belarusian-run cyber ops collective. Vanished at 24. Resurfaced on the darknets two years ago under the handle "Spine." And last month, your bitcoin wallet moved $4,800 to a Chrysalis test node in Ufa."

The operative's jaw tensed.

Z's tone dropped, soft now. Intimate.

"See, you don't need to tell us who you are. You already did that by showing up. What I want to know is who she is."

Silence.

Z placed a small white object on the table. A cube. Simple. Blank.

Viktor looked at it.

Z said: "She's in here."

Now there was fear. Barely. But it showed. A flicker.

Will stepped forward. "We're not asking you to name her. We already have one: Chimera."

The room went still.

Z pressed the cube once. A soft hum.

Viktor spoke for the first time, hoarse.

"You... don't know. Not even close."

Will crossed his arms. "Try us."

Viktor smiled grimly. "She's not on any server. Not in any file. She speaks only through fragments—signals stitched from thousands of echoes. There is no voice. No face. Not even we know her name."

Sara leaned forward. "How do you follow her?"

He looked at her—almost reverently.

"She doesn't command. She resonates."

Will glanced at Z. "Encrypted hierarchy?"

Z nodded. "Nested across mirror mesh. Self-destructing key layers. If Chimera dies, Chrysalis doesn't crash—it fragments. The vectors keep moving."

Will exhaled slowly.

"We'll confirm the metadata," he said. "But thank you, Viktor. That's the first true thing you've said."

Z stood.

"Have someone bring him water," he said . "We won't need to ask again, eh?."

Viktor didn't look up.

He didn't need to.

Z closed the door behind him and stood in the corridor for a moment with his hand still on the handle.

The corridor was lit the way Nusquam lit everything below grade — cool white, even, no shadow to read. He'd asked Helena once whether that was deliberate. She'd said yes without elaborating.

Viktor would talk again tomorrow. Z already knew the shape of the next conversation. Viktor would test one lie to see if it landed, and when it didn't he would offer a second piece of truth, smaller than the first, to keep some sense of control. They always did. The interrogation wasn't the part where you broke them. It was the part where they discovered, on their own, that they had nothing left to protect.

Z pulled off his black field jacket and folded it over his arm.

His grandfather had read faces in a Warsaw rail yard in 1946, sorting people coming back from places they did not name. The old man had told him once that the trick was never to look at the eyes. The eyes were what people had practiced. You looked at the hands, the throat, the place under the jaw where the pulse showed.

Z had been thirteen.

Granville, VT

Cecil Brandon had a love-hate relationship with modern tech. He adored the NSA-supplied surveillance gadgets, the kind of gear that could sniff out a burner phone from two counties away and bounce microwave pulses off windows for conversations in sealed rooms.

But Cecil was also old-school enough to know that sometimes the only real solution was to go back to the basics—like telephone poles.

They stood like sentinels across rural America, placed at regular intervals along county highways, draped with cables, and overlooked by most. Every farm road had at least one—old wooden monuments to a simpler surveillance age. And in Granville, Vermont, that meant opportunity.

Cecil sketched it out in his notebook—the kind he still carried despite encrypted tablets.

Route 100, the main artery cutting through Granville's eastern edge, would be the first. Then Butz Road, then North Hollow Road. Every access route to and from the quiet village would be covered. He coordinated with power and utility companies, disguising his work as a line maintenance project with "pole integrity reinforcements."

On each selected pole, he'd install dual camera systems: high-mounted, angled for long-range license plate capture, capable of resolution clarity even in a snow squall.

One at driver height, placed in inconspicuous weatherproof housings, tuned for facial capture with low-light infrared capability for 24-hour operation.

Each image—each pixel—would route to SYBIL, where deep-learning classifiers trained on over a billion facial patterns would run them through threat-profiling overlays.

It would become impossible to approach Granville unseen.

SYBIL wouldn't only identify you. She'd know who you were pretending to be—and who you really were.

Once a face was captured, tracking would begin immediately—pulling from DMV records, international arrivals databases, even obscure online forum appearances. If you came near Nusquam, you were already known.

Cecil looked up from his plans with a quiet smirk.

The Green Mountain Power crew had the bracket halfway up the pole before Cecil finished his coffee.

He stood across the road in the lay-by, hands in his coat pockets, watching the lineman work. The man was young, maybe twenty-eight, moved on the spikes the way someone moves when they've been climbing for ten years rather than two. Good. Cecil had asked for him by name.

The driver-height housing went on first. Cecil tracked the angle from the road. A car came through at maybe forty and he held his eyes on the housing, not the car, watching whether the camera face showed. It didn't. Good again.

Twenty years ago this would have been a man in a parked car. Three shifts. Logbook on a clipboard. Coffee in a thermos that lost heat by ten. He'd run that detail in Bosnia and again in a quiet park in Maryland, and he could still feel the specific ache in his lower back from sitting still for sixteen hours.

The poles, he thought, didn't get sore backs.

A pickup slowed coming north. The driver lifted two fingers from the wheel in the way Vermonters did. Cecil lifted two fingers back without taking his other hand from his pocket. The pickup went on. The lineman, twenty feet up, didn't even register it.

Cecil pulled his notebook out and wrote the pole number, the time, and a single word next to it. Clean.

Then he capped the pen and walked to the next site.

The Green Mountain Power crew had the bracket halfway up the pole before Cecil finished his coffee.

He stood across the road in the lay-by, hands in his coat pockets, watching the lineman work. The man was young, maybe twenty-eight, moved on the spikes the way someone moves when they've been climbing for ten years rather than two. Good. Cecil had asked for him by name.

The driver-height housing went on first. Cecil tracked the angle from the road. A car came through at maybe forty and he held his eyes on the housing, not the car, watching whether the camera face showed. It didn't. Good again.

Twenty years ago this would have been a man in a parked car. Three shifts. Logbook on a clipboard. Coffee in a thermos that lost heat by ten. He'd run that detail in Bosnia and again in a quiet park in Maryland, and he could still feel the specific ache in his lower back from sitting still for sixteen hours.

The poles, he thought, didn't get sore backs.

A pickup slowed coming north. The driver lifted two fingers from the wheel in the way Vermonters did. Cecil lifted two fingers back without taking his other hand from his pocket. The pickup went on. The lineman, twenty feet up, didn't even register it.

Cecil pulled his notebook out and wrote the pole number, the time, and a single word next to it. Clean. Then he capped the pen and walked to the next site. "Let 'em try," he muttered.

CHAPTER TWENTY-ONE

Two Houses

Beijing – Ministry of State Security Annex

The conference room was windowless, polished in black glass and red lacquer. A single wall-mounted screen displayed satellite reconnaissance from the northeastern United States. Six faces surrounded the table: three MSS officers in tailored civilian suits, three PLA cyber operations officers in olive green.

The temperature in the room was civil, but only barely.

Deputy Director Sun Tao, MSS Bureau 10, tapped the table lightly to begin.

"We have received an intelligence fragment routed from academic correspondence out of New Hampshire. It references a test environment for cryogenic vector isolation, terminology consistent with prior flagged R&D nodes."

He gestured, and the screen split: a forged spec sheet, an equipment manifest, and a GPS coordinate—one of the possible decoy nodes near Plattsburgh, NY.

Major General Li Shun, PLA Strategic Support Force, glanced sideways.

"This site is not on our active watchlist. Why were we not informed?"

Sun didn't blink.

"Because it was routed through a civilian academic funnel—MIT graduate researcher, Taiwanese passport. That places initial purview under Bureau 10."

Li frowned.

"The phrasing—'modular coherence test chamber'—that's not civilian. That's S&T-level development. Military-grade. Why hasn't your bureau actioned this?"

"Because we believe it's a decoy."

A sharp intake of breath from one of the PLA colonels.

Sun leaned in.

"It's too perfect. The terminology is textbook. The funding trail leads nowhere. The shell company matches patterns from past U.S. disinformation campaigns. If this is real, they've left it exposed for us to find."

General Li crossed his arms. "Or you're letting bureaucratic suspicion blind you to a lead that's already cost us three years of lag in superconductive architecture."

"We don't chase bait," Sun said flatly.

"You missed the F-35 plans until we recovered them on our end. How many more opportunities will you dismiss out of—what?—professional paranoia?"

The tension cut through the air like a piano wire.

From the far end, MSS senior analytical officer Zhao, spoke. "If we investigate the site, and the Americans detect our attention, we could trigger an operational lockout. If it's bait, we give them a win. If it's real..."

He let it hang.

General Li looked at his aides. "We'll launch a parallel operation. Unilateral. You do not own the domain on scientific espionage, Director Sun."

Sun's face remained still. But his knuckles paled as his hands clasped. "I advise your team prepare for the diplomatic fallout. The CIA is watching every node east of Buffalo."

"Let them," Li said. "They're already watching you."

The screen dimmed. The room went silent.

——

Fort Meade-Ops Center

SYBIL's interface glowed amber. A silent alert pulsed:

MSS-PLA divergence confirmed. Target: Parallax Veil Node PLT-03 (Plattsburgh)

Sara Brandt leaned over the shoulder of a SIGINT technician.

"They both saw the bait."

Will Morgan entered behind her. "Question is—who takes it first."

Genevieve, watching a filtered satellite trace on a nearby screen, murmured:

"They both blinked at the same time."

Will's jaw tensed. "Good. Now we know where to apply pressure."

——

ACIC HQ – Commander's Secure Conference Room

The walls were paneled in matte acoustic suppressors, the kind used for operational privacy. The room was small, cold, and sealed with a biometric lock.

A smart screen lit the table's center with two logos: MSS in red. PLA SSF in green. A thin black line flickered between them.

General Edwards, Commander of the Army Intelligence and Security Command (INSCOM), leaned over the edge of the briefing table, sleeves rolled, glasses tossed aside.

Will Morgan sat opposite, arms crossed, watching SYBIL's live analysis cascade across the interface. Divergence graphs. IP skims. Meta-intrusion profiles. Subtle. But widening.

"We fed them one leak," Will said. "And they split. Not cleanly—but enough."

Owen nodded once.

"MSS is in wait-and-verify mode. The PLA's moving ahead with a test probe."

"Good. Let the soldiers blunder in first. We widen the gap by giving MSS a reason to resent them."

Will turned to the table, tapped the console.

"SYBIL—generate a controlled leak. Reference an experimental constraint mismatch. Something that would only appear if you'd interfered physically with the site."

SYBIL replied:

"Constraint signature prepared. Key phrase: 'phase noise irregularities detected in superfluidity test post anomaly event.' Releasing under flag of MIT robotics researcher."

Will looked to Owen.

"MSS will read that as sabotage. Like the PLA triggered detection."

Owen's grin was faint.

"And when they accuse each other, we get to observe who the real field agents are."

"It's not just data anymore," Will muttered. "It's behavioral telemetry."

"Perfect," Owen said. "If we keep them chasing ghosts, they'll never find Shen Ke."

——

Plattsburgh, NY – Parallax Veil Node PLT-03

A nondescript building on the edge of a rural campus, lights dimmed, driveway still dusted in early frost. Inside, two ACIC tech officers, posing as night-shift lab staff, manned the interior of the false node.

They weren't physicists. They were Tier-4 decoy operators, trained to act, observe, and mislead.

An alert pinged on the embedded thermal monitor.

Unmanned drone. Low-altitude. Direction: From Canadian border. Flight profile: PLA-style pattern.

One tech murmured into a secure throat mic.

"Falcon-3 visual confirmed. Passive scan sweep, narrow spectrum. They're looking for heat dispersion."

On a nearby rooftop, a SIGINT team monitored the PLA drone's comms back channel. "Encrypt batch incomplete. They're masking this run, but it's crude. They're probing—nothing persistent yet."

At the fake lab entrance, a hidden panel inside the doorframe began cycling a signature burst: a custom electromagnetic footprint that mimicked anomaly behavior—the kind a bad actor would trigger by accident.

Inside, the ACIC team logged the probe.

"Telemetry injected. 'Ghost trace' uploaded to buffer. It'll show up as synthetic phase noise if they tap it."

One of them turned, smiled. "PLA's about to look real stupid in their next debrief."

In the distance, the faint buzz of the drone faded away into the dark.

——

Ministry of State Security Bureau 10 – Beijing

The room was dimly lit, soundproofed, and lined with acoustic panels. Thick air. No windows. A low-frequency hum vibrated from the floor, part of a Faraday dampening field built into the architecture. Only voice. No signals.

Seated at the oblong conference table were six officers of Bureau 10, China's division tasked with foreign scientific and technical intelligence. The briefing monitor displayed a distorted image from the Plattsburgh site: a spectral phase pattern—nonlinear, oscillating, unstable—precisely the kind of signal that would be left behind by a miscalibrated or tampered quantum system.

Deputy Director Sun Tao stood, jaw tight. "This anomaly was triggered forty-eight hours after Strategic Support Force Unit 4 performed an unauthorized low-altitude flyover of Sector Echo-Twelve."

He tapped the screen. The anomaly looped. Again. And again.

"This is not academic noise. It is a signature pattern, engineered. Either the Americans planted it in anticipation of detection, or the SSF triggered it during their intrusion."

A younger operative, analyst Zhao, sat forward.

"We confirmed that the signal appears on the lab's telemetry mirror. If this was bait, it was designed to look like a field compromise. They want us to suspect one another."

"And we have cause to," Sun said bluntly. "This was not cleared through inter-agency coordination. No permissions. No protocol. And now we're contaminated."

An older officer, Director Liu, head of internal security for Bureau 10, looked across the table. "Do we believe the Strategic Support Force acted alone?"

Zhao hesitated. "Unknown. But their technical signature is consistent with PLA-style surveillance drones, not civilian interceptors. They used military-grade shielding, but not well."

"So they were clumsy," Liu muttered. "Or arrogant."

Sun closed the file.

"We are opening an internal security review. All MSS field sites with PLA adjacency will be audited. I want operational logs, intercept footprints, chain-of-command authorization for every overlapping node."

Zhao asked, "And the Americans?"

"They are watching," Sun said. "But we will not give them the show they want. Quiet discipline. Not theater."

Liu added:

"Begin passive surveillance on all PLA-linked research delegates stationed abroad. Particularly any with visibility into quantum or cryogenic computing projects."

Sun nodded. "And notify the liaison at the embassy. We will begin rotating clean assets into the region. No further probes until we reestablish chain integrity."

As the lights dimmed, Sun's final words hung in the air:

"If they're playing shadows against us, we must be the fog."

——

Beijing - PLA Strategic Support Force – Command Facility

The Operations Briefing Room of the Strategic Support Force's cyber-intelligence wing sat deep inside a fortified campus west of Beijing. The walls were reinforced titanium laminate, the lighting sterile and bright. Digital display banks wrapped the perimeter, showing live metrics of foreign signal interception, reconnaissance scheduling, and cyber-range simulations.

At the head of the room, Major General Li Shun, stoic, decorated, and fiercely loyal to the military chain of command, stood before a tactical whiteboard. He held a red laser pointer and a copy of the MSS incident dossier, marked Classified: Internal Only.

He tapped the pointer against the screen, where the MSS's accusation pulsed in bold Hanzi:

Operational Breach: SSF Flyover of Echo-Twelve (Plattsburgh Sector)
Result: Signal Anomaly. Presumed Compromise
Filed by: Bureau 10, Ministry of State Security

Murmurs rose among the officers at the oval table—colonels and intelligence captains in dark-green uniforms, all bristling at the tone of the report.

Colonel Ren Kai, lead on technical surveillance doctrine, spoke first.

"They're accusing us of sloppy intrusion with no evidence of compromise. This reeks of posturing."

"They want control," muttered Lieutenant Colonel Zhou, cyber-defense specialist. "They're angry we moved first."

General Li said nothing for a few seconds. Then said, "They're trying to consolidate the scientific battlefield under their own fiefdom. But this is not only about surveillance, it's about credit. If this Plattsburgh site is legitimate, they want ownership of the find. If it's fake, they want plausible deniability."

"And if we're right?" Zhou asked.

"We were first," Li said flatly. "And that terrifies them."

He turned to the table.

"Prepare our internal counter-analysis. Full report on the anomaly signature. If it was engineered, we will identify the synthetic pulse. If it was legitimate, we retain first-contact rights."

Colonel Ren added, "And what about their audit?"

"Let them audit," Li said coldly. "We'll open only what we choose. But no more sharing forward reconnaissance."

He stepped away from the board. "We will deploy a parallel probe on the Orono and Schroon Lake sectors. Quiet, compartmented, fully deniable. No electromagnetic telemetry. Only satellite and terrain proxies."

Zhou paused. "General... what if this is a deception operation?"

Li looked at him, calm but cutting. "We'll trace the lies back to their architects."

He turned and addressed the entire table. "Let the MSS chase ghosts. We will find the machine."

CHAPTER TWENTY-TWO

The Peak

From Ferry to the Peak – A Measured Ascent

Star Ferry at Tsim Sha Tsui - Morning

She moved with quiet determination, her cane tapping gently on the tile as she stepped onto the Star Ferry at Tsim Sha Tsui, the Kowloon side terminal. The morning harbor air carried a faint trace of diesel and sea salt. Tourists clustered at the rails for selfies, but she stayed back—balanced, deliberate. Her black coat, long and tailored, swept above polished flats that had seen cities on three continents.

As the ferry glided across Victoria Harbour, the skyline unfolded like circuitry: glass, steel, and motion stacked into vertical grids. The ferry horn gave one long, low groan as it approached Central Ferry Pier No. 7 on Hong Kong Island.

She disembarked with care. The concrete dock sloped slightly downward—an uneven surface she took slowly. Her cane clicked against the painted safety lines as she passed under the terminal's low awning and emerged into the light.

Ahead: IFC Tower, bustling streets, and the beginning of her ascent.

She turned right onto Man Yiu Street, up toward Connaught Road Central, waiting patiently at crosswalks, watching for taxis that ignored red lights. Her cane tapped a steady rhythm over curb cuts and yellow tactile paving blocks.

Soon, she reached the entrance to the Central–Mid-Levels Escalator System—the world's longest outdoor covered escalator system, a spine through the vertical city.

She stepped onto the first moving walkway. It hummed beneath her.

From there, her climb became mechanical—escalator by escalator, 800 meters uphill.

Past Queen's Road Central, where bankers spilled out of Pret and Pacific Coffee.

Past Hollywood Road, where the scent of incense from a nearby temple mingled with wet concrete.

Past Staunton Street, where delivery men ducked under the canopy of hanging laundry.

At Shelley Street, she paused to rest. The escalators operated only uphill until 10 a.m. After that, it would all be on foot. She checked her watch. 09:52. Close.

She stepped off the escalator at Conduit Road, the last station. The city was far below now—filtered by haze and humid light.

From here, it was a short but steep cab ride to the Peak Tram Lower Terminus at Garden Road.

She boarded the tram with a quiet nod to the conductor. The old funicular groaned and lurched upward at a sharp incline, climbing past dense foliage and concrete retaining walls. As the tram climbed, the buildings outside tilted unnaturally—optical illusions from the steep grade.

At the Victoria Peak Upper Terminus, she disembarked and stepped slowly onto the platform.

A final path wound through shaded trees to a quiet overlook—a private ledge slightly off the main tourist promenade. There, shielded from view but high above the city, she waited.

Her cane rested across her lap like a forgotten relic.

Below, Hong Kong shimmered—alive with movement, none of it able to reach her.

——

Hong Kong Island

Li Shun did not take the ferry.

He arrived at the Four Seasons Hong Kong by back entrance—his car unmarked, escorted only by a civilian staff driver rotated weekly through the embassy pool. Inside, he walked straight through the lobby in civilian dress, not once glancing at the sweeping harbor view offered to guests.

A short passage through Central MTR Station's unpaid zone led him into the heart of Hong Kong's underground artery. No CCTV from his entry point to the next crossover. He timed it to the minute.

He exited near Hong Kong Park, emerging behind a cluster of uniformed schoolchildren chattering in Cantonese. He didn't stand out—just another tall, well-kept man in his fifties, walking with a tourist's idle pace but eyes that never rested.

His destination was the Peak Tram Lower Terminus on Garden Road.

Instead of boarding inside, he waited outside the terminus at the operator's side entrance—where his reserved tram was ready, sealed and timed outside of public operating hours.

Inside the car, alone, he stood without holding the rail, letting the incline rise around him.

No entourage. No phone. No digital footprint.

Li Shun, Senior Strategist for the PLA Strategic Support Force, gliding silently toward a meeting that officially would never exist.

Victoria Peak – The Voice in the Fog

The lookout was quiet—only the occasional distant click of a camera shutter beyond the trees.

She sat with her back to him, facing the drop. Her coat motionless in the breeze.

Between them only a low stone bench and five feet of gravel path.

Chimera (Yasha Moravec) said, "You came alone. Good."

Her voice reached him not from her mouth, but from a small transducer clipped beneath the bench. Fragmented slightly, phase-shifted. A digital whisper.

Li Shun said, "Your protocols are dramatic."

"My protocols are safe."

He didn't sit. He remained standing—still, alert, hands in pockets.

"You know what I want."

"Yes. Surveillance and soft penetration of six U.S. sites. Possible decoys, you believe. You want confirmation."

"I want signal fidelity, not guesswork. I want to know if we're chasing noise."

A pause.

Chimera said, "You'll have it. Chrysalis doesn't recruit. We signal. The ones who respond will tell us what you want to know."

"And if they fail?"

"They burn. That's the difference between an asset and a variable. We don't train loyalty. We trigger it." She stood slowly now, but turned away from him. The mist cloaked her form, hiding everything but the tip of her cane. She began walking into the misted grove that led deeper into the Peak trail system.

He did not follow.

Li Shun studied the silhouette of her back. "And when this is over? When the U.S. sites are confirmed?"

"You pay the second tranche, and we never speak again."

"And the ghost drive?"

A pause — just long enough to register. "Burned years ago," she said. "Industrial accident. You read the report yourself." She let him hear the smile in her voice. She wanted him to hear it. A reminder, delivered as deniability: she knew the lie because she was the one who'd written it.

Li's jaw tightened almost imperceptibly. He had hired her precisely because she was the only person alive who could deliver Chrysalis at this scale. He had also hired her knowing she could end him with a single transmission to the wrong inbox. The contract was protection money dressed as a service agreement, and they both knew it.

"Wire your deposit," she said. "Monero. Same channel. Same code. No back channeling. If you're traced, I will erase this initiative with a whisper."

"Understood."

The Strategic Support Force was newer to the game than the men she'd worked for in Prague, or the ones in Moscow who'd thought they owned her. Their money spent the same. What they bought with it was their business, until the day it wasn't.

Behind him, the wind shifted. Far below, the Star Ferry sounded its horn—one long, low note. The city moved as always. But something had changed.

The Disappearing Woman

Victoria Peak, Hong Kong Island

Chimera walked past one of the twelve surveillance agents Li Shun had positioned along the Peak Trail system. The agent didn't flinch—he'd been briefed on how little they'd have to go on. Still, the sight was unsettling.

She wore a silver-streaked black wig, tucked under a wide oversized sunhat with ear flaps, the kind favored by tourists hiking on ultraviolet-wary doctor's orders. Her sunglasses were reflective and large enough to obscure most of her brow and cheeks. Prosthetic latex reshaped her jawline, subtly widening the base. A flattened bridge and a swelling of the nostrils distorted her nose from surveillance files. Her lips remained bare—the only visible feature.

Facial recognition had nothing to work with. No eye data. No brows. The only persistent biometric available was the proportional size of her head and the general contour of her mouth—barely enough for a low-confidence open-set guess in fog and motion blur. And that was by design.

She moved with deliberate asymmetry, her cane tapping every third step like a soft metronome. That, too, was a choice.

She followed the fog-lined trail off the main overlook and ducked into a public restroom built into the hillside, out of view from most of the tourist angles. The cameras noted her entry. Then the wait began.

Inside, she lingered for long enough to suggest plausible use of the facilities—but not long enough to undress or fully change.

And then... she exited.

And another woman followed. Same oversized hat. Same gait. A second cane. Then, a third. They were nearly identical. Three middle-aged women with a slight right-side limp, dressed in muted outdoor attire.

Now, three Chimera shadows split across the park:

One settled on a bench, visible to drones.

One joined the queue for the Peak Tram, casually descending with tourists.

The real Chimera—undetected—slid into the back of a waiting red taxi.

She never looked back.

The taxi wound down steep roads to the Aberdeen Marina, passing under cameras already fed false license plate IDs via an onboard jamming relay. At Dock 4, she stepped into a sleek mid-sized speedboat, where the driver—an older woman with no visible tattoos and a dead SIM phone—nodded once.

Moments later, the boat peeled across the harbor, disappearing into the lattice of sea traffic between Hong Kong Island and Lamma.

By the time Li Shun received word of her movement, all three surveillance tails were locked on decoys.

And Chimera was gone.

——

Beijing – PLA Strategic Support Force HQ – 1125 Hours Hotel

Li Shun stood alone in the dim operations suite, back to the bank of monitors still playing the final seconds of Chimera's vanishing act. The SCIF melted into the haze of Victoria Harbor, swallowed by fog and reflection. She was gone.

"She outplayed us," he said aloud, voice clipped. "But the game is not over."

Two benches from the waterfront rendezvous point—seemingly innocuous—had been ripped from the concrete within two hours of her disappearance. They now sat inside a sterile PLA forensic lab outside Guangzhou, surrounded by analysts in clean suits. Every screw, fiber, and embedded chip was under scrutiny.

Two hundred new PLA cyber recruits, fresh from orientation, were tasked with analyzing CCTV footage across a five-block radius. One hundred twenty-four cameras. Two hours each. Frame by frame. Their orders were simple: find any deviation from the ordinary. No AI filters. Just human pattern recognition.

At the boat rental kiosk, investigators tracked down the owner who leased the SCIF used in the escape. "Paid in cash. Neutral accent. Gloved hands." Still, the boat was hauled from the marina, its every surface swabbed and vapor-screened.

Meanwhile, behind layers of operational compartmentalization, Li Shun watched the balance update in the PLA's crypto shadow wallet. ¥7,154,002.06—the amount he had transferred to Monero for Chimera's services. He hated it. But the job was done, and the transaction was final.

Monero (XMR) was no ordinary currency. Its backbone was cryptographic obscurity—ring signatures, stealth addresses, RingCT. The perfect cloak. Transactions weren't just encrypted; they were invisible, undecipherable, and by default, deniable.

But Chimera had left behind one thread.

After eight days of silent failure, a technician on hour fifteen of her shift shouted from across the lab:

"We've got something!"

The currency seized at the boat rental exchange had been vacuum-sealed for evidence. Swabs from several bills revealed traces of skin oil and epithelial tissue—not uncommon, but usually too degraded.

This time, one small, coarse strand had been trapped under the foam pad of the voice-changer device hidden beneath the park bench.

It was an eyebrow hair.

By morning, after a full-spectrum mitochondrial and nuclear profile run, the match hit an old, partially redacted archive out of Belgrade and confirmed by a Czech backchannel biometrics feed.

Yasha Moravec. Tradecraft: elite. Czech-born. Exfiltration specialist. Known alias network: six verified, eleven suspected. Unconfirmed ties to Chimera.

Li Shun closed the file and muttered:

"Now to find her."

He turned to his aide.

"I want her name flagged on all ICAO and IATA manifests. Facial variation masks. Behavioral motion traces. Run passive asset sweeps in Belgrade, Amsterdam, and Lisbon."

He looked out the window into the heavy Beijing haze.

"She took our ghost coin. Let's see what she buys next."

——

Belgrade, Serbia — 2300 hours local

Rain shimmered across Kalemegdan Fortress, its ancient stones slick with history and drizzle. Below, the Sava and Danube met in quiet defiance of borders, and the pulse of Belgrade's nightlife vibrated through the city's veins. Music echoed from splavovi—those floating river clubs chained along the banks—where neon blurred across water and secrets changed hands over glasses of rakija.

In a nondescript gray telecom facility leased under a shell company, four floors beneath Vračar, the PLA's Strategic Support Force had repurposed an old Ministry of Interior data node. Officially, it was a civil–military "tech exchange." Unofficially, it was a covert SIGINT relay station, wired directly into the Safe City surveillance grid—an expansive Huawei-designed network of over 10,000 facial-recognition cameras across Serbia.

A crimson warning blinked on one of the operator stations.

> MATCH: 82.6% Confidence — Subject: MORAVEC, YASHA (codename: CHIMERA)33
> Camera: Terazije Crossing, Belgrade
> Timestamp: 22:44 Local

Captain Li Yuan squinted at the frozen image. The woman was older now. Hair darker, shorter. The cheekbones and gait matched. The subdermal model, reconstructed using previous Europol intercepts and a Berlin customs scan from 2017, was holding up.

"Replay with gait overlay. Run time-delta on timestamp and last public transit sensor hit," he ordered in Mandarin.

The system obeyed. An AI trace sketched a projection of her walking pattern—left shoulder tilt, hip torque, irregular stride—into the scrolling video of Belgrade's busy pedestrian zone. The match jumped to 92.1%.

Li nodded once.

"Confirm cross-feed with Novi Sad node. Query last 48 hours for matching stride signature or partial face."

Twenty PLA cyber recruits, barely out of the Kowloon training loop, now worked in tight rows on Serbian soil. Their previous mission had been dissecting Hong Kong MTR camera logs for dissident overlays. Here, they scanned cafes, tram stations, hotel lobbies—anything within the Huawei grid.

They didn't need cooperation from Serbia. Not when China had built the infrastructure.

"Belgrade Metro is due for full facial sync upgrades in Q4," said the senior engineer beside Li, watching the cascading feeds.

"We won't need to wait," Li replied. "Her signature is embedded. She won't pass a streetlight without waving at Beijing."

Within moments, three additional sightings triangulated. Hotel Moskva. A corner kiosk at Knez Mihailova. A fleeting reflection in a jewelry shop mirror near Studentski Park.

They found her.

——

Outside — The Street

Yasha Moravec exited a dim gallery space near the university, face partially hidden under a plum-colored shawl. Her stride was casual. Confident. She paused to light a cigarette, unaware—or perhaps uncaring—that she had been claimed by an algorithm six thousand kilometers away.

She crossed toward the river.

A nightclub's bassline thudded in the distance, and the Serbian rain began to fall harder.

——

Belgrade, Serbia — PLA Strategic Support Force 2318 Hours Bravo

The rain had intensified, blurring streetlights into smeared halos. From beneath the hood of his charcoal windbreaker, Major Zhu Wen watched Chimera from across the street. He walked with a tourist's posture, camera bag slung loose over one shoulder, but his eyes were fixed and cold.

She didn't check behind her. Didn't hesitate at intersections. That told him two things: she was either overconfident—or she wanted to be found.

They'd confirmed the biometric hit less than an hour ago. Li Yuan had kicked the feed to Zhu's burner the moment three separate nodes—each at least a kilometer apart—had clocked the same signature. The probability curve was tight. Chimera had resurfaced.

Zhu adjusted his pace as she passed a late-night bakery, her silhouette briefly glowed in the warm window light. She bought nothing. Just observed. Clocked the exits. He made a note of it.

Sava Quay — 23:34 Bravo

Yasha's route looped back toward the river. She passed three splavovi before pausing outside one—Plava Reka, a low-slung club popular with Belgrade's underground DJ scene. She didn't enter. She leaned on the railing, finished her cigarette, then turned and crossed Karadjordjeva without looking.

Zhu followed at a steady interval—fifty meters, varying angles. He used mirrored panels, car glass, convex security bubbles on ATMs. Not once did she give any indication she'd made him. If she was baiting, she was good.

Savski Venac — 00:03 Bravo

She reached a cluster of prewar apartments perched above the old Yugoslav Ministry of Defense ruins. A single blue door. No markings. Residential intercom panel with several blank nameplates.

She didn't buzz. She used a key.

Zhu slowed and passed on the opposite sidewalk, head dipped. A microcamera stitched into his collar snapped six photos per second. Wide-angle, low-light optimized. The door, the buzzer plate, the threshold step — all logged.

Timestamp 00:04

Subject enters 12 Makedonska Street. Door code or key access confirmed. Ground-level residence.

Zhu circled once and returned to the next block. The rain masked his breath, and the whine of a distant tram provided cover for the soft crunch of his boots.

He moved to a vantage point above the residence, tucking into a gap between a stone retaining wall and a hedgerow. From there, he had a clear view of her window: sheer curtains, faint movement, light from a desk lamp. Books stacked on a sill. A kettle boiled. She was settling in.

Zhu keyed a silent message into his phone:

Asset CONFIRMED. Subject MORAVEC, YASHA (CHIMERA) resides 12 Makedonska, Apt A. Recommend passive monitoring until active directive issued.

He didn't send it yet. Not yet.

He waited for her light to turn off.

It never did.

Zhu had been in position for five hours.

From the outside, the small apartment looked the same as it had when he arrived—quiet, and almost too ordinary. The single upstairs light remained on, glowing faintly through the thin curtains. It had not flickered once.

He shifted feet constantly and sat on an empty garbage can in the alley across the street, careful not to create movement that might draw attention. His notebook rested open on his knee. The entries were repetitive.

18:05 – Light on. No movement.

18:40 – No activity.

19:20 – No visitors.

20:10 – No change.

21:03 – Still no movement.

The street had grown colder as the evening deepened. A light wind pushed dry leaves along the curb. Twice a neighbor had walked a dog past the house. Once a delivery truck had turned around at the end of the road. Nothing else.

Zhu lifted the small encrypted handset from his pocket.

He waited for the line to establish.

"Zhu."

Li Shun's voice came through calm and even.

"Reporting observation status. Five hours continuous surveillance. Target structure unchanged. Interior light still active. No movement observed. No visitors. No departures."

"You believe the structure is empty?"

"I cannot confirm occupancy." Zhu glanced again at the quiet house. "However, continued stationary observation may compromise position if neighbors become attentive."

Another brief silence.

Zhu chose his words carefully. "I request authorization either to reposition or to be relieved."

On the other end, Li Shun considered it for only a moment.

"Your discipline is noted," he said. "Remain in place. Replacement is already en route."

Zhu allowed himself the smallest breath of relief. "Estimated arrival?"

"Seven minutes."

The line clicked dead. Zhu set the handset down and returned his eyes to the house. The upstairs light was still on.

CHAPTER TWENTY-THREE

Sun Tao

Beijing-MSS Headquarters – 10th Bureau (Counterintelligence)

Yidongyuan government compound Xiyuan area of the Haidian District.

The air in the conference chamber of the 10th Bureau was recycled, too cold, and deliberately sterile. On the wall behind them, the red and gold seal of the Ministry of State Security loomed over the oval glass table like a silent judge.

Three senior officials sat, stone-faced, around the polished surface.

Director Huang Jintao, Vice Minister for Counterintelligence Strategy, glanced down at the tablet displaying the most recent Western intelligence press leaks. Nothing direct. Nothing concrete. But troubling implications.

Deputy Director Cai Yuren of the Americas Desk was livid.

"We invested sixteen years in Shen Ke. Sixteen years! Millions in transfer protocols, years of dead drops and signal meetings. And now they claim he died in prison?" His voice cracked, emotion spilling into his cadence. "There's no body. No photographs. No chain-of-custody. Nothing."

Across from him, Zhou Lin, Liaison to the Military Intelligence Bureau (MID), remained calm.

"Which is precisely why you should assume he's not dead. Not until the Americans give us something more than a newspaper whisper."

Huang raised a hand.

"Let's dispense with the shouting. The question is not whether Shen Ke is dead. The question is whether he was ever truly ours."

That silenced them.

Even Cai.

A low hum from the air vent filled the pause.

"There are anomalies," Zhou said, steepling his fingers. "The information he gave us—while valuable—always pointed away from actionable breakthroughs. Delays. False patterns. We spent three years chasing a dead quantum branch because of him."

"That's disinformation," Cai spat. "We were misled by other Western leaks. That's not on Shen Ke."

"Or it's exactly on Shen Ke," Zhou countered. "And you let it happen."

Cai stood abruptly.

"You're questioning the integrity of my entire section."

"I'm questioning your judgment," Zhou replied icily. "Not your patriotism. Though if your failures cost the Republic time and strategic positioning, history won't differentiate."

Huang cut in again — quieter this time.

"The Foreign Ministry is already drafting talking points. If Shen Ke is alive, and they've faked his death, they'll use him. Somewhere, somehow. His silence is weaponized. We cannot be reactive."

A long silence.

Huang looked at Cai.

"From this moment forward, Shen Ke is treated as a compromised asset. Assume he was flipped as early as 2007. Reverse-engineer everything he touched."

Cai sat slowly, pale now.

"That's half our network in Silicon Valley."

"Then you'd better start pruning."

Huang stood.

"We will not admit betrayal. We will not confirm death. We will not appear confused. We will proceed with containment."

Cai said, "For the record, Yasha Moravec's name has surfaced in PLA chatter as an unrelated commercial problem."

He closed the folder on the table, and walked out, leaving silence and ruin behind.

Outside, Beijing's skyline flickered with controlled light. Inside, the war of shadows sharpened its knives.

Fort Meade-ACIC Headquarters – Secure Briefing Room

The room was small, windowless, and far below the ground floor of Fort Meade—Briefing Room Gamma, where the walls were triple-lined with active acoustic countermeasures and even SYBIL's logs were set to manual only.

Will Morgan sat at the far end of the narrow conference table, sleeves rolled to his forearms, posture deceptively relaxed. But his eyes scanned the field report on the screen in front of him with cold precision.

Ed Perry, Commander of ACIC, leaned on the edge of the table, sipping coffee that had gone cold three hours ago.

Owen Edwards, Commander of INSCOM, stood near the whiteboard, arms folded across his chest, flipping through a thin classified file. The Chinese transcript was still fresh.

"So," Owen said, closing the folder. "Beijing's throwing elbows. Zhou and Cai nearly came to blows in the MSS 10th Bureau."

"Not surprised," Will said, calm. "They've got three scenarios and no proof which one is real."

Ed glanced at him.

"Run them."

Will held up a hand, ticking them off as he spoke:

"One: Shen Ke's dead. A clean, tragic end—no leverage left, no revenge to exact. They're hoping for this."

"Two," he continued, "he was a double all along and the U.S. flipped the table on them. If that's true, they've got to assume everything he touched was contaminated. Sixteen years of sunk cost and internal fallout."

"Three," he said, voice cooling, "he's alive. And we've built something around him—quiet, expensive, and far from D.C. That one scares them most. Because it means we're still playing the board and they don't know where the king is."

Owen scratched his chin. "How long can we bluff?"

Will answered without hesitation. "As long as they keep yelling instead of shooting."

Ed sat down. "The problem is, when the yelling stops. They'll test us. Use a proxy. An accident. Maybe a diplomat gets dragged into something at customs. A lab gets interlocked. Nothing traceable, just pressure."

Will leaned back. "We let them chase shadows. Send their tail teams upstate, see what they find in Barre or Littleton or Schroon Lake. Meanwhile, Nemo's buried under layers they can't reach."

Owen tapped the table. "This only works if we don't overplay it. If we start flexing Shen Ke as a live asset, they'll know. They're paranoid, but they're not stupid."

Will nodded. "We won't surface him. No leaks only silence."

Ed folded his hands. "What about Echo Reef's expansion?"

"Cover holds," Will said. "It's a remote R&D contract for DoD cryptographic research. All budget references are black chest code. SYBIL's already generating controlled anomaly noise—something sketchy enough to distract but not confirm."

Owen smirked. "You're enjoying this."

Will's expression didn't change. "I'm buying us time. Time is the only thing China can't steal."

A quiet settled in the room.

Ed stood. "Alright. We hold posture. No new signals. Let the MSS stay confused. But the moment they shift from surveillance to shaping—"

"I'll be ready," Will said.

Ed looked at him.

"No. We'll all be ready."

Owen gave a half-grin.

"You realize we've built an entire intelligence deadfall around a man who just wants to walk his dog and build superconductors."

Will cracked the smallest smile.

"Good cover, isn't it?"

Lights dimmed automatically as they stepped out.

Behind them, the map of Vermont flickered to standby—one glowing red node pulsing beneath layers of operational silence.

——

Beijing, China - PLA Headquarters

The secure briefing room in Beijing had no insignia, no flags—only a matte wall and a projection surface that showed rural Vermont in winter grayscale. A farmhouse. A barn.

The PLA analyst did not speculate. She narrated.

"CHIMERA maintains three subcontracted technical collectors in North America. One was compromised six weeks ago in Vermont."

The slide changed.

A grainy still image: a man being escorted down concrete steps. Basement level. Restraint posture. Military control, not police.

"Held off-books," she continued. "Interrogated, arrested by U.S. Army Counterintelligence. Not FBI. Not DHS."

That mattered.

Another slide. Satellite imagery—commercial resolution, legally acquired, deniable.

A lone figure crossing the property at dawn.

Same height as the detainee. Same stride length. Same asymmetrical shoulder drop.

Gait analysis overlaid in pale vectors.

"Post-arrest," the analyst said. "The subject disappears. But activity at the location increases. Power draw. Communications discipline. No visible research staff. No signage."

She paused just long enough for the conclusion to form on its own.

"CHIMERA suspects Shen Ke survived. Her people believe he is being concealed."

One of the generals leaned back. "Suspects," he repeated. Not a question.

"Yes," the analyst said. "No confirmation. But Army CI does not build rural holding sites for farmers."

Silence.

Then another voice—older, flatter.

"If Shen Ke is alive, he would not remain idle."

The screen shifted again.

A name appeared. Not a face.

NEMO

— *Unregistered researcher*

— *No academic affiliation*

— *No digital footprint post-2015*

— *Power usage consistent with high-density compute*

— *Location overlap with CHIMERA compromise*

"Probability?" the general asked.

The analyst didn't hesitate. "Enough."

That was the standard. Not proof. Not certainty.

Just enough to act.

The Decision

The next room was smaller. No analysts. No slides.

"CHIMERA was wrong once," he said. "We will not make the same mistake twice."

He stood.

"Engage a contractor. Rural terrain. Winter window. One target."

A pause.

"If this man is Shen Ke," he continued, "we end a liability."

"And if he is not?"

The general's expression didn't change.

"We remove whatever the Americans are hiding."

He turned toward the door.

"Good enough," he said.

And somewhere, half a world away, an assassin would receive coordinates.

CHAPTER TWENTY-FOUR

The Wolf

The weapon of the advocate is the sword of the soldier, not the dagger of the assassin." - Alexander Cockburn.

Beijing-PLA Strategic Support Force Headquarters

The room was windowless, buried deep beneath the National Defense Science and Technology Complex. Digital red clocks glowed silently across the wall. A 3D map of northeastern America hovered midair—New England lit up in latticework.

Major General Bai Zongren stood with arms crossed. The cyber-operations chief of the PLA's shadow tasking group, he answered only to the Central Military Commission.

“We're not discussing arrests anymore,” he said. “This is now a counterforce directive. We need deniable hands.”

Around him: a senior colonel from the Technical Reconnaissance Bureau, two uniformed officers from Unit 61398, and Colonel Yu Jinhai from PLA liaison.

A file loaded into the holoscreen. Three dossiers.

1. *DARIUS "WOLF" STRAKER: “The ghost hunter,” said Bai, flipping the image with a gesture.*

“Rural terrain, mountain background, speaks enough Mandarin to navigate southern Africa. Perfect fit for the Vermont target.”

Colonel Yu frowned. “He demands real-time coordinates. No recon. No improvisation.”

“We'll provide them,” Bai snapped. “If we can't, we're the problem.”

2. *ZOË KOWALSKI: The room dimmed slightly as the projector cycled her file.*

"Polish-American," said the TRB officer. "Disguised poisoning, electronic masking, may leave no trace. Ideal for neutralizing Moravec.

Yu interjected, skeptical.

"She's unreliable with unstable operations. Her work in Slovakia drew NATO interest. Too subtle for field termination."

"We don't need overt," the TRB officer replied. "She can fabricate SVR fingerprints. Let the Russians wear the blame."

3. HENDRIK "BASTION" REIMANN

Reimann's image flickered: a glowering man, buzz-cut, scar on his temple.

"Effective only when subtlety is irrelevant," Bai said dryly. "He's a street warhead. Loud. Messy."

Yu nodded. "He's a final option. If we want to provoke American reaction, he's the one."

A beat of silence. "But if he's caught—it's uncontainable."

Major General Bai exhaled.

"It's settled. Straker for Vermont. Kowalski for Moravec. Reimann remains in reserve."

He tapped the secure tablet. "Initiate Ghost Paper. Tasking routes through Paraguay."

——

"There is no faith which has never yet been broken, except that of a truly faithful dog."

Granville, VT=Nusquam Late Autumn

Nusquam was quiet.

A brittle wind combed through the late-autumn trees, sending dry leaves skittering across the gravel path like whispers of forgotten conversations. Frost laced the edges of the trail from the lab to the greenhouse, and Shen Ke—Nemo—walked alone, hands buried in his coat pockets, shoulders hunched against the chill. He'd insisted on his solitude this morning, needing clarity for a delicate procedure. No escort, air and distance.

Runa trotted parallel to him, ranging ahead, then circling back—her gait relaxed, but eyes sharp. She was seven now, but still lean. The old Malinois had adopted the rhythms of Nusquam easily, but she never dropped her vigilance.

Cecil's man Leandro Cruz, former Marine Scout Sniper, watched from the edge of the comms hub, coffee in hand, eyes followed the dog more than the man.

"You let him go alone?" Genevieve asked beside him.

"He insisted. SYBIL's perimeter's green," Leandro said. "Runa's with him. That's never alone."

Genevieve gave a faint nod. "Let's hope she's enough."

Nusquam Fields - 1,000 Yards Out

Darius Straker lay beneath a mat of pine needles and synthetic camo netting, his body sculpted against the Vermont hillside as if he belonged to it. His breath barely fogged the air inside his half-mask. He'd been in position for hours. Motionless. Patient. The kind of patience you learn when your life depends on how long you can lie still while something else dies.

His eye hovered behind a Steiner scope. The crosshairs centered on a slim figure walking an exposed curve in the trail. One thousand yards. No wind. Subsonic .338 Lapua would hit center mass in silence. The target would crumple before anyone even heard the crack. It was almost elegant.

He watched for the perfect cadence in the walk. The exact point of breath cycle. The cleanest trajectory.

Nusquam Fields - Runa Stopped Walking

It was subtle—a pause mid-stride, a tilt of her head. Then the shift: ears forward, nostrils flaring.

Leandro noticed it first on the surveillance screen. "Something's off. Look at her—"

Runa froze, tail down, muscles tight. She sniffed again—sharp, three quick inhales. Her head turned northwest.

Darius didn't see her yet. He saw only the man, framed in certainty.

Runa bolted.

Darius's gloved finger took up slack on the trigger. Slow breath. Calm heartbeat. Perfect shot.

Then a blur.

A tan shadow exploded into his scope — Runa, closing from an oblique angle, too fast to track, too sudden to plan for.

Instinct jolted his aim— The suppressed round snapped into a water pipe six inches from Nemo's chest.

Metal rang like a bell. Nemo flinched, stumbled, dropped.

Will's voice cut through comms. "Gunshot! Vector Runa's heading! Full lockdown!"

Runa didn't bark. She didn't growl. She placed herself between Nemo and the shot, teeth bared, chest heaving.

Darius pivoted, chambered another round, scanned— No shot. Too exposed. His position had seconds left before response teams vectorized.

He ghosted back, slipping into the trees, erasing footprints, dragging a heat-dampening tarp behind him. But he knew: the moment was lost.

He hadn't counted on the dog.

Nusquam - Compound

Nemo sat on the gravel, stunned but unhurt. His glasses were missing. Runa pressed against him, panting hard.

Genevieve sprinted the last stretch, skidding to her knees beside them. "Are you hit?"

Nemo shook his head, still dazed. "No... no. She jumped in front of me."

Runa whined once and nuzzled under his arm.

Leandro arrived seconds later, rifle in hand, eyes sweeping the perimeter. "SYBIL's triangulating origin point. We'll have a vector in thirty seconds."

He dropped to one knee and pressed his hand to Runa's side. "You good, girl?"

She licked his hand once, then turned back to watch the woods, eyes locked.

Nusquam Operations -The Debrief

Later, in the operations room, Cecil's drone expert Rami Al-Sayid's drone feed painted a heat trail — faint, fading fast, but visible. It showed a lone thermal shadow moving up the ridge minutes before the shot. A sniper perch hastily abandoned.

Karen dropped a data spike on the table. "Found this embedded in the tree bark near the greenhouse."

Leandro picked it up—a rifle casing. The etching was faint, but there: Cyrillic initials, professionally marked.

"Runa smelled him from a thousand yards," Genevieve said. "She saved his life."

Leandro looked at the screen, then at the dog curled at Nemo's feet.

"She saved him," he said. "And she gave us a ghost's footprint."

The hillside had gone quiet again in the predator's shadow.

Darius Straker moved fast, but not chaotically. Every step was chosen. Every stride a calculation. He dropped low, used gullies, creek beds, frost-patched moss. Thermal discipline mattered now. He tugged the thermo-shield tarp over his back and shoulders like a second skin, the fibers designed to scatter infrared and confuse drones.

His exfiltration path snaked west, toward a shallow ravine where a camouflaged e-bike was hidden beneath deadwood. He would not be fast — but he would be invisible. He'd memorized woodland density maps, studied the temperature variances, logged the security team patrol intervals. He hadn't come to Vermont to improvise.

But he also hadn't come to miss.

Nusquam Operations - SYBIL Acquires Target

Karen's voice was low but sharp. "Let's get him."

In the operations hub, SYBIL's tactical interface pulled in real-time data: acoustic triangulation, thermal variance, drone flight logs, weather overlays, and directional scent patterns from Runa's pursuit arc. It displayed a dispersed motion corridor stretching northwest from the shooter's perch.

"Straker's no amateur," Karen muttered."

Marcus "Shiv" Kwan, Cecil's Technical surveillance expert, fingers flying across his tablet. "No track, no trash, no sweat residue on the trunk bark. But Runa's trajectory gave us the opening vector."

Karen nodded. "And this shell casing?" She rotated the polished brass. "Match-etched, Cyrillic. Covert GRU procurement or PLA special purchase. Either way—foreign signature."

Nusquam Sniper's Nest - Forensics in the Wild

Cecil Brandon and two field agents swept the sniper's perch. The spot was pristine. No cigarette butts, no food wrappers. But not perfect.

"Hold on," Cecil said, crouching. "He left us a sliver."

He held up a thin ceramic shard the length of a fingernail. A sliver from a custom suppressor baffle — the kind designed to withstand multiple disassemblies and subsonic gas venting.

"This isn't field-issue," Cecil said. "This is bespoke."

Nusquam Fields - Thermal Ghosting

Rami Al-Sayid launched a microdrone from a gloved palm. It buzzed up, hovered, its lenses sifting lingering thermal shadows like a crime scene scanner at altitude.

"Found his wake," Rami said, tapping a screen. "There's a residual heat print in the creek bed — see the left heel pattern? He turned east to mislead, doubled back into the ridgeline."

"Classic Recce move," Leandro said. "He's trying to walk the thermal signature out of range and double back once our sweep overshoots."

"SYBIL," Shiv Kwan said, turning toward the AI's screen, "give me a ten-minute forecast window — atmospheric density, drone coverage grid, and optimal intercept points."

SYBIL's voice came cool and clear.

"Projection complete. Nearest viable intercept zone is a reforested slope north of Echo Hollow. Wind conditions favorable. Estimated target velocity: 3.4 km/h. Arrival at exfil point in twenty-two minutes if unimpeded."

Shiv nodded. "Then we impede."

Nusquam Security Ops - The Interdiction Plan

"We don't need to catch him," Cecil said to the team. "We need to make him run hot."

Genevieve looked up. "You want to flush him?"

"I want him to feel the noose. Push him toward his fallback exit. Every pro has one."

Cecil said, "Which means someone helped stage it. Extraction logistics, burner comms, alternate identities. We find that network—we corner him."

Genevieve looked down at Runa, curled at Nemo's feet, eyes still locked toward the forest.

"We have the scent now," he said. "He was hunting. Now he's prey."

Nusquam

The forest was still alive with data.

Overhead, two tactical drones hummed beneath the canopy line, their propellers masked by acoustic baffling. Infrared mapping bled across SYBIL's screen in pulses—a digital heartbeat tracking residual warmth across moss, lichen, creek water, and disturbed earth.

In the ops center, Will's jaw was clenched. "He's faster than we projected."

Sara pointed to the updated terrain model. "He's cutting diagonally—see that ridge? If he hits the eastern slope in under five minutes, we lose drone LOS unless we push now."

Will nodded. "Rick, get me topography on the elevation east of Echo Hollow."

"On it." Rick's fingers blurred over the control surface. "Steep grade, rocky switchback. Limited mobility. But there's a thermal void halfway up — he could be using it to mask his ascent."

"SYBIL," Will said, "what's the probability that slope leads to a planned exfil?"

"Eighty-four percent. Supporting data: angled stone deposits consistent with ski-pack rigging, heat-ablation residue on two ledges, and aluminum stress markers—possible foldable launch frame."

Will's eyes narrowed. "Paraglider."

Darius: Seventeen Minutes Out

Darius Straker paused beneath a granite overhang and unclipped the tarp cinched to his back. He worked fast but smooth, unfolding the compact thermal-shielded paraglider frame. The chute—matte black with silver filament mesh—shimmered faintly in the shadows.

He glanced at his satellite-linked burner. A blue LED blinked once.

Transmission acknowledged.

From a moss-covered stump ten meters away, a thin black spike extended—the uplink beacon he'd embedded twelve hours earlier. long enough for the satellite to cross overhead, short enough to avoid detection.

So he thought.

Fort Meade-NSA TAO

Miles away, inside a hardened operations suite beneath Fort Meade, Sloane Merrick, supervisor at NSA's Tailored Access Operations (TAO) unit, sipped coffee as her screen pinged an anomaly.

"Unregistered burst on Band 4," one of her analysts said. "Duration 0.91 seconds. Narrow-band, encrypted. Spike intersected a Chinese relay satellite over Vermont grid six."

Merrick tapped a control. "Isolate."

The waveform was faint, but unique.

"Coordinates," she said.

A moment later, she picked up her phone. "Get me ACIC. Tell Will Morgan we caught his ghost."

Skies above Nusquam - The Drone Chase

Rick's watched Leandro's drone camera as it snapped to life — a blur of motion over icy stone. "I've got him!"

The screen locked onto a thermal silhouette sprinting uphill with unnatural grace — a perfect predator's economy of motion. Straker was almost to the ridge's peak.

Cecil's voice crackled through comms: "We've got a Quick Reaction Team two klicks out—"

"Won't be fast enough," Will cut in. "Cecil, drop the second drone and box him in. Drive him east. Leandro call it."

Leandro watched the slope, calculating angles. "He'll launch in under ninety seconds if he clears that crest. We need obstruction above—cut thermals, blind descent."

Rick nodded. "EMP-pulse chaff—low yield, tight spread. Give me thirty seconds."

The drone dumped a burst of silver mylar chaff that exploded mid-air, glittering like snow. It hung above the slope like a fractured halo—distorting the thermals, skewing descent planning.

Darius saw it, and for the first time, cursed.

——

The Escape

He launched anyway.

Straker clipped into the glider, sprinted the last ten meters, and leapt—as the drone tagged his back with a tracking pulse. The chute flared open with a whoosh, catching the fractured wind.

He spiraled, dipped, corrected — and vanished into the misty valley beyond.

Rick slammed his fist on the console. "Dammit—he's out."

Will stared at the screen. “No. He’s marked now. And we have his gear.”

Nusquam Ridge - The Cache

Later, while sweeping the ridge line, one of the agents called out.

“Something in the tree root!”

Rami Al-Sayid moved in, crouching. Hidden inside a hollow cedar root system was a signal cache — a hardened ceramic capsule with digital wiring soldered into a transmitter no larger than a thumb.

She opened it carefully — no active encryption now, just embedded code. Her brows lifted.

“Oh, this is good.”

Nusquam - Operations

Back at Nusquam, Rick projected the decrypted payload onto the wall.

“Meet your next breadcrumb,” he said. “This was a one-time code beacon, a frequency tuned to a very specific backscatter bounce. But inside? Coordinates. And a name.”

He clicked.

A location blinked onto the screen:

Cayuga County, NY.

Then a second name:

Chrysalis Node – Safehouse Σ-9.

Silence fell in the room.

Will looked at Sara. “We just cracked a door.”

Sara said, “Now we kick it in.”

CHAPTER TWENTY-FIVE

Breach Protocol

Nusquam Barn Ops Room 1800 Hours R

The corridor outside the operations room still smelled faintly of gun oil and rain-dried wool. The mood inside was worse.

Nemo was safe, but the fact he'd been targeted—at Nusquam—shattered the illusion of sanctuary.

Ed Perry had flown in by chopper the hour after the drone footage came back. He paced the length of Will's operations office now, voice cold.

"You told me Vermont was cold storage. That this place was off-grid. Unreachable."

Will stood motionless. "It was."

"Not anymore," Ed said. "You have thirty hours to clean this up. After that, DARPA and INSCOM are going to want their pound of flesh."

Genevieve sat at the table, Runa's head resting on her boots. "That shot came from one thousand yards. It was surgical. That's not a leak — it's a tracker with command access."

Perry's expression hardened. "Find whoever gave him the keys."

Nusquam Ops

Karen Bolanowski worked two laptops at once, flipping between satellite logs, FOB surveillance reports, and internal badge activity. "There's no breach in the Nusquam schedule. No visitor entry outside the cleared support teams."

Rick chimed in on the secure line, "Then it's signal-based. Someone outside is monitoring when we let Nemo walk."

She nodded grimly. "Then they have environmental markers. Probably scraping our greenhouse HVAC readings or kinetic telemetry from the lab doors."

Grace Roberts chimed in from a nearby terminal. "I'll pull the HVAC sensor logs. If they're spoofed or mirrored, we might find the matching pattern."

"Do it," Will said. "I want every electromagnetic signature from the last 48 hours run through SYBIL. If someone's fingerprinted our schedule, find the pattern."

——

Fort Meade - Watchtower Ops

Grace Roberts was nothing if not thorough.

If Lavi Alon and Viktor Ardelean were the only two known operatives physically in the area, one of them had to be carrying Chimera's schedule-intelligence source. Unless, of course, they weren't the only two. Unless there were more Cicadas already in place—quiet, patient, waiting for instructions.

She refused to believe this much movement had happened without leaving a trace.

Somewhere inside SYBIL's mountains of harvested noise—intercepts, anomaly flags, metadata bleed, infrastructure logs, ingestion artifacts—there had to be a clue. PEREGRINE-NULL was still embedded inside Chrysalis's evaluation pipeline, still feeding its stolen little trickle of insight back to Watchtower. If Chimera had used Chrysalis infrastructure to collect the targeting intelligence, SYBIL might already have seen part of the collection event without recognizing what it was.

Which meant the answer might already be in the building.

She needed the right mind to find it.

And she knew exactly where to go.

Derek usually preferred to work in dim light with his door closed, as if bright rooms made thinking too easy and therefore less precise. His office was washed in the cool glow of the large aquarium against the far wall, shifting blues and deep purples moving across the furniture like reflected thought. The low hum of the motor, the soft rush of circulated water, the gentle gurgle from the air stones gave the room a strange calm, almost submarine in its effect. Derek sat motionless in front of his six-monitor array, eyes fixed, fingers still, as though the real activity was happening somewhere behind his face.

Grace tapped lightly on the doorframe.

He looked up at once and smiled.

Derek had always liked her. Sara too. At LaserTech, they had been the first to treat him as more than the odd brilliant man down the hall. They had drawn him into the mole hunt before anyone else fully understood what he could do, and in ways neither of them had meant to, they had changed his life.

"Derek, I need your help."

That got his full attention.

She stepped inside, crossed to his desk, and handed him a page of notes already covered in her small, disciplined handwriting. He took it carefully, reading in silence while she explained.

"Chimera had schedule intelligence," she said. "Not just broad opportunity windows. Specific timing. Enough specificity to put the threat in motion. If that intelligence came through Chrysalis infrastructure, PEREGRINE-NULL may have brushed against it. SYBIL may have logged the shape of it without understanding what it was."

Derek's eyes moved back to the page.

"PRISM-THRESHOLD," he murmured. "Hmm."

He said it again, quieter.

"PRISM-THRESHOLD."

Grace watched him make the turn—the moment the phrase stopped being a label and became a possible structure in his mind.

"Could that be a location?" he asked.

She smiled faintly. "I've been wondering the same thing."

He nodded once.

"Okay. Leave it with me."

Then, a beat later, softer, almost to reassure himself as much as her he repeated. "Leave it with me."

The echolalia surfaced when he was locking onto something. Grace had learned that early. It wasn't uncertainty. It was alignment.

Derek hit the intercom button on his desk. Rick Huang's office was directly next door, close enough that Derek could have called out without raising his voice. But Derek liked the intercom. It allowed him to remain where he was, inside the architecture of the problem.

"Rick."

A crackle. "Yeah?"

"I need parser support. False Constellations plus PEREGRINE-NULL. Cross-domain correlation. Priority now."

There was no complaint in Rick's voice. "On it."

They really were a remarkable pair. Rick brought structure, speed, systems logic. Derek brought instinct for hidden pattern, the kind that could feel accidental until it solved something no normal analyst would have even seen.

Within minutes Rick was at his own terminal next door, building the query architecture Derek wanted. He fed the False Constellations data, PEREGRINE-NULL's returns, and relevant Chrysalis pipeline fragments into SYBIL's pattern parser, widening the tolerance bands, then narrowing them again, forcing the machine to compare both content and behavior—timing, reuse, signatures, semantic wrappers, reference fragments, routing echoes.

On Derek's center screen, SYBIL began to work.

"C'mon, girl," Rick said over the open intercom channel. "Find me some common data."

Grace stayed by the desk, arms folded, saying nothing. The aquarium light shifted across Derek's face. Onscreen, candidate matches populated in cascading columns—facility tags, shipping metadata, abbreviated routing lexicons, procurement stubs, local inventory notations, ghosted cross-references. SYBIL ranked them by confidence score and contextual relevance, throwing up a long, ugly list that only another machine could have loved.

Rick leaned into Derek's doorway just long enough to glance at the first wave of output.

"She gave us a lot," he said. "Too much, maybe. But there's signal in there." He tapped the doorframe once. "Let me know if you need anything else. I've got to get back to the fingerprinting algorithm."

Then he was gone again.

The office fell quiet except for the hum of the aquarium, the whisper of cooling fans, and Derek's occasional soft repetition of certain terms as he sorted.

"Threshold... threshold..."

"Null ingress..."

"Warehouse... no..."

"Supply node..."

Grace waited.

She knew better than to rush him. Derek did not move faster when pushed. He moved deeper.

Nearly an hour passed before he turned in his chair.

He was smiling openly now, with the unmistakable bright satisfaction of a man who had found the one clean thread in a tangled knot. Without a word, he held out a sheet of paper.

Grace took it.

Most of it was dense with what Rick jokingly called SYBIL-speak: parser trails, confidence bands, cluster references, inferred node relationships. But one line had been marked in thick yellow highlighter.

Cayuga County. vineyard supply warehouse

Grace looked up sharply.

Derek pointed to it. “That's your PRISM-THRESHOLD,” he said. “Or as close as SYBIL can prove.”

Her eyes dropped back to the page. The warehouse sat almost absurdly close to one of the False Constellation sites. Not inside it. Not directly attached to it. But near enough to exploit the deception, hide in the noise, and borrow legitimacy from the decoy footprint.

Which meant Chimera had not merely penetrated their environment.

She had understood it.

Grace felt the shape of the problem change in her hands.

Derek, still smiling, added, “Right next to one of your False Constellations.”

She said nothing, then she looked at him and smiled back, not because the answer was comforting, but because it was real. And real was something they could hunt.

The door closed and the aquarium hum filled the office again.

Derek did not go back to his monitors right away. He stood where he was, hands at his sides, watching the angelfish track a slow figure-eight past the driftwood. PRISM-THRESHOLD. Cayuga County. Vineyard supply warehouse.

It fit. That was the part he kept circling. It fit the way a piece of code fits when you've forced it. Clean on the surface, load-bearing only because nothing had tested it yet.

He sat down. Pulled the SYBIL trail back up. Started reading from the bottom this time, the lowest-confidence matches first, the noise the parser had discarded. If Chimera had wanted to hide something near a vineyard warehouse she would not have hidden it cleanly. She would have hidden it under something the system was trained to ignore.

The angelfish completed another figure-eight.

"Threshold," he said softly. "Threshold."

Fort Meade-Watchtower Ops

Grace did not linger.

The paper Derek had handed her remained folded once in her hand as she walked down the corridor toward the Will's officer. She could still hear the soft aquarium hum fading behind her as the door closed.

When she stepped into Ops, the lighting shifted from Derek's cool underwater blues to Watchtower's familiar dim amber glow. Screens cast quiet reflections across the glass office walls. Analysts spoke in low voices over headsets. Data moved silently across the wall displays.

Cathy looked up first.

She had the particular instinct of someone who noticed when a room changed temperature.

"Gracie?"

Grace held up the paper. "Derek found something."

Cathy's chair rolled back before Grace had finished the sentence.

Will Morgan stood at the long operations table in the conference room reviewing a cluster of satellite images when the two women approached. He didn't look up immediately. He finished marking something on the tablet in front of him first—his usual discipline about not abandoning one thought mid-stream.

He glanced up. Grace handed him the sheet.

"PRISM-THRESHOLD," she said. "It's a location."

Will read the highlighted line without expression.

Cayuga County — vineyard supply warehouse

His eyes moved once across the rest of the SYBIL annotations. Then he looked up at Grace.

"How certain?"

"High confidence correlation between PEREGRINE-NULL telemetry and the False Constellations dataset. Rick built the parser. Derek confirmed the pattern."

Sara leaned in closer to read the sheet over Will's shoulder.

"A vineyard supply warehouse?" she said.

Grace nodded. "Farm equipment. Fertilizer shipments. irrigation hardware. Bulk deliveries. Seasonal labor traffic. Trucks moving at all hours."

Sara exhaled slowly. "Perfect camouflage."

Will said nothing.

His gaze had shifted to the wall display showing the regional map of the False Constellations decoy sites.

He tapped the screen once. The Cayuga County point appeared. Another tap brought up the nearest False Constellation node.

The two markers glowed on the map.

They were close. Very close.

Cathy saw it at the same moment.

"Right next to one of the decoys," she said.

Grace nodded. "Yes."

Will studied the display for several seconds longer. Then he said, "Not next to it."

The two women looked at him. He tapped the screen again, expanding the logistics overlay.

"Inside its shadow."

Sara tilted her head slightly. "Meaning?"

Will rested his hand lightly on the table.

"Meaning Chimera didn't stumble across our deception architecture."

He looked at the warehouse marker again.

"She studied it."

Grace felt a small chill at the back of her neck.

Will continued, calm as ever.

"A vineyard supply warehouse would generate a predictable logistics signature—agricultural freight, seasonal equipment shipments, high truck traffic during harvest months. That noise blends perfectly with the supply footprint of a research site."

Cathy finished the thought. "She's hiding in the logistical background radiation."

Will nodded once.

Grace crossed her arms.

"So either Viktor Ardelean or someone else is operating out of that warehouse."

Will shook his head. "Possibly."

The word hung there. Gracie knew that tone.

"What are we missing?" she asked.

Will looked at the map again.

"Two things."

Grace waited.

"First," he said, "Chimera obtained schedule intelligence precise enough to trigger an operational deployment."

He tapped the warehouse marker again.

"If that intelligence was collected from Chrysalis infrastructure, whoever is operating from that location isn't just staging there."

"They're collecting there," Grace said.

"Yes."

Sara's eyes narrowed. "And the second thing?"

Will turned the tablet around so both of them could see the overlay Derek had printed.

The yellow highlight. PRISM-THRESHOLD.

"Chimera didn't name that location randomly."

Grace felt the realization forming even before he said it.

Will spoke. "Threshold means a transition point."

Gracie looked back at the map. "Collection to action."

Will nodded. "Exactly."

Grace's mind moved through the implications rapidly. "That means there could be more Cicadas nearby."

"Yes," Will said.

"Waiting for instructions," Gracie added.

Will leaned back from the table. His voice remained calm, but there was a sharpened edge beneath it now.

"If Chimera built a threshold node there, the warehouse isn't just a hiding place."

He looked from Grace to Sara.

"It's a trigger."

A moment of silence passed. Then Sara asked the question all three of them were already thinking.

"How fast can Cecil get eyes on it?"

Will reached for the secure line.

"Let's find out."

——

Granville - Marlene Dufresne Safehouse

Cecil Brandon answered on the second ring.

"Brandon."

"Ops," Will said.

Cecil heard the tone immediately. Not urgency. Something worse, precision.

"What do you need?"

Will brought the Cayuga County map up on the secure display and pushed the data packet to Cecil's tablet.

"Location just came out of SYBIL pattern correlation. Vineyard supply warehouse outside Aurora. We believe it may be connected to Chimera's schedule intelligence source."

A pause.

"Confidence?"

"High."

Cecil didn't waste time with speculation.

"Understood."

Will continued.

"We need eyes on it without lighting the place up. No overt presence. If there are Cicadas in the area, I don't want them spooked."

"Already thinking the same thing."

Cecil was standing now, headset sliding on as he walked toward the small tactical planning station in the surveillance wing.

"Let me look."

The file finished loading.

Satellite overlay. Logistics signature. Rural road grid.

Cecil zoomed in.

"Farm belt," he muttered. "Low-density traffic. Good concealment. Lots of legitimate freight movement."

He switched to thermal satellite archives.

Night traffic patterns. Trucks. Pickup trucks. Agricultural equipment.

But something else caught his eye.

"Interesting."

Back in Watchtower Ops, Gracie leaned closer to the speaker. "What is it?"

"Warehouse footprint matches commercial storage, but truck arrivals are wrong."

"How wrong?" Gracie asked.

"Too regular."

He highlighted a series of timestamps.

"Three arrivals last night. Exactly forty minutes apart."

Will didn't move.

"Delivery schedules don't behave like that," Cecil continued. "Farm supply runs stack. You get clusters, not metronomes."

Gracie said. "Staging."

"Maybe," Cecil said. He zoomed further. "Give me ten minutes."

The channel clicked silent.

Eight minutes later the line clicked open again.

Cecil's voice had sharpened. "Will."

"Go."

"I've got traffic camera coverage on Route 90 about two miles south of the warehouse."

Gracie straightened slightly. "License plate hits?"

"Yes."

"Good?"

"Interesting."

He pushed the data. The Watchtower screen updated. A pickup truck appeared. Followed by its travel path.

"Vehicle arrives at warehouse at 01:12," Cecil said.

"Departs?"

"01:47."

Will watched silently.

"Then it heads north," Cecil continued. "Toward the False Constellation site," Gracie said.

"Yes."

Gracie leaned closer. "But it never reaches it."

"No."

The map zoomed out. Rural roads spidered across the screen.

Cecil marked three points. Three barns. Three farm outbuildings. All within a five-mile radius.

The path line fractured between them.

Gracie understood first. "It didn't miss the destination."

"No," Cecil said. "It divided the route."

Gracie exhaled. "Dead drops."

"Or staging nodes," Cecil said.

Gracie felt the shift in the room.

"How many vehicles?"

"Three last night."

The silence that followed was heavier now.

Will studied the map. Three red markers glowed across the farmland.

He spoke calmly. "Cecil."

"Yes."

"Put eyes on the warehouse."

"Already working on it."

"How?"

"Passive."

Cecil zoomed the satellite image again.

"There's a wooded ridge six hundred meters west of the building."

He marked the position. "Perfect overwatch."

Will nodded. "Line of sight?"

"Partial during daylight. Clear thermal at night."

Will asked, "Team?"

"Two-man surveillance element. Long lens. Passive thermal. No RF transmissions."

Will approved immediately. "Good."

Cecil continued. "I'll also launch a microdrone once the team confirms the pattern."

"Altitude?"

"Below treeline."

Gracie folded her arms. "And if we're right?"

Cecil answered without hesitation. "We'll know how many Cicadas are actually operating in Cayuga County."

Will looked again at the three red markers. Then he said, "Because I don't think it's two."

Cecil's voice came back. "Neither do I."

A beat passed.

Cecil added: "Will..."

"Yes?"

"If that warehouse is the collection node..." He zoomed the map once more. "And those barns are distribution points..."

Gracie finished the thought. "We're not looking at two operatives."

Gracie looked at the glowing map. Three barns. One warehouse.

A small rural grid that suddenly looked like infrastructure.

Will spoke the conclusion. "We're looking at a nest."

——

Fort Meade - Watchtower Ops

Later that night, the operation board lit up with a full readout on Safehouse Σ-9.

"Cayuga County," Cecil said, "rural, sparsely patrolled. The target structure is an old apple distribution center re-permitted as a vineyard supply warehouse."

He tapped the screen, showing satellite renders. "No obvious guards, but the thermal's suspicious. Heat bloom's too high for the generator size. Basement activity. Air turnover in the attic. We're looking at minimum three, maximum seven occupants. Possibly reinforced substructure."

Rick pointed to the southern wall. "That antenna? It's spoofing a feed to a nearby Verizon tower. It's pushing intermittent pulses. I think it's phoning home to Chrysalis. Low-band signaling. Maybe even dead-man."

Will glanced at the clock. "ETA for Quick Reaction Force units?"

Cecil replied, "DHS Special Response is an hour out staging from Albany. FBI SWAT already embedded with locals. We're running point."

"NSA TAO?" Will asked.

Cecil nodded. "They're on passive intercept. No direct action."

Fort Meade - ACIC Legal Office

ACIC legal counsel Marisol Vega was already on the encrypted line with the Eastern District of New York's U.S. Attorney.

"You will have an affidavit-ready intel packet listing probable cause within the hour," she said crisply. "You are not authorizing action under FISA-702 Tier One provisions. This is a domestic law enforcement. This is a foreign threat embedded on U.S. soil. We move, or they disappear."

She glanced at Will as she ended the call.

"You're covered," she said. "But you better find something we can hold them with."

Fort Meade-Watchtower Ops Morgan's Office

Will walked the team through the layout.

Cecil would lead exterior breach coordination and drone overwatch. Rick would handle comms jamming, local signal masking, and real-time decrypts of any uplink attempts. Talia Moreno would roll with the entry team to perform on-site intelligence triage; flash drives, maps, codebooks, laptops. Runa would be leashed but in the van, ready for scent work or trail pickup on escapees. Genevieve and SYBIL would manage the server sync from Nusquam.

Cayuga County, NY-Chrysalis Node – Safehouse 0314 Hours R

The old apple distribution warehouse sat hollow under a gray sky, its corrugated metal panels rust-stained and weeping brown streaks down crumbling concrete block. The eastern wall hadn't seen a coat of paint since 1987. Along the loading ramp, fragments of weathered wood pallets lay scattered, split and warped, their surfaces slick with the residue of decades-old fruit. The only sign of current occupation was a dented pickup beside the dock and a thin heat shimmer rising from the roof vent—a telltale sign that something was running inside.

The orchard beyond the warehouse loomed dark, rows of dormant trees casting long shadows across rotting mulch and fermented soil. The smell hit first: decay, feculent and sweet, the ghost of apples that had gone to brown sugar and vinegar in the darkness. It clawed at the back of the throat.

But the thermal bloom didn't lie. There were people inside.

"Final check," Will said, donning his vest. "We move at 0325 Hours local. Any last feeds?"

Rick raised a hand. "SYBIL just flagged an outbound bounce. 12.1 milliseconds ago. It left Σ-9 and pinged a relay outside Warsaw. Coded burst."

Will nodded once. "We don't have time to wait."

The ACIC convoy cut its lights a half-mile out. The engines idled down. Every movement from then on was muscle memory.

Will stepped out first, dressed in matte-black field gear, his vest rigged for command, sidearm holstered high, his voice calm through comms.

"Watchtower actual. We go in silent. First contact team takes the south wall. Cecil—confirm drone visual on the attic vent."

"Confirmed," Cecil's voice came through. "Minimal movement up top. Subsurface motion still strong. Generator room's live."

Rick's voice overlaid. "Comms sweep clean. No outbound pings in the last 40 seconds. TAO's got the backscatter link on a hair trigger. SYBIL's synced."

Cecil nodded to Leandro Cruz beside him. He adjusted his rifle sling and gave a silent signal to the second team.

The orchard beyond the warehouse loomed dark, rows of dormant trees casting long shadows. Wet soil clung to boots. It smelled like cold iron and fermented mulch.

Cecil's team reached the south side in formation, moving through the overgrown property where apple storage crates lay scattered and decomposing. They moved like liquid—quiet, precise. The tech on point dropped to one knee, placed the cutting charge against the corroded metal wall, and stepped back.

A dull pfft—no flame, no light. Just the hiss of fast vaporized steel.

The side door fell inward.

A dull pfft — no flame, no light. Just the hiss of fast vaporized steel.

The side door fell inward.

Will's team flowed in, muzzles sweeping arcs. The outer warehouse space was what the cover suggested: dust-thick, damp, reeking of spoiled fruit and mold. Racks of old palletized crates lined the walls—rotting wood, burlap, the sickly-sweet stench of fermentation. Just for show. Just for cover.

They passed through the back office.

And the environment transformed.

The moment they stepped into the interior passageway, the smell shifted from agricultural decay to the sharp, metallic bite of ozone. The temperature dropped fifteen degrees. The air changed texture—crisp, cooled by industrial HVAC.

Ahead, a reinforced concrete stairwell descended into the sub-basement. And below, visible from the landing, came the glow: soft blue-white light reflecting off stainless steel cooling racks and the LED indicators of server cabinets. The hum—a low, steady thrumming that made the air vibrate.

Chrysalis's nerve center, hidden beneath layers of rot and agricultural camouflage.

"Vault entrance," Karen called, pointing to a false wall behind what looked like an old control office. Her voice seemed to cut through the ozone-tinged air.

Leandro was already on it, gloved fingers sliding over the sealed floor. "Pressure plate. Fiber optic tripwire. Layered failsafe."

Rick's voice cracked through comms. "Hold breach. SYBIL's analyzing lock logic now."

SYBIL's tone was clinical. "Tripwire bypass in three... two... one. Safe to proceed."

Leandro stepped through, rifle raised.

The stairs into the sub-basement weren't built for apples. They were purpose-built, reinforced. Cold concrete descended twenty feet into a hardened, climate-controlled chamber. The descent felt like entering a vault—each step downward took Will further from the decaying agricultural world above and deeper into the precision architecture of modern espionage.

At the bottom: server racks lining both walls, their cooling systems working overtime, exhaust fans screaming. The LED displays cast stuttering blue and red light across the concrete floor. The ozone smell grew sharper—the bite of electricity in air, the smell of solder and high-temperature component failure just barely averted by constant refrigeration. Humidity gages. Temperature monitors. Everything tracked, everything controlled.

Inside this hardened subterranean space: six people, two of whom bolted immediately toward a secondary exit.

The stairs into the sub-basement weren't built for apples.

Cold concrete descended twenty feet into a reinforced level lined with military-grade server racks and insulated compartments.

Inside: six people.

Two bolted.

The first didn't get far—tackled hard by Cecil's point man. The second made it five steps before Runa, unleashed and descending fast, took him down by the thigh, fangs sunk deep. He screamed—but never reached his pistol.

Will swept in behind. "Hands where I can see them!"

Three men and one woman raised their arms. One of them was already trying to swallow a pill — Karen punched his jaw sideways, dislodging it onto the floor.

Genevieve moved straight to the desk—laptop open, but not yet wiped. Her fingers flew. "Local server's hot. They didn't have time to trigger the burn."

Rick patched into her feed from the van. "Copy that. Send me directory structure."

A moment later: "Holy hell—this is a Chrysalis drop point. Comm logs, payment ledgers, alias registries."

Karen was scanning papers taped to the wall. "Shipping manifests. Data storage units labeled as glassware packing, eleven shipments through Michigan, four through Nevada."

Will holstered his weapon and took a breath.

"This wasn't just a safehouse," he said. "This was a syndicate relay."

——

FBI Transport Van 0425 Hours R

The detainees were in transport vans under FBI custody.

Rick secured a sealed box from under the floor, inside was a Lithuanian-made suppressor baffle, identical alloy composition to the shard recovered from Nemo's attempted hit. That was the link they needed.

One of the agents tapped Will on the shoulder. "We found something else."

He pointed to a walk-in cold room.

Inside, packed in crates lined with dry ice, were drives. Dozens of them. Each labeled with just a single character and number.

B-9, D-12, E-7, S-3

Will stared at them, then at Cecil.

"Sigma-series routing nodes," he said. "Each of these drives probably links to a different Chrysalis sub-network."

Will exhaled once.

"This wasn't the end," he said. "It's the beginning."

CHAPTER TWENTY-SIX

The Quiet Request

Arlington, VA-DARPA Director-Secure Line 0742 Hours R

Helena Quinn sat alone, her screen locked in direct-to-NSC encryption. No staffers. No record. Just a whisper request passed through ACIC channels at Will Morgan's insistence—one she hadn't expected to grant, but now couldn't ignore.

The screen flickered, then steadied.

President Jonathan Stratton appeared, tie off, sleeves rolled. It was early, but he looked like he'd been at his desk since dawn.

"Helena. What's the nature of the call?"

"A non-operational matter, sir. But one I think you'll want to hear."

She paused. Chose her words precisely.

"Two months ago, a retired Army service dog—Belgian Malinois, name is Runa—intercepted and alerted on an inbound assassin at a DARPA-aligned research site. That warning gave the on-site physicist and his security team enough time to avoid what would have been a confirmed kill shot. The target was Shen Ke."

Stratton's eyes sharpened. He knew the name, even if the cover story had erased it.

"The Chinese defector. Thought dead."

"Exactly. Runa didn't just detect. She pursued. Engaged. Forced the asset to break cover and flee. She likely saved the only man on Earth capable of advancing what we've buried under ECHO REEF."

A beat of silence.

"She's not on active duty. Her record is sealed. She's not eligible for public commendation. But Will Morgan believes she deserves something... enduring. Quiet. Presidential."

Stratton's jaw set. Then softened.

"You're asking me to authorize a confidential Presidential Medal for an animal."

Quinn, with a ghost of a smile. "No, Mr. President. I'm asking you to acknowledge a sentient act of defense by a soldier who doesn't know she's not in the fight anymore."

Stratton looked off-screen. Then back.

"Approved. I'll have the mint strike a custom medallion. Full seal. No ceremony."

"She wouldn't like one anyway."

Nusquam, Vermont – Barn Lab Compound 20 Days Later

The black case was delivered via non-military courier under a flat cover manifest: Scientific Recognition Plaque – USDA Division 12. It bypassed every logging system, flagged only by SYBIL and handled directly by Watchtower personnel.

Sara Brandt carried it into the barn. Nemo was at his desk, calibrating cryogenic controls on a side monitor. Runa, as always, lay curled beneath his feet.

Sara set the box down without a word.

Nemo asked, "What's this?"

Sara: "Open it."

He did.

Inside: a navy velvet-lined case containing a circular medallion. Presidential seal, engraved in silence.

On the reverse:

For Loyalty Beyond Command

Runa – Defender, Watcher, Ghost-Saver

Nemo stared. His fingers moved gently over the inscription.

"She didn't even bark."

"She didn't have to."

Barn Lab – Nemo's Office Wall -Time: That Evening

It now hung beside a dusty schematic of a superconducting qubit array and a framed still of the Apollo 8 Earthrise photo.

The medal was modest. No lighting. No plaque.

But everyone who passed it—Sara, Genevieve, Rick, even Will—stopped, just briefly.

Runa, of course, never looked up.

But every time Nemo sat down, he'd glance once toward the wall.

And remembered.

Nusquam–Back Field Behind the Barn Lab 0612 Hours R

The grass was still wet with dew. The early fog clung low over the treetops, softening the Vermont hillside into blurred shapes of green and gray. Will Morgan stood with his hands in his jacket pockets, facing east toward the rising sun. Genevieve Larsson approached slowly, coffee in one hand, scarf loose around her neck.

She stopped beside him and handed him the second mug without speaking.

They stood in silence for a while.

Genevieve said, "She doesn't know what it means, you know. The medal."

Will, said, "She doesn't have to."

"Then why push for it? Presidential recognition? That's not your style."

Will sipped the coffee. It was hot and bitter—just how he liked it. He let the words settle before answering.

"Because she wasn't deployed. Wasn't trained for this environment. No orders. No handler. No fallback. But when it counted... she moved. She acted without hesitation. Without doubt."

"And saved him."

Will nodded once.

"Saved him clean. No muzzle flash. No alarm. Just instinct and timing and complete selflessness."

Genevieve looked off toward the barn.

"She's bonded to him, you know. She watches him like he's something breakable."

"He is."

Another pause. The birds were just starting to wake in the trees. A breeze stirred the edges of Genevieve's scarf.

"I've given out ribbons. Pinned medals on soldiers who did half as much, under full command, with a squad behind them and a medevac inbound. Runa had none of that. Just training, loyalty, and choice."

"You're not wrong. But it's unusual—for you to ask for something symbolic."

Will turned to look at her fully now. His voice dropped to something more raw, more human.

"Because we keep asking people to do impossible things. In secret. With no promise of thanks. And sometimes... someone does the right thing without being asked."

He looked toward the barn now.

"She deserves to be remembered. Not in a file. Not in a classified report. But in a way that says—we saw what you did."

Genevieve was quiet for a long time.

Then she smiled, barely.

"She'll never know it's for her."

"No. But he will."

CHAPTER TWENTY-SEVEN

Pattern Drift

Unknown (Node: COTERIE-9 / Chrysalis Signal Fork)

The interface was minimalist. No operating system, no keyboard, just a black field and a spectral editor that manipulated data like music.

Yasha Moravec—Chimera—began to compose.

"No vectors. Only listeners.

No orders. Only pattern."

She selected a base waveform: random fluctuations modeled on solar flare entropy. To the untrained eye, it was cosmic noise. To those attuned to the Layer 3 lattice encryption, it was invitation.

She encoded the phase-shift headers with recursion keys, buried below steganographic camouflage:

A medieval poem in Breton

A fake bug tracker on a defunct GitHub repo

A digital restoration of a broken weather satellite file

Each fragment on its own meant nothing.

But when aligned... it sang.

She added activation metadata:

Phase Window: 13 days

Target Coordinates: Schroon Lake, Carthage, and Sunapee

Priority Threads: Thermal inconsistency, anomalous signal decay, sensor spoofing attempts

Buried Test Thread: Echo Reef perimeter breach

Her voice, modulated and fragmented, recorded the final line into the encoded payload: "Let the signal wake the quiet minds."

She deployed it to the zero-trust propagation net—a swarm of nodes that would deliver fragments globally, recombining only inside the minds of those conditioned to see.

Chrysalis was now listening.

——

Fort Meade - Watchtower Ops 0820 Hours R

Dr. Adrian Keller—code-named Pythagoras—was not a run-of-the-mill genius.

He had been born in Basel, Switzerland, to a mathematician father and a concert violinist mother, and from the beginning his education had followed no straight line. Chess clubs gave way to physics Olympiads; philosophy debates bled into probability theory. He resisted academic lanes with quiet stubbornness, drifting between disciplines until MIT noticed him during a visiting lecture he was never formally scheduled to give.

By twenty-four, Keller had authored a landmark paper on decision theory in adversarial systems—work that DARPA would later classify, with some understatement, as dual-use intelligence methodology.

After that, he lived everywhere and nowhere. Short fellowships in Oxford. A research stint in Tel Aviv. A consultancy role with Singapore's Future Systems Initiative that ended without explanation. He maintained no permanent address, no institutional loyalty, and no interest in tenure. His name surfaced only in footnotes and classified annexes, spoken across multiple agencies by people who knew better than to put it in writing.

At Watchtower, he appeared the same way he lived—intermittently and without warning.

Some days he simply showed up, coat over one arm, already mid-sentence, as if he'd only stepped out for coffee and wandered into a classified facility by accident.

Officially, Keller followed interesting problems.

Unofficially, interesting problems followed him.

The conference room lights softened. A schematic of Chrysalis-7 glowed on the screen, ten labeled boxes connected by arrows: Bait, Path, Mirror, Breadcrumb, Telemetry, Fork, Façade, Snapshot, Isolate, Reveal.

Adrian tapped the first box with a stylus. Nothing happened. Sara handed him the working one without comment, and he laughed at himself.

"Think of it like poker with invisible cards."

Rick was already at the side console, three monitors up, fingers moving. He hadn't been told to start. He'd read the schematic on the way in.

"Seed the bait," Adrian said. "Something credible. A plausible dataset, a half-finished notebook. Curiosity, not suspicion."

"Pushing now," Rick said. On his middle screen, a folder structure assembled itself: quarterly margin projections, a draft NDA, an internal memo flagged DRAFT—DO NOT CIRCULATE. The timestamps staggered themselves across six weeks. "Aging it backward. SYBIL's writing the edit history."

"Author metadata?" Sara asked.

"Three contributors. Two real names from public LinkedIn scrapes, one composite. The composite has a Slack history we built last quarter for a different op. Recycling."

Adrian moved to the next box. "Step two. A visible path in. An exposed dev node, an old account that looks like an honest mistake."

SYBIL's voice came through the room speakers, level and unhurried. "Provisioning subdomain. TLS certificate aged to fourteen months. Last login backdated to a Tuesday evening, consistent with the cover identity's calendar."

Will watched the screen. "Who finds it first?"

"Anyone running standard recon," Rick said. "Shodan scrape would catch it inside forty-eight hours."

"Good." Will's jaw set. "Keep going."

"Mirror the environment," Adrian said. "Once they're in, it has to feel like they're somewhere real. Ticketing, share drives, colleague names. Comfort makes them dig."

Sara leaned against the table. "So you calm them down."

"Pride does the rest."

Rick's left monitor populated with a Jira clone, real-looking tickets, half of them resolved, two flagged as bugs that any decent engineer would want to read. "Pulling the colleague directory from the composite Slack now. SYBIL's giving everyone a birthday and a coffee order."

"Step four," Adrian said. "Breadcrumb recursion. Each artifact points to another. Not a line out. A spiral in."

"Logged," SYBIL said. "First breadcrumb live. Depth metric initialized at zero."

"Telemetry next." Adrian tapped the box. "Invisible observers. Timing, mouse patterns, what they ignore. The behavioral picture builds itself."

Will leaned forward, eyes on Rick's right screen. "You want mistakes, not destruction."

"Right." Adrian moved to the next box. "Behavioral forks. Give them choices that tell you who they are. Brute force or quiet lateral move. Their choice is a fingerprint."

"Fork logic is running off the same engine we used for the Carthage profile," Rick said. "If they hit the export script, we log it as opportunist. If they map the network first, we log it as state-trained. SYBIL's got a confidence threshold at sixty-eight percent."

Sara cut in. "What if they're patient enough to do both?"

Adrian looked at her, then at Rick.

"Then we learn something new," Rick said. "SYBIL flags the deviation and we update the model in the next pass."

Will nodded once. Move on.

"Seven," Adrian said. "Recursion pain. At some point the breadcrumbs circle back. They see their own footprints. Confusion slows them. Stress makes them improvise. Improvised moves expose tools and habits."

Sara's eyes didn't leave the screen. "You're making them dig their own grave."

"Step eight." Adrian's tone shifted, more careful now. "Synthetic exfil façade. Something that looks like success. An outbound queue, a ghost repository. They think they pulled the data. We get the transfer trail."

"Façade's already spun up," Rick said. "Pointed at a dead drop in our sandbox. Anything that touches it gets stripped, hashed, and routed to attribution."

"Outbound attempt would register as—" Adrian began.

"Outbound attempt registered," SYBIL said.

The room went still.

Rick blinked at his screen. "That's a test packet. I queued it ninety seconds ago to confirm the trap was live."

Will exhaled, slow. "Good."

"Step nine," Adrian said. "Escalate and contain. When triggers fire, sever paths to real assets. Snapshot the session. Keep feeding illusions so they keep working for you instead of burning cover."

"Snapshots, recordings, attribution," Will said. "Everything for the file."

"Step ten is the reveal." Adrian set the stylus down. "You take the session, the transfer headers, the behavioral profile. You package it. Then you decide. Hand it to partners. Bait the handler. Build the indictment. Chrysalis turns curiosity into confession without breaking anything you actually care about."

A long silence. SYBIL printed a small line at the bottom of the screen: Trap stack initialized. Awaiting first contact.

Sara spoke first. "You let them win, and they bring you the rope."

"You let them feel clever," Adrian said. "You let them take the trophy. Pride makes them predictable."

Will studied the schematic, then Rick's monitors, where the whole architecture sat live and breathing.

"Run it on Chrysalis-7."

Adrian's expression didn't change. "We've been running it. The bait went live during step three. The path opened during step five. The first reconnaissance ping came in while you were watching the fork logic."

Will looked at him.

"Now we decide," Adrian said, "whether to bait the handler or hand the file to the courts."

"Telemetry complete," SYBIL said. "Session archived."

Will nodded once. "Then we play their applause and follow the hands that clap."

——

SYBIL Detects Anomaly Spikes

Nusquam – Sublevel Ops Room - 2244 Hours R

Operator: Genevieve Larsson

Codename: ECHORITHM WATCHPOINT

SYBIL's voice was almost too calm for the magnitude of the alert.

> *"Environmental anomaly detected. Sites: Carthage, ME and Sunapee, NH.*
>
> *Signal Type: Probabilistic EM Pulse*
>
> *Entropic Signature: Non-natural*
>
> *Pattern deviation: +5.3σ baseline————"*

Genevieve stared at the console. The monitor pulsed with twin overlays—heat shift anomalies on passive IR arrays paired with minor fluctuations in electromagnetic noise that mimicked powerline hum. At first glance: trivial.

But they weren't.

SYBIL flagged a match with a long-dormant dataset:

> *"Chrysalis Phase Signal – Lattice 3B: Fragmentally Aligned. Confidence: 82.4%"*

He tapped the secure channel.

"Will—it's Gene. You need to see this. Carthage and Sunapee both pinged within five minutes of each other. SYBIL says it's Chrysalis."

"Live?" Will asked.

"Not vector contact. Signal prep. The lattice is waking."

There was a pause.

Will's voice hardened. "Assume we've been found."

Fort Meade=Watchtower Conference Room 0814 Hours R

The whiteboard was covered in cross-linked diagrams—vector threads, anomaly maps, signal spikes. Genevieve sat near the console, eyes bloodshot. Cathy scrolled through packet captures from the Carthage breach.

Adrian Keller paced. He stopped mid-step, coffee forgotten in his hand.

"I've been thinking about it all wrong."

Will looked up from the secure laptop. "Go on."

"Chrysalis doesn't recruit," Adrian said, gesturing to the board. "They signal. Their people self-select. Anyone who gets inside proves they can see what others miss."

Will nodded slowly. "Initiation by perception."

"Exactly. Cicada 3301. Layered steganography. Public artifacts with private meaning." He exhaled once. "But here's the part I was missing."

He turned toward the console.

"We don't need a human."

The room went quiet.

Genevieve looked up first. "You're saying—"

"SYBIL creates the candidate," Adrian said. "A full-spectrum digital persona. Academic footprint. Open-source publications. Years of forum arguments, half-finished theories, correct insights buried under noise. Someone who looks brilliant but unfinished."

Cathy frowned. "A sock puppet?"

"No," Adrian said. "A person."

He typed, and the screen filled with a dossier header:

SUBJECT: PEREGRINE-NULL

STATUS: SYNTHETIC / UNATTRIBUTABLE

ORIGIN: SYBIL-GENERATED

Will stood.

"You're proposing we let an adversarial intelligence syndicate recruit an AI."

Adrian nodded once. "They'll never know. Chrysalis doesn't run background checks the way we do. They look for pattern recognition, curiosity thresholds, tolerance for ambiguity. SYBIL can model all of that—better than any human."

Genevieve leaned back slowly. "And if they test her?"

"They already do," Adrian replied. "Every puzzle they release is a behavioral probe. SYBIL solves some. Misses others. Argues publicly with herself under different aliases. Leaves fingerprints that feel human."

Cathy's voice was quiet. "What about the breadcrumb?"

"We seed it," Adrian said. "An academic preprint. Open access. Hosted overseas. Inside it—an incomplete Chrysalis fragment. Real enough to be recognized. Broken enough to require intuition."

"No metadata," Will said automatically.

"None," Adrian agreed. "SYBIL handles distribution entropy. She finds it the way Chrysalis expects someone like her to find it."

"And once they notice?" Genevieve asked.

Adrian met Will's eyes. "We do nothing. Chrysalis watches. Evaluates. And if they like what they see..."

"They activate her," Will finished.

A long silence.

Will walked to the window, mist rolling off the fields near Nusquam. When he spoke, his voice was steady.

"This keeps civilians out of the blast radius. No coercion. No bodies."

He turned back.

"And if Chrysalis feeds her poisoned insight?"

"SYBIL sandboxes everything," Adrian said. "Nothing reaches us without being stripped, modeled, and cross-validated."

"Attributes?" Will asked.

"Elior Navarro," Adrian said. "Nomadic — Valencia, Montréal, Reykjavík. High-signal intellect, unfinished profile, ideologically aligned."

Will looked at the dossier again.

PEREGRINE-NULL.

SYBIL had created a complete Legend.

"They won't be recruiting an asset," he said. "They'll be interrogating a mirror."

A cunning grin crossed his face.

"It's a brilliant idea."

He nodded once.

"Let's give Chrysalis what they want. Someone who sees the pattern."

——

Fort Meade - Secure Server Room

SYBIL generated a simulated laptop, indistinguishable from a real one. To the outside world, it behaved like any commercial machine with a camera and microphone present, switchable by an external intruder if they tried. Elior Navarro (PEREGRINE NULL) spoke with a synthetic voice, tuned to an Icelandic English accent. SYBIL made his gender male.

A PDF appeared on the screen:

Emergent Behavior in Lattice Dynamics of Photonic Crystals – Vol. 8, Issue 1 (Open Access Translation, Qingdao Archive, 2021).

SYBIL hadn't searched for it. The file had surfaced on its own, buried in an abandoned Git repository mirrored at a Finnish university. The account hadn't been touched since 2019. The commit date, however, was two weeks old.

Odd.

A string flashed briefly in the metadata:

01100011 01100001 01111001.

"Decay"

Fourteen pages in, the word appeared again—hidden inside the pixel noise of a Bragg mirror diagram. Not text. Not an image. Phase distortion.

SYBIL ran a spectral reassembly tool he'd written years ago to hunt steganographic artifacts. The signal resolved—chaotic, uneven—but with a harmonic that didn't belong. He inverted the slope and ran an FFT pass.

A phrase emerged:

COALESCE://INITIATE::RECURSION SEED::HEAR_US

No matches anywhere. Not even the dark web.

This wasn't a file. It was an invitation.

No ads. No traps. A pattern—elegant, recursive.

In the synthetic voice Navarro said, "I see you."

SCOTERIE-7 / Chrysalis Signal Observation Node 1117 Hours R Unknown (spoofed to Rostov, relayed via Lagos and Reykjavík)

The room was not a room. It was an enclave of silence, black glass walls, no visible doors, and only a single circular machine, upright, and glowing faintly with pulse rhythms that matched no known server OS.

Chimera stood behind the terminal, eyes hidden beneath an augmented diffusion visor. Her face was calm, her breath slow, and her body completely still. Her only movement was the soft flex of her fingers across the air-projected interface.

The signal tree was live.

Dozens of shards pulsed across the global map—fragments of encoded phase logic sent out like pollen. Most had gone untouched. Others had been scraped by automated crawlers and dismissed.

But one had been read. Interacted with. Altered.

NODE ACTIVATION: FLAGGED VECTOR (UNREGISTERED)
DEVICE SIGNATURE: UNENROLLED
IP ORIGIN: Maine, USA
RESPONSE TIME: 63.2 seconds
BEHAVIORAL DEVIATION: +2.1σ above mean
ENTROPIC COLLISION AVOIDANCE: MANUAL

The Maine origin didn't match Navarro's nomadic cover—Valencia, Montréal, Reykjavík—but Chimera had seen this before. Operators rerouted. The question was whether his response patterns held to the legend even when his geography didn't.

Chimera tilted her head. "Manual avoidance," she whispered.

A signal reassembly animation appeared on-screen a blurred outline of Navarro's process: the waveform filter, the flipped FFT, the brute-force spectral match.

VECTOR CANDIDATE: TAG AS OBSERVER-7B
ESCALATE FOR CONTINGENT CONTACT?

Chimera said nothing at first.

Then said, "Initiate passive evaluation. Route challenge fragment through mirror mesh 6A. Embed further recursion layer into next push."

The system replied with a soft chime. Confirmation.

SEED DEPLOYED: OBSERVER-7B
EXPECTED WINDOW: 96 hours
RESPONSE TYPE: SELF-VALIDATING

Chimera removed the visor. Behind her, audio whispered from a hidden speaker. It was Navarro's synthetic voice captured through ambient spill from the simulated laptop mic. Sybil knew it had been activated.

"I see you."

She smiled faintly. "Do you?"

She turned off the screen.

CHAPTER TWENTY-EIGHT

Inside the Wire

Leadership is the capacity to translate vision into reality.

DARPA Headquarters – Helena Quinn's Office, Morning

Helena Quinn had never thought of DARPA's budget as spending.

Portfolio, she corrected herself silently as she scanned the columns on the screen. National investment portfolio.

Returns just happened to arrive in strange forms—algorithms, materials science, physics experiments that looked pointless until they didn't.

She leaned back in her chair.

Every now and then someone on the Hill would ask the same question: What are we getting for all this money?

Helena usually resisted the urge to laugh.

Take ARPANET.

The story still amused her because the seed of it had been so... small. Not a grand strategic doctrine. Not a white paper. Just an observation.

A spider web.

Someone had noticed that when a stone hits a web, the web doesn't collapse. The shock doesn't spread evenly. The force localizes. The rest of the structure keeps working.

Networks that survive damage.

That idea had turned into packet switching.

Packet switching had turned into ARPANET.

ARPANET had turned into the internet.

Helena stared at the budget number again and gave a faint shake of her head.

"Not a bad return," she murmured.

Last time she checked, the internet accounted for something like three or four percent of GDP across the major economies. McKinsey had run the numbers years ago. The World Bank had gone even further—fifteen percent of global GDP tied to the digital economy now.

Sixteen trillion dollars a year.

All of it, in some indirect way, traceable back to a few DARPA researchers asking what would happen if you built a network that behaved like a spider web.

Helena tapped her pen lightly against the desk.

"Best venture capital firm in history," she said to the empty office.

And most of the world still thought DARPA was just another government expense line.

Its charter wasn't to chase market trends, but to fund "blue-sky" research—high-risk, high-reward scientific ventures that could change the future or protect it.

Which is why Helena didn't hesitate to expand Nusquam.

She called it Nusquam Nation now—a quiet but powerful build-out of America's most secret research enclave, hidden in the folds of rural Vermont. She had already acquired two adjacent farms and secured first refusal rights on three more. That meant five hundred acres under DARPA control, with another five hundred lined up.

To Helena, the benefits were obvious:

– Remote, defensible terrain.
– Proximity to Canada's vast hydroelectric grid.
– No seismic fault lines, no wildfires, no hurricanes—just snow. And snow c
be managed.
– Even climate change played in Vermont's favor.

She kept the old farm leases in place for cover. Cattle still roamed the pastures, and fields were still tilled. It all looked the same from above. Even paid a few bills.

But underground, she saw the future being written.

Long-term, Helena envisioned Nusquam Nation as a strategic defense asset—a sovereign slice of innovation cloaked in farmland. A place where the rules could bend, where breakthroughs could breathe, and where the next trillion-dollar idea might once again begin with a question no one else was asking.

The sunlight through the window slanted across the matte finish of the architectural blueprint now unrolled across Helena Quinn's conference table. Lines crisp, ink still smelling faintly of heat-set toner, it stretched nearly edge to edge — the future anatomy of Nusquam laid bare like a surgical diagram.

She didn't sit. She stood over it like a general reviewing campaign terrain.

To an outsider, it might seem strange for the Director of DARPA to obsess over the layout of a single covert research site buried in rural Vermont.

But this wasn't just any site.

This was Operation Echo Reef.

And Helena Quinn did not outsource importance.

She moved a weighty brass paperweight to pin the corner of the schematic flat. Her eyes scanned the fine print with a precision honed in war rooms and laboratories alike.

Fifteen feet below grade, the blueprint revealed a vaulted, blast-resistant subterranean chamber. Its walls were layered in alternating composites — tungsten-laced steel, boron-infused polymers, and micro-structured ceramic insulation designed to cancel electromagnetic bleed.

"The walls were layered in alternating composites—tungsten-laced steel, boron-infused polymers, and micro-structured ceramic insulation designed to cancel electromagnetic bleed. A Faraday shell wrapped around a cryogenic core."

Quantum Lab: Tier Zero Classification
Dilution Refrigerator Bay (Cryomech LF-70)
QPU Isolation Modules (3x Superconducting Array Pods)
EM-proof power bus with redundant thermal drains
Vibration-dampened flooring on gyroscopic shock supports

Every component necessary to build and test a next-generation quantum processor — and hide it from the world.

The ground floor included a fully compliant SCIF, offices, a compact conference room, and a simple galley with enough space for mission-critical staff to eat without disappearing into town.

Second floor: a modest lounge with sleeping quarters — enough for six personnel, maybe eight in a pinch. Modular bunks, folding desks, hardwired secure uplinks. Comfort by necessity, not indulgence.

She ran her fingers across the margin notes in blue ink. Some were hers. Others, added later by Will Morgan or ACIC's infrastructure lead. Every mark mattered.

She unraveled the next set of prints for the farmhouse expansion. It included an expanded kitchen and dining room together with a brand new wing. She referred to as the in-laws suite. It was hardly that but rather more like a good sized three bedroom apartment. The basement would house a new power plant with backup, a small SCIF and infirmary.

And now, looking at it as a whole, she smiled — not out of pride, but satisfaction.

“Everything it needs to be,” she said aloud, mostly to herself. “Nothing it doesn’t.”

She stepped back from the table, arms crossed, gaze lingering on the clean geometry of the barn—its new silhouette, the hidden complexity inside it.

"She stepped back from the table, arms crossed, gaze lingering on the clean geometry of the barn. A clandestine lab built around one very rare mind. Nemo's."

And maybe... for the team growing around him.

She tapped a finger against the table, once. Then reached for her secure tablet and typed a single directive:

“Greenlight construction. No further delays. — HQQ”

Outside her office, Washington pulsed in its usual controlled chaos.

Inside, a blueprint waited to become real — and with it, the next chapter of a war no one dared admit had already begun.

Fort Meade - Commander Perry’s Office - Late Evening

The room hummed with the soft drone of filtered air and hidden electronics.

Ed Perry sat at the end of the polished conference table, jacket off, tie loosened, the fatigue of command heavy in his eyes.

Across from him, Helena Quinn stood before the wall screen, hands clasped behind her back, the ghostly blue light of Echo Reef’s simulation playing over her face like phosphorescence.

She had been speaking for several minutes, outlining the quantum lattice expansion metrics, but there was a tone—a note beneath the technical precision—that made Perry tilt his head.

“You sound almost proud,” he said.

Helena turned slowly. “Wouldn’t you be? It’s... extraordinary, Ed. The architecture is self-correcting. It’s learning without deviation. Nemo has built something that listens, adapts.”

Perry studied her. “You make it sound alive.”

She smiled faintly, stepping closer to the image. "Maybe it is. Every generation has its miracle, Ed. Radar. The transistor. The microchip. This is ours. Except this one knows us back."

"That's what worries me," he said.

Helena's eyes softened — the look of someone who'd already had the same argument with herself. "You're thinking in terms of control. I'm thinking in terms of potential. You don't teach a child to walk by locking the door."

"Helena," Perry said evenly, "this isn't a child. It's a classified defense construct tied into systems we barely understand. And the people behind it — Nemo, Genevieve — they're not soldiers. They're human. That means they'll make choices we can't predict."

She leaned on the back of a chair, the faintest flicker of something maternal in her tone. "They're brilliant, Ed. Fragile, but brilliant. That's why I keep them close—to keep them safe. From interference. From politics. From themselves."

He gave a short, weary laugh. "That sounds less like leadership and more like... ownership."

Her smile didn't fade. "You say that like it's a bad thing."

Perry's gaze sharpened. "I'm saying if you start believing it's yours, you'll stop seeing when it becomes something else."

For a long moment, Helena said nothing. She turned back to the screen—the shifting light painting her expression in glints of silver and blue.

Finally:

"Every miracle begins with arrogance, Ed. The trick is knowing when to stop believing it's yours."

The simulation pulsed—a soft, harmonic glow like a heartbeat.

Neither spoke again.

Perry walked out into the corridor, the air cooler than the SCIF, his thoughts heavier than before. The fluorescent lights hummed overhead—steady, indifferent. Helena's words replayed in his head: "Every miracle begins with arrogance." She believed that, and worse, she believed she could master it. That kind of faith could move mountains—or bury people under them.

He paused at the end of the hallway, looking through the reinforced glass toward the courtyard. Somewhere down the chain, Nemo and Gayle were pushing boundaries Helena no longer seemed eager to define. She wasn't guarding a project anymore—she was guarding a legacy. And legacies, he knew too well, had a way of consuming their makers.

He exhaled, straightened his shoulders, and muttered to himself, "We'll need a tighter leash before the miracle bites." Then he turned toward the secure elevator, already drafting in his head what he'd have to tell Will Morgan—and how little time they might have to act.

——

Granville VT- March 9 0700 Hours R

It was only early March, and already the snowmelt had begun—the earliest in recent memory, even for Vermont. Mud season, usually a six-week ordeal of thawed earth and axle-snapping ruts, had arrived early. For Helena Quinn, that wasn't a problem. It was an advantage.

Because construction had officially begun on Nusquam Nation.

Bulldozers and backhoes carved deep into the frozen hillside behind the barn, pushing aside snow, shale, and dirt with mechanical indifference. The excavation for the new farmhouse extension and the doubling of the barn's footprint was ahead of schedule.

Twenty feet down, the foundation was being poured for a subterranean Faraday cage, its reinforced latticework designed to block even the most sophisticated electromagnetic surveillance. While the cage itself would do the heavy lifting, Helena knew the underground siting offered something even more valuable: natural shielding.

Underground, the new lab would benefit from:

Reduced cosmic radiation, which could cause decoherence in qubits

Minimized electromagnetic interference, from both civilian and military sources

> Stabilized temperatures, critical for maintaining cryogenic systems near absolute zero

> Dampened low-frequency vibrations, which could degrade quantum signal integrity

To further suppress microseismic noise, the mudsill—the structural beam connecting frame to foundation—was being bolted directly into the concrete, locking the lab into the earth itself.

Normally, a project of this scale would take six months. Helena had given them ninety days. Bonus incentives were built into the contract for every week shaved off the schedule.

To speed things up, the subgrade was cleared free of snow, ice, and frost. Ground heaters and insulated blankets were used to warm the ground before pouring the special mix of concrete with warm water.

With luck—and some unrelenting pressure—the new lab would be operational by Independence Day.

Waiting in a trailer on-site was the core of the system: a $3 million Bluefors Ankaa™-3 dilution refrigerator, capable of maintaining stable temperatures within a few millikelvins of absolute zero. Nearby, still sealed in its custom shipping crate, sat Rigetti's 84-qubit Ankaa™-3 chip—valued at $950,000 and still humming with factory-calibrated entanglement potential.

Nemo was excited. He could admit that much, at least to himself.

The eighty-four-qubit machine sitting in the trailer was not just an upgrade from his nine-qubit testbed. It was a leap. A violent one. The kind that changed the scale of what was possible so completely that it made the old work feel like sketches in the margin of a real design. With that much power, the horizon moved. Problems that had once looked theoretical now felt close enough to touch.

That was the point, of course. No ceiling. No artificial limits on what might be built, solved, or broken open. And that was what unsettled him.

Power was one thing. Operating it was another. Could he do it alone? Probably not. Could he do it with a small staff? Maybe. But every new hire widened the circle. Every résumé, every interview, every background check was not just an administrative nuisance but a possible breach point, a possible catastrophe. Around ordinary companies, a bad hire meant incompetence, theft, maybe embarrassment. Here, it could mean exposure. Prison. Death.

He forced himself to stop there.

He had come too far to start trembling at variables he could not control. Worry was a habit, not a strategy. The machine was here. Helena had made her move. Will had made his. The expansion was no longer hypothetical. It was sitting outside in a trailer, heavy as fate.

And he was not entirely alone.

He had Genevieve. He had Karen. However uneasy the arrangement still felt at times, those facts mattered. As for Helena and Will—trust was too generous a word, maybe. But reliance was unavoidable, and in his world unavoidable things had a way of becoming their own kind of faith.

So he drew a slow breath, let it out, and made himself think the only thought that mattered now:

It was here.

Which meant it was time to begin.

——

Nusquam

Nemo stood alone in the lab long after the call ended.

The quiet at Nusquam was different from the quiet in cities. In Brooklyn, silence had always been relative—traffic breathing through the streets, distant sirens, the mechanical pulse of eight million lives stacked in layers above and below each other. That had been the anonymity he wanted. Density was camouflage.

Here, in Vermont, the quiet was absolute.

Outside the lab windows the forest had already gone dark, the late winter sky fading into a flat iron-gray that seemed to swallow sound itself. Inside, the racks hummed behind their shielding panels. Cooling fans. Power supplies. The low electric whisper of machines doing what they were designed to do.

Predictable. Contained. Secure. Safe.

Nemo rested his palms on the edge of the console and stared at the diagnostic traces scrolling across one of the monitors. He wasn't really seeing them.

Helena Quinn's voice replayed in his mind.

Expansion. Partnerships. Facilities. Replication.

The words had come easily to her. To Helena, scale was proof of success. That was the language of DARPA—the assumption that if something worked, you built ten more of it, then a hundred.

A national asset.

He exhaled slowly. Nusquam. He had chosen the name carefully. Not just because it sounded right, but because it meant something precise. Nowhere. That had been the entire point.

First Brooklyn—Bay Ridge, specifically. Dense enough that nobody noticed anything. Thousands of apartments, thousands of signals, thousands of people minding their own lives. You could disappear there simply by existing normally.

Then Vermont. Distance instead of density. Faraday shielding layered into the walls. Fiber lines buried deep enough to be indistinguishable from the surrounding infrastructure. A place so deliberately unremarkable that satellites would pass over it without curiosity.

Nusquam wasn't supposed to be important. It was supposed to be invisible.

He pushed away from the console and walked slowly across the lab, the rubber soles of his shoes making almost no sound on the epoxy floor.

Helena's proposal wasn't wrong. In fact, technically speaking, it was the logical next step.

ECHO REEF worked.

Not theoretically. Not in simulation.

It worked.

The mathematics held under stress. The quantum layers behaved as predicted. The architecture scaled in ways that even he hadn't entirely expected when he first sketched the idea out on a yellow legal pad in a Brooklyn apartment kitchen three years ago.

Recognition should feel good.

And part of him—the younger part, the one who had once presented papers at conferences and waited to see if anyone in the room understood what he had just said—felt something dangerously close to pride.

He had built something that mattered.

Something that people like Helena Quinn took seriously.

But pride wasn't the dominant feeling.

What he felt, mostly, was exposure.

He stopped beside the equipment rack where the shielding mesh disappeared into the wall panels. The layered copper lattice gleamed faintly in the LED light.

Visibility was risk.

Always had been.

When something became important, people started asking questions.

When people asked questions, they started looking.

And when people looked long enough...

They eventually found things.

Nemo folded his arms.

Helena saw Nusquam as a seed. A prototype. The first node in a larger network. But that wasn't what Nusquam was supposed to be. It was a refuge. A laboratory. A place outside the map.

He found himself thinking about the word again. Nowhere. Nowhere meant safety. Nowhere meant nobody cared enough to interfere. Nowhere meant you could work.

He looked back at the glowing rows of monitors.

Helena wanted to turn nowhere into somewhere. Into infrastructure. Into something that would show up in briefings and budgets and congressional oversight hearings. Somewhere people could point to.

He rubbed a hand slowly across the back of his neck.

The irony wasn't lost on him.

He had spent most of his life trying to disappear into systems large enough that nobody noticed the individual pieces. And now he had built something so effective that it could no longer remain hidden. Success had a way of doing that.

Nemo returned to the console and leaned forward, studying the quiet cascade of data. If Helena succeeded, Nusquam wouldn't stay nowhere. It would become the first coordinate in a map. And maps attracted travelers. Some of them friendly. Some of them not.

For a long moment he said nothing.

Then, almost unconsciously, he spoke the word aloud. "Nowhere."

For the first time since Helena had outlined the plan, he realized the real question wasn't whether expansion made sense. Technically, it did.

The question was something else entirely. What happened to a man who built his life around disappearing...

when the world suddenly decided he mattered?

——

Fort Meade - Will's Office

Sara enters Will's office without knocking—the only person allowed to do so. "Boss, got a minute?"

Will completes what he was writing on his computer turned and responded, "Sure."

"Genevieve is concerned about Nemo. With his new 84-Quibit bit unit the possibilities just took a quantum leap. "

"And..."

"She feels he is distressed and concerned about lack of staff while at the same time being leery of new people."

Knowing that Sara rarely presented a problem without a solution or at least a course of action, he asked, "Got a plan?"

"Yes, but you are going to hate it."

"Wonderful."

"Let him borrow Derek. At least for awhile until the anxiety passes."

"So, that's what the two of you cooked up?"

Sara just smiled.

"Why Derek?

"Genevieve knows what Derek can do and can't do. They like each other and she thinks Nemo and he will work well together."

"Well, he's got a fish name Nemo."

"Is that a yes?

"I'm outnumbered,"

"But if Derek doesn't want to go I won't force him."

"We wouldn't ask."

"We? So it is a conspiracy."

Sara left before he would change his mind and headed to Derek's office.

Derek's Office

Sara didn't knock.

She never did.

Derek's office door was half closed, the room beyond lit almost entirely by the soft, shifting glow of the aquarium. The low hum of the filter motor blended with the gentle hiss of air stones bubbling through coral and driftwood.

Six monitors curved around Derek like the cockpit of a small spacecraft. Lines of code crawled across one screen. Satellite telemetry flickered on another. SYBIL's analytic dashboards pulsed in the background.

Derek himself barely moved. He sat forward in his chair, elbows on the desk, eyes fixed on the center monitor. The glow from the screens caught the lenses of his glasses, turning them briefly opaque. Inside the tank, the orange-and-white clownfish named Nemo drifted lazily between two coral arches.

Sara stepped into the room and leaned against the doorframe. "Working in the dark again," she said.

Derek didn't turn immediately. His fingers tapped three keys, waited for a response, then he leaned back. Only then did he look over. "Sara."

He said her name the way he always did—flat, but unmistakably pleased.

She walked in slowly, hands in the pockets of her jacket, pausing beside the aquarium.

The fish circled once through the coral, tail flicking.

"I need to ask you something," she said.

Derek swiveled slightly in his chair, giving her his full attention. That alone said a lot. Derek rarely gave anyone his full attention. "What?"

She glanced at the tank, then at him. "Do you want to go to Vermont for a while?"

His eyebrows rose just a fraction. “Why?”

“To help with a project.”

Derek’s eyes flicked briefly to one of the monitors, where SYBIL’s interface glowed faintly.

"I've never been to Vermont."

"Neither has most of Vermont, emotionally."

“How long?”

“Not sure yet.”

He nodded once. “Okay.”

Sara immediately shook her head. “No.”

Derek blinked.

“You didn’t even ask what the project is.”

“You asked.”

“That’s why I’m stopping you,” she said gently. “Don’t say yes because I’m asking.”

Derek tilted his head slightly, processing that. Then he asked the question she knew he would. “Will you be there?”

Sara smiled faintly. “I’ll take you up there. But Genevieve is permanently assigned now, and Karen’s there on temporary rotation. So you won’t be a stranger.”

Derek nodded again, thinking it through.

“The only person you won’t know is Nemo.”

Derek frowned slightly. “Nemo?”

Sara gestured toward the fish tank. “Different Nemo.”

Derek glanced at the clownfish drifting through the coral. “That’s confusing.”

Sara laughed. “That’s the code name for a brilliant quantum scientist.”

He leaned back slightly in his chair. “Do they have fish?”

Sara folded her arms. “I’m sure that can be arranged.”

Derek’s expression changed instantly. “Cool.”

"Those are historically dangerous words from you."

She added, almost as an afterthought: “They do have a very cool dog.”

That caught his attention too.

Derek considered this information carefully. “I’ve never been to Vermont,” he said. “Is it nice?”

Sara stepped closer to the aquarium, watching the clownfish slip through the anemone.

“It’s beautiful,” she said. “Mountains, lakes, rivers... small towns that look like postcards.”

She smiled slightly. "And a general store staffed by a really nice lady."

Derek pictured it. His world was usually cables, signals, packet traces, and the quiet glow of monitors. Vermont sounded... different. He looked back at her. "When do we leave?"

——

Middlebury Airport

The UC-35B Citation Encore hummed steadily through clear skies, its cabin quiet except for the low whir of engines and the occasional soft crackle from the cockpit intercom.

Derek Wilshire sat beside Sara Brandt, six seats empty around them—standard procedure, unspoken but understood. No one had needed to say the word escort. The seating arrangement said it for them.

It was Derek's first time in an aircraft, and the wonder of it sat openly on his face.

He leaned close to the window, forehead nearly touching the glass, watching the world rearrange itself beneath them. Roads bent into long vectors. Rivers curled like loose wire. Fields resolved into grids and rectangles, shifting color with the winter light.

"Everything looks like code from up here," he murmured at one point, half to himself.

Sara glanced over. His eyes weren't just watching the scenery—they were tracking it, following patterns as they moved.

"Code?" she asked.

Derek nodded, still looking out the window.

"Repeating structures. Constraints. Landowners drawing boundaries. Highways optimizing travel time. Even the rivers... they look chaotic but they're following gradient descent. Water solving equations."

Sara smiled faintly. She had learned early that Derek didn't speak metaphorically. If he said something looked like code, he meant it literally.

Below them, the farmland of upstate New York slowly gave way to rougher terrain. The geometry softened. Forest spread across the landscape like spilled ink. Low mountains rose in long ridges, snow tracing their contours.

Derek leaned back slightly, absorbing the shift. "The algorithm changes here," he said.

Sara raised an eyebrow. "Less human optimization," he explained. "More geological."

"Vermont," she said.

He nodded, as if that confirmed something. For a few minutes neither of them spoke. The cabin remained still except for the vibration of the engines and the gentle sway of the aircraft in the cold air.

Derek eventually glanced toward the cockpit door.

"Does it bother you?" he asked.

"What?"

"That the plane stays up."

Sara laughed. "No."

"It should," Derek said thoughtfully. "Lift is counterintuitive. Density differences creating upward force. We trust it because it works every time."

"Military aviation prefers things that work every time."

"That's the same rule as cryptography."

Sara studied him. Derek didn't look nervous. If anything, he looked calm in a way that only appeared when his mind was fully engaged.

"You okay with where we're going?" she asked.

He turned back to the window.

"I think so."

"You think so?"

"Well," Derek said carefully, "you asked me not to say yes just because you asked."

Sara nodded. That had been deliberate.

"So?" she prompted.

Derek considered the question with visible seriousness.

"There's an eighty-four qubit machine waiting in a trailer in rural Vermont," he said. "A physicist who hides from the world. A cryptologist who used to work against the Russians. And a dog."

Sara smiled again.

"You forgot Genevieve."

Derek shook his head slightly.

"No, I didn't."

The airplane banked gently as the pilot began the descent.

Outside the window the ridgelines grew sharper. Frozen rivers cut bright lines through dark forest. Small towns appeared—clusters of roofs and church steeples tucked into valleys.

Derek watched them closely.

"People built those towns near water," he observed. "Transport first. Then power. Then roads."

"Pattern recognition?"

"History leaves footprints."

The landing gear deployed with a low mechanical thud. Derek felt it through the floor and looked down, fascinated.

"Is that normal?" he asked.

"Perfectly."

The aircraft descended through a thin layer of cloud, and suddenly the runway appeared—long, gray, and surprisingly small compared to the immense sky above it.

Middlebury Airport.

The Citation touched down with a firm but smooth bounce. Reverse thrust roared briefly before fading back into a quiet hum as the aircraft slowed along the runway.

Derek blinked once. "That was... efficient."

Sara unbuckled her belt. "That's the idea."

The cabin door opened a few minutes later, and cold Vermont air poured inside—clean, sharp, carrying the scent of snow and pine. Outside, the mountains rose in quiet blue layers along the horizon.

Derek stepped onto the tarmac and paused. The air was different here. Thinner. Quieter.

Every sound felt sharper.

He looked around slowly, taking in the empty airfield, the small terminal building, the dark forests beyond the runway.

"This is very far from Brooklyn," he said.

Sara zipped up her coat and nodded toward a black SUV waiting near the hangar.

"Welcome to Vermont."

Derek watched the mountains for another moment.

Somewhere out there was a man named Nemo.

A physicist hiding from the world.

A machine that might change it.

Derek felt the familiar spark in his mind—the sense of a puzzle about to reveal its edges.

"Do they really have fish?" he asked.

Sara sighed.

"Yes, Derek."

"Good."

He followed her toward the SUV, the cold air crunching under their shoes as the quiet airport closed behind them.

——

Nusquam Lab

Sara did not introduce them. She could have. It would have been the normal thing to do. But normal introductions were for normal people, and neither of these men operated very comfortably inside that architecture. Instead she opened the lab door and stepped aside.

The quantum system satin the lab. Inside, the air was cool and dry. Racks of control electronics lined one wall. Fiber ran in carefully organized bundles to the dilution refrigerator housing the 84-qubit processor. A whiteboard filled with equations occupied the far side of the room.

Nemo stood there, sleeves rolled, studying a waveform on a tablet.

Sara gestured casually. "Derek, take a look at the control interface."

That was all she said. She stepped back into the hallway.

Karen noticed immediately. "You're not introducing them?"

Sara folded her arms, leaning against the wall. "They'll figure it out."

Inside the lab Derek moved slowly, absorbing the room the way he always did—quietly, completely. He didn't start with the machine itself. He studied the cables first. The separation of control buses. The shielding around the timing lines. The careful physical spacing between certain components.

His head tilted slightly.

Interesting.

Across the room Nemo sensed someone else in the space. He glanced up briefly but said nothing. Whoever Sara had brought in was studying the racks like a man reading a language.

Good.

Derek stopped in front of the interface console. "You separated the control bus from the timing bus."

Nemo answered without turning. "Yes."

"To reduce cross-talk."

"Mostly."

Derek studied the waveform scrolling across the screen. "The error rate dropped."

"Eight percent."

Derek nodded once.

"Worth it."

Now Nemo turned.

The two men regarded each other for the first time.

Derek's expression was neutral but intensely focused. Nemo's gaze carried the same quiet analytical weight—less social curiosity than structural evaluation.

For a few seconds neither spoke. In the hallway Karen leaned toward Sara. "Should we... intervene?"

Sara shook her head.

Inside the lab Derek gestured toward the equipment. "Eighty-four qubits."

Nemo nodded.

"New upgrade."

"From nine."

Nemo's eyes narrowed slightly. "Yes."

Derek tilted his head again.

"How long did that take?"

"Too long."

Derek considered the machine another moment. Then he said, almost casually: "You're Nemo."

Not a question.

Nemo blinked. "Sara told you?"

Derek shook his head. "Architecture."

"You think like me."

Nemo studied him more carefully now. "You're Derek."

This time it was a question. Derek nodded.

Nemo absorbed that. Then he noticed something behind Derek. A soft scratching sound on the floor. Runa had entered the lab. The Belgian Malinois moved with quiet confidence, nails tapping lightly against the concrete floor. She paused in the doorway, scanning the room the way working dogs do—quick, deliberate assessments.

She walked directly to Derek. Not cautiously. Not hesitantly. She sat down beside him and leaned against his leg.

Nemo frowned. "That's unusual."

Derek looked down at the dog. "Hello." He reached down and scratched behind her ears with gentle precision, exactly where dogs prefer it. Runa's tail thumped once against the floor.

In the hallway Genevieve watched the scene unfold. She smiled. "She doesn't do that."

Karen looked surprised. "Ever?"

"Not with someone she just met."

Inside the lab Nemo crossed his arms, studying both Derek and the dog. "She reads people."

Derek looked mildly confused. "She's a dog."

Nemo shook his head. "No." He nodded toward Runa. "She's an algorithm."

Derek processed that. Then he nodded thoughtfully. "Biological."

"Yes."

Another silence settled between them. But this one was different. Less awkward. More... calibrated.

Derek glanced around the room. "Do you have fish?"

Nemo stared at him. "Fish."

"Yes."

Derek gestured. "Tanks."

Nemo took a moment to process that question. Then he pointed toward the corner where a small aquarium sat on a side table. Inside, a bright orange clownfish drifted through coral.

Derek walked over and crouched to examine it. "You named it Nemo."

"Yes."

"Why?"

Nemo shrugged. "Seemed appropriate."

Derek studied the fish. "For what?"

Nemo leaned against the rack behind him. "For someone who hides in plain sight."

Derek looked back at him. Really looked this time. Something clicked behind his eyes.

Across the hallway Sara watched the moment land.

Karen whispered. "You planned this."

Sara nodded.

Inside the lab Derek stood again. He extended his hand.

"I'm Derek."

Nemo shook it. "I know."

Runa stayed right where she was, sitting beside Derek, as if she had already decided he belonged there.

CHAPTER TWENTY-NINE

Quantum Persistence

Nusquam Lab

Nusquam slept beneath a blanket of snow that morning, its metal roof sheened in frost. Inside, the lab pulsed with quiet life, fans, cooling pumps, and the faint hum of cryogenic compressors.

Genevieve sat at the console with a steaming mug of coffee while SYBIL's spectral display rippled across the curved glass. Nemo stood nearby, arms folded, watching the oscillations of two linked qubits dance in elegant symmetry.

The waveform trembled, a reminder that perfection, even here, was an illusion.

"Preserving coherence," Nemo said, as if reciting a creed. "That's the real trick. Everything else is just noise management."

Genevieve looked over. "You mean keeping it alive long enough to matter."

"Right. A qubit's state is fragile, every stray photon, every vibration, every tenth of a degree of thermal drift tries to tear it apart. Decoherence isn't failure. It's gravity in another form, the universe pulling quantum back into the classical world. But, you know that."

He moved to the control rack, fingers trailing over the screen. "We fight it with control systems, optimal control theory, adaptive feedback loops, active error suppression. We're basically whispering to the qubit: stay where you are, stay coherent, stay pure."

SYBIL's voice joined in:

> *"Real-time feedback stabilized. Noise suppression algorithms maintaining fidelity above 99.4 percent."*

The waveform steadied, holding like a breath that refused to fade.

The Integration

The heart of the system rested inside a small cryogenic chamber, a slice of diamond fused to a silicon photonic chip no larger than a postage stamp.

Nemo nodded toward it. "This was the hard part. Marrying diamond quantum memories to silicon photonics."

Derek, hovering at the door with his ever-present mug, frowned. "Why silicon?"

"Because it behaves," Nemo said simply. "Circuits on a solid-state platform don't rattle apart every time the Earth sighs. Vibrations, temperature drift. All of that kills entanglement. But silicon, if engineered right, doesn't flinch. It gives us a stable stage for the photons to perform."

Genevieve smiled. "And that performance gives us entangled memory qubits, the building blocks for large-scale, long-lived networks."

He nodded. "Spot on. We're not just storing quantum information, we're linking memories, synchronizing them. Once entangled, they can communicate over distance without a fiber line screaming for maintenance every few kilometers."

On SYBIL's monitor, an entanglement fidelity map bloomed across the screen — a constellation of interconnected nodes.

"Robust generation and distribution confirmed," SYBIL intoned. "Vibration susceptibility negligible. Temperature drift within stable parameters."

Miniaturization and the Real World

The following week, the lab felt different. Tighter. More purposeful.

The prototype had shrunk — from a full optical table to a module barely the size of a paperback. Wires fed into it like veins.

Derek stared at it, impressed despite himself. "That's it? The whole thing?"

"Integrated photonics," Genevieve said. "It's all inside the chip now — no more fiber jungle."

"Miniaturization," Nemo added. "It's what makes quantum clock synchronization actually deployable. Field units, aircraft, orbital relays. If this works, you could synchronize time across continents with quantum precision — no GPS drift, no relativistic lag."

He turned toward the display, his tone quieter. "It means command and control systems that never desync. Secure networks that never lose phase."

Derek let out a low whistle. "Which also means every intelligence service on Earth will want it."

SYBIL didn't disagree.

"Predicted applications: defense, space communications, precision navigation, and strategic deterrence."

"Threat assessment: elevated."

Nusquam Lab

Late one night, only the glow of monitors lit the lab. Nemo sat at the control console, eyes fixed on the shifting traces of data.

He spoke more to himself than to anyone else. "The classical-quantum interface — that's the real bridge. The control system doesn't just monitor; it negotiates between worlds."

Genevieve, tired but still curious, joined him. "Bridge how?"

"Classical electronics send signals — microwave, RF pulses — that steer the quantum state. It's like conducting an orchestra with a baton made of mathematics. Then the readout electronics convert the qubit's whisper back into a digital pulse we can interpret."

She watched the rhythm of data flow on the monitor, the seamless translation from quantum indeterminacy into classical certainty.

"We're standing at the edge," she said. "Between what can be known, and what can only be measured once."

Nemo smiled faintly. "And we're building the language that lets both sides speak."

SYBIL's final report scrolled across the screen:

System Status: Quantum Control Active.

Coherence Stability: Sustained.

Platform Integrity: Solid-State Photonic.

Operational Readiness: 94.7%.

Designation: Quantum Persistence Node – Prototype A.

Outside, snow fell in silence, each flake a brief coherence event, collapsing softly against the glass.

——

Nusquam Research Facility — Four Months Earlier

The diamond wafer gleamed beneath the microscope's polarized light, flawless to the naked eye and, as Nemo suspected, too flawless.

Genevieve adjusted the laser's aim, her breath fogging the viewport as Derek watched the coherence trace rise.

"Ninety microseconds and climbing," Derek said. "This could hold—"

The spectral line jittered, then flattened. Entanglement gone. Another run dead.

Genevieve swore under her breath. Derek hit the console with an open palm.

Nemo only took off his glasses and looked at the silent monitor. "Diamond's too pure," he said at last. "No nitrogen-vacancy imperfections, no anchoring spins. We've engineered away the memory."

Genevieve turned, half incredulous. "You're saying we need less perfect diamonds?"

He nodded, subtle, knowing smile ghosting across his face. "Imperfection gives it a story to tell. The universe forgets when it's flawless."

SYBIL's interface flickered to life behind them, lines of failed coherence trials scrolling like epitaphs.

"Run 1272 terminated. Decoherence complete," she reported.

The lab went still. Outside, the mountain wind rattled the aluminum siding. Inside, Nemo's mind kept spinning.

Two Months Later — Clean Room Delta-3

The new assembly floated in liquid helium at near-zero kelvin. A web of fiber couplers connected the diamond chip to a silicon board etched with micro-scale photonic circuits.

Everything was tuned. Everything was fragile.

Genevieve initiated the entanglement sequence, fingers hovering over the console like a pianist striking a hesitant chord.

The signal bloomed — a perfect spectral peak, coherent and sharp — then vanished with a hollow pop.

A faint hiss followed. The laser shutter tripped automatically. Derek sprinted to the rack. "The photonic bridge burned out!"

SYBIL's voice filled the sterile air:

"Thermal drift exceeded tolerance. Cause: uncontrolled Joule heating."

Nemo leaned on the console, calm in that unnerving way that made Genevieve uneasy.

"We built a quantum violin," he said, "and snapped the string."

Genevieve removed her gloves, tossing them onto the bench. "That was three weeks of alignment."

Nemo glanced at the fractured wafer. "Failure is still data. The system's telling us what it won't allow."

He picked up a broken fragment of the diamond and held it against the light.

"Next time," he murmured, "we'll listen better."

Three Weeks Before Breakthrough — Lab B-1

The hum of the new silicon-photonic board filled the room like static breath. Derek monitored the waveguide channels as Genevieve adjusted the polarizers.

"Signal routed through channel seven. Coherence holding..."

A pause. The trace on the monitor plunged.

"Photon loss again," Genevieve said.

SYBIL's projection summarized the damage:

"Attenuation rising. Entanglement time: zero."

Nemo pinched the bridge of his nose. "It's not the waveguide. The photons can't decide whether they belong to silicon or diamond."

Derek looked up from the monitor. "So we're mediating a custody dispute between two materials?"

Nemo didn't answer. He turned to the whiteboard, uncapped a marker, and began sketching, refractive indexes, phonon interactions, dopant gradients.

He circled one phrase: Resonance Coupling. He underlined it twice.

Genevieve watched the loops of his handwriting, calm, deliberate, the way he always became when his mind was steps ahead of everyone else.

"What if," Nemo said, "we stopped forcing the interface to choose? Let them share the state, not fight over it."

The room was quiet except for SYBIL's low system hum — a sound like patience learning to breathe.

Nusquam=Present Day — Breakthrough

The lab lights were dimmed now. Only the low-frequency hum of the refrigerator and the soft pulse of indicator LEDs filled the space. Through the viewport, a single diamond wafer glowed beneath the alignment laser.

Genevieve stood at the console, monitoring the entanglement log. SYBIL's interface projected a calm blue halo over her face.

SYBIL announced:

Qubit A entangled Stability at ten to the negative four seconds and holding

Nemo leaned closer, eyes fixed on the trace. "Ten to the negative four," he whispered. "Still coherent. That's stable and...communicable."

He rerouted the photon stream through the silicon waveguide. A shimmer appeared on the secondary wafer — the other half of the quantum pair. Entanglement confirmed.

Genevieve's smile broke before she could stop it. "You've done it."

Nemo stood motionless, watching the waveforms steady into a perfect harmonic lock.

"Diamond quantum memory integrated with silicon photonics," he said. "Stable entangled memory qubits. We just gave quantum information a home that doesn't decay."

SYBIL displayed the projections: coherence lifetimes measured in years.

Derek, standing in the doorway with a coffee that had gone cold an hour ago, stared at the numbers.

"If this leaks," he said, "MSS, SVR—hell, everyone will light up the planet trying to steal it."

Nemo didn't respond. The glow from the wafers caught in his eyes, small twin constellations reflected in silence.

For the first time, the network held.

CHAPTER THIRTY

Protecting the False Flag

Fort Belvoir, VA-Commanding General Owen Edwards Office 0820 Hours

The blinds were drawn, the overhead fluorescents humming faintly in the silence before the meeting began. The room held four men, all used to secrets. But today, something felt different.

Judd Lockwood, CIA Counterintelligence Liaison, stood near the head of the conference table, his face unreadable. Opposite him sat General Edwards, Commander of INSCOM. Ed Perry of ACIC and Guy Zarelli, his top operations deputy, were already leafing through their notebooks but paused when Lockwood placed a sealed envelope flat on the polished walnut surface.

"This isn't just a courtesy drop," Lockwood said, tone clipped. "Langley requested this meeting at the Director's direction."

Owen gave a nod. "We're listening."

Lockwood drew a controlled breath. "We have a new asset inside the Ministry of State Security. Codename: Snow Lantern. Embedded at the Second Bureau. Counterespionage division. Tier Omega-3."

Guy gave a low whistle.

"He's already given us valuable intel," Lockwood continued. "This morning, we received confirmation from him that the MSS is aware of something called Operation Parallax Veil. They don't know what it is yet, but they know it exists, and they're escalating. We believe we may have a leak."

Owen's expression didn't shift. "What makes you think the leak is on our end?"

"Because we haven't told anyone in Beijing about Parallax Veil. The program name was never supposed to be exposed outside of highly limited compartments within INSCOM and ACIC. If it's being discussed in MSS boardrooms, someone talked or something leaked."

He looked directly at Ed. "So, I'm here for confirmation. We don't need the details. I just need to know if is Operation Parallax Veil real?"

Ed Perry glanced at Owen, who gave a subtle nod.

Ed spoke evenly. "It's real."

Lockwood exhaled slowly. "Good. That's what we needed. You've just verified our mole."

He collected the envelope and closed his folder. "I won't ask you for details. I'm not here to breach compartments. I'll report to Langley that Snow Lantern's intel checks out...so far."

He stood. "Let me know if anything changes."

The moment the door shut behind him, silence reclaimed the room for a few beats.

Guy turned to Owen. "How the hell did they penetrate the MSS at that level?"

Ed leaned back in his chair. "Doesn't matter. What matters is we've got an asset inside MSS feeding the CIA, and now they're watching one of our black programs. This is only going to tighten."

Owen folded his hands. "I want Will Morgan in the loop. This is going to need containment, and maybe some proactive maneuvering. His team has the experience—and the flexibility—we'll need if this spreads."

He turned to Guy. "Work with Will. Craft a plan. I don't want this spiraling into a mole hunt inside our own walls unless it has to."

Owen looked at Ed and asked, "Agreed?"

Ed smiled. "Good idea. Will's team trusts Guy. They'll bring him in clean."

Owen gave him a knowing smile. Crafty to create harmony before it even started he thought.

Fort Meade – Watchtower Conference Room 0830 Hours R

The Watchtower conference room was quiet except for the faint hum of SYBIL's secure wall display, which showed a closed digital map of the Northeast with six glowing points.

Will Morgan leaned forward, his arms braced on the table. Sara Brandt sat beside him, flipping through a thin classified file. Across from them, Guy Zarelli adjusted his reading glasses and tapped his stylus against his notes.

"Look," Guy began, "thirty thousand suspicious contact reports—SCRs—every year. Between all agencies. When you're dealing with that volume, it's a statistical certainty that some succeed. The problem is, we usually don't know where—or how bad it is—until something breaks."

Sara looked up. "You think this is one of those breaks?"

Guy nodded. "We've got a name leak. Parallax Veil. The MSS knows the phrase, but they don't know it connects to. Yet. So, I asked myself—if they penetrated the operational file, what would they see?"

Will answered calmly. "What the Chinese have started calling Operation Parallax Veil is in fact our False Constellation. They'd see Gracie's six black-budget decoy research sites. That's it."

He gestured toward the screen as SYBIL rendered the list in white text on blue.

Horizon CryoSolutions LLC – Orono, ME – Quantum Algorithms

Silvershore Research Partners – Carthage, ME – Quantum Error Correction

Triton Analytical Systems – Schroon Lake, NY – Quantum Simulation

IronNest Technology Group – Plattsburgh, NY – Quantum Communication

Whitecap Systems LLC – Lowville, NY – Quantum Cryptography

Starlight Vector Labs – Sunapee, NH – Quantum Hardware Development

"They're credible fronts," Will continued. "Even our own In-Q-Tel contact—the Director of Strategic Investments—doesn't know the op name. His files only show legitimate DARPA sub-contracts and financial disbursement trails. Nothing labeled Parallax Veil."

"So," Guy said, "the leak came from someone with verbal exposure. Loose tongue. Or a mole. But not at the top levels."

"Right," Sara agreed. "Someone low enough to be invisible, but close enough to touch classified programs."

"I've already tasked SYBIL with filtering potential vectors," she added. "It's a brute-force run—access logs, project rosters, known MSS interest maps. It's going to be a long list."

Will nodded. "Put Tech and Cathy on it. Let them sort it. Derek's the best we've got on pattern deviation and outlier behavior."

Guy closed his folder. "I'm pulling SCRs for the last three years, cross-referencing any contact reports tied to DARPA, In-Q-Tel, or DCSA personnel with access to Northeast quantum portfolios."

A brief silence followed. Each of them thinking the same thing.

If MSS got the name, someone cracked the perimeter. The only question now was—how far in did they get.

Fort Meade–Watchtower Operations Room 1002 Hours R

The low light in the operations cell gave the space a submarine quality—rows of angled monitors casting soft blue and green glows across the workstations. SYBIL's diagnostics scrolled across the largest wall display: lines of metadata, timestamps, user hashes, and access events, all updating in real time.

Sara stood at the whiteboard, her sleeves rolled up. Her handwriting was fast and angular—clusters of names, acronyms, and oblique connections scrawled across the surface like a battlefield map.

"Run that again," she said without turning. "But drop the Tier-1 clearances. I want mid-range certs—contractor liaisons, deputy analysts, and assistant schedulers."

Cathy Wang, seated at the main terminal, narrowed the filter on the SYBIL interface. "Done. We're down to 11,844 unique IDs across all six shell sites. That's still a forest."

"Start thinning it." Sara pointed to a new section of the board. "Sort by anyone who had multiple site interactions but no mission-justified reason to cross-pollinate. No Temporary Duty Assignments, no joint-tasking memos."

Cathy raised an eyebrow. "You're thinking curiosity?"

"I'm thinking drift," Sara said. "Moles don't always pull the trigger. Sometimes they just circle the target, waiting for the right cue."

SYBIL chimed—two new anomalies surfaced in the enhanced data.

Cathy turned to look. "One DCSA admin assistant filed itinerary clearance to both Plattsburgh and Carthage within the same fiscal quarter. No project tie-ins. Travel marked as 'logistics recon.'"

Sara frowned. "Too much coincidence. Flag it."

"And this one," Cathy added. "Mid-level compliance officer. Accessed IronNest's files from a shared secure node in Arlington—after hours. Not part of his job role."

"Now we're getting warm," Sara murmured, circling both with a dry-erase marker. "Let's keep digging."

The camera feed caught the two women in a moment of perfect sync—analyst veterans a generation apart, triangulating the leak not with weapons, but with pattern recognition and patience.

Down the hall, SYBIL's algorithm watched it all.

And behind its digital stillness, it had already begun to model the likely breach vector.

Fort Meade–Rick's Office – one week later 1050 Hours R

The fan noise in the Rick's office was white and constant, a soft wall of sound beneath the blinking LEDs and stacked quantum-array terminals. Rick Huang sat alone, hunched over three side-by-side displays. A stylus twitched in his right hand as he flipped through SYBIL's deep metadata sweep like a cardiologist examining the electrical echo of a heart.

"Okay, girl," he muttered. "Show me the arrhythmia."

SYBIL had just flagged two access events from within the DCSA Arlington enclave—one from a travel node, the other from a Tier-2 clearance badge routed through a shared enclave cache that should've triggered a lateral movement alert. Rick leaned forward.

Access Point: DCSA Arlington Secure Node

Time: 0203 EST

Credential: DCSA—Tier-2 / Compliance Oversight

Files Accessed: IronNest / Quantum Comms briefing deck – (Unscheduled)

Cross-reference pattern: 93% match with known MSS vector timing (exfil attempt, 2022)

"Bingo. IronNest is IronNest Technology Group—Plattsburgh, NY. Quantum Communication Research. Subtle. Real low-profile. Might as well have named themselves QuantumSecretsRUs and put a billboard on I-87."

Rick tapped into the real-time terminal audit trail. "This guy wasn't just poking around. He was pulling structured packets—bundled queries, segmented over multiple sessions. That's espionage tradecraft."

He keyed his mic.

"Sara, you've got a smoking heat trail here. Your compliance guy isn't just anomalous—he's replicating MSS scraping behavior from a prior incident we ran with NSA in Singapore. Same timing, same staggered pulls."

"Your definition of 'good news' remains inspiringly flexible."

Sara over comms,"We've got travel overlap and unnecessary site recon too. Cathy and I are backtracking his comms tree next."

"Let me know when you get any hits on message frequency or unexplained protocol jumps. I'll dig into side-channel traces."

He leaned back, one hand over his mouth.

If this was what it looked like, they'd found the first human node that connected a leak to MSS signal behavior.

And SYBIL... was watching it propagate.

——

Fort Meade – Watchtower Conference Room – 1214 Hours

The door shut with a soft hydraulic hiss. Will Morgan stood at the head of the conference table, arms folded, watching as Sara laid down a crisp summary dossier in front of him.

Sara sat to his left, flipping through the pages. Guy Zarelli paced behind her, reading off the digital board as Cathy's visual annotations flicked across the screen.

Primary Contact Identified: Alias: Joseph Lin

Vector Behavior: MSS tradecraft—short duration VoIP, staggered interval comms

Endpoint Movement: Toronto → Istanbul, last six months

Comms Linkage: DCSA compliance officer, Tier-2 clearance

"We've confirmed the pattern matches the MSS consular routework we saw in 2021," Sara said. "And the alias 'Joseph Lin' is a legacy shell. Shows up in shell company layers flagged by NSA and Treasury—Yǒuquán Holdings, front for at least three intelligence transfers out of Vancouver and Macao."

Will gave a curt nod. "So we have the handler."

"Yeah," Guy added, "but we don't have the one taking the handler's calls. Not for certain."

Sara leaned back, eyes on the screen. "How confident are we that it's the compliance officer?"

"Eighty-six percent match based on SYBIL's pattern crosslink," Sara replied. "But we don't have definitive attribution—no physical meet, no cash trail, no burner activation. The smart ones never use a single point of failure."

Will looked to Guy. "We can't burn an innocent man. And if it's not him, we spook the real one."

Guy stepped forward. "We tighten the circle. We don't confront—we constrain."

Will arched a brow. "Walk me through it."

Guy turned to the board. "We build a digital bottleneck. Use the alias 'Lin' again—leak a slightly modified file to just six mid-clearance users including the compliance officer. The bait is a restricted access alert, routed through a side-channel. Looks accidental, looks juicy."

"And if our guy bites?" Sara asked.

"We set passive flags," Sara said. "We won't catch him pulling it—we'll catch the beacon it activates."

Will looked thoughtful. "A canary trap. Old school. Different versions to multiple suspects. Subtle variations to trace the source of a leak by identifying which version was compromised."

"Modified," Guy said. "Digital canary plus SYBIL tagging—metadata residue baked into the file. No one sees it, but the moment it's mirrored, we get a time, a path, and a new behavioral vector."

Will stood silent, then nodded.

"Let's do it. Cathy builds the doc. Rick and SYBIL seed the trail. Sara—choose your six with care. I want cross-agency, cross-department, and enough white noise to keep it credible."

Sara added, "And what if we catch someone other than the compliance officer?"

Will gave a grim smile. "We update our threat profile."

He tapped the table twice with his knuckle.

"We're not just chasing a traitor. We're baiting one."

Fort Meade – Watchtower Ops Cell – 1345 Hours

Cathy hunched over her terminal, two monitors glowing with classified template files. On one, she duplicated a real presentation deck from IronNest Technology Group—the company fronting the Plattsburgh decoy quantum comms site. On the second screen, she introduced subtle alterations.

She murmured aloud as she worked. "Three genuine graphs. One plausible lie. Just enough signal to look leaked... just enough poison to matter."

She changed the title:

> DISTRIBUTION RESTRICTED – Q-DEF SATCOM Overlay: Phase 2

Then inserted a fake acronym: SINEGATE – Signal-Nested Encryption for Geo-Adaptive Transmission Environments.

"SYBIL," she said, "highlight falsified segments in green overlay, archive real structure in blue for reference."

SYBIL:

> *"Working. Confirmation: structure integrity preserved. Falsified indicators embedded in visual layer metadata."*

Cathy added a dummy author name—"K. Liddell, DARPA Liaison, Signal Architecture"—then embedded access logs from a supposed Q-cleared system on the West Coast. She gave it just enough cred to trip interest, but too irregular to trigger formal reporting.

She saved the file to a secure shared node accessible to six handpicked mid-tier staffers, including the suspected compliance officer.

Filename: IronNest_P2_SINEGATE_Alert.pdf

Tagline: "FLAGGED – For Strategic Tech Assessment Clearance Review"

She pinged the file over to Rick.

"Your turn to make it radioactive." Said Cathy.

Fort Meade-Watchtower Ops Metadata Tagging 1410 Hours R

Rick received the decoy doc and loaded it into a forensic sandbox. The room lights dimmed as SYBIL's node interface adjusted for code-level injection.

"Injecting triple-layer pattern tag...

Layer One: Hash alteration, 17-character deviation to flag duplication.

Layer Two: Metadata mimicry embedded in page transitions.

Layer Three: Recursive signal echo—silent beacon, unique to file structure, be copied clean."

SYBIL: "Propagation tracer installed. Silent echo active. Pattern will replicate on forward transmission, including encrypted containers."

Rick smiled. "Good girl."

He opened a command window and injected a unique tag signature:

Tag ID: RS-9e21fc74a–watchtrail

Fingerprint: Nonlinear data compression bounce pattern

Payload: 23-byte replication vector, echoes to SYBIL node once handled

"SYBIL, begin passive monitoring of all six nodes starting... now."

SYBIL: "Monitoring active. Four of six accounts accessed file header. No duplication detected. Tracker armed."

Rick stood and stretched. "Time to see if curiosity kills the mole."

Rick stayed at the console after Cathy left.

Six nodes. Four had already touched the file header. He set up a side window the way he used to set up a side bet, one column per node, timestamps in the left margin. Not because SYBIL needed it. Because he did.

The casino floor in Atlantic City had taught him this exact posture. You watched the table you were working and you watched the three around it, and the second your attention narrowed to one you started losing money. Peripheral was the whole game.

He pulled a strip of beef jerky out of the drawer and tore it with his teeth.

Node four moved first. He saw it before SYBIL flagged it — half a second, maybe less, the kind of margin that didn't matter unless you'd spent a decade training your eyes to catch it.

He chewed slowly and waited for the system to catch up.

——

Fort Meade – Watchtower Operation – 0318 Hours

The room was dark, except for the soft blue hum of SYBIL's live diagnostic interface. Rick had gone home. Cathy was sleeping on a cot in the corner.

SYBIL's voice cracked through the stillness—flat, clinical, unstoppable.

SYBIL:

"Anomaly detected.

Tag RS-9e21fc74a has replicated.

Forward vector established: Node 4 – Internal Clearance Path AC-22237."

The screen lit up, revealing a mirrored copy of the decoy file. But the original metadata signature had fragmented—duplicated across a mobile container.

SYBIL:

"Secondary hop initiated. Obfuscated shell routing detected.

Origin match: suspect node traced to Q4 compliance terminal.

Final echo confirms: traitor active."

By the time Will and Sara arrived twenty minutes later, Guy Zarelli was already reviewing the digital trail. Cathy slid into her chair, eyes wide.

Cathy said, "That's our guy. Same terminal. Same timing pattern. He took the bait."

"It's not just bait. It's a breadcrumb trail now." Replied Guy.

Will folded his arms and nodded. "Follow it."

SYBIL:

"Exfil path incomplete. Awaiting outbound relay."

——

Istanbul – Secure Apartment, 0831 Hours Charlie

A narrow shaft of sunlight leaked through old Venetian blinds in a quiet apartment overlooking the Bosphorus.

The man known as Joseph Lin sat in silence before a retrofitted laptop, its screen flickering with cascading blocks of scrambled data. He wore reading glasses—unnecessary, but helpful for disguises.

He read the silent alert:

[NODE ECHO: INJECT RECEIVED. CONTENT FWD-SAFE. REPLY ROUTE ACTIVE.]

His fingers hovered over the keyboard for only a second before opening a virtual network interface—a custom MSS transmission relay with a three-minute open window.

He selected the response payload:

ACK: ITEM RECEIVED. CONTINUE SIGNALING THROUGH AUTH VECTOR. ID CONFIRMED.

Below it, a new instruction line:

REQUEST: VERIFY ACCESS TO VECTOR SITES IDENTIFIED AS HORIZON, TRITON, and WHITE

Lin pressed send.

The signal vanished into encrypted ether, headed for someone embedded within U.S. systems—someone now fully activated.

Fort Meade-Watchtower Secure Briefing Room 0730 Hours R

The door locked with a solid mechanical thunk. Will Morgan stepped inside, coffee in hand, trailed by Sara Brandt and Guy Zarelli. Gussie Brindisi was already at the head of the table, scrolling through SYBIL's trace overlay.

"He accessed the file at 0314, local. Four minutes later, we got a replication ping in the diagnostic shell. SYBIL confirmed a layered export through an encrypted air gap—burner drive only."

She flipped the screen. The name lit up in red.

NAME: Samuel Cardenas

Position: Compliance Oversight Liaison – DCSA Contract Security Division

Clearance: Tier 3 / SCI Peripheral

Will's jaw tightened. "He's got access to all six decoy projects through his site audit files. Just enough to flag them as real, but not enough to know they're bait."

"Which is what makes him dangerous," said Sara, "The MSS won't know they've been misled—yet."

Guy nodded. "He doesn't even know what he's giving them. That makes it clean."

Gussie added, "And expendable."

Will leaned over the table, his voice flat. "Okay. We can't detain him here. He hasn't tripped legal thresholds, not yet. But we can freeze him."

He turned to Guy. "Flag him for an in-person audit. Gently escalate a reporting discrepancy—something that pulls him off the net. We give him thirty-six hours to sweat."

Guy said, "Meanwhile we plant passive audio in his home and pull his last six weeks of burner metadata. NSA's already backstopped the phone that bounced off Istanbul."

"If he reaches out again, we get confirmation," said Sara, "If he doesn't, he burns himself trying to cover it up."

Gussie said, "One more thing—he's scheduled to visit Whitecap Systems next week for a mock recert."

Will looked up sharply. "We intercept that meeting. He'll try to verify if the leak led to consequences. That's our squeeze point."

He stood, eyes narrowed. "No early arrests. No spooks with windbreakers. We catch him trying to climb back in. And we leave the door cracked just enough... to follow him out.

CHAPTER THIRTY-ONE

Floating Box

Washington, D.C.–Dupont Circle 1812 Hours R

The afternoon rush hour was thinning, streetlights just starting to glow. Cardenas stepped out of a nondescript office building on New Hampshire Avenue, a canvas messenger bag slung over one shoulder. He wore khakis, a navy windbreaker, and aviator sunglasses—classic mid-grade civilian contractor.

But five ACIC agents were already in place. The floating-box formation surrounded him—vehicles ahead, behind, and across the intersections. They never followed directly. They floated, like ghosts.

"Box Lead, this is Echo 1. He's headed east on Q Street, walking fast."

"Copy. Echo 1 in position at 21st."

"Echo 2 set at Massachusetts."

From a silver Subaru a block away, Agent Cecil Brandon adjusted the IR lens on his custom dash-cam. A tablet screen showed a live facial index—Cardenas's profile pulsing green as SYBIL revalidated the scan every five seconds.

Cecil muttered, "No wiggles. Pulse steady. No sign he knows he's boxed."

Inside a parked food truck posing as "DC Falafel Joint," Agent Andrea Velasquez (Echo 3) sipped tea and tapped on a secure laptop.

Echo 3 said, "He pinged off two cell towers in the last six minutes. No encrypted apps open. Watching podcast clips. Junk data stream."

Echo 3 scrolled through the secondary tab — Cardenas's HR file, pulled an hour earlier under expedited authority. Passed over for GS-14 twice. Performance reviews clean but unremarkable. A formal complaint filed two years back about a contractor — Booz Allen, six-figure billable — getting the lead on an audit Cardenas had built the framework for. Complaint went nowhere.

Echo 3, "He's been carrying water for people who out-earn him three to one. Watched his complaint die in HR. That's the door MSS walks through every time."

Cecil: "Money?"

Echo 3: "Not primarily. Bank records are clean. This is a man who thinks he was robbed of a career. They told him he matters. That's all it takes."

From the rooftop of an adjacent brownstone, sniper-trained observer Callen Briggs (Echo 4) watched through a telephoto lens.

Echo 4 reported, "Contact approaching 22nd. He's checking windows now—habitual. Not paranoid yet. Hand's twitchy near the bag."

Cardenas entered a small Lebanese café, glanced around, and took a seat by the window. The team gave it a beat—a decoy patron entered three minutes later. Cardenas ordered coffee, typed briefly on his phone, and looked up every twenty seconds.

Cecil said, "Watch his fingers. If he starts typing in a chat window, I want timestamps, characters, compression pattern. SYBIL can match the echo."

Echo 3 said, "Copy. SYBIL's hot on packet sniff."

Outside, Agent Briggs adjusted his scope.

Echo 4 said, "Still alone. No meets. But I'd bet good bourbon he's waiting."

The tension was coiled. The team didn't need him to move. They needed him to signal. Or better—receive one.

Then Andrea's screen lit up.

Echo 3 alerted, "Heads up. Phone just pinged a dormant packet relay—IP out of Brno, Czech Republic. 2 seconds later, the phone ran a decoy app: 'Transit Schedules.'"

Cecil said, "And that, my friends, is a drop signal."

Echo 4 said, "Someone's watching their boy."

Cecil keyed his radio.

Cecil said "Lock him in the box. We don't spook him, we don't squeeze him. We watch. The real asset's about to step into view."

Rick monitoring on SYBIL Rick came over comms, "He just pinged Brno. The Czech Republic. Because nothing screams 'I'm not a spy' like routing through 2009."

Foggy Bottom – Just Off 22nd Street – Late Afternoon

The café's door shut behind Cardenas with a whisper of hydraulics and the scent of espresso still clinging to his coat. The clatter of M Street traffic carried over the brick buildings—buses groaning at stoplights, the distant wail of a siren threading down K Street like a warning.

He turned onto 22nd and cut east—past shuttered art galleries and boutique law offices whose names were etched in brass. This part of D.C. didn't shout its secrets. It whispered them.

Three blocks south, just off I Street, a narrow alley opened between a shuttered framing shop and a dry cleaner's. At its end, tucked under a soot-streaked cornice and half-hidden by creeping ivy, was a black awning stamped with fading silver script:

Adams Morgan Back Room, Books & Relics

Rare. Obscure. Not for the general public.

Cardenas paused, checking the alley's mouth behind him. The sidewalk was empty except for a dog walker and a cyclist fiddling with a lock. Still, his hand stayed close to the inside pocket of his coat.

He approached the door and knocked—not on the wood, but the brass inlay just below the handle. Three short, two long. A code. A tradition.

The door unlocked with a soft mechanical click. No one answered.

He stepped inside.

The secondhand bookstore smelled of incense and mildew. A cracked sign above the window read: closed. It was 6 pm unofficially, still very much in operation.

Cardenas hesitated outside the second door, glanced around casually, and knocked twice, then once—pausing between. The same pattern he'd used before.

A buzzer sounded. The deadbolt clicked.

Inside, the lights were dim. A battered globe sat beside an old card catalog. The man behind the counter was not the usual handler.

This man was Agent Micah Trask, dressed in vintage corduroy, with precisely mismatched spectacles. His posture was wrong for retail—too square, too watchful. He didn't smile.

Trask said, "You're late."

Cardenas stiffened but covered it quickly. "Metro stalled. Purple Line construction."

Trask (gesturing): "Back room."

He led him through a false wall between sagging shelves and into a quiet study space, supposedly for rare manuscript review. But a hidden ceiling mic and micro-cameras were already recording every movement. SYBIL was transcribing in real time from Fort Meade.

Cardenas sat. “The asset... vector access confirmed. Horizon, Whitecap, and Triton are warm. Silvershore needs deeper scrape. We’re waiting on a DCSA vector there.”

Trask asked, “Details?”

Cardenas replied, “Horizon has a new comms shell. They’re pushing updates using off-the-books fiber. It’s not on standard DARPA backhaul, so I flagged it.”

Trask nodded once, letting the silence hang. “You ever met Chimera?”

Trask let the silence sit. "Why are you still doing this?"

Cardenas's mouth tightened. The question was old between them, a checksum, asked every meet.

"Because the people who built this country sold it to the highest bidder thirty years ago," he said. "And I'm done being the one who files the paperwork while they cash the check."

Trask nodded once. The phrasing matched the file.

Cardenas blinked. The name wasn’t supposed to be said out loud. “Only proxies. Voice once. Through the training layer.”

“What did she say?”

“She said—‘Obedience is an illusion. We calibrate for disruption.’”

That was it. The code. SYBIL’s alert went live.

SYBIL: MATCH CONFIRMED – SIGNAL VECTOR ACTIVE. ENCRYPTED PROTOCOL OPEN.

Back at Fort Meade, Will watched the screen with Sara, Cathy, and Guy Zarelli. The digital signature blinked green. Cardenas was now fully tagged.

Will said, “We let him walk. He takes the infection home. That’s how we ride the pattern.”

Sara nodded. “And if Chimera’s watching—she just entered the trap.”

Arlington, Virginia – Cardenas’s Apartment – 2113 Hours

Samuel Cardenas stepped into his modest apartment just off Columbia Pike, locked the door behind him, and dropped his keys in the dish by the door.

His shades came off. The quiet hum of a nearby air purifier filled the room.

SYBIL DIAGNOSTIC LOG – WATCHTOWER NODE 004

SIGNAL HANDSHAKE CONFIRMED

NODE VECTOR STATUS: LIVE

PROTOCOL CHRYSALIS VARIANT A2.3 FOUND

PASSIVE ECHO TAG REPLICATING...

REPLICATION PATHWAY INITIATED

In the background, a simple network switch blinked its green LEDs. A small Lenovo laptop sat closed on the kitchen table. Cardenas opened it, waking it from sleep.

SCREEN: "Welcome, Samuel."

Last Sync: 6 minutes ago.

He didn't notice the subtle distortion in the sync process. He didn't notice the slight delay in his virtual machine's load time.

But SYBIL did.

Fort Meade–Watchtower Operations

Rick Huang leaned forward as his custom analytics interface lit up.

Rick said, "Replication confirmed. We're inside his exfil pipe."

Sara, standing beside Will, read the stream with practiced eyes. "And it's self-reinforcing. Each ping he sends—each heartbeat—rides SYBIL's tag with it."

Rick pointed to a new signature blooming on the secondary monitor. "We've got movement. The tag just hit a second node. East Coast, looks like a proxy server obfuscated through Quebec—likely one of Chrysalis's handoff points."

Guy Zarelli said, "That's fast."

"No. That's vulnerable. They think they're inside our walls." Will said, " They never planned for us to be inside theirs."

Back at Cardenas's apartment, the man himself scrolled through what he believed were harmless OSINT aggregates. He fired off a sanitized metadata packet through his exfil console—automated, compressed, and embedded with invisible Chrysalis signature markers.

Unbeknownst to him, that very action confirmed the live trace.

Will exhaled slowly. "And now we let SYBIL map the entire shadow network."

——

Fort Meade–Watchtower Ops 2122 Hours R

The walls of the Watchtower operations glowed in low blue light, broken only by the steady flicker of terminal screens and the quiet murmur of processing fans. In the center, a 12-foot display screen showed SYBIL's live trace—an abstract neural map pulsing like an ECG across the digital void.

SYBIL ALERT — TRACE INITIATED

Origin: ARL-105.9 (Cardenas)

Secondary Node Found: 185.47.XX.XXX [Rotterdam, Netherlands]

Subnet Cluster: ORCHID-MIRROR

Replication Status: Expanding

Rick Huang slid his chair sideways across the console bank, pulling up a 3D topology model. "SYBIL's riding the beacon through ghost nodes—server shells set up for Chrysalis's internal comms. Each one is a false front, but the routing tables are real. She's mapping the trails. That's Rotterdam... next stop could be Bucharest, maybe Tblisi."

"Are we inside or just following?" asked Will.

"Inside. Not deep yet—but we've got keystroke drift, input buffering, even shadow DNS calls." replied Rick, "They're not clean."

SYBIL's display showed a branching architecture: red pulses for confirmed Chrysalis hosts, yellow for suspected proxies, and green for newly infected nodes. It looked like a growing nervous system—recursive, redundant, but now compromised.

Guy Zarelli reading out loud, "Glasshouse. That's been in two SCRs flagged as dark-hat servers with no clear owner."

Sara said, "Chimera-root. She's in there."

Will stepped closer to the screen. The words felt like prophecy. "SYBIL's inside the machine. Now we don't chase Chimera... we watch her move."

Rick said, "We'll have the whole Chrysalis backbone by dawn... unless she sees it first."

Fort Meade – SYBIL Operations Core – 0045 Hours

The operations floor had quieted to a low hum of focus. Coffee cups sat abandoned beside consoles. Soft clacks of keys punctuated the silence. On the wall display, SYBIL's network map had evolved—no longer a branching tree, but a latticework of obfuscated pathways, self-erasing links, and quantum key-rotors—what Rick had once called "paranoid architecture."

But SYBIL was built for paranoia.

Cathy Wang, seated at the east terminal, leaned toward the screen. "SYBIL caught their recursion countermeasure. They seeded a logic bomb in one of the deeper comms tunnels. Classic zero-trace backburner protocol."

Guy asked, "It didn't trigger?"

Rick said, “SYBIL forked the tag and burned the loop in simulation. She absorbed it like a vaccine.”

Will stood behind them, hands folded. “She’s not just tracing. She’s learning them.”

Cathy glanced over. "You called the recursion trap before SYBIL flagged it. How?"

Rick didn't look up from his terminal. "Same way you call the next card in a six-deck shoe. You watch what's already been played, you count what's left, you bet the math."

A beat.

Cathy asked, "You counted cards?"

"Allegedly."

Sara, passing behind them with her coffee, didn't break stride. "He's been escorted out of three casinos on two continents. Don't get him started."

Rick: "Two casinos. The third was a misunderstanding."

On the screen, the lattice map folded inward. Three nodes pulsed blue—verified command-and-control layers. One of them labeled:

CHIMERA-ROOT [Narrowband Quantum Uplink - Passive Awaiting Trigger]

SYBIL ASSESSMENT: [CHIMERA-ROOT] houses rotating encryption schedule. Physical disconnect suspected. Awaiting external packet pull.

Rick turned. “She’s got Chimera’s command node. It’s cold, but it’s real. This is the first hard target we’ve seen in her uplink layer.”

Cathy asked, "How do you keep guessing the right node?"

"Card counting. Different deck, same math."

Cathy stared. Rick shrugged. "Long story."

Sara, passing through: "Short story he's unwilling to tell."

Cathy said, “Also, we found an admin shell—‘Fenwick’—isolated, but tagged. We think he’s her top human relay.”

“Can we move on him?” asked Will.

“No way to physically locate him yet. His packets come from looped darknets. But he just became the golden thread.”

As dawn edged over the horizon, SYBIL continued her silent work.

SYBIL ALERT – 0521 Hours:

NODE 44 – CORSICA – IDENTIFIED AS C2 REFLECTOR

NODE 46 – DAR ES SALAAM – SINK NODE FOR INFECTED SCRs

TOTAL CHRYSALIS NODE ESTIMATE: 71

Sara entered with fresh coffee, scanning the display. “How many have we found?”

Rick answered, “Over half. And three of their mirror nodes. We have their architecture, Will. We’re inside.”

Will looked up at the map glowing across the ops floor. “Now we start building the kill chain.”

CHAPTER THIRTY-TWO

Chrysalis Takedown

Fort Meade-Watchtower Conference Room 0730 Hours R

The lights were dimmed. A 3D holomap shimmered above the conference table, casting soft azure and crimson glows onto the gathered faces.

SYBIL's latest overlay rotated slowly—an evolving mesh of Chrysalis network nodes, each pulsing with heat-sig intelligence. Blue marked known contact points. Yellow indicated tagged nodes. Red... was still active command infrastructure.

Will stood at the head of the table, flanked by Sara, Guy Zarelli, Rick Huang, and Cathy Wang. Thomas Carrone leaned against the wall, arms crossed.

Will said, "We've cracked their architecture. Not all of it—but enough. SYBIL confirms 71 active nodes, three confirmed command mirrors, and one root cold node labeled CHIMERA-ROOT. That's our zero point."

He pointed to a glowing node just offshore near Cyprus—Node 28.

"First, we isolate the relay sinks. These are their log buffers—places where data slows before moving upstream. We'll kill those first. Hit them fast, burn their logs, leave nothing to backtrace."

Rick asked, "You're thinking vector churn? Break their relay tempo, force overcorrection upstream?"

"Yes. Every relay they lose forces them to reroute traffic faster than they can verify node integrity. They'll expose vulnerabilities just trying to stay afloat."

Rick said, "SYBIL's already modeled six likely choke routes once Nodes 11, 14, and 28 go dark."

Rick brought up a subpanel. "These three—Corsica, Tbilisi, Kuala Lumpur—they're fragment-mirroring external signal vectors. Hit those at the same time and Chimera's going to feel it in her optic nerve."

Sara leaned forward, arms on the table. "We have one chance to hit hard before she disappears again. The second we start burning her scaffolding, she'll go underground. That's why we need concurrent action—not cascade."

"And we need human plays too.: said Rick, "`Several of these nodes are managed by assets. People. We tag them, interrogate where we can, ghost where we can't."

Will added, ""Node 44 is an NSA target. Sloane Merrick's already queuing for the malware injection. Thomas?"

Carrone stepped forward. "We're putting Navarro 's channel on ice after this phase. He's too hot. The moment Chimera senses node collapse; she'll check her variables. We make sure he doesn't flinch."

"What about CHIMERA-ROOT?" asked Sara.

Everyone turned toward Will. "That node is disconnected. Cold. But it's tagged. And when it wakes up—when they try to re-centralize—we ride the signal home."

The SYBIL display zoomed in on the root node's last known quantum uplink. A message blinked below it:

PASSIVE STATUS CONFIRMED. NO EXFIL SEQUENCE DETECTED.

TAGGING RESIDUE: STABLE.

"So, we wait." Said Guy.

"We wait. And when they come back online..." Sara said flatly, "We erase them."

CHAPTER THIRTY-THREE

If you hear the gunshot...

If you hear the gunshot it wasn't meant for you.

Various Countries 0500 Hours R

In five countries over three continents a highly coordinated take-down unfolded involving seven state agencies. Precise timing was critical over the eleven time zones, but these agencies were highly professional, and it came off without a hitch.

NODE 11 — Tbilisi, Georgia 0107 Hours Delta

Operation Name: SCORPION BRIDGE

Location: Abandoned Soviet-era health spa in the hills above Mtatsminda

Projected thermal overlays flicker across the stone walls of a safe house basement. Will Morgan, flanked by Cecil Brandon and Lt. Col. Breck Langston of the Joint Special Operations Command (JSOC), reviews the structure's layout.

Cecil Brandon said, "Three data points—one uplink node, two short-range mesh routers. They're not broadcasting. This is a vetting platform."

Breck Langston added, "And guarded. Georgian SSSG intercepted a coded traffic burst—shortwave spectrum. Likely a failsafe."

Will Morgan nods. "We hit it hard. We don't give them time to burn the archive."

The abandoned rusted health spa sits like a relic of empire—decaying murals, shattered balconies, and vines curling over radiation signs from a defunct boiler room.

Three black-out SUVs idle behind trees. Field officers of the Georgian state intelligence agency (SSSG) prepare breaching charges on a side annex while ACIC team members deploy jammers and facial capture arrays.

Drone footage shows a sentry smoking on the second-floor balcony.

SSSG Officer (in earpiece): "Visual confirmed. Primary server chamber believed to be in sub-basement. Infrared shows movement—two awake, others sleeping."

Moments later a muffled detonation on the west wall shakes dust loose. Flashbangs roll across the tiled floor of the sub-basement, stunning two Chrysalis operatives seated at consoles. One dives for a magnetic drive, but Cecil Brandon enters fast behind the breach team and draws down.

Cecil says, "Don't even think about it."

Breck Langston, behind him, isolates the central rack:

"It's encrypted but not volatile. This node was listening—not transmitting. It's a filter node."

One of the detainees—a young man, Sergo Gvishiani—blinks rapidly, trying to track everyone's movements. Cecil scans his face and gets a soft SYBIL ping.

Cecil said, "We've seen him before. Istanbul vector leak, three years ago. He's a repeater."

In the control room minutes later, An American JSOC tech pulls thermal shielding off a concealed cabinet behind a false panel. Inside is a data vault of high-frequency optical plates—a type of storage used for non-clouded identity tokening.

SYBIL (remote voice-over): "Passive echo node. Operative pattern references confirmed: Nodes 28 and 61. No central directive ID. Possibly receiving from autonomous handler."

With the dawn fighting with the darkness for attention, Sergo is zip-cuffed and led down cracked spa balcony marble steps. A Georgian officer lights a cigarette and leans toward Will.

Georgian officer in accented English said, "Your American ghost network... this is only the skin."

Will responded, "We're cutting deeper."

NODE 14-Corsica, France 0252 Hours Bravo

Operation Name: BLACK SALT

Location: Abandoned satellite tracking station, coastal ridgeline west of Sartène

Rain slashes the windows of a converted farmhouse nestled in the hills, a covert staging house, French DGSI field commander Capitaine Élodie Charvet stands at a weathered table covered in printed blueprints and SYBIL's node map. Direction Générale de la Sécurité Intérieure is the French General Directorate for Internal Security.

Charvet (in French): "Intel says they still think the uplink is operational. Their relay pulses at irregular intervals—an adaptive pattern. They're hiding from someone. Maybe us."

Behind her, a two-person NSA SIGINT team, embedded under diplomatic cover, confirms that the Corsican node acts as a packet manipulator, rerouting, and re-sequencing downstream data for Chrysalis vector pathways.

NSA TECH (to Charvet):"This is a repeater hub. No local command structure. But there are people—someone's tending the stack."

DGSI operators move under the cover of coastal fog, slipping through brush and rockfall. The satellite station is a rusting steel monolith from the Cold War, topped with two inoperative dish arrays and encircled by downed fencing.

A ground team splits: One pair circles east to block escape routes while another inserts a passive fiber disruptor through an underground telecom tunnel.

The rain conceals their thermal signature.

Inside, at the basement server bay, a lone Chrysalis operative named Hristo Valev, ex-Bulgarian signals officer turned freelance systems cleaner, taps out hex code beside a glowing cooling tower.

As SYBIL's latent tagging residue surges the uplink, his console flashes:

"NODE 61 COMPROMISED // INITIATE MANUAL BURN"

Valev reaches for a vial taped under the desk.

Too slow.

The trapdoor to the maintenance corridor blasts open. Charvet herself leads the takedown.

CHARVET (in Corsican French): "Step away from the node. Hands where we can see them."

He lunges. Two suppressor bursts to the leg drop him fast. Agents swarm.

A black transport chopper lands on the cracked helipad as Valev, now zip-tied and conscious, is hauled aboard. His encrypted laptop, stuffed into a waterproof sleeve, contains relay logs from five downstream Chrysalis mirrors, including a defunct signal path to Brazil.

After the breach SYBIL's remote payloads begin cleaning and cloning the node's internal logs. Heat-mapping shows recent human presence—meaning others had been there, or are planning to return.

SYBIL (V.O., filtered): "Node 14: compromise complete. Signature artifacts mirror Tbilisi. Relay patterns matched. Tracking forward propagation."

NODE 28 — Kuala Lumpur, Malaysia 0120 Hours Hotel

Operation Name: LANTERN TRACE

Location: Upper floors of a high-rise co-working space in Bukit Bintang

The U. E. Embassy Joint Ops Center was a tight room lit by muted monitors. Members of the U.S. Regional Security Office (RSO) coordinate with Malaysian Special Branch (SB) and NSA TOS Supervisor Sloane Merrick via secured relay. A SYBIL diagnostic runs silently across one screen, revealing unusual outbound traffic from a known Chrysalis signature cluster—buried within anonymized freelancer traffic.

Sloane to SB commander: "The node's embedded in a mesh of gig economy shell startups. Data laundering. Your guys go in first—we follow with the claw."

She taps a screen.

Target: Floor 43 – ApexWorks Ventures.

What looks like a small logistics startup is a front for Chrysalis uplink segmentation and vector identity obfuscation.

Bukit Bintang High Rise 0150 Hours Hotel

The building looms above neon streets and noodle stalls still busy past midnight. Two Malaysian plainclothes officers block the service lift at ground level. Upstairs, a Special Branch insertion team prepares for breach—guided by SYBIL heat map feeds patched through NSA surveillance balloons orbiting the KL metro grid.

Inside the forty-third floor Apexworks darkened office, three Chrysalis assets are awake. One—Adilah Tan, a Malaysian AI engineer turned activist—types into a narrow console. A message flashes across the glassy black monitor: "Node 11, 14 breached. Manual lockdown pending. Shift pattern."

The words flicker and vanish.

A second asset, Willem Graaf, ex-Dutch military signals tech, watches a secure uplink to a fiber router blink red. He picks up a burner phone—doesn't dial.

Then: CRACK.

The entry door is blown inward with a fluid breaching charge.

Malaysian SB storm the room, shouting in Malay. One Chrysalis operator throws himself at a hard drive rig. He's intercepted mid-air by a kinetic takedown and restrained.

SB Officer to FFICER to Graaf: "Hands behind your head! Sekarang!"

Moments later NSA techs in full gear arrive via secured stairwell. From the server cage they extract three encrypted SSDs and a quantum-resistant authentication dongle logged into a sandboxed experimental OS—unknown origin.

Sloane Merrick's voice crackles in via sat relay: "We've got uplink schedules—targeting Brazil, Istanbul, and an unused DNS tunnel pointed at upstate New York. SYBIL's tagging signal propagating."

Fifteen minutes later helicopters hover above, lights off. It lands on the rooftop and three captured operatives—Tan, Graaf, and a third silent figure with no ID—are bagged and boarded for rendition under joint U.S.-Malaysian custody.

A hardcase of evidence is sealed with a triple sig chain. Graaf looks up and mutters in Dutch: "You don't get it. We don't recruit. We recurse."

Embassy Ops Center – SYBIL Feed – 0250 Hours Hotel

Node 28 dissolves into the network map, tagged and neutralized. New branches light up on the screen like veins—an outbound route to Lisbon and a dormant circuit tagged "Fenwick."

SYBIL (automated whisper): "Node 28 down. Vector integrity compromised. Residual signals infected."

NODE 44 — São Paulo, Brazil 0812 Hours Papa

Operation Name: VIOLET VEIL

Location: Abandoned telecommunications substation repurposed as a tech repair warehouse, outskirts of Vila Leopoldina

Fort Meade — Watchtower Ops Conference Room

Will Morgan stands at the operations board, flanked by Sara Brandt and Guy Zarelli. A blown-up image of the São Paulo substation flickers onscreen—thermal overlays from SYBIL, revealing routine heat signatures in the midnight hours despite being off-grid.

Will said, "They're using the site as a clean lab for obfuscated storage and identity re-spoofing. Node 44 is a regenerator—scrubs opsec trails and assigns new operational metadata."

Guy said, "If it's a regen node, it's probably also a catch basin—reused identities, safe zone signals. Capture here might expose half the network's foot traffic."

They greenlight joint action with Brazil's ABIN (Agência Brasileira de Inteligência) and GRU's COT (Comando de Operações Táticas) for breach and rendition.

The Vila Leopoldina substation building squats behind razor wire and graffiti-tagged fencing, its antenna mast long stripped. Three security lights glow dimly, masking the infrared-coded transmission system SYBIL first picked up.

Inside the tech bay. Aline Vilar, ex-cybersecurity expert turned Chrysalis logistics node coordinator, packs an encrypted Pelican case. She's assisted by "Mateus" a former telco engineer who thinks he's working freelance airgap data repair jobs.

A third figure—tall, silent, and masked—is monitoring uplink spikes. A suspected Chrysalis senior operative.

SCREEN: "Node 28 flagged. Reset ID pool now. SYBIL anomaly suspected."

Then: Four EMP microbursts go off around the building's perimeter—standard protocol to disrupt exfil equipment and deep-sleep countermeasures.

Seconds later, COT operators in full tactical gear breach two access points simultaneously.

COT Commander in Portuguese: "Segurança nacional! Deite no chão agora!"

Mateus goes rigid. Aline drops her bag and runs, but is brought down in a clean intercept maneuver by a COT agent using a magnetic capture net.

The masked figure? Gone.

Moments later in the upper loft NSA agents, arriving under joint cover, sweep the loft and find the regen racks—five microservers loaded with repurposed ID data, scrubbed MAC addresses, and burner biometric templates.

SYBIL has already seeded these systems via airborne signal contagion.

SYBIL (V.O., faintly filtered): "Replication achieved. Regeneration matrix now deterministic. Locating signature collisions."

Lead agent peers at a grid of pseudo IDs—dozens mapped to known regions, including DC, Berlin, Tel Aviv, and Seoul.

Sara turned to Guy and said, "This...when they call home... we'll be listening."

NODE 61 — Prague, Czech Republic — 0248 Hours Bravo

Operation Name: GLASS WOLF Basement archives beneath a defunct language institute in Malá Strana.

U.S. Embassy, Prague – Joint Field Briefing Room

Two walls of screens show architectural scans of a centuries-old building across the Vltava. SYBIL's diagnostics highlight thermal irregularities, inconsistent signal decay, and a mirrored file transfer loop pinging off Reykjavik and Singapore.

U.S. liaison officer: "It's quiet, low-frequency, high-value. Our partners at Bezpečnostní informační služba (BIS) confirm no official Czech registration for the sublease."

Remoting in from Fort Meade, Guy Zarelli, reviewing Chrysalis fragment packets, frowns.

"They're not transmitting. They're validating. This node doesn't speak—it listens."

Sara Brandt nods, catching on. "It's a passive trust node. Probably runs vetting models for field assets. That makes it... command-adjacent."

Will Morgan said, "Then we take it intact."

Malá Strana, Prague

The picturesque district is cloaked in fog. Narrow cobblestone streets. Yellow lamps glowing like ghosts. A joint ACIC-BIS surveillance team moves in stealth—plainclothes, with neural comms.

Two blocks over, SYBIL tracks a data ping from an anonymous Czech VPN — and instantly flags a behavioral signature match: "Operative Fenwick: observed cadence drift."

Inside the building, Node 61 is live.

In the basement archive David Kubek, a Czech-born systems linguist and Chrysalis operative, operated alone. He sat at a micro-console surrounded by archived volumes and silent fan units—some of them fakes, housing encrypted storage arrays.

SYBIL began a latency mirroring exploit, simulating Chrysalis-paired authentication requests. Kubek stared at the prompts, confused. The sequences were all valid—but they didn't conform.

He grabbed a red key and reached toward the wipe button—

A whispered voice (filtered through ceiling vent): "That would be a mistake."

From above, the BIS commander spoke through a surveillance drone mic. At the same time, an electromagnetic restraint round fires from the shadows, striking Kubek's console and frying the control port.

The BIS moved in, guns drawn.

Kubek froze, blinking. He nodded once—acknowledging he's been outplayed.

Kubek said, "You're not supposed to see us. We're the ones who vet your ghosts."

Moments later the team uncovered a black glass array—multi-surface reflective boards containing quantum-originated cryptographic seeds, used to "burn" vector IDs onto new Chrysalis assets through visual contact or auditory imprint.

SYBIL immediately began to map seed overlaps, revealing links to Node 11 (Tbilisi), Node 44 (São Paulo), and Node 7 (Bucharest).

SYBIL (V.O.): "Passive seed node. Vector crossover detected. Contagion protocol initiated."

EXT. CHARLES BRIDGE – NIGHT

As Kubek is led away under cover, a soft mist drapes the river.

From Charles bridge a distance away, a lone watcher — possibly Chimera herself — stood just beyond camera range. Her silhouette merged with the shadows. She vanished before a drone could pivot to track her heat signature.

Watchtower Ops – Live Coordination – Night

Will, Sara, and Guy oversee the whole board. One by one, red nodes ex on SYBIL's tactical display.

SYBIL: "58% of identified relay nodes disabled. Tagging residues replicating at 93% projected efficacy."

——

Finishing the job

Fort Meade-Watchtower Conference Room 1015 Hours R

Will Morgan said, 'We've taken down nodes. We've captured cells. But the signal keeps regenerating. Like it's... self-healing."

Sloane Merrick said, "It is. Recursive systems don't depend on structure. They depend on behavior. On activation logic. On trust."

She tapped the glass. A cluster of nodes reconfigures.

Sloane (cont'd)

"These are all second-gen activations—unconnected to Chimera but still acting like extensions of her will."

"You don't kill a behavior. You must make it turn against itself. " said Rick.

"So how do we do that?" asked Will.

"Baited recursion."

Rick pulls up a side window labeled: RECURSION VECTOR X-57: "Cascading Mirror".

"We take a real challenge layer from Navarro clean it, modify it, lace it with a signal that appears genuine to Chrysalis sensors. But the moment it gets passed to a second node..."

Sloane, nodding said, "It triggers a vector echo—a traceable, time-stamped loopback. Like a honeypot with teeth."

"And the node that spreads it?"

Sloane said, "Believes it's passing a legitimate activation. But it's rebroadcasting a signature that SYBIL can track, record, and recursively map."

Sybil (V.O.) Prediction: 91.3% probability recursive echo will reveal tertiary backbone infrastructure.

Will said, "Give me an example."

"Navarro receives a new activation challenge: a fake quote from an obscure novel encrypted with a Fibonacci rotation. When he solves it, it returns a location: a "drop spot" for the next signal.

"But we intercept that return path, overwrite it, and insert a false challenge layer. Something tantalizing. Slightly off."

"We make it appeal to recruitment logic: a challenge about loyalty and secrecy. Something so pure to Chrysalis doctrine, they must pass it on." Said Thomas.

"And the moment they do, SYBIL attaches a latent residue tag to the outbound signal., said Rick, "It "rides the recursion home," mapping each relay node and triggering micro-signals that wake up our passive listeners."

Rick clicks a key. The graph shifts, tracing a simulation, each bounce lights up in green.

"And Chimera?"

Thomas said, "She won't see it. Not at first. Recursive systems assume trust—they verify structure, not origin. That's their blind spot."

Sybil: Estimated network degradation: 43% within first 36 hours post-dissemination.

Will leans in, folding his arms, asked, "Anything else?

"Yes, "said Sloane, "Erode Trust Mechanisms. In a non-hierarchical model, trust replaces structure. Disrupt trust, and the system begins to fracture. We will leak news of a compromised key activation node to shake faith in the network.

"If he is game, we could use Navarro as a covert asset to deliberately "turn" and create visible internal chaos.

"Lastly," said Sloane, "Denial through noise. Flood likely vectors with over stimulation or lookalike triggers, creating activation confusion.

"Do we do all of them at once?" asked Will.

"I would recommend doing the "baited recursion first, followed closely by the leak and then noise.

"With any luck. Chimera may be distracted enough at that point to make Navarro's job a little easier." suggested Sloane.

Will looked around the room and took in each agreeing face and said, "That's the way we will have it. Let's light the match and step back."

——

MSS Headquarters – Beijing – Zhongnanhai Sub-Level Command Room

The air in the subterranean command room was thick with anger and cigarette smoke. On the central screen: footage from the public arrests of Chrysalis operatives—Georgia, France, Germany, Malaysia, Brazil, and Kuala Lumpur—all within a few hours. Flashes of faces being pinned on pavement. Federal agents in windbreakers. Black bags over heads.

A brutal, surgical purge.

Deputy Director Sun Tao, MSS Bureau 10 (Science & Technology) stared at the footage in silence, arms crossed, his jaw tight. Around the polished black conference table, several senior directors from Second, Seventh, Eight Bureaus.

"Chrysalis was compromised," he said. "Not by ACIC alone. This was bait."

A young analyst tried to clarify.

"Sir, it's likely the Americans used those decoy sites—Plattsburgh, Schroon Lake, Sunapee—as trap points. PLA cyber units attempted passive signals analysis on them... the response was disproportionate."

Tao snapped his eyes toward him.

"Attempted? They used full-spectrum probes. Against our targets. Without coordination. Without authorization."

Silence.

He tossed a manila folder onto the table. It slid halfway down the lacquered surface and stopped in front of Director Xu Jianhong, Director of MSS Foreign Operations Bureau.

"The PLA used Chrysalis as a tool to vet the decoys. And they did it without ever informing us."

"To what end?" Xu asked.

Li looked straight at him. "To assess whether our sources were legitimate... or corrupted. The military is trying to verify our failures by co-opting our networks. This is a blatant move to assert dominance over foreign intelligence.

Xu exhaled sharply. "They're treating us like a liaison service. Like we're their clean-up crew."

Tao leaned forward, voice cold and calm. "No more. Effective immediately, we are severing shared analysis with PLA Strategic Support Force on all Echo Reef–related traffic."

He turned to a senior aide. "Reassign the handlers for Phoenix Arch and White Bridge to internal MSS-only oversight. I want a complete Tier 1 audit of PLA sources feeding into our targets."

"And Chrysalis?" someone asked.

Tau tapped the screen, which now displayed the ACIC seal over a blurred arrest photo.

"Dead. Or dying."

He paused. "We build something better. Ours."

MSS Special Projects Wing – Later That Night

A plain file marked Project KAITEN was placed in a locked steel drawer, flanked by encrypted drives and the glowing core of a biometric scanner.

The file inside bore one line:

"Rebuild autonomous infiltration architecture. No PLA access.

CHAPTER THIRTY-FOUR

A Wrong Word

Rochester, VT - Country Store - Monday 1500 Hours R

Late afternoon on a gloomy Monday was the slowest time at the Country Store, the hour when even the old refrigerator hum seemed louder than usual. Marie-Claire sat behind the counter with a stack of invoices, pen poised, half her attention on the numbers and half on the window fogged with the promise of rain.

A late-model sedan rolled into the gravel lot and stopped squarely in front of the store. Metallic gray. Clean. Newer than most things that found their way out here. She noticed the way you notice anything unfamiliar in a place where familiarity is the rule.

The driver stepped out as the engine went quiet. Tall. Late twenties. Well put together—casual jacket, jeans, shoes that hadn't seen mud. He passed directly beneath the overhead night light, the one that doubled as a security camera, and pushed through the door with an easy confidence that suggested he wasn't in a hurry.

He wandered the aisles without browsing, selecting toiletries with purpose. Toothpaste. Travel-size soap. A razor. Nothing that justified a special trip, which struck her as faintly odd. At the counter he smiled, friendly in a practiced way, and made light conversation while she rang him up.

Quiet day, he said. Weather like this always slows things down.

She agreed. Locals knew better than to linger on Mondays.

Then the questions came, lightly enough to pass as curiosity. Was she from around here—born here, not just living here now? Did she live nearby? How long had she worked at the store?

Marie-Claire answered without thinking much of it. People passing through often wanted to place you, to anchor themselves by mapping the town onto a person.

After a pause, he asked, almost as an afterthought, if she knew what had happened to the Lavoie farm.

She looked up at him then. "I heard a company bought it," she said. That was the truth, or at least the version that had filtered through town.

"Oh?" he said, interested but not surprised. "Anybody living there now?"

"I don't think so. Maybe tourists. That kind of thing."

He nodded, considering. "So maybe it's available as a summer rental?"

Marie-Claire turned and gestured toward the corkboard near the door, crowded with overlapping business cards and fading flyers. "I don't know," she said. "But you can check it out."

He smiled again, thanked her, and wished her a good evening. The bell over the door jingled as he left.

She watched through the window as he got back into the sedan and pulled away. Only then did she notice the license plate was Maine, not Vermont and felt the small, belated prickle of unease that came when a conversation replayed itself with different emphasis.

Odd, she thought, returning to her paperwork. Just... odd.

Rochester, VT - Country Store - Tuesday 0930 Hours R

The next morning, Gayle/Genevieve stopped briefly at the Rochester Country Store for essentials—milk, bread, butter, the usual things you forgot only after you were already home. She greeted Marie-Claire warmly. Over time, she'd grown genuinely fond of the French-Canadian store manager, whose calm competence anchored the place as much as the building itself.

Marie-Claire rang up the items, hesitated, as if deciding whether something was worth mentioning. "Had a visitor asking about the farm yesterday," she said. "Nobody does. Only the locals even remember it was the Lavoie farm and that it was recently sold."

She looked up. "Really? What did he want?"

"Wanted to know who bought it. And whether it was available for rental."

That made Gayle/Genevieve pause. "What did he look like?"

Marie-Claire described him carefully as tall, well put together, late thirties or early forties and then the car. A newer gray sedan. Maine plates. Nothing overtly strange, she added, just an odd line of questions. Sometimes conversations wandered in that direction on their own.

"Yeah," she said after a moment, forcing a light tone. "I'm sure. Thanks for telling me. Probably the IRS."

She laughed, paid, and gathered her bag.

But as she stepped back out into the morning air, the laughter didn't quite follow her.

She made a note to tell Will.

——

Washington, DC - FISC Court - next day

From a technical standpoint, the National Security Agency (NSA) could tap into the Country Store's security cameras without difficulty. Legally, it was another matter entirely. Even something as mundane as a rural convenience store required a warrant—and in this case, one that would withstand intense scrutiny.

That responsibility fell to Marisol Vega, Chief Counsel for Operations at Army Counterintelligence Command.

Vega was well known to the judges who rotated through the Foreign Intelligence Surveillance Court (FISC) bench. She had earned that familiarity the hard way—by never overreaching unless it was absolutely necessary. She was disciplined, and allergic to embellishment. That restraint gave her credibility—and, on rare occasions like this, just enough latitude when she asked for something unusual.

Judge Harlan Pryce had seen every flavor of overreach in twenty years on the FISC bench. He recognized ambition dressed as urgency. He recognized fishing expeditions with classified bait. He leaned back now and studied the woman across the table from him, trying to decide which this was.

Marisol Vega let him look.

"Five minutes of footage," she said. "One entry camera. One checkout camera. No audio."

"From a convenience store."

"Yes, Your Honor."

"In connection with a project you can't name, involving an individual you can't fully identify, tied to a directive you can't enter into the record."

"That's correct."

Pryce set down his pen. "Ms. Vega, I've granted you some unusual requests over the years."

"You have, Your Honor. I've tried not to waste them."

He held her gaze for a moment longer. Then he picked the pen back up. "Five minutes only."

She thanked him without smiling and left before he could reconsider.

Washington, DC - FISC - Later that day

The National Security Agency moved quickly.

From the five minutes of authorized footage, analysts extracted several clear frames of the subject's face—clean angles, good lighting, no obstructions. Within minutes, the images were run against NSA holdings comprising more than three billion indexed facial records.

The footage was clean. Better than they'd hoped, good angles, steady light, no obstructions. Within the hour, analysts had pulled a dozen usable frames and run them against three billion indexed faces.

Then someone flagged a problem.

The subject's citizenship status was unconfirmed. Which meant every second they spent analyzing the footage was a second they were potentially running facial recognition on a U.S. person, and the Fourth Amendment didn't care how good your reason was.

Vega was back in front of Pryce by noon.

He read her submission twice. Then he granted it, and slid the order across the table with two fingers.

"If this person is American," he said, "what you find stays in a drawer. No criminal use. Intelligence only."

"Understood."

"I mean it, Counselor."

"So do I."

CHAPTER THIRTY-FIVE

Smirnov Frustration

Moscow - SVR Headquarters

The file wasn't tagged as operational.

That alone caught SYBIL's attention.

It sat in Kir Smirnov's private workspace buffer—never transmitted, never referenced in tasking, never opened during duty hours. A legacy-format image file, degraded, scanned decades ago.

A photograph.

Black and white. Late Soviet era. Two men in winter coats standing beside a river embankment, ice broken along the edge. One of them is young—early twenties, hair too long for regulations, smiling at the camera as if the world has not yet taught him caution.

Metadata reconstruction identifies him as Sergei Mikhailovich Smirnov.

Older brother.

Filed cause of death: industrial accident, 1993.

Location: a closed research facility later absorbed into a joint Russian–Israeli optics initiative.

Official report: equipment failure. No disciplinary action. No prosecution.

What never made it into the file is what Kir learned years later—through a favor, paid carefully and never repeated.

The accident occurred three weeks after Sergei attempted to block a data transfer he believed was unauthorized.

The destination node was never logged.

The supervisor who overruled him emigrated six months later.

SYBIL flags a pattern not of grief—but of fixation.

Kir does not speak of his brother. He does not visit graves. He does not drink on anniversaries.

He does, however, show a statistically anomalous intensity when operations involve:

– Photonics research

– Quantum-adjacent systems

– Western laboratories operating under dual-use cover

Especially when the Americans insist they are only doing defensive work.

Kir closes the file.

His next message to the team is clipped, professional, and precise.

"Proceed. I want the Vermont node understood completely. No assumptions. No shortcuts."

There is no mention of Sergei.

But SYBIL adjusts her threat model accordingly.

Kir Smirnov is not hunting secrets.

He is hunting closure.

——

Moscow - SVR Headquarters

It took six weeks for the Russian satellite to arrive.

A Luch-Kh / Olimp-K platform—officially a "communications relay," unofficially a roaming SIGINT collector—slowly adjusted its orbit until Vermont sat beneath its gaze. The maneuver consumed fuel, favors, and political capital. Assets like that were never idle for long. For three days only, the SVR had the sky.

It was wasted.

From orbit, Genevieve Larsson might as well have been a ghost.

She never appeared in daylight except for a brief, irregular run to the country store. Even then she moved with discipline—head down, huge floppy sun hat regardless of weather, angles denied. She transitioned from farmhouse to lab without ever fully exposing herself outdoors. The lab's windows were one-way. The farmhouse shades were permanently set halfway down, a deliberate geometry: standing faces erased, lenses defeated.

No usable imagery. No patterns. No mistakes.

The SVR escalated.

A FedEx driver arrived with a camera stitched into the brim of his cap—only to discover the "front door" was a disguised sally port. It was always answered by Karen Bolanowski... or someone who looked and moved suspiciously like Secret Service.

Three days burned. Millions spent. Nothing to show.

Kir Smirnov stabbed the secure-channel key hard enough to rattle the desk.

"Report, comrade."

Jacob "Jax" Miller—codename затвор (zat-vor) Shutter—answered immediately.

A trusted non-official cover, late twenties, American on paper and in accent, constructed through years of layered residency fraud. Charismatic, restless, precise. Street eyes. Human sensor array.

"According to building permits," Jax said evenly, "the farmhouse underwent extensive renovations shortly after purchase by a foreign corporation. Likely a capital storage vehicle. No rental activity. Minimal foot traffic. Only two women regularly visit the nearby country store."

Smirnov exhaled sharply through his nose.

"The Middlebury State Airport recently extended its runway and installed new landing equipment," Jax continued. "Nothing unusual given the college and ski traffic."

A pause.

"That's it?" Smirnov asked. "That's all you have?"

"Yes, sir. Other than"—a fractional hesitation—"they adopted a dog."

Smirnov froze.

"A dog?"

He opened Sable's file and searched a single word.

DOG.

There it was.

Subject pauses to pet every dog encountered during jogging routes.

"How do you know this?" Smirnov demanded. "Did you see the animal?"

"No, sir. I searched the White River Valley Herald. A classified ad for a retired Army Belgian Malinois. Also appeared on Craigslist. I called. The sellers said the dog was adopted by a nice young woman in the area."

The room went quiet.

"The satellite gave us nothing," Smirnov said at last. "We need confirmation. A photograph."

"Yes, sir."

Jax waited.

For days he watched Route 100, patient as a hunter, until the car appeared—the same vehicle flagged by the satellite, unremarkable and therefore perfect.

He passed it once.

He turned into the empty church lot across from the country store and waited.

When she stepped out of the car, Jax already had the camera raised. A Russian-made JUPITER-6, KMZ glass, heavy and unforgiving. No stabilization. No forgiveness.

She exited the store minutes later.

He took the shot again.

Perfect. Head-on. Unobstructed.

At last, the SVR had a face.

——

Moscow - SVR Headquarters

Kir Smirnov played the long game. Meticulous, patient, every contingency weighed and rescored until the odds tilted in his favor. After the Radiant Sentry fiasco he had one priority: find Sable and close the chapter on ACIC's meddling. Who knew what she'd already deduced from SVR inquiries? He wouldn't leave that to chance.

His patience paid off. A face exiting a country store matched to Genevieve Larsson—Sable.

He assembled a three-man hit team and staged the operation out of Montreal, close enough to Lake Champlain for a quick, quiet approach into New England, and useful because the consulate offered discreet logistics. Equipment and papers moved in diplomatic pouches; personnel and visas were timed months apart so nothing read like a single, traceable wave. Small rehearsals and benign staff swaps at the consulate normalized the team's comings and goings.

The plan was surgical: land near Venise-en-Québec, meet the waterfront contact, run the eighty-mile lake transit under cover, land at Button Bay, slip inland to the safe house and move on the target. Clean, fast, deniable.

Local cutouts and on-the-ground handles were already vetted and in position:

1. GULL — Montreal sleeper contact (meets team on arrival; handles local transport).
2. SKIPPER — Venise-en-Québec waterfront contact and 28-ft speedboat operator.
3. BUTTON — Safe-house handler near Button Bay for staging and layover.

The team itself was compact and purpose-built:

- MOROZ /moh-ROHZ/ — Team lead / planner. Calm, clinical, calls the shots.
- VIKHR /VEE-kher/ — Breacher / close-assault. Fast, violent, the point man.
- ZMEY /ZMEY/ — Exfil/driver/boat operator. Steady hands, navigation, and escape.

Smirnov's signature was in the details: staggered visas, diplomatic transfers, practice switches to desensitize local watchers, and a single clear rule—no loose ends. The operation would be invisible on paper and ruthless in execution.

— —

Moscow — SVR Operations Directorate S — 2210 Hours Charlie

The underground chamber had the air of a surgical theater: windowless, climate-controlled, its light flat and unforgiving. Three officers stood when Kir Smirnov entered, a small, automatic motion of rank rather than reverence. They straightened as if gravity itself demanded it.

Smirnov set his tea glass on the table and slid a slim black folder across to the officer at the center—a field controller with the cool, practiced face of someone who had shepherded operations through worse weather. He did not bother with preamble. His voice was low, measured, each word a metronome.

"Target designation: Sable."

The name landed like a stone. In that room even a whisper could sound like an edict.

"Last known alias: Genevieve Larsson. Confirmed location: northern Vermont. She is under the protection of the United States Army Counterintelligence Command. Possible connection to Nusquam — classified facility." He let the hush bloom, watched the Colonel's eyes flick to the map on the wall where a patch of Vermont glowed like an exposed nerve.

Smirnov's tone never hardened; it simply sharpened. "We will not strike for spectacle. We will restore symmetry."

He tapped the folder once, sending a sound that was almost ceremonial. "A three-man cell will approach via the Lake Champlain axis. They will be discrete. Their insertion will be small, surgical. A separate diversionary element will move by road toward Burlington — backroads, local traffic patterns, the sort of convoy that draws routine eyes and makes no one look twice."

The Colonel's jaw tightened, not with surprise but with appreciation for the clarity of the order. "Decoy to draw attention inland," he said. "Water team to cut the veil where the land thinks itself safe."

"Correct." Smirnov folded his fingers together. "No flags. No chatter. Use only preexisting local networks and covers. Avoid our standard communications. No trace that leads back to S. No public victory. The objective is singular."

He walked slowly to the projected map, his shadow elongating across roads and shoreline. "Entry through Montréal, cross at secondary points into the Champlain corridor. The Americans trust their wilderness; that trust will be the camouflage we exploit."

Mirov, the Colonel, swallowed whatever comment he might have made and inclined his head. "Yes, Comrade Director."

Kir's gaze lingered on him a heartbeat longer than necessary. "You will not fail," he said. The words were a scalpel. "Failure is noise. Noise draws light."

He lifted the tea glass, drank what remained with the precision of a man who measured everything, and set it down as if sealing an agreement. He added, not as an aside but as doctrine, "Do not harm any auxiliary personnel. The objective is her alone. If death is the outcome, it must appear as chance — not reprisal."

He rearranged the papers into a single, clean stack, the movement small and exact. Before he reached the door he spoke again, his back to them now, voice travelling across the table like a commandment.

"When it is done, erase the line that tied her to us. No record. No remembrance. She never existed."

The door sealed behind him with a hiss, leaving Mirov and his team staring at the file. On its cover: a single, embossed name. SABLE.

And beneath it—a single handwritten signature in blue ink. Кир Смирнов.+

Moscow-SVR Private Directorate Buffer — 2241 Hours Charlie

The corridor outside was empty.

Smirnov walked it without hurry, his footsteps absorbed by the concrete, and stopped at the terminal alcove he used when he did not wish to be seen thinking. A habit of thirty years. The SVR had built him an office with a view. He rarely used it for anything that mattered.

He set his palm to the reader. The screen populated with the overnight queue — signals traffic, asset reports, two flagged intercepts from the Helsinki station that could wait until morning.

And one automated intelligence notification, priority low, tagged for his profile by a keyword filter he had set so long ago he no longer remembered doing it.

He opened it.

Yevgeni Borisovich Larin. Born 1941, Novosibirsk. Died 14 March, Haifa, Israel. Natural causes. Survived by a daughter and two grandchildren. Private interment.

Kir read it once. Then again.

The supervisor who had overruled Sergei had spent thirty-two years eating breakfast on a terrace somewhere above the Mediterranean, watching his grandchildren grow, dying in a bed with clean sheets and people who loved him nearby.

Natural causes.

Kir sat with that, not with rage, rage was for men who had not yet learned that emotion was simply energy without direction. Not with satisfaction, there was nothing here that constituted an ending. Only the flat, administrative fact of a man who had made one decision in 1993 and lived a complete life anyway, untroubled, unaccountable, unavailable.

The thread was gone.

He had always assumed, somewhere beneath the methodology, that there would eventually be a thread to pull. Not justice — he was not naïve enough to call it that. Something more precise. A reckoning that could be engineered, timed, made to feel like consequence rather than accident.

Larin had denied him even that. Simply by dying first.

Kir closed the notification.

He did not flag it. Did not forward it. Did not add it to any file.

He sat for eleven seconds, long enough that the screen's idle timer dimmed the display and then he opened the Helsinki intercepts and went back to work.

There was still Vermont.

There was still the particular category of Western deception that dressed itself as defensive research and called the dead collateral.

Sergei had known. Had tried to stop it. Had been overruled by a man now buried in Israeli soil with grandchildren weeping at the graveside.

Kir would not weep at anyone's graveside.

But he would finish what the file had started.

He always did.

Fort Meade-Cyber Operations Command 0342 Hours R

The room was dark except for the glow of curved monitors and the slow pulsing of status LEDs — a digital aurora that breathed in silence.

Rick Huang leaned forward, a steaming mug forgotten beside the keyboard. SYBIL's console wasn't alarming—not yet—but the numbers in the corner had begun to drift.

Something subtle. Something alive.

On-screen, the system displayed a sequence of transmission bursts — each under 300 milliseconds — bouncing off public routers in Québec, skipping through a pattern that, to most analysts, would look like background noise.

"SYBIL," Rick murmured, "expand anomaly delta-one."

The AI's voice was soft, cultured — the sound of reason in a storm.

"Pattern variance confirmed. Entropy deviation: 0.0197 above baseline. Signature suggests hand-shaped routing. Probable covert relay."

Rick frowned. "Source?"

"Triangulation incomplete. Canadian uplink, but origin signal fragmented. Partial overlay—Montreal corridor."

He exhaled, long and low. "That's north of the Vermont line."

The chair beside him slid back. Sara Brandt entered, barefoot in sweats, eyes still fogged with sleep but already sharp. "What've we got?"

Rick zoomed in on the frequency waterfall. "Ghost traffic. Tight burst. Too clean to be commercial, too short for civilian encryption. Smells like an SVR hop."

"Destination?"

"Southbound," SYBIL replied, "vectoring toward ACIC grid region seventeen... which includes the Nusquam node."

That woke her fully. "Get Will."

Fort Meade–Watchtower Secure Channel 0349 Hours R

Will's voice came through calm, gravel-thick from lack of sleep.

"Talk to me, Rick."

Rick's fingers danced over the keys. "We caught a microburst from Montréal. Quantum-resonant encryption—handmade, not commercial. Not one of ours."

Sara cut in. "Trajectory lines up with the Champlain corridor, and SYBIL flags it as inbound to region seventeen."

Rick added, "On the bright side, whoever built this respects their own tradecraft. Bad news is they respect it enough to use it on us."

Will was silent for three seconds— long enough to measure risk, triangulate consequences.

"Probability of coincidence?"

"Less than one in ten million," SYBIL answered.

Will's tone flattened, controlled. "So we have a foreign signal near Nusquam, cloaked under a noise envelope. Could be staging, could be recon, could be the real thing."

Rick said, "It's too disciplined for recon."

Will nodded to himself, unseen. "Wake Cecil. Prep drones and ISR. Nobody in the clear until we know what's moving."

Sara heard the sound of him moving—the scrape of a chair, a door opening, night air pouring in.

"If this is what I think it is," Will said, "they're not coming to look. They're coming to kill."

The line went dead.

CHAPTER THIRTY-SIX

Ivan

Moscow, Russia

For more than a decade, Ivan had existed where no one was supposed to exist at all: inside the confidence of the SVR. Not a courier. Not a cutout. A voice that survived meetings, votes, and purges. He had been seeded during the Radiant Sentry years—silently, patiently—when the program was still an argument rather than a weapon, and Moscow was still deciding whether it was real or American theater. Ivan did not steal secrets in bursts; he accumulated trust. His reporting was never late, never embellished, never wrong. In a system that devoured its own on suspicion alone, that record was not merely rare—it was impossible.

His access followed the arc of credibility. Operational rosters, first. Then routing logic—how messages were moved, delayed, laundered. Eventually, the conversations no file ever captured: the doubts spoken after the doors were sealed, the rivalries masked as ideology, the moments when generals hesitated and analysts reframed reality to survive the room. Ivan heard the arguments before they hardened into orders. He knew which proposals would die, which would be reborn under different names, and which were dangerous precisely because no one argued against them.

Most valuable of all, Ivan understood how the SVR thought—what it feared, what it underestimated, and what it was prepared to sacrifice when certainty failed. When his messages arrived, they did not read like warnings. They read like inevitabilities, written by someone already standing on the far side of the decision. That was why they were trusted

——

Moscow — ACIC Undisclosed Safe House — 1414 Hours Charlie

The safe room smelled of cigarette smoke and cheap coffee, the kind of small comforts intelligence officers let themselves keep when the rest of life is rationed to protocols and pseudonyms. A single, dim lamp threw an amber pool over a battered desk. Maps, red threads, and photographs lay scattered like an accusation.

Across the table, the station chief thumbed a secure SCIF handset to Judd Lockwood CIA Special Agent, voice low and measured. The line clicked into place with the soft authority of government hardware. He did not like to waste words.

"Judd, this is Moscow Station," he said. "I have a message from Ivan. Urgent."

There was a pause. Langley's end of the line exhaled—paper rustle, the micro-movement of someone leaning forward.

"Go on," Lockwood answered.

"He says Sable has been targeted." The station chief's voice hardened. "Confirmed location: northern Vermont, possibly connected to a Granville facility."

Silence settled over the call. On the far side, the name arranged itself into strategy and risk.

"Who's moving?" Lockwood asked, flat, professional. "SVR footprint or local cutouts?"

"Three-man cell," the chief replied. "Deep cover. No chatter, no sigs on traditional wideband channels. Ivan's note is terse: this team will avoid SVR nets entirely. They'll use civilian transport vectors and local assets already embedded. Entry through Montréal, secondary roads into the Champlain corridor. They'll use the wilderness as a veil."

Lockwood pinched the bridge of his nose. "So operationally clean it looks surgical and invisible until someone's dead."

"Exactly." He tapped a thumb against the desk, thinking aloud. "No flags in the comms. No courier noise. Whoever set this up knows how to move without leaving the bread crumbs we usually track."

"Any idea who's sponsoring?" he asked.

The line hummed. "Not directly. The way it's staged—precision, the avoidance of SVR channels—suggests Moscow wants plausible deniability. But that could be a red herring. Could be a third-party cutout, state-backed, or a private hand with deep tradecraft. Ivan insists urgency—he believes the window is narrow."

Lockwood closed his eyes for a microsecond and let the picture form: a three-man cell threading across borders, night-driving through snow, closing on a target the Americans believed safe behind trees and trust. He pictured Sable moving through a Vermont lab or a rented farmhouse, unaware that a knife had been laid along her path.

"All right," he said, voice cold with decision. "We'll coordinate with London, Canadian

Security Intelligence Service and Homeland Security. No direct Moscow channel—no signals back to the station.

"You want us to avoid SVR channels even in reporting?" the chief asked.

"Absolutely," Lockwood replied. "Treat this as a covert extraction-in-waiting. If Moscow's involved, we don't feed their bureaucracy. Keep it tight—MI6, CSIS, ACIC liaisons, and my desk. And—" he hesitated, the weight of what he was about to ask making the rest of the sentence small and precise—"don't let the Bureau know the source channel. Not yet. If this is a setup, exposure kills the asset."

Another pause. The station chief, who had wired nations and whispers, gave a soft, reluctant assent. "Understood. We'll move clean and fast. Ivan will stand by on a one-time secure burst for confirmations only."

Lockwood let the words settle, then closed the line. The lamp hummed. Outside, Moscow's night kept its slow, indifferent watch.

He rose and pulled on a dark coat—no ceremonies. In this business, decisions were necessary and irreversible.

If Sable was the prize, the coming hours would decide whether she walked out alive or became another ghost in the intelligence ledger.

Lockwood dialed the director's number.

——

Fort Meade - Watchtower Operations

The urgent flag on Will's secure line blinked red before the message even finished downloading. He read it once, then again, each pass stripping a little more air from the room.

FROM: NSA — SIGINT ALERT

TO: Major Will Morgan, ACIC

SUBJECT: URGENT — SVR KILL ORDER (KIR Smirnov) — TARGET: G. LARSSON (SABLE) — LOCATION: NUSQUAM / VERMONT

Will set the tablet down. The watch room seemed to sharpen into focus, LEDs colder, voices farther away. He didn't have to look up to know who was already in the loop; faces turned toward him automatically.

Rick Huang was the first to speak, voice taut. "How did they get a positive ID?"

"Long-lens photo at the country store," Sara said. "An SVR NOC named Miller, calls himself Shutter. Caught her face on a single pass and got it back to Moscow before we ever saw him. Cecil's pole cameras picked him up the next day, but by then the image was already on Smirnov's desk."

Rick's jaw went hard. "Smirnov? He's not the kind who asks twice."

Will rubbed his brow. "He issued orders. Kill team. Targeting instructions attached."

——

Langley, VA—CIA Headquarters

Jennifer Mansky watched the alert roll through her console again as if the words might rearrange themselves into anything less urgent. The bulletin had been blunt: imminent assassination threat, She had signed it and pushed it—DHS, FBI, state partners. Protocol screamed caution first.

Now, with the hits piling into her inbox—dozens of agency acknowledgments, a scattering of urgent replies—she felt the room tighten. Half the people on the distribution list would call for posture and boots on the ground. She knew what that looked like on a map: every sensor lit up, every local sheriff deputized, news vans rolling toward Button Bay. That cascade would endanger whatever fragile advantage they still had.

She rubbed her temples and tapped a secure channel. If anyone in the chain could make the authorities slow their stride, it was her.

"Temporary hold," she wrote into the ACIC uplink, fingers precise. "Hold tactical escalation pending classification verification. Public safety priority, but minimize footprint. I'm sending a brief to the Director." She hit send before doubt could stall her.

Minutes later the secure line lit: the Presidential ring. The caller ID read simply: POTUS. Her throat went dry. She glanced at the alert, then activated the connection.

"Jennifer," President Stratton's voice came through, flat, measured, not the bluster she'd expected from television. "I just read the DHS dispatch. Walk me through it."

She summarized fast, clinical: the source, the timestamps, the SIGINT signature Derek had flagged, the risk assessment they'd drafted. She didn't mention Nusquam. She emphasized civilian risk, the potential for panic, the need to thread the needle between warning and escalation.

Stratton listened, no interruptions. When she finished he asked one direct question that made her stomach clench: "Are you sure your release won't compromise a larger program?"

Her own voice had the steadiness she cultivated in public. "If it's what we think, sir, a wider release risks every asset and program we have on that corridor. But if it's real and imminent, we risk lives by waiting."

Silence held for three slow beats.

"I'm putting this under ACIC's lead. Major Morgan and Commander Perry will coordinate the field response. DHS will maintain situational awareness and provide civilian protections, but operational control rests with ACIC. No broad public release. No interagency ops without ACIC concurrence."

Mansky's insides, taut with the posture of the last hour, relaxed fractionally—and then tightened again. The President's words were a cold clearance: she had authority to push the alert, but the President was pulling the reins in. He'd defused a potential political explosion by centralizing command, but he'd also removed the last line of latitude she'd hoped to use to force immediate, wide action.

"Mr. President," she said, because she needed to fill the silence with something competent, "if ACIC is leading, I need them to keep us informed. If I'm going to be fielding state and local inquiries, I can't be blind."

"Agreed," Stratton said. "You stay in the loop. You do not initiate first-responder directives that have not been coordinated through ACIC except to protect life. That is an explicit order. Keep your people ready. And Jennifer—if you think we're leaving someone exposed by containing this, tell me now."

Mansky looked at the line item on her screen—several dozen agency nodes that were already awake because she'd punched the bell. Her instinct had been to err on the side of warning; the President had chosen containment. She felt the tug between two professional absolutes: protect the public at all costs, and preserve the integrity of classified operations that might save countless more lives if handled properly.

She squared her shoulders. "Understood, Mr. President. ACIC has the lead. I will maintain civilian protective posture and stand ready to escalate if directed."

He acknowledged it with a single, crisp "Good." The line clicked and the secure channel closed.

Mansky sat in the after-silence, hearing the low thrum of servers and the distant shuffle of an agency waking to an alert she had sent. She'd doubled down—had pushed the button that made people move—but the President had just rerouted the motion. She did not know what Nusquam was, who Genevieve

Larsson really was, or what secrets ACIC was protecting. That ignorance left a cold taste.

She opened a secure chat to Perry, fingers steady now. "Commander Perry—Presidential directive routed ACIC operational control. DHS and FBI on situational awareness only. I'm standing by to coordinate civilian protective measures and will defer tactical moves to your command. We need a unified comms posture now."

She hit send and watched the message pass into a queue keyed to titles and clearances. Outside, city lights glowed on the horizon; inside, the alert still pulsed like a small, dangerous heart. She had doubled down to save lives—now she had to trust the men and women in the field to do the thing she could not.

——

Fort Media-Watchtower Ops -Secure Line

The overhead lights were too bright for how tired Will Morgan felt. He stepped into the secure one person booth, the door sealing behind him with a dull magnetic thud. The red phone blinked once—a priority line. He didn't hesitate.

"Ed," Will said, his voice low, clipped. "We've got a problem."

There was a pause. The faint hum of encrypted static. Perry's voice—cool, composed, edged with irritation. "What's up?" he asked.

"The CIA pushed an interagency alert. DHS, FBI, even NCTC. Full distribution." Will exhaled. "They flagged an imminent threat against Sable."

A long silence. He could almost hear Perry calculating on the other end—the implications, the breach of compartments.

"Goddammit," Perry muttered. "They don't even know who Sable is."

"Correct," Will said. "They don't know about Genevieve only FNI does and they don't know where she is. Or Nemo. Or Nusquam. But if DHS or FBI start tripping sensors in northern Vermont, it's going to bring every alphabet agency within fifty miles. That'll blow the cover and the program."

Perry's voice sharpened. "We stay in control. ACIC runs point, period."

"Agreed. I can keep the field command contained through Harlan and Hayes, but we'll need an immediate kill order on DHS notifications above clearance level five. Otherwise, the chatter reaches Langley."

"I'll handle it," Perry said. "You keep your team dark and local. If anyone asks, the operation is a domestic counterintelligence intercept, nothing more. DHS can monitor at the state border but no boots, no drones, no locals briefed. Copy?"

"Copy," Will said. His tone was steady, but beneath it ran the flicker of something colder—the knowledge that one wrong report, one DHS sensor ping, and everything they'd built at Nusquam could collapse in hours.

Perry's final words came tight and final. "I'll put a lid on CIA and DHS. You focus on the lake. And Will—if they reach Vermont first, you don't call for permission. You act."

The line went dead.

CHAPTER THIRTY-SEVEN

Aurion Secure Vaults

Inner Mongolia Autonomous Region, China — Classified Black site: Jīngzé Facility- one Year Ago

The wind howled outside the hardened concrete installation, a soundless scream muffled by sound-dampened walls and two meters of insulation. Inside, fluorescent lights buzzed overhead, casting a clinical pallor over the narrow lab chamber.

Dr. Yasha Moravec stood before a modified terminal built with custom Field Programmable Gate Array modules. The interface was written entirely in Mandarin, but she didn't need translation.

Behind her, the walls pulsed with heat, not from ambient temperature, but from the superconducting cavity of the device embedded beneath the floor. A hybrid quantum-classical accelerator. The prototype.

Her handler, Li Shun, head of the PLA Strategic Support Force's Quantum Exploitation Division, entered the room behind her. His footfalls were measured. Slow.

"You were not cleared to access the lattice control node," he said.

Yasha didn't turn.

"Your implementation of Recursive Braiding is inefficient," she said curtly. "It's based on a flawed interpretation of the Girvin-MacDonald-Platzman transform. You're building a keyspace from noise."

Li stepped closer. "We are building hegemony."

She turned now. No fear. Just contempt.

"You're building a machine that will never work unless someone feeds it truth. And you've run out of liars smart enough to pretend it's functioning."

Li studied her. "You don't believe in the work anymore."

"You don't pay me to believe in the work, you pay me for access to my Chrysalis network. Besides, I believe in physics. Not hubris."

There was silence before Li said, "And yet you kept the schematics."

That was the moment. Her expression flickered—so brief most would miss it. But Li was a predator trained to spot it.

He stepped forward, leaning in.

"Tell me where the ghost drive is."

She smiled thinly.

"You won't find it. Not in Guangzhou. Not in Zürich. Not even here, where you had me ghostwrite your pseudo-scientific press to keep your funding flowing."

He moved too fast to see—a strike across the face. Open-handed. It split her lip. She staggered back.

"The moment you walked into this lab," he said, voice low and shaking with rage, "you ceased being an asset. You became a liability. And I don't tolerate liabilities."

She wiped the blood from her chin, eyes shining not with tears, but certainty.

"Then you'd better kill me now."

He didn't. That would have required clearance.

She watched him weigh it and saw the answer in his stillness. He wouldn't go to Beijing for permission. Not for her. Which meant he'd already convinced himself she was more useful breathing than buried — at least until he could find what she'd hidden.

Good.

She had spent eleven months building the inventory in her head: every fabricated benchmark, every paper she'd ghostwritten under a Politburo byline, every supplier Li had cheated, every name on the funding chain that would not survive daylight. The schematics were almost incidental. The schematics were what he thought she had.

What she actually had was leverage. And leverage was a currency you could spend more than once.

She had also spent eleven months preparing the door.

Li left her in the lab under guard. Two men outside the chamber. A third at the corridor junction. Standard rotation, ninety-minute intervals, last shift change at 22:00. She had timed it across forty-three nights.

She returned to the terminal as if resuming work, blood drying on her chin. The FPGA modules accepted her credentials without comment. They had no reason not to. She had written half their boot logic, and the audit subsystem reported to a log file she had quietly redirected to a buffer that overwrote itself every six minutes.

She opened the lattice control node Li had accused her of breaching. He had been right about the access. He had been wrong about the purpose.

For the last three weeks she had been feeding the superconducting cavity beneath the floor a thermal regulation profile with one tiny lie embedded in it — a phase drift on the helium recirculation pump, well below the alarm threshold, accumulating. Tonight, on her command, the lie would finish becoming the truth.

She entered fourteen characters and pressed return.

Beneath the floor, the cavity's coolant loop went from nominal to critical in under ninety seconds. The fault would read, to anyone reviewing it later, as a degraded compressor seal — the kind of failure that had taken down two other PLA cryogenic rigs in the last decade. Nothing exotic. Nothing suspicious. Just physics catching up with cheap procurement.

The first alarm began to chirp at 21:47. By 21:48 it was joined by three more. By 21:49 the chamber's overhead lights cycled to amber and the ventilation hoods reversed to evacuate boil-off helium before it pooled.

The guards opened the door.

She was already at the threshold, lab coat on, tablet in hand, speaking before they could.

"Cavity breach. Get the floor cleared. Now. If the cryogen reaches the FPGA bay, the prototype is gone."

She said it in Mandarin, fast, with the impatience of a scientist who had no time for soldiers. They were not trained to argue with the woman who had built the thing they were guarding. They moved.

She moved with them, but not where they expected. While the senior guard radioed the corridor station and the junior unlocked the secondary blast door for the emergency evac route — the route she had insisted on during the facility's safety review eight months earlier — she peeled off at the second junction.

The evac route had two branches. One led to the surface muster point. The other led to the loading bay where the cryogen trucks resupplied. She had argued for the second branch on the grounds of redundancy. Li had approved it without reading the engineering memo.

The loading bay biometric scanner accepted her palm because she was on the maintenance authorization list. She had added herself in March, buried inside a batch update of fourteen technicians whose names Li had signed off on without checking.

The ghost drive was already in the bay, inside the maintenance kit she had positioned three weeks earlier — a sealed diagnostic case left in a rack of identical sealed diagnostic cases. She lifted it, walked past the idling resupply truck whose driver was watching the alarms strobe through the loading bay windows, and slipped into the unheated equipment corridor that ran beneath the perimeter berm.

The corridor was a service tunnel for the buried fiber trunk. It had no cameras, because cameras required power conduits, and power conduits compromised the EMP hardening Li had personally specified.

At the far end, two kilometers later, was a maintenance hatch that opened onto the access road behind the perimeter fence. She had walked it twice, in coveralls, during scheduled fiber inspections.

She walked it a third time now, in the dark, with the ghost drive in one hand and her lip still bleeding.

By the time the cryogen alarm was confirmed as a non-critical incident — the cavity was fine, the readings false, the compressor seal intact — she had been gone for ninety-six minutes.

By the time Li reached the lab and understood what the lie in the thermal profile had actually purchased her, she had crossed into Mongolia

She was gone.

CHAPTER THIRTY-EIGHT

NATO Alert

NATO Headquarters-Brussels, Belgium — 0042 Alpha

The Joint Intelligence and Security Division liaison wing was quiet at this hour. Cecil Brandon sat in a borrowed office on the third floor, reviewing a folder of signals tradecraft summaries that NATO wanted Watchtower's read on by morning. Across the room, Z had his boots up on a credenza, scrolling through what looked like a Polish football forum.

"You realize you're at NATO Headquarters," Cecil said without looking up.

"I am aware."

"And you're reading about Lech Poznań."

"They are 2 and 7 against Legia this season. It is a tragedy of national proportions."

Cecil turned a page. "Two more days of this and we go home."

"Two more days." Z stretched. "Then I am going to eat a proper sausage and forget Belgium ever existed."

Down the corridor, a phone began to ring.

It rang for a long time before someone answered.

A minute later, the duty officer knocked on Cecil's open door. "Major Brandon. Colonel Bohm is asking for you on a secure line. He says it's about a Tier One."

Cecil set the folder aside.

Z's boots came off the credenza.

——

Fort Meade-Watchtower Morgan's Office 1844 R

The lights were low. SYBIL's interface hovered across the embedded wall display in calm blue arcs. Will Morgan sat in his chair, jacket slung over the backrest, shirt sleeves rolled. He was reviewing a cross-domain threat assessment when the door buzzed—twice.

Sara Brandt entered without waiting.

"Midnight intercept just came in from NATO SIGINT. Brussels is flagging it Priority One."

Will stood immediately.

Sara handed him a sealed folder and nodded to the screen. "They're patching through to your secure line. SYBIL's already decrypting the relay."

Will pressed his palm to the biometric plate, and SYBIL's audio link clicked on.

"This is Colonel Alaric Bohm, NATO JISD—Joint Intelligence Support Division, Signals Section. We have a real-time alert on your Tier One target: codename Chimera."

Will's posture sharpened.

"Where?"

"Belgrade, Serbia. Local intercepts from the Chinese-operated Huawei 'Safe City' grid were scraped by a German SIGINT bird running above the Balkans. Cross-ref matched a PLA image packet against one of our retained signals channels from Operation Hexfinder. Chimera's facial structure pinged 91.7% confidence. They're tracking her."

Will frowned. "You're reading their internal recognition traffic?"

"Correct. It's embedded in a steganographic heartbeat signal between their Belgrade relay node and Guangzhou. We wouldn't have caught it if our scraper hadn't been tuned to Huawei's heartbeat frequency—credit to your man Rick Huang."

Sara raised an eyebrow. "They're burning her?"

"Not yet. But they've got boots on the ground. One confirmed PLA agent trailing her. Probably more in reserve. And here's the kicker: they haven't alerted MSS. Not even on the dark relay lines."

Will's expression darkened. "PLA wants her silenced. Maybe she saw something she wasn't supposed to."

Sara added, "Or something she was supposed to survive."

Will looked at SYBIL's screen, where the coordinates of 12 Makedonska Street were already being cross-referenced with NSA's Balkan HUMINT map.

"Tell NATO to maintain passive observation. No contact with her unless we say so. I want SYBIL to scrape every outbound packet from that relay node. And get me a whisper team in-country. Larsson and Nemo need to be briefed on this immediately. If Chimera's compromised—"

Sara finished it for him. “The entire Chrysalis decryption thread might die with her.”

Fort Meade-Watchtower Secure Channel 1932 Hours R

The room was already humming when Will entered. The secure comms hub had been lit red—live op status—and SYBIL's central display had begun dynamically mapping 12 Makedonska Street in Belgrade. Satellite pass schedules. PLA electronic footprints. NATO HUMINT feeds. Everything was coming online.

"Close the door," Will said, and Sara did.

Cecil Brandon and Z were already on the secure video link from Brussels, the JISD watch floor visible behind them. Cecil had a coat in his hand. He hadn't put it on yet, but it was clear he was about to.

Will didn't waste motion.

"Cecil, you and Z are ground lead. NATO has a fast-mover spinning up at Melsbroek. Wheels up in forty minutes. You'll land at Nikola Tesla under diplomatic cover."

Cecil nodded once. "Understood."

"Sara runs the room here with me. Rick on the grid. Cathy on overwatch and deception routing. Cecil, you're the only voice on the ground I want making calls in real time."

"Copy."

Z leaned in toward the camera. "Cover identities?"

"Already being walked through the embassy. Andrew Wallace, Defense Attaché. Katherine Reyes, USAID. You'll get them on the plane."

"I am Katherine Reyes?" Z asked.

"You are Andrew Wallace's interpreter," Sara said dryly. "Try to look serious."

"I always look serious."

"You look like a man reading about Polish football."

Will didn't smile, but the corner of his mouth moved. He turned back to the map.

"Initiate Directive IRON LANTERN."

SYBIL responded in calm neutral tone.

> *"IRON LANTERN confirmed. Objective: high-risk asset exfiltration from hostile surveillance zone. Target: Moravec, Yasha — codename CHIMERA. Authority override: Morgan, W."*

Will looked around the room. "We don't ask permission for this. We don't wait for Brussels or Langley to greenlight it. NATO has their hands full and CIA has no operational teeth in Serbia right now. That makes it ours."

Sara stepped up to the console. "Team Watchtower only?"

Will nodded. "Layered ghost signature. No joint op with JSOC or CIA SAD. We keep this deniable."

He turned to each station.

"Cecil, ground extraction. You and Z get her out. If she's already compromised, you recover whatever she's holding and you go."

Z gave a single nod from the screen.

"Rick, Spoof the Belgrade CCTV feeds with a looped image set. Give them a ten-minute corridor during extraction."

"Already loading the patterns."

"Cathy, overwatch and deception routing. Runpoint alternates every thirty seconds. You're the air controller."

"On it."

"Cecil, SIGINT decoy team out of Aviano will spoof a signature toward Novi Sad. PLA should chase it for at least an hour. That's your window."

Cecil tilted his head slightly. "Exfil?"

Will tapped the screen—highlighting Corridor TANGO-17, an unregistered NATO logistics road near the Iron Gate Gorge, straddling the Danube.

"Old rail spur. Shielded tunnel. No electronics. NATO used it during Balkan Phase 2 in 1999. Nobody's looked at it in twenty years. Get her to the train."

Sara looked up from the file on the table. "You really think she still has it?"

Will didn't blink.

"I think she's the only person alive who can prove the PLA's entire quantum program is a bluff. And I think they know it."

On the screen, Cecil shrugged into his coat. Z was already moving off-camera.

Will held Cecil's eyes.

"Move fast."

"Always do."

The link cut.

——

Belgrade Nikola Tesla Airport — 0418 Alpha

The NATO transport touched down hard on a wet runway, taxiing fast to a remote stand where a black Škoda Octavia waited with its engine already running. The driver, a Serbian national on the embassy's quiet payroll, didn't speak. He handed over the keys and walked away across the apron toward a maintenance hangar.

Cecil took the wheel. Z dropped into the passenger seat, already pulling up the apartment schematic on a hardened tablet.

"Forty-one minutes from here to Makedonska if I do not hit a tram," Cecil said.

"Do not hit a tram."

The drive in was quiet. Belgrade at four in the morning was a city of wet stone and sodium light. Cecil ran the route SYBIL had pushed to the tablet — minor streets where the Huawei grid had blind spots Rick had identified during the inbound flight.

Z spoke once, halfway in. "She is dead already."

Cecil glanced over.

"SYBIL just dropped the thermal," Z said, turning the tablet so Cecil could see. "Apartment registered a body-heat decay starting nineteen minutes ago. The trace is flattening fast."

Cecil's expression did not change. He pressed the accelerator a degree harder.

"How fast is the PLA off the X?"

"Unknown. But the heat signature in the stairwell vanished four minutes after the decay started. They are gone."

"Gone where?"

"Gone in a hurry."

Cecil ran a calculation in his head and didn't like the answer. They had been moving since the moment Bohm's call landed in Brussels. There had been no slack in the line. And it had still not been enough.

"Something pulled them," he said.

"Something pulled them," Z agreed.

The Škoda turned onto Makedonska.

12 Makedonska Street — Belgrade, Serbia — 0459 Local

The old blue door hung ajar.

Cecil went first, sidearm low and concealed beneath his jacket. He cleared the front room silently and nodded once. Z entered behind him, pulling the door closed.

The air was still warm.

A kettle sat on the stovetop, steam rising in thin uneven curls — past boiling, past whistle, settling. Two mugs on the table, untouched. A long wool shawl on the floor near the desk. The lamp glowed beside the bed. None of the books were disturbed.

And then Yasha Moravec, slumped on the floor beside the desk, face turned away.

Z crouched without touching her. He looked first, before anything else.

"Puncture at the base of the skull. No exit. No blood pooling." He spoke half to himself. "Long needle. Maybe ten centimeters. Single thrust, upward through the brainstem. She was standing when it happened, then they lowered her. Her knees did not strike the floor."

Cecil glanced at the angle of her hand. "Two-man job?"

"One holding, one striking. They knew exactly where to enter. This is rehearsed. Not improvised."

Z moved around the body without disturbing the scene. His eyes did the rest.

"Kettle is past its boil cycle but the steam is still cohesive. Six to eight minutes since shutoff." He glanced at the mugs. "Tea bags in both, but neither poured. She had a visitor expected. Not a stranger. She made the cups before she heard them come up."

Cecil scanned the room. "Search pattern?"

Z turned slowly, taking it in. "Drawer half-pulled. Books face-down on the shelf, but only the bottom row. Cabinet hanging open. Desk cushion displaced." He pointed at each thing in sequence. "They went fast and shallow. Surface only. No floorboards lifted, no ceiling panels checked, no false-back inspection on the cabinets. This is not a complete search. This is the first ninety seconds of one."

"They got interrupted."

"They got yanked."

Cecil moved to the laptop still open on the desk. A single line of code blinked on the screen.

init_echo_prism//root/threadset=sybil

He leaned in. "She was not transmitting. She was finishing a sale."

Z came to stand beside him.

"To whoever could pay the price she had set," Cecil said. "Which, given what is on it, was always going to be us."

Z exhaled slowly. "So they killed her, started tossing the place, and ran. Before they found whatever she actually left behind."

Cecil straightened and walked toward the bookshelves. The Serbian translation of Introduction to Braiding Statistics sat reshelved upside-down — wrong against the orderly bottom row, wrong in a way that only mattered to someone looking for it.

He pulled it gently.

Click.

A soft, metallic shift behind the shelf.

Z's head came up.

"Cecil."

"I see it."

"We did not arrive in time to save her," he said quietly. "We arrived just in time to keep them from finding what she left behind."

He turned to the wall.

Cecil held the cold capsule in his gloved hand for a long moment, weighing it. Z was already on the secure handset to Watchtower.

"Ops, Z. We have the package. Cold capsule, intact. Lattice-lock signature. We are moving to secondary."

Will's voice came back clipped over the link. "Confirm secondary?"

"Embassy-routed safehouse, Dedinje. We want a deeper sweep on this apartment before we leave the country. She built this place over years. Whatever else is in here, the PLA was not going to find it in ninety seconds and neither did we."

A pause on the other end.

Cecil glanced at the body, then at the bookshelf, then at the kettle that had finally gone silent.

"Z is right," he said. "There is more here. She would not have left only one breadcrumb."

Sara's voice came through, behind Will's. "Tri-band thermal rig is en route from Aviano. ETA your safehouse, ten hours."

Cecil nodded once. "We will be waiting for it."

Z keyed the handset off and looked around the apartment one last time. At the shawl on the floor. At the two mugs Yasha had set out for a meeting that was never going to happen.

"She knew we were coming," he said quietly.

Cecil sealed the cold capsule inside a Faraday pouch and slipped it into his inner coat. "She held on. Long enough to leave us this."

He glanced once more at Yasha Moravec.

"And whatever else she left, we are going to find."

He opened the door just enough to check the street.

The hallway was empty.

They moved.

12 Makedonska Street — Belgrade, Serbia — Next Day, 1640 Alpha

The body was gone. Embassy contract cleaners had moved it before sunrise, quietly, under the cover of a fictitious estate dispute. The apartment had been resealed and guarded, and the only people in it now were Cecil, Z, and two ACIC technical specialists who had flown in overnight from Aviano with the tri-band thermal rig packed into a pair of unmarked Pelican cases.

The rig sat on a folding tripod in the middle of the living room. Its monitor displayed the apartment in layered false color—visible spectrum, mid-IR, magnetic resonance—overlaid into a single composite map of every density, every thermal gradient, every metallic anomaly within the walls.

Z worked the controls. Cecil watched the screen.

For two hours, nothing.

Then, beneath a structural beam that should have been cold steel, an anomaly appeared. A faint bloom — two degrees above ambient — pulsing on SYBIL's overlay like a heartbeat trying to hide.

"Hold the scan," Cecil murmured.

Z froze the frame. "That should not be warm."

"No. It should not."

The beam looked solid, untouched since construction. But Z ran the magnetic resonance overlay against the visible-spectrum image and the discrepancy sharpened. Behind a false tile, precisely counter-weighted to cancel its magnetic signature, something was embedded flush into the concrete.

It took the two specialists forty minutes to extract it without triggering whatever it was.

A Faraday-sealed capsule. No seams. No RF bleed. It should not have existed, and yet it did.

By protocol, NSA TAO was summoned under Title 50 authority. The capsule was flown to Fort Meade in an isolation cradle, unpacked under white-light containment.

Inside lay a single folded sheet of paper. No watermark. No fibers traceable to any known manufacturer. Just an address:

Aurion Secure Vaults AG, Im alten Riet 139, 9494 Schaan, Liechtenstein.

Two names followed—Dr. Elias Bregenz, Zurich-based attorney, and Notarin Helena Wüst, notary public in Vaduz.

It was the kind of clue Yasha Moravec would leave. A breadcrumb wrapped in silence.

The Ghost Drive, once decrypted by TAO's deep kernel rig, yielded only a small payload—Chimera's passphrase and a twelve-digit account number tied to Aurion Secure Vaults. No metadata. No digital twin. Every byte scrubbed down to the quantum layer.

Both physical keys to the box were accounted for—one held by Dr. Bregenz, the other by Helena Wüst. Neither ever duplicated, neither stored on-site.

Folded inside the capsule's lining was a single handwritten instruction, written in Yasha's unmistakable script:

> "Presenter of passphrase + account number + codename EIDOLON = release both keys."

Cecil read it twice.

No signature. No flourish.

That final word—EIDOLON—like a ghost whispering its own name.

Beijing, China — Strategic Support Force HQ

Li Shun stood alone before a wall-sized feed of the Belgrade apartment. Drone footage. Real-time.

He said nothing.

An aide approached.

"She's been confirmed. Dead. No trace of the ghost drive."

Li replied, "Then it still exists."

He turned away. "Burn every known contact. Start with Vermont."

CHAPTER THIRTY-NINE

Liechtenstein Retrieval

Fort Meade - Will's Office

Chimera had hidden the existence of her Liechtenstein vault the way a careful conspirator hides a blade—two pieces, never in the same place. The vault itself in one location. The passwords somewhere else entirely.

Now Watchtower had both.

Retrieving what was inside, however, was not a job Will intended to scatter across agencies or committees. Some operations only worked when fewer people knew they existed.

He turned, almost automatically, to the one man he trusted with his life.

The man who had already saved it twice.

Once in Afghanistan.

Once in a quiet park in Maryland.

He had already asked enough of Cecil this week. He was about to ask more.

Sara didn't need to ask who he meant. She had already reached the same conclusion.

Will wouldn't hand this to Langley. Or the Bureau. Or any of the other alphabet soups that inevitably turned a clean operation into a bureaucratic autopsy.

"It's less than a two-hour flight from Belgrade to Zurich," Sara said, glancing at the map on the wall display. "But getting from Zurich to Liechtenstein will take about the same amount of time once he's on the ground."

Will's mouth bent into the faintest smile.

Sara saw it immediately.

"But the ride home is a killer," he said.

She shrugged. "He's got to make that trip whether he stops in Liechtenstein or not."

The room held the small, familiar quiet of two people who had worked together long enough to think along the same lines.

Then the console chimed.

A new message appeared across the secure Watchtower display—SYBIL's stark white text cutting across the screen.

ANOMALY DETECTED – NUSQUAM NODE

VERMONT PERIMETER SIGNAL DISRUPTED

REEVALUATE THREAT VECTOR

The room seemed to tighten.

Will and Sara looked at each other.

The humor drained from Will's expression first.

"Someone just found Nemo."

Zurich, Switzerland

"Snow drifted over the Rhine valley as Cecil Brandon stepped off the train from Zürich." His coat collar was turned high against the alpine wind, his expression unreadable—a mask honed from years of surveillance briefings and cold-weather operations.

He had come armed with nothing more than a leather folio, a diplomatic cover letter from Fort Meade, and three words that would open whatever Yasha Moravec had locked away: the passphrase, the account number, and the codename—EIDOLON.

Dr. Elias Bregenz's office overlooked the Limmat River, a place where discretion was architectural. Heavy wood paneling, muted carpets, no photographs. The lawyer himself was a tall, spectral man with surgical diction—one of those Europeans who could make silence sound contractual.

Cecil laid the folio on the desk.

"Cecil Brandon, United States Army Counterintelligence Command. Acting under joint ACIC–NSA directive."

Bregenz adjusted his half-rim glasses. "You have documentation?"

Cecil opened the folder. Inside: a single sheet containing the account number, the passphrase, and beneath them, handwritten in block print—EIDOLON.

The lawyer's eyes flicked once to the word. He rose, crossed to a concealed drawer behind a wood panel, and withdrew a small velvet-lined case.

"This key," Bregenz said, "was not to be surrendered except under those precise conditions. Dr. Moravec was explicit."

He placed it on the desk—an ornate steel key, stamped with a microscopic Aurion crest.

Cecil took it with a gloved hand. "Then the condition is met."

Vaduz, Liechtenstein

Vaduz was smaller, colder, cleaner.

Helena Wüst's notarial office sat on a cobblestone street behind the cathedral, every surface polished to quiet perfection. She was in her late fifties, composed, with the calm of someone who had notarized secrets heavier than gold.

"You understand," she said in flawless English, "Liechtenstein notarial code forbids release of any key without absolute verification."

Cecil slid the second document forward.

The passphrase. The account number. EIDOLON.

Wüst studied it, lips pressed thin. After a long breath, she unlocked a recessed wall safe and removed a narrow black key, identical in make to the first.

"She told me this day might come," Wüst said. "And that if it did, whoever stood where you are now would already be late."

Cecil pocketed the key.

"She was right about that."

Outside, dusk was coming down off the mountains. Cecil stood on the cobblestone a minute longer than he needed to, the weight of two keys in his coat. Then he started walking.

Schaan, Liechtenstein — Aurion Secure Vaults AG

The security director at Aurion Secure Vaults AG met Cecil Brandon in the marble atrium with the composure of a man who had seen every kind of client—except one like this. Two armed plainclothes agents shadowed Cecil through biometric locks, iris scans, and a final steel corridor lined with vault doors—each one identical, anonymized, and silent as a tomb.

Vault 312-A.

Moravec's compartment.

He inserted both keys—Bregenz's and Wüst's—into twin slots and turned them simultaneously.

A muted click.

An internal relay cycled once, then again.

The drawer slid open with a hiss of negative pressure.

Inside: a matte-black data vault the size of a paperback book, its casing stamped with the EIDOLON glyph—Yasha's private sigil, etched so faintly it caught light only at an angle. No visible ports. No serials. The surface absorbed light like Vantablack.

Cecil placed it into a lead-lined containment case and keyed his transceiver.

"Asset recovered. Codeword: EIDOLON. Extraction commencing."

Within three hours, the drive was airborne under NSA diplomatic courier, destination Fort Meade.

Fort Meade — TAO Secure Operations Center

Inside the isolation bay the EIDOLON module sat mounted on a chilled forensic rig, its housing clamped open like a dissected instrument.

A fiber tether ran into the rack where SYBIL mirrored the device bit by bit, the stream unfolding across the analysts' displays in dense columns of entropy.

At first there was nothing recognizable in it.

Noise.

Perfect, deliberate noise.

One of the TAO engineers leaned closer to his screen.

"Hold on."

Across the room the quantum emulator had begun mapping the bitstream against its simulated lattice environment. Patterns appeared for a fraction of a second and collapsed again, like interference fringes.

The emulator stabilized.

The data didn't decrypt.

It inverted.

A mirrored key architecture—something designed to unlock only when reflected through a quantum state identical to the one that created it.

Cecil felt the room shift before anyone spoke.

The screens brightened simultaneously.

SYBIL spoke into the quiet.

"Decryption complete."

A pause.

"Dataset identified: PLA Directorate of Quantum Systems. Operation designation: ZHENGYI."

The projections spread across the wall displays.

Not documents.

Evidence.

Benchmark curves appeared first—entanglement performance graphs that the global scientific community had argued about for years.

The curves didn't match.

SYBIL highlighted the discrepancies in red.

"Original laboratory measurements embedded beneath published values."

A second layer opened.

Raw data streams from Chinese quantum testbeds.

Grace Roberts' voice came through the secure line from Maryland.

"Those numbers are impossible."

SYBIL answered calmly.

"Correct."

The overlay shifted.

"Published benchmark data altered to simulate entanglement fidelity beyond demonstrated capability."

Silence settled over the room.

On another screen a chain of financial routing diagrams began assembling themselves.

DARPA subcontractor code repositories.

A siphon through a cutout company.

A second handoff.

A third.

Each arrow eventually converged on a single infrastructure cluster.

Chrysalis.

SYBIL continued.

"Stolen algorithmic frameworks repurposed to generate simulated benchmark outputs."

Another window opened.

European laboratories.

Swiss.

German.

Dutch.

Each node marked with a sudden unexplained collapse in experimental replication.

"Competing research results suppressed through corrupted peer datasets."

Science itself had been rewritten.

Grace spoke again, slower now.

"You're telling me the entire quantum supremacy announcement was fabricated."

Cecil didn't look away from the screen.

"Not fabricated," he said. "Engineered."

The wall display filled with one final dataset. Metadata signatures. A familiar name appeared at the top. Moravec, Yasha.

SYBIL's voice softened almost imperceptibly.

"Authentication verified."

A final data fragment detached from the archive.

"Embedded annotation detected."

The analysts leaned closer as the system rendered it.

Not a sentence. Not a message.

A short string of characters.

46.8523 N 9.5328 E—Y

No explanation. Just coordinates.

Cecil exhaled slowly.

One of the TAO analysts whispered, "What's there?"

Cecil already knew. The Alps. Liechtenstein. The safe box. Yasha hadn't written a philosophy. She had written a map.

CHAPTER FORTY

Rezdiffra

Odenton — Will's Home

Saturday morning, and for once, Gracie arrived before Will was up.

As she made coffee, she gathered the mail off the counter. On top lay an open bill from a doctor's office she didn't recognize—not one of Will's. Three of them marked paid each eight thousand dollars and change. Rezdiffra.

Curious, she searched for the name on her phone.

A new liver treatment drug.

At that instant, she understood who Gussie's "research fund" really was.

She knew Will had saved carefully, invested wisely, was secure—but that was still big for anyone.

She slid the envelope to the bottom of the stack, out of sight.

Of course he'd do it.

Gussie was Watchtower, and Watchtower was family.

Gracie smiled softly.

"My man," she whispered. "My steely-eyed, tough-as-nails pushover. God, how I love him."

Fort Meade -Watchtower Ops One Month Later

The corridor outside Watchtower was unusually still.

Sara leaned against the doorframe of Will's office, holding a single sheet of paper. No briefing tabs, no red stamps—just a printout.

Will looked up from his monitor.

Something wrong?"

Sara shook her head, smiling faintly. "Something right, for once."

She crossed the room and handed him the paper.

He read in silence.

Liver enzyme counts. Platelet recovery. Normalized bilirubin levels.

He didn't say anything for a long time, just exhaled through his nose and set the paper down like it might break.

"She's responding," Sara said. "Doctor says it's still early, but... it's working."

Will leaned back and looked past her through the glass wall of his office. In the bullpen beyond, the team was busy at their desks.

"Good," he said. Then, softer: "She deserves that."

Sara nodded, lingering in the doorway. "She wanted me to tell you she's sorry she couldn't keep the secret longer. She figured you'd notice eventually."

He almost smiled. "She's terrible at covert work."

Sara laughed once. "Yeah. But good at everything that matters."

When she left, Will sat there a while, turning the paper over in his hands. He folded it neatly and slid it into the top drawer with the same quiet care he reserved for mission orders and personal letters.

Odenton, MD-Will's House Late Evening

Will stepped inside, the kind of tired that went deeper than muscle. The lamp over his desk glowed softly, the one Gracie always left on.

There, among the day's mail, was a small ivory envelope addressed in looping cursive. No return address. He knew the handwriting.

He sat down and opened it carefully.

Inside was a single card—no date, no signature line. Just a short note written in a shaky but determined hand:

> Major,
> For once, the mission's going well. The numbers look good, the nurses laugh much, and I'm starting to believe I might just outlive my paperwork.
> You gave me time, and I intend to use it wisely. Tell the team I miss them—
> don't you dare let them get soft.
> With love,
> —G.

Will read it twice, folded it back into the envelope and set it in the drawer beside the lab report.

He leaned back, eyes closed, and let the quiet settle around him. Outside, the wind moved through the trees, whispering like distant radio static, the kind of silence that didn't need to be filled.

Fort Meade — Watchtower Operations Center - A Week Later

Sara stayed late, long after the rest of the team had cleared out. The ops floor was a dim constellation of standby lights and idle monitors, humming like distant crickets.

She stepped into Will's office to drop off a file, meaning to be quick. His desk was as it always was—precise, impersonal, except for one small drawer left slightly ajar.

Sara hesitated. Then she gently pushed it closed—but something caught her eye. An ivory envelope.

Her name wasn't on it, but she knew she shouldn't need one.

She drew it out just far enough to see the handwriting on the card inside. G.

Sara read the first line, then stopped. It wasn't for her—and it didn't need to be.

She slid it back, shut the drawer carefully, and stood there a long moment, eyes softening.

She smiled to herself, shaking her head.

"Damn it, Will," she whispered. "You really can't help yourself, can you?"

CHAPTER FORTY-ONE

Zhengyi Complex

Fort Meade — ACIC SCIF / Post-EIDOLON Debrief

The air inside the vault-level SCIF was dry and still, the kind of silence that hummed against the skin. A holographic schematic of the Chrysalis network glowed in suspended light, dozens of nodes scattered across continents, pulsing faintly like neurons in a sleeping brain.

Major Will Morgan stood at the head of the table, jacket unbuttoned, the fatigue behind his eyes offset by the precision in his tone. Across from him sat Cecil Brandon, the keys from Liechtenstein still sealed in an evidence pouch beside his tablet. Sara Brandt leaned forward, pen tapping against her notes, her expression tight—analyst focus fused with disbelief.

"We always suspected the numbers didn't line up. The PLA couldn't have jumped that far ahead that fast." He lifted a hand, gesturing toward the display, the glow of it reflecting faintly in his expression. "But this... this isn't just deception. It's strategic fiction. Entire labs, entire theories—manufactured to make the rest of us chase ghosts."

"Yasha figured it out years ago. That's why they came for her," Cecil said, nodding toward the EIDOLON dossier.

"The data shows Chrysalis wasn't just a target, they used it. Hijacked nodes to seed false benchmarks. Every 'failure' we thought was a hardware fault was actually sabotage designed to suppress us from overtaking them."

"So, the PLA's 'quantum supremacy' never existed," Sara said, flipping through decrypted data sheets. "They created the illusion of superiority so they could control the tempo and decide when Western research felt obsolete, and when to leak 'advances' for political leverage."

"And while we argued over funding and export controls, they built an empire out of smoke." Said Will.

He paced once around the table, arms folded, watching the node-map rotate slowly.

Each red pulse represented a compromised Chrysalis site. Each green light, one they'd reclaimed. Too many still flickered amber.

"Yasha's logs name every compromised conduit," said Cecil, "Three in Europe, five in Asia, one here. "Helios Advanced Materials, Nemean DataWorks, Echelon Dynamics. They all tie back to the same encrypted transport key: ZHENGYI."

"Meaning the same PLA ghost architecture was used across all their shells," added Sara.

"That's where we burn it down," said Will.

He stopped in front of the holographic projection, the reflection of data scrolling across his face.

Will continued, "SYBIL cross-correlates every signature, any resonance matching EIDOLON's payload gets flagged as hostile. We isolate the Chrysalis framework, trace their suppression cascade, and reverse-engineer every falsified data fork they've buried."

"We expose the myth, or we inherit it," said Sara. "And if we do?" asked Cecil.

Will looked at both of them, the weight of what they'd uncovered hanging between words.

"ACIC becomes the firewall between science and shadow. Because if the world's running on counterfeit physics—somebody's got to rewrite the truth."

Will looked around the table.

"Chrysalis ran for years because nobody saw the full ledger. Every node, every courier, every funding channel—they kept the books in the dark."

"We're opening Operation Shadow Ledger."

The lights dimmed slightly as SYBIL's voice entered the room, low, and calm:

> *"Operational framework recognized. Initial Chrysalis cleanup protocol designated:*

"Objective?" Sara asked.

"Balance the books."

No one spoke.

Outside the SCIF, Fort Meade slept under snow, unaware that the balance of technological power had just flipped—in silence, by ghosts, and by the woman who refused to stay dead.

PLA Directorate of Quantum Systems (Zhengyi Complex)

The Ministry compound lay buried beneath a mirrored skyline, its facade indistinguishable from any of the glass towers that ringed Chaoyang District. But inside—beneath five sublevels of biometric security and negative-air corridors the Directorate's war room was anything but ordinary.

A dozen holographic tables projected real-time telemetry from network monitors across the Pacific and Europe. Quantum relay indicators blinked red. The silence that followed was the kind that no one dared to break.

At the head of the table, General Zhao Renwei, Director of the PLA Quantum Systems Command, stared at the array of failing nodes as if willing them to revive. To his right sat Colonel Su Qi, head of Technical Counter-Operations. Across from them, the gaunt figure of Dr. Liu Chang, chief architect of Operation Zhengyi, stood rigid, eyes hollow.

"How long has it been compromised?" said General Zhao Renwei.

Colonel Su Qi said, "Seventy-three minutes since the intrusion vector first registered. The pattern doesn't match any known foreign offensive toolset. It's recursive—adaptive. Almost as if it was written by our own framework."

Dr. Liu Chang hesitated and then said, "That's because it was. The signature belongs to Moravec's algorithm. The EIDOLON key."

The room stiffened.

General Zhao replied, "Impossible. Moravec was neutralized."

Dr. Liu Chang, gesturing to the feed said, "Neutralized, yes. Silenced—no. She left a trigger buried in the false datasets. Whoever holds EIDOLON just activated it."

A map unfolded in mid-air: red nodes cascading across Europe and the United States. The Chrysalis suppression architecture, the mechanism that falsified every "quantum supremacy" result was unraveling live on screen.

Colonel Su said, "The Western systems are exposing the deception publicly. Their analysts have authenticated the fabrications. Within hours, they'll trace every relay back here."

General Zhao, through clenched teeth. "Initiate defense cyber protocols. Burn the servers, the backups, the archives."

Dr. Liu Chang, "That won't matter. The moment EIDOLON decrypted, it began propagating. Every checksum in the suppression layer now reports its true state. He paused and then continued, "They will know it was all simulation."

Zhao's jaw tightened. He looked to the far wall where a steel door led to the Directorate's command annex.

General Zhao, "Get me the Ministry of State Security.

If our empire of ghosts is collapsing—he glanced to the holographic ruins of their network — so must every witness."

Outside, the Beijing skyline shimmered in early dawn. What had once been the proud digital citadel of Chinese "quantum supremacy" was now slowly dying, its illusions peeled apart, byte by byte. And as the last of the red nodes blinked out, a single phrase surfaced on the Directorate's primary console, a final echo from Yasha Moravec's buried code:

"EIDOLON RETRIEVES THE TRUTH."

——

Fort Meade — Media Operations Briefing

Helena Quinn, 55, had been misquoted, mischaracterized, and, once, outright fabricated by a columnist looking for clicks. She'd learned the hard way that facts alone didn't win narratives—control did.

Now she played the political press like a symphony: deep-background briefings, selective on-record remarks, and strategic silences that spoke louder than any quote.

When the PLA began flooding international media with boasts of quantum supremacy—claims of computational leaps that would render Western encryption obsolete overnight—most of the world panicked.

DARPA didn't. Helena knew their internal assessments: the Chinese claims were exaggerated, stitched together from misinterpreted patents, academic half-truths, and state propaganda. Still, the optics were disastrous.

She moved calmly, offering trusted reporters just enough direction. Names of legitimate scientists, citations to public but overlooked research, hints at open-source conference data to sow skepticism without ever breaching secrecy. Each whisper became an anchor of doubt in an otherwise hysterical news cycle.

Then came the interview that shifted everything.

Live on C-SPAN, under the soft glare of studio lights, Helena smiled faintly when the host asked if America was falling behind.

"Let's just say," she replied, "the United States isn't playing catch-up. We're racing ahead without fanfare."

No leak. No breach. Just a single calibrated sentence that rippled through every embassy and think tank before sunrise.

The White House — Oval Office, Late Afternoon

The late sun washed the Oval Office in amber, through the floor-length curtains. The hum of the air vents was the only steady sound—everything else was the rhythm of argument and restraint.

President Jonathan Stratton sat behind the Resolute Desk, jacket off, sleeves rolled, a folder of briefing papers fanned out before him like discarded playing cards.

National Security Advisor Robert Maddox stood by the window, restless, one hand tapping a folder against his leg.

Julia Branson, the President's competent and observant special assistant, hovered near the credenza, tablet in hand, her eyes moving constantly between the faces in the room.

Helena Quinn sat opposite the President, hands clasped, expression unreadable.

CIA Director Jennifer Mansky and Elena Raine, Director of NSA, flanked her on either side.

The conversation had already gone three laps around the same question: how to answer Beijing's boldest lie yet.

"Let's be clear," Maddox said, pacing. "The PLA's claiming computational parity. They're saying their quantum system can decrypt our defense lattice in real time. It's nonsense—but the world doesn't know that. The markets are skittish. Allies are nervous. We look flat-footed."

Julia interjected without looking up. "And if we say nothing, the narrative hardens. By next week, it'll be quoted in every defense journal as fact."

Maddox turned sharply. "So we issue a counterstatement—something simple. We call it disinformation and move on."

Jennifer Mansky's voice cut through the air, low and surgical. "You issue that statement, and Beijing calls it a cover-up. They want us to react. Every word we say gives their propaganda legitimacy. Silence is smarter."

Maddox bristled. "Silence looks like guilt."

Helena Quinn leaned forward slightly. Her tone was calm, precise.

"Gentlemen, we're missing the point. The PLA's campaign isn't designed to convince scientists—it's designed to convince governments. They're seeding perception of inevitability. If everyone believes China's already won the quantum race, funding dries up, partnerships stall, and trust in our tech leadership erodes. They don't need the physics to be true. They just need the optics to be believable."

Stratton watched her intently, fingers steepled beneath his chin.

"So what's your move, Helena?"

She let a breath pass before answering. "We don't chase their story—we redirect it. I've already spoken on C-SPAN, carefully. The right people noticed. The rest will speculate."

Maddox frowned. "Speculate? That's our national strategy now?"

Helena met his gaze. "In the information age, ambiguity is strategy."

Elena Raine spoke, her voice mild but weighted. "NSA traffic confirms their psyops division's been amplifying those claims through state-linked media. We've flagged the pattern—they're pushing 'quantum supremacy' hashtags through academic proxies. Coordinated."

Stratton's jaw tightened. "And the public thinks they've leapfrogged us."

"They think," Helena said, "because we let them. But there's value in that. If the PLA believes their own narrative, they overextend. They expose what's still aspirational."

Maddox exhaled, unconvinced. "So you're suggesting what—more press teasers? Whisper campaigns?"

"Not whispers," Helena said. "Signals. Carefully placed. A paper here, a symposium there, a funding leak from a plausible contractor. Nothing classified, nothing confirmable—but enough to shift the gravity back toward reality."

Jennifer Mansky nodded slightly, appreciating the precision. "Controlled ambiguity. Let them chase shadows while we hold the high ground."

Stratton leaned back, studying Helena. "You think you can manage that line?"

Her smile was faint but deliberate. "I already have."

The room fell still. Even Maddox stopped pacing.

The President turned to Julia. "Draft language for a quiet background statement—no quotes, just context. Let it circulate through the usual media conduits."

Julia typed without comment.

Stratton rose, stretching the stiffness from his shoulders. "The goal isn't to prove we're ahead. It's to remind the world we're not behind."

He looked directly at Helena. "And if they push harder?"

She met his gaze, unflinching. "Then we stop hinting."

POTUS gave a faint smile. "God help them when we do."

——

Later – Outside the West Wing

As Helena stepped into the fading light of late afternoon, her phone vibrated. A secure text, single line, unsigned:

They've taken the bait. Quantum press echo increasing. PLA analysts chasing citations you planted.

——

Beijing — Zhongnanhai Compound, Midnight

The rain fell in fine silver lines across the old courtyard stones, pooling at the base of the crimson walls. Inside a secure conference room in the State Council compound, a circle of men and women watched Helena Quinn's C-SPAN interview replay on a muted screen.

The image froze on her faint smile.

General Lu Jian, commander of the Strategic Support Force, stood with his hands behind his back, eyes narrowed. "The Americans have chosen ambiguity," he said softly. "That is not weakness—it is camouflage."

Across from him, Minister Lin Heng, head of the PLA's Quantum Strategy Division, adjusted his glasses, his expression analytical rather than defensive. "She said 'racing ahead without fanfare.' It's deliberate. She's provoking curiosity, not confidence. That means their program is further along than we estimated."

Lu turned toward him, voice edged with irritation. "Your projections said otherwise."

Shen didn't flinch. "Our projections were based on observable data. What she's offering is a nonverbal, calibrated signal to suggest technological maturity and narrative control."

A civilian analyst from the Ministry of State Security interjected, scrolling through a feed of social metrics. "Her interview has already tripled engagement across Western media. They're quoting her as reassurance. Investors are stabilizing. The propaganda effect of our quantum claims is collapsing."

Lu's fist landed softly on the table. "Escalate. Release the simulation footage."

Shen shook his head. "Footage without verification invites scrutiny. They'll find the flaws. Quinn is forcing us into overexposure."

Silence spread across the room. Outside, thunder rolled over the city.

Vice Minister Tang Ruifang, the Party's liaison to the Central Propaganda Department, spoke from the corner. "She's not speaking to the world," Tang said. "She's speaking to us. She wants us to believe we've miscalculated."

Shen's tone was colder now. "And she may be right. Her narrative discipline is surgical. Every word she speaks has an echo built in. It ricochets through analysis loops faster than our countermeasures can dampen."

Lu's jaw tightened. "Then we silence the echo."

Shen looked up, eyes expressionless. "You cannot silence suggestion, General. You can only replace it with something louder."

He turned back to the paused screen—the American strategist frozen mid-sentence, gaze calm, unflinching.

"She's telling the truth in a way that sounds like misdirection," he murmured. "That's the most dangerous kind of lie."

——

Zhongnanhai Operations Wing — Later That Night

A courier entered silently, handing Shen a sealed file. The cover bore a single line of text:

Subject: DARPA – Project Chrysalis cross-referenced with civilian contractor *"LaserTech."*

Shen read the header once, then again, slower. He looked out through the rain-slick glass toward the floodlit reflection of the Forbidden City beyond the wall.

"Find out," he said, "what they mean by racing ahead without fanfare."

The courier nodded and left.

Shen remained at the window, his reflection merging with the city's glow—a man staring into both the future and the trap already closing around him.

——

Fort Meade — SCIF, Next Morning

The morning sky was pale and windless over the compound, the kind of quiet that felt engineered. Inside the SCIF, the walls hummed faintly with filtered air and white noise.

Helena Quinn entered carrying a single folder, no tablet, no aides. Her heels echoed once on the composite floor before the door sealed behind her.

Around the table sat Major Will Morgan, Ed Perry, and Sara Brandt—each with a cup of black coffee and the unmistakable posture of people who hadn't slept much.

On the central monitor, SYBIL's interface pulsed in low amber, visualizing live sentiment graphs drawn from global media feeds.

Helena set the folder down. "They took the bait."

Will leaned back slightly. "Zhongnanhai?"

"Confirmed," she said. "NSA intercepted chatter at 0300. PLA's Strategic Support Force met overnight. Lin Heng himself attended. They're second-guessing their own propaganda."

Sara exchanged a look with Will. "So your little line on C-SPAN—'racing ahead without fanfare'—wasn't improv."

Helena smiled faintly. "Nothing on live television is ever improv, Agent Brandt."

Ed Perry rubbed his temple. "Their analysts are good. If they start to believe we're ahead, they'll start searching for proof—and in doing so, expose what they're actually working on."

"That's the plan," Helena said simply.

She tapped the table and SYBIL projected a thin ribbon of headlines—Western, European, and Asian press—all repeating variations of her remark: U.S. Quantum Lead Confirmed?; DARPA Official Drops Hint of Supremacy. The narrative pendulum had already swung.

Will studied the patterns, eyes narrowing. "We can map the reaction tempo. SYBIL's echo analytics will show where Chinese cyber-ops are trying to counter the story. Every new rebuttal gives us a node to trace."

"Quite," Helena said. "Their defense becomes a confession."

Ed folded his hands. "You've just launched a full-spectrum perception op, Helena. Without a single classified disclosure."

She met his eyes calmly. "You don't counter a lie with a denial. You counter it with a more believable truth."

Sara leaned forward, elbows on the table. "What if Lin Heng decides to retaliate with something tangible—an actual data leak, or worse, a staged demo?"

Helena's tone stayed even. "Then he overplays his hand. And when he does, we'll already know where to look."

Will rose, walked to the monitor, and stared at SYBIL's fractal network pulsing across the screen.

"Let's feed this through Watchtower's signal analysis. I want every relay of the PLA narrative mapped and timestamped. If they try to amplify a new story, we pivot before it matures."

Helena nodded. "I'll coordinate with State and the Pentagon's media cell."

Perry gave a thin smile. "You enjoy this too much."

"I enjoy precision," she said. "This isn't propaganda. It's inoculation."

The room fell silent for only SYBIL's pulse filled the space, a heartbeat of data translating human intent into measurable light.

Will turned back. “Helena—how long before they realize you wanted them to see it?”

Her eyes met his. “They already do. They just can’t agree why.”

——

NSA Operations Annex — Later

Rick Huang and Derek Wilshire watched the same sentiment graph from their workstation. Derek’s fingers drummed against his keyboard, reading the feedback curve.

“Look at that spike,” he murmured. “They’re trying to drown the signal with noise—but it’s recursive. Every denial reinforces the suggestion.”

Rick grinned. “Quinn just made Schrödinger’s press conference.”

Derek frowned. “Meaning?”

“She said something that’s both true and false until observed,” Rick replied. “Classic quantum communication.”

Across the hall, Will Morgan stood at the glass, watching the team. The operation had started as containment; now it was turning into something larger—something Helena had understood before any of them.

——

Zhongnanhai, Concurrent

Lin Heng watched a bank of monitors displaying Western headlines. The same phrase—racing ahead without fanfare—appeared in eight languages.

He exhaled slowly. “She’s teaching the world to doubt us.”

General Lu Jian’s reply was cold. “Then teach the world to fear us.”

Shen looked up. “Fear burns fast. Doubt lasts longer.”

He turned off the screen.

CHAPTER FORTY-TWO

The Accident

Genevieve Larsson — The Accident

By day, Genevieve Larsson chased ghosts in the ocean—modeling quantum algorithms that could detect submarines through the faintest disturbances in magnetic and electric fields.

By night, she hunted a different phantom entirely: the dream of reducing monstrous prime numbers to rubble, breaking public-key encryption through sheer, relentless ingenuity.

The lab around her was dark except for the harsh LED above her desk, a pale square of light cutting into the midnight gloom. She sat hunched in it like a lone pilot in a cockpit, surrounded by silent whiteboards and cold equipment that gleamed faintly in the shadows.

Her eyes burned. Her fingers trembled. She had been at this for sixteen straight hours—reworking Shor's algorithm, stripping out clutter, adjusting quantum phase estimation parameters until the lines on the page blurred. Fatigue made the equations unsteady, like waves shifting under her.

Still, she pressed on.

Her handwriting, usually sharp and rigid, had softened at the edges. Numbers leaned into each other, decimals drifted, and at one point she caught herself overwriting a term with a completely different one. She squinted at the mistake, annoyed at her own slipping precision, and forced herself to rewrite the sequence.

But in her exhaustion, the correction came out crooked. A "1" collapsed into a "7." A phase shift she meant to center ended up offset—just slightly, just enough to look wrong.

She frowned at the page.

Her eyes fluttered shut—not in thought, but in surrender. When she opened them again, the room felt tilted, unsteady. She reached for her mug without looking.

Her hand clipped the rim.

The mug toppled.

A flood of lukewarm coffee spilled across her notes, fanning outward like a sepia sunrise over her months of calculations.

"Damn it."

Her voice was a hoarse whisper.

She lunged for the notebook, pulling it free of the puddle, blotting at the edges with her sleeve. smearing ink in streaked arcs. Whole rows of numbers washed into shadow.

She flipped backward, looking for a clean step to anchor her reconstruction. Paused.

The fatigue-distorted page. The sloppy correction. The displaced phase term she'd been meaning to fix.

Under the smeared ink, it didn't look careless.

It looked different.

She traced the altered sequence with her finger, slow, careful, the way you handle something you don't yet trust. One factor off. Exactly where the dead ends ended.

She'd missed it for weeks. Of course she had. She'd been looking at it the way she always looked at things — rested, precise, the symmetry holding. The mistake had broken the symmetry. That was what she needed.

Genevieve stared at the page. Her hand was shaking, which she noticed in the abstract way you notice weather.

Not the solution. But the doorway.

She'd just stepped through.

——

Nusquam Lab - POC

It was generous—borderline optimistic—to call it a prototype. But Nemo did anyway.

In truth, it was a proof of concept, a small internal experiment meant to answer one question: Can this idea even work?

Against the odds, it did—at least partially. The system managed to decrypt roughly twenty-five percent of the intercepted messages. But those fragments—half phrases, broken keys, incomplete codes—were enough to prove the impossible was suddenly possible.

Some of the decrypted lines were trivial. Others were tantalizing—hints of something far larger hidden just beyond the noise.

Slowly, begrudgingly, the algorithm began to learn.

Thirty percent.

Thirty-five.

Forty.

Not perfection—just enough to make educated guesses, to trace patterns through the noise.

They began narrowing their scope, filtering for specific origins—certain call signs, encrypted relays, and packet signatures that kept reappearing. Each partial decryption was a fragment of a larger voice trying not to be heard, and now, for the first time, they were starting to listen.

——

Nusquam Lab

Genevieve paced the lab, eyes bright, a pen still in her hand though she'd stopped writing long ago. The idea had come fast—like static collapsing into signal—and now it was spilling out faster than she could form the words.

"Nemo, listen, Derek Wilshire. I know he's not a quantum theorist, but that's why we need him. The partial decrypts—twenty-five, maybe forty percent—they're not random. They cluster. The gaps aren't noise; they're structure. It's like the algorithm's hitting a harmonic node in the key space but skipping the dissonant factors. If we can map which decrypts succeed versus which fail, Derek could see the hidden pattern. He's wired for that—pattern topology, non-linear inference—if anyone can see it, it's him—"

She barely breathed between words, her brain outrunning her mouth. Nemo leaned on the counter, arms folded, expression half amusement, half admiration.

When she ran out of breath. He smiled. "I know."

They both laughed, the tension breaking. Genevieve grabbed her phone. "We're calling Will."

When Will Morgan answered, his tone was already cautious. "What do you want him to do?"

"He's not a quantum theorist, but he understands signal processing and pattern topology better than anyone. He'll see the structure, not the physics."

"Yes, of course," Genevieve said quickly. "But he doesn't need to. If he can see why we can decrypt some messages and not others—just one small insight—he might unlock something the math's been hiding."

Nemo grinned faintly. "And knowing Derek, he'll probably do it before we finish explaining what the problem is."

Will sighed, resigned but curious. "All right. Bring him in."

Genevieve smiled—the kind that meant she already knew this was going to work.

CHAPTER FORTY-THREE

Closing Ranks

Fort Meade - Nusquam - Secure comms

"We're capped," Nemo said. "Coherence collapses before fidelity."

Will didn't hesitate. "Cause."

"Shielding. Without Radiant Sentry–grade niobium stacks, the system fails."

Grace came in smoothly. "The composites LaserTech developed were the only ones that held. We don't need their system knowledge—just materials behavior."

"You're talking about reaching back to LaserTech," Perry said.

"Not operationally," Will replied. "Expertise extraction only."

"University cover," Grace added. "Materials science scope."

Will's voice hardened. "No reference to Nusquam. No reference to Echo Reef."

"And if they correlate anyway?" Perry asked.

"We terminate," Will said.

A brief silence.

"Authorization granted," Helena said as she joined the channel. "Project Shiny Spire is active."

"Scope," Will said.

"Niobium multilayers only. Named personnel. Neutral sites."

"Compartmentalization."

"Sealed," Helena said. "One anomaly—we pull the plug."

"Proceed," Will said.

——

Linthicum Heights, MD - Fort Meade - Arlington - Secure Comms

"You're asking us to consult without knowing the application," George Lee said.

"Yes," Grace replied. "And we're doing it deliberately."

John Jankowitz frowned. "That's not how we usually work."

Helena's voice was calm, precise. "You're not being asked to support a system. You're being asked to evaluate materials behavior."

George folded his arms. "So we're blind."

"You're bounded," Grace said. "To superconductive layering, thermal drift, and resonance stability. Nothing else."

John scanned the data packet. "This is incomplete."

"By design," Helena said. "You have everything you need—and nothing you don't."

John looked up. "You're seeing collapse under load."

Grace nodded. "That's correct."

"It's not the niobium," John said. "It's phonon coupling. Mechanical energy folding back into the lattice."

George glanced at him. "So what's the fix?"

"Damping," John said. "You bleed the resonance before it feeds back."

Grace didn't smile, but her voice softened. "That's exactly the insight we needed."

——

Nusquam Dinner Table

The farmhouse dining room was warm with low light and easy conversation—Genevieve, Nemo, Karen, and Sara exchanging quiet jokes over roast chicken and wine. It felt almost normal, the kind of evening that briefly disguised the scale of what they were working on.

Only Derek Wilshire sat apart, eyes unfocused, fork idle on his plate. Sara noticed but didn't press; she'd seen that expression before—his mind wasn't here, it was orbiting somewhere deep in the math.

The laughter faded when Derek spoke, almost absently.

"Have you noticed," he said, "that all the successful decrypts use highly totient numbers?"

He frowned, muttering again under his breath. "Highly totient numbers..."

Sara tilted her head. "Totient what?"

But Genevieve froze, wineglass halfway to her lips. Across the table, Nemo's eyes widened. The same realization struck them both at once—the missing link between quantum phase estimation and key distribution.

Without a word, they pushed back from the table, chairs scraping the floor.

Karen blinked. "Did I miss something?"

Sara sighed, half-smiling. "Yeah," she said. "About three months of math in one sentence."

By the time she looked toward the hallway, Genevieve and Nemo were already gone—racing back to the lab.

Derek just kept staring at his plate, whispering, "Highly totient numbers," as if tasting the phrase that had just changed everything.

——

Nusquam Lab — Three Days Later

The hum of processors filled the underground lab, a low mechanical heartbeat under the Vermont cold. Genevieve Larsson hadn't slept much—no one had—but she didn't care.

Using Derek's insight into highly totient numbers, she'd rewritten key sections of the quantum code. What they were now calling Derek's Algorithm was performing far beyond expectation—eighty percent of encrypted traffic decrypted cleanly, the rest falling in fragments that hinted at near-total success.

It was no longer a proof of concept, yet not quite a prototype either—something in between.

They'd looped in Sloane Merrick, head of NSA Tailored Access Operations, for validation and containment.

Now, across the wall of monitors, streams of Mandarin text scrolled by in real time—PLA and MSS transmissions peeled open after years of silence.

Each decoded message was a window into the unseen machinery of a rival superpower, and as the data poured in, Genevieve felt the weight of what they had built—an accidental miracle turned weapon of intelligence.

——

Fort Meade - Morgan's Office

The Portrait, the Trireme, and Three Very Curious Analysts

Rick Huang leaned back in his chair, spinning slowly as he stared at the open doorway of Will Morgan's office. The boss wasn't in—rare, valuable, a window of opportunity. Derek hovered beside him with a coffee the size of a ballistic missile.

Derek squinted toward the credenza.

"You ever notice the angle between that portrait and the trireme? It's precisely forty-five degrees."

"Please don't say that out loud," Rick groaned. "If SYBIL hears that and decides to audit all of us for alignment bias, I'm blaming you."

Derek ignored him, walking halfway into the office to study the ship model more closely.

"It doesn't make sense. Why a trireme? He has zero nautical hobbies. I checked his social posts and purchase records—he's never bought a fishing pole."

Rick snorted. "Will Morgan doesn't fish. Fish confess."

Cathy, walking by with a stack of reports, paused. "Are you two seriously conducting unauthorized desk anthropology?"

"Not unauthorized," Rick said. "Just... unsanctioned adjacent."

Cathy shook her head and left before she became part of the conspiracy.

Derek folded his arms. "Okay, working theory: the woman is his wife."

"Incorrect," Rick said immediately. "You're assigning him a whole love life. He barely has a lunch life."

"Fine. Sister?"

Rick considered this. "Possible. But Will's emotional architecture is—how did Gracie put it?—'opaque, but load-bearing.' Hard to see sibling softness there."

Derek pointed at the portrait again, studying the woman's expression.

"She looks... important."

"Everything in his life is important," Rick replied. "He's the kind of guy who organizes his vitamins alphabetically."

Derek frowned.

"Vitamins aren't alphabetical."

"You think that stops him?"

Before Derek could respond, Sara Brandt stepped into the ops floor, a stack of case files tucked under one arm, her tone preemptively exasperated.

"Oh God," she said. "Please tell me you two are not speculating about the portrait again."

Rick gestured defensively. "We're engaging in constructive interpersonal pattern analysis—"

Sara gave him a look that could extinguish streetlights.

"Rick. It's his mother."

Rick blinked. Derek blinked. Cathy—now pretending she wasn't listening from ten feet away—blinked too.

"Oh," Derek said softly.

"That... makes sense," Rick admitted, deflating like a balloon that had discovered gravity.

Sara walked past them into Will's office, adjusted the portrait by a hair's breadth (a gesture of respect more than necessity), and stepped back out.

"What about the ship?" Derek asked. "You know anything about that?"

Sara shook her head. "Nope. Total mystery. I asked him once, years ago." She mimicked Will's understated delivery perfectly:

"It's a question I'm still answering."

Rick threw up his hands. "See? This is why we can't figure him out. He drops riddles like breadcrumbs, except the breadcrumbs explode ."

Derek stared at the trireme again, brow furrowing with increasing intrigue.

"Maybe it's symbolic. Or historical. Or something psychological."

Sara shrugged lightly. "Whatever it means, he hasn't told anyone. So let it sit. He'll tell us when he wants to—if he ever wants to."

She moved off toward the glassed-in operations room, but paused just long enough to add:

"And if you two rearranged anything in that office, SYBIL will know before we take our next breath."

When she was gone, Rick exhaled.

"She definitely knows what it means."

"She definitely does not," Derek countered. "If she did, she'd have smirked. Did you see a smirk? I didn't see a smirk."

Rick leaned back again, staring at the silent trireme.

"We're missing something."

They were.

——

Nusquam Lab

The lights in Nusquam's subterranean lab hummed with their steady LED brilliance, reflecting off steel consoles and glassy cryogenic housings. Nemo sat alone, a notebook balanced on one knee, scribbling symbols in black ink the way others might jot grocery lists. Equations cascaded across the page—probabilities, error rates, photon polarizations.

On the central display, a simulation flickered: streams of photons fired through a fiber channel, half-red, half-blue, dancing like fireflies against the black screen.

Sara Brandt entered, coffee in hand. She paused, watching the display. A cascade of red and blue photons scrolled across the central screen—orderly, pulsing, hypnotic. But something was off about the rhythm.

"You've been at it for sixteen hours," she said.

Nemo didn't look up, fingers flying across a secondary keyboard. "Trying to break my own system. Third attempt. If I can't crack it, maybe no one can."

Sara moved closer to the display. "What am I looking at?"

"Simulated quantum key exchange. I'm sending a key through a fiber channel, encrypted with photon polarization states. Red means horizontal. Blue means vertical." He tapped the screen. "See that blip? Test interceptor just tried to read the stream."

Sara watched the blue photons flicker. "What happened?"

"The measurement changed the state. The key registered tampering." Nemo's voice quickened. "That's the whole point. Anyone tries to listen in, the quantum state collapses. We see it immediately. No hidden eavesdropping. No 'harvest now, decrypt later.' The key becomes useless the moment it's observed."

Sara processed that. "So the adversary knows they've been caught."

"Yes. Which means they either intercept clean—and we know about it—or they get nothing." Nemo pulled up a second window showing cascading data. "Now watch. I'm generating a new key. Fifty thousand photons per second. Each one carries a random polarization state."

The red and blue stream accelerated on screen, almost a blur.

"But here's the problem," Nemo said, his tone shifting. Urgent now. "Quantum decoherence. Noise in the channel. Photons don't survive fiber optics perfectly. Temperature fluctuations, signal scatter, environmental interference—they all degrade the quantum state. We lose maybe forty percent of our photons to the environment before they reach the receiver."

Sara leaned in. "That's a forty percent failure rate."

"Was." Nemo's fingers moved faster. "Until Genevieve and Derek figured out how to encode redundancy into the polarization states. Rather than one photon carrying one bit, we now use clusters—spatial and temporal encoding. A single corrupted photon doesn't kill the key."

He pulled up a new display: a reconstruction algorithm in motion, photons aggregating into stable patterns.

"Watch the algorithm rebuild it."

The corrupted and clear photons sorted themselves on screen. The corrupted ones faded to gray. The clear ones brightened.

"The receiver processes the cluster, discards the degraded measurements, reconstructs the key from the clean photons. Error correction on the fly." Nemo leaned back, breathing harder than before. "We're now at ninety-eight percent key recovery rate. Quantum channel is unbreakable, and we can actually use it."

Sara absorbed that. "So theoretically, someone could jam the channel entirely. Flood it with noise."

"Yes. Denial of service, not decryption. But that's obvious. You'd know you were under attack."

"How long does it take to generate a usable key?"

Nemo gestured at the screen. "This simulation? Fifty thousand photons, ninety-eight percent recovery, one-time pad generation—thirty seconds. Live system with actual cryogenic hardware, maybe two minutes. Handshake, validation, deployment."

Sara was quiet, thinking tactically. "If someone steals the apparatus—the actual quantum generator, the fiber channel, the receiver—can they replicate it?"

"They can try. But the code isn't just the hardware. It's Genevieve's algorithm. It's Derek's error-correction framework. It's months of calibration specific to our environmental conditions." Nemo's voice took on an edge. "You copy the hardware and you get a dead box. The math has to be spot on with the physics, or nothing works."

Sara nodded slowly. "And if they try to force it?"

"The key fails to generate. System lights up red. You know you're being attacked." Nemo turned to face her. "That's the beauty of it. With RSA or traditional crypto, you don't know you've been compromised until years later when someone decrypts your secrets. With QKD, you know in real time. Seconds. Immediate certainty."

"Whoever controls unbreakable, real-time-verified communication controls the intelligence conversation. Our adversaries can't harvest our secrets. Can't crack them later. Can't even listen in without us knowing."

Sara picked up the coffee she'd set down and pushed it toward him. "Then you need to finish this. Before someone decides to steal it."

Nemo smiled a devilish smile. "Well... thanks to Genevieve and Derek's new algorithm, we actually have a working prototype.

——

Will Morgan's office - later

Will stood at the head of the table, his tie loose, his sleeves rolled. Nemo's data scrolled across the plasma wall—streams of photons, error-correction models, key generation rates. The Watchtower team sat in silence as Will distilled it into strategy.

"This isn't just an encryption upgrade," he said, voice low and deliberate. It's a weapon," Nemo said. "Whoever controls unbreakable, real-time-verified communication controls the intelligence conversation. Our adversaries can't harvest our secrets, can't crack them later, can't even listen in without us knowing."

He gestured toward Nemo. "He's just given us something the Russians, the Chinese, the Iranians—every hostile actor on the planet—will do anything to steal. And if they can't steal it, they'll try to burn it down before we deploy it."

Grace Roberts leaned forward. "Then the question isn't if we can build it. The question is can we protect it long enough to matter?"

Will's eyes met hers. "Yes. SYBIL will integrate QKD into our next-generation secure channels under codename Echo Reef. From now on, no assumption of safety unless it's quantum."

He paused, letting the weight settle. Then he smiled faintly—the rare kind that carried both resolve and warning.

"Ladies and gentlemen, welcome to the next battlefield. The war for silence."

CHAPTER FORTY-FOUR

"Silencing the Wolf"

"You were never one of us."

Remote Border Road – Northern Myanmar, 14km from the Yunnan Frontier -- 19:04 Local UTC +630

The jungle dusk had settled like a smothering shroud. Insects buzzed in waves. Steam rose off the cracked clay road as the last heat of the day bled into the undergrowth.

Darius "Wolf" Straker stood beneath the tin awning of an abandoned border weigh station. He wore a sweat-soaked field shirt, dust-caked boots, and a black pack slung over one shoulder. His .338 Lapua was gone. He'd ditched it three borders ago.

His eyes stayed fixed on the road.

They were late.

A single Chinese military SUV pulled up. No markings. Windows dark. It rolled to a stop ten feet away and idled.

Straker didn't move. He was used to handler games.

The rear door opened. A thin man in a fitted linen jacket stepped out. No insignia. No name.

Colonel Ren Kai. Strategic Support Force. Internal Action Liaison.

Ren in a calm voice said, "You failed."

"I wounded him."

"He lives."

Straker stared at him, the edge of his jaw ticking.

"Mission was compromised. Intel was bad. Terrain wasn't what you—"

"Stop."

A second man stepped out. Quiet. Compact. Gloves on. Carrying a case.

Straker's body instinctively shifted—weight over the balls of his feet, breath low. But he didn't draw. Not yet.

"The Party doesn't reward failure. You were contracted to remove a liability. Instead, you became one."

"I never signed up for political theatre. You wanted it clean, I made it disappear. You want me gone, just say it."

"Very well."

The second man opened the case. Inside: a suppressed QSZ-92, wiped of serial, magazine loaded.

He held it out to Straker—grip first. Straker stared at it.

He smiled. The corner of his mouth curled just enough to hint at his contempt.

"Of course. You'd rather I do it myself."

Ren didn't answer.

Straker took the weapon. Weighed it in his hand. It was light. Balanced.

He looked up at Ren Kai with something that almost resembled pity.

"You're scared of people who think for themselves. That's why you'll always need us... and always kill us."

Then he moved.

Not to his own temple.

He spun, low and fast, bringing the gun up toward Ren's aide.

But the man was faster.

One suppressed round. Center mass. Another to the throat. A third through the right orbital socket.

Straker hit the ground hard. Face-first. Legs twitched once. Then went still.

Ren Kai stepped forward and stared down at the body.

"You were never one of us."

He turned back to the car. The aide knelt and retrieved the pistol, wiped it clean, and placed it back in the case.

No words were exchanged.

The SUV turned around and disappeared into the tree line.

Within hours, satellite data would be overwritten. Straker's alias scrubbed from the Thai border logs. The weigh station would catch fire in the night, and no one would come to investigate.

By dawn, Wolf was just another ghost in the jungle.

CHAPTER FORTY-FIVE

Mossad Assessment

Fort Meade -SCIF 2245 Hours R

Cecil was alone at his terminal when the compartmented channel chimed—two soft tones, the kind that asked for attention but not alarm. He pulled up the encrypted buffer and entered his authentication phrase.

The message had routed through three cutouts. The origin was compartmented—nothing but a label:

[COMPARTMENTED/TLV].

But Cecil knew the source before reading the first line.

[ENCRYPTED CHANNEL — ROUTING: COMPARTMENTED → FTM]

FROM: [COMPARTMENTED]

CLASSIFICATION: EYES ONLY

SUBJECT: Infrastructure pattern match—quantum application

—Begin message—

Re your recent inquiries regarding distributed command-and-control architecture in quantum networks. We've been tracking similar development patterns across multiple threat actors. Same broker network, different regional vectors, but coordinated acquisition strategy.

"Our assessment: whoever is building this infrastructure isn't trying to steal quantum computing capability. They're trying to build an undetectable surveillance system using quantum cryptography as its foundation. The architecture suggests someone who understands both quantum physics at the highest level AND intelligence tradecraft... Find

the person who thinks like both scientist and spy, and you'll find your infrastructure."

You should know what you're hunting. And you should know we're interested in the outcome.

An old professional who respects capabilities when he sees them.

—End message—

Cecil read it twice, the second time slower. Then he heard the SCIF door hiss open behind him.

"You got something?" Will's voice was level, but alert.

Cecil didn't turn. "Tel Aviv."

Will moved closer but didn't look at the screen—compartmented information required deniability. "And?"

"Mossad's been watching Chimera's infrastructure builds. Same pattern we're seeing. Same quantum-crypto angle we've been suspecting."

Will absorbed that, his posture tightening slightly. "They've identified the pattern."

"More than that. They've assessed her objective. She's building an undetectable surveillance capability and using quantum cryptography as the foundation. Whoever designed it works fluently in both quantum physics and tradecraft. That's the combination that matters."

Will was quiet for a second until he said, "So Chimera understands both registers."

"Mossad has been tracking infrastructure like this across multiple regions for months. They're confirming what we're hunting is the real thing."

Will nodded slowly, processing the implications. "And they're telling us because we handled the asset professionally six months ago."

"He reported back what happened at Nusquam. Apparently, the fact that we detained him, questioned him, and released him without aggression—that counted for something in Tel Aviv. Counted enough that when they had something we needed to know, they found a way to tell us."

Will nodded slowly, understanding the full calculus. "Professional courtesy becomes an intelligence channel."

"It does. And right now, it's validating what we've suspected—that Chimera is uniquely dangerous because she holds both pieces in her mind at once. Log it. And Cecil—make sure only you and I can read that message. Compartmented stays compartmented."

"Already done."

Will left the SCIF with a clearer understanding of what he was actually hunting. The person who could hold the physics and the tradecraft in her mind at the same time, and weaponize the seam between them.

CHAPTER FORTY-SIX

Target designation Sable

Nusquam Lab

Nemo stood, hands flat on the console, the recent work on Apparition Echo Reef and the prototype Shor-accelerator still glowing on his screen. "We fed the NSA hundreds of intercepted Russian messages—bulk decrypts came through this week. The model flagged recurring keywords: Nusquam, Sable, Nemo, quantum. When the analysts translated, we had confirmations."

He didn't need to say more: the machine had handed them Moscow's intent like a wrapped blade.

Will flipped to the next pages in the message. There, in terse NSA prose, was the why: Smirnov—already convinced Larsson had been Sable for years, the mole that had skewed Russian understanding of Radiant Sentry—had closed the file. The SVR wanted finality. The order left no hint of delay.

"Where does China stand?" Rick asked.

Grace answered before Will could. "Zhou Lin MSS flagged the Vermont Service presence weeks ago. He was suspicious about Shen Ke—thought he might still be alive and somewhere in the U.S. When the Russians pinned Larsson, the Chinese cooled on the manhunt. Their focus shifted to finding the quantum program. They want the tech; the kill doesn't help them much. They'll watch rather than strike."

The practical questions arrived in a drumbeat: Who knew Larsson's presence? How quickly could she be moved? Could they intercept the kill team in transit? Should they brief Stratton now? Call the FBI? The Secret Service? MI6?

Will's face hardened into command clarity. "First: protect Larsson. Lock Nusquam down now—no in, no out without me. Two: NSA stays on our pipe. Rick, send me any Network Operations Center telemetry that shows unusual movement from Boston north. Grace—coordinate with Sarah at Secret Service liaison. If this smells like an assassination under domestic cover, we need federal jurisdiction and fast. Sara, figure our extraction options for Sable—nonkinetic routes first. Notify Perry and get Stratton's token-level read-in."

Rick's fingers flew across keys. "I'm dumping all Sable-related packet signatures into SYBIL. If the SVR cutouts signal, I'll light it red. We'll know. We'll see movement before they're on the ground."

Sara closed her eyes for a second, then opened them with the practiced calm of someone who'd seen too many fast-moving catastrophes and learned how to steady the ship inside them. "We don't give them the luxury of surprise," she said. "Not now."

The quantum arrays hummed, oblivious. For the first time in months, the lab felt less like a sanctuary than a target. Will felt the weight of the choice: hide the woman who'd once been a weapon and a mole, or risk letting the swift calculus of Moscow rewrite a darker margin of history.

He tapped the secure network once, routing a single line to London and one to Tel Aviv—silent, procedural calls to allies who could help and to allies he might have to trust with a life. The kill order read like the last act of a long, cold drama. The response would have to be cleaner, faster, and as invisible as the channel that had carried the Russians' intent.

"Move," Will said, voice low. "Do it clean."

——

Fort Devens -ACIC New England Field Office 04:07 Hours R

The field office smelled of coffee and printer toner. Dawn gray crept across the parade ground. Major Nathan Harlan stood by the window, palms on the sill, waiting for the secure line to blink. In his work, odd hours were normal; surprises were rarely benign.

The line answered with Ed Perry's voice, direct, flat, the tone of a man who'd been awake long enough to make clear decisions. "Major Harlan. Sorry to wake you. I need you up."

"On my feet, General," Harlan said.

Ed wasted no time. "We've got an urgent from Homeland Security via a trusted channel that one of our people codename Sable has been targeted. Last known alias: Genevieve Larsson. Location confirmed: northern Vermont. She's under ACIC protective watch. This is ACIC compartmented—do not raise Nusquam outside your chain."

Harlan's face stayed calm. "By whom?"

"Three-man kill team," Ed replied. "Clean tradecraft. No SVR chatter. They'll avoid standard comms, use civilian transport, local cutouts. Entry through Montréal, secondary roads down the Champlain corridor. They intend to use the wilderness as cover. The window is narrow.

"You are authorized to activate a Threat Detection Operations Team."

Harlan absorbed it. "So surgical the locals won't see it till it's over. You want interdiction or perimeter defense?"

"Both," Ed said. "But keep it off official channels. We need deniability. ACIC handles Nusquam knowledge—FBI and others don't get that layer. You run this low-profile. Use civilian vectors, local liaisons in Québec and Vermont, clean rentals, and cash payments through our CSIS contact in Montréal. No direct signals back to Moscow. If this is a setup, exposure kills the asset."

Harlan flipped open his notebook. "I can mobilize road watches under routine public-safety pretexts—Massachusetts State Police, Vermont detachments. We can interdict along the Champlain corridor within an hour if needed."

"Good," Ed said. "I'll send a Montreal coordinator through CSIS they'll coordinate with MI6's Canadian liaison arm. Air medevac is authorized only as last resort; ground movement preserves cover. You'll have medical assets on standby under preexisting agreements. Remember: custody must remain ACIC. If you take them, you certify the chain of custody."

"Chain of custody stays with ACIC," Harlan confirmed. He shaded a line in his notes. "Who's my SIS contact, and what's the pickup plan if the cell moves fast?"

"We'll push the contact details in five minutes," Ed replied. "Primary plan: intercept civilian arrival, escort to a clean pickup point, transfer to Fort Devens custody. If the cell accelerates, hold perimeter and call me. And Major—if you see signs that the team isn't SVR but a crafted third party, pull back and notify me immediately."

Harlan closed the notebook and nodded to himself. "Understood. Minimal footprint. Maximum deniability. Pick up if feasible; contain if not."

Ed's voice went quieter, more deliberate. "We're counting on you, Nate. This stays tightly compartmented. Nusquam is ACIC-only. Don't let it show up where it doesn't belong. Godspeed."

"Copy that, sir," Harlan said. He closed the line, ordered three unmarked SUVs, and began moving—maps in hand, contingencies already running through his head.

——

Fort Devens — ACIC New England Field Office

The operations floor hummed with controlled urgency. Rows of screens threw shifting light across the faces of analysts and operators. Major Nathan "Nate" Harlan stepped out of his glass-walled office, phone still in hand, the decision already made.

"Spin up Threat Detection," he said.

A subtle ripple moved through the room. Chairs rolled. Coffee cups were pushed aside. This wasn't a drill.

Within moments, a dozen specialists slid into position. The Threat Detection Operations Team—TDOT—was online.

Green icons blinked on the tactical display as field assets acknowledged. The room's quiet transformed into a low, efficient buzz—ACIC's version of combat readiness.

Harlan paced to the center of the floor, voice steady.

"Tasking is Vermont corridor. We're supporting Fort Meade and ACIC HQ. Objective: early warning, interdiction, and neutralization. Assume multiple foreign actors.

"Priority zero," Harlan added. His voice was calm but iron-edged. "Eyes on every ingress. If they're coming, we see them before they see her. Let's move."

The overhead displays burst into coordinated life—satellite overlays, traffic nets, and drone telemetry feeding through a secure NSA relay. A green circle blinked over Essex Junction, another over Nusquam.

"Rina, I want an air picture. If a mosquito crosses the border, I want to know what color its wings are."

Captain Rina Halvorsen, Signal Intelligence/Electronic Intelligence (SIGINT/ELINT) lead, already had her headset on. "Copy that. Pulling live radar and satellite sweeps from Montreal sector."

"Jules, pattern correlation. Look for any overlapping comm bursts or encrypted traffic along the Champlain corridor."

Sergeant Jules Kwan, CyberOps specialist, fingers flying over three keyboards, murmured, "On it. Ghost packets already pinging at the forty-eight border nodes."

"Monroe, spin the drones. Silent pattern. Keep altitude under two hundred feet."

Warrant Officer Dale Monroe, Drone Operations Lead, smirked. "Already warming them up, sir. Vermont's about to get a new flock of birds."

"And Hana—get me human eyes."

Staff Sergeant Hana Ruiz, Human Intelligence (HUMINT) coordinator, lifted a phone to her ear. "Local law enforcement and two plainclothes teams inbound. ETA fifteen."

Harlan looked up at the wall clock.

"Fifteen minutes to eyes-on. After that, we lock the board."

The massive central monitor flickered as SYBIL's remote telemetry joined the feed, voice cool and neutral:

> *"Integration complete. Quantum surveillance channels synchronized. Target field visibility at 96.2%."*

Harlan folded his arms, gaze hard.

"Good. Now let's find whoever thinks they can hunt on U.S. soil."

——

Outside, the wind swept across the Devens parade ground, scattering dry leaves against the chain-link perimeter fence. Inside, the hum of the ops floor steadied into rhythm—screens alive, systems syncing, threat feeds spooling in real time. Major Harlan said nothing more. He didn't need to. The team was in motion now—quiet professionals doing what they did best: watch, analyze, and wait for the tremor no one else could see coming.

Three states south, at Fort Meade, Will Morgan would soon feel the first echo.

CHAPTER FORTY-SEVEN

Exfiltration

Fort Meade, SCIF Room 7 -Eight hours before Button Bay

No windows. No clocks. Just the kind of silence that belongs to decisions too heavy for daylight.

Ed Perry stood with his jacket off, tie loosened, staring at the map display. Will Morgan leaned on the edge of the table beside him, expression unreadable, while Grace and Sara waited by the console. SYBIL's soft pulse lit the walls like an artificial heartbeat.

"She's the target, Ed. SVR's confirmed it. Smirnov's kill team is already inbound," said Will.

"I know," Perry replied. His voice was quiet but carried the iron weight of command. "We can't keep her here—not with that kind of heat closing in."

Sara glanced at the map. "Where?"

Perry tapped a location on the holographic overlay—Wales. A coastal dot on the A487.

"Penrhyndeudraeth. MI6 maintains a secure safe house there under a joint program with GCHQ. Minimal footprint. Population just over two thousand. Nearest city—Porthmadog. She'll vanish into the hills."

Grace folded her arms. "And what about her work? She and Nemo are joined at the neural core of Echo Reef. You cut her off, the whole project loses balance."

Perry looked at her, then at Will. "We're not cutting her off."

Will understood before anyone else. "You're invoking Stratton's order."

Perry nodded once. "Special Executive Directive 014. Presidential authority. She enters WitSec under modified parameters—dual classification. Her new identity becomes permanent, but she retains restricted operational access."

"Meaning," Sara said slowly, "she disappears from every database except SYBIL's."

"Exactly. Officially, Genevieve Larsson ceases to exist. Unofficially..." Perry paused, "She continues to work with Nemo. Under her alias, Gloria Jansson."

Sara mumbled, " I guess I'll just call her 'G'."

The room was still.

Will broke the silence first. "What about extraction?"

"MI6 owes us for Singapore," Perry said. "Langley's out of the loop, and Stratton's keeping DHS quiet. London Station will handle the lift. She'll move under Tier-Zero security through RAF Valley, then ground transport to Penrhyndeudraeth. Only two handlers on the British side know who she really is."

Grace's tone softened. "She'll be alone."

Perry's reply was low. "Safer than dead."

——

Fort Meade - Secure Conference Room

The blinds were drawn. Only the wall clock moved.

Will Morgan sat across from Ed Perry, a sealed folder between them marked

EYES ONLY // PROTECTIVE RELOCATION.

"She can't stay who she is," Commander Perry said. His voice carried the weight of procedure, but his eyes held something closer to regret. "After Vermont, every Russian cutout in the hemisphere will be looking for her. The hit team might be gone, but the signal's out. She's burned."

Will leaned forward, elbows on the table. "Genevieve doesn't have family. Her mother's gone, her father's in memory care. There's no one left to disappear with her."

"That's what makes her the perfect candidate," Perry said. "Clean extraction, clean reinvention. WitSec is the only program airtight enough to hide her—and the only one that won't raise questions inside the community."

Will stared at the folder. He already knew what was inside: new IDs, a background built from fragments of erased lives. It always felt like a small death.

"What's the alias?"

"Gloria Jansson," Perry said. "Born in Duluth, Minnesota. Environmental-data consultant. Nothing about her draws attention."

Will exhaled through his nose. "She's earned better than hiding behind a fake résumé."

"She's alive," Perry replied. "That's better than most get."

The secure line to Nusquam buzzed and Perry clicked on the speaker button.

"Hello Genevieve. I'm here with Will. We've considered all the factors and your safety trumps everything. "

Perry explained the decision in plain terms—no jargon, no politics. When he finished, he clicked on send and transmitted the folder to her.

Genevieve stared at it, the embossed seal a tombstone of her old life.

She didn't reach for it.

Across the room, her Secret Service detail waited silently.

Genevieve let out a slow breath. "This wasn't the plan.' This wasn't what anyone promised when I risked her life for her country—when I spent years walking a razor-thin line as a double agent inside Russian intelligence, feeding false information to buy time for Radiant Sentry to become functional."

She continued, voice steady but edged with something sharp and cold.

"I did what my country asked," she said. "Every order. Every risk. Every lie I told was for the flag on your lapel." Her eyes noticed Ed Perry glancing down at his lapel. "And now you're telling me the only way to keep me alive is to vanish. To become a... what did you call it?"

Ed Perry swallowed. "A shrouded doppelganger. A complete overwrite. Zero public footprint, zero discoverable identity anchors. The highest level of protection we can offer."

"Protection," she echoed, the word a bitter laugh. "I already have Secret Service protection. They said that was enough."

"Agents can be outmaneuvered," he said carefully. "Your situation is... unprecedented. You're not just a target. You're unfinished business for two different intelligence services who both believe they own a piece of you."

She flinched—not visibly, but inwardly, where the truth struck deepest.

"Genevieve," he continued, "the only way to guarantee you survive the next year is to become someone else entirely."

Genevieve looked at the man, then at the folder. A new name. A new past. A new future.

An erasure disguised as mercy.

She folded her arms, chin lifting. The steel in her voice returned.

"You're asking me to disappear because I was loyal," she said. "Because I did the right thing. Because I served."

"Yes," the general admitted. "Because you served."

Silence filled both ends of the call, dense, suffocating, official.

When Genevieve reached for the envelope she didn't open it. She simply rested her hand on top of it, fingers unmoving. Gently patting her heart she said, "Will, I owe you so much for trusting me and standing up for me when no one else would. I will never forget it. If you agree there is no other way, then I must now trust you."

Placing his hand on his heart Will acknowledged with a slight nod of sad regret.

"When this is done," she said, "when I am whoever this folder says I am... I want it noted." Her eyes sharpened, blue fire under ice. "I want it remembered that my country didn't save me. It hid me. And that's not the same thing.

Perry hesitated. "I can make that notation."

Genevieve stood, the chair legs scraping softly across the floor. "Good," she said. "Because if I'm going to become a ghost, someone should at least write down who died."

"If this keeps the work safe," she said, Looking at the name inside the folder, "then Gloria Jansson it is."

Will met her eyes. She managed a small, brittle smile the kind that hides everything it costs.

Outside the room, the corridors of Fort Meade hummed as if nothing had changed.

Inside, one life had just ended so another could stay invisible.

——

Nusquam / Echo Reef Lab

The world outside had already forgotten Genevieve Larsson. Inside Nusquam's glass corridors, however, the air still carried her name.

She stood in the dim lab light, the envelope from Fort Meade unopened on the workstation beside her. Across the room, Nemo adjusted calibration feeds on the quantum array—pretending to be lost in code. He wasn't.

The hum of the cryostat filled the silence between them.

"So," Nemo said finally, not looking up, "is it official?"

She nodded once. "As of midnight, Genevieve Larsson no longer exists."

Her voice was even, but the words landed heavy in the air.

She set the envelope down and opened it carefully—inside, the new passport, driver's license, and credentials.

GLORIA JANSSON.

Her face, her eyes, her signature. But not her.

Nemo turned toward her, the cool light from the monitor catching the faint exhaustion around his eyes. "Gloria Jansson," he said, tasting the name like something unfamiliar. "Doesn't sound like you."

"It's supposed to sound like no one," she replied. "That's the point."

He hesitated, then crossed the space between them, stopping close enough that she could see the reflection of her false name in his pupils. “And yet,” he said softly, “I still see Genevieve.”

She smiled, small and fleeting—a moment of warmth in the sterile hum of Echo Reef.

“Careful, Nemo. That kind of talk gets people reassigned.”

He almost smiled back. “Then I’ll work harder at subtlety.”

They stood there for a long moment—the hum of the quantum servers their only witness.

For now, she would remain at Echo Reef under full ACIC protection. Under order from President Stratton the lab’s cover rewritten so deeply that not even DARPA’s audit bots could trace it.

To the outside world, Gloria Jansson was an environmental-data consultant assisting a defense climate-modeling pilot.

To Nemo, she was still the woman whose insight he trusted more than his own algorithms.

She picked up the new ID, studied it, then slid it into her pocket like a secret she hadn't agreed to keep.

There was more in the envelope. A second packet, thinner. She opened it. A trade paperback. Pink and cream cover, embossed title in cursive: The Long Way Home. The author's name on the cover read GAYLE PERSSON. On the copyright page, in small print, the rights holder was listed as Gloria Jansson.

"What's this?"

"Your legend," Nemo said. "ACIC seeded it eighteen months ago. Ghostwritten by a contractor in Phoenix. Twenty-three reviews on Amazon. A small but believable sales history." He almost smiled. "Apparently you're a romance novelist now. Your pen name is Gayle Persson. The publisher's records list Gloria Jansson as the author of record."

She turned the book over. The back-cover blurb was generic. Two strangers, one cottage, a complicated past.

"It's not very good," Nemo added.

"Did you read it?"

"Three pages."

She let out something that was almost a laugh. "So in Granville, I was Gayle. That's where she's been already."

"And now you're Gloria. Same person. The book solves it if anyone asks."

She set the paperback down beside the new passport. "Guess we should tell SYBIL."

"Already did," Nemo replied. "SYBIL says Gloria Jansson has Level 4 clearance."

"Guess we should tell SYBIL," she said lightly.

"Already did," Nemo replied. "SYBIL says Gloria Jansson has Level 4 clearance."

A pause. Then softer: "And Genevieve Larsson?"

Nemo's gaze lingered on the floor, his voice almost inaudible. "She's off the grid. But not gone."

Genevieve let the words settle. Somewhere deep inside the system, her new identity was already propagating—a ghost overwriting the living.

But here, in this room, between the hum of machines and the faint pulse of unspoken attachment, she still existed—at least to one person who refused to forget her.

——

London Station-MI6 Exfiltration Brief

Rain on the windows. An aging building that still smelled faintly of paper and gun oil.

Edward Langley stood across from Jennifer Mansky's British liaison, folding the final transmission from Fort Meade.

"Priority clearance for one civilian scientist, alias Gloria Jansson," he read aloud. "American national. Sensitive counterintelligence cooperation. Full blackout authority."

"Destination?" asked the liaison.

Langley smiled faintly. "A place no one will think to look. Penrhyndeudraeth. Quiet town. Beautiful coastline. And absolutely no chance of running into anyone who's ever heard of Radiant Sentry."

CHAPTER FORTY-EIGHT

Kill Team

Champlain Border Corridor 0417 Hours R

Snow flurried across the black ribbon of Route 7, whispering against the hood of a matte-gray Land Cruiser with stolen Vermont plates. Inside, four men rode in silence. No radio. No lights. Just the hum of tires on frost.

Their driver, Viktor Gurevich, former Spetsnaz, kept his breathing steady and his eyes fixed on the narrow beam of headlights ahead.

Behind him sat Sasha Novik—comms and overwatch—methodically checking the charge on a palm-sized scrambler rig.

In the third row, a hard-eyed man known only as Mitya cleaned the suppressor threads of his rifle with the care of a jeweler.

In the front passenger seat, Alexei Baranov—team lead—watched the forest roll by through night-vision lenses.

"Signal link verified?" he murmured.

"Confirmed," Sasha replied. "Burst relays every twenty minutes. Moscow wants confirmation within two hours."

"Target?"

Baranov opened a folded photo. Genevieve Larsson. Smiling, mid-stride, unaware of the death warrant that had crossed three borders to find her.

He refolded the paper carefully. "Orders are simple. In and out. No noise."

A pause. Then, said, "If anyone else is there... collateral."

——

Venise-en-Québec 2347 Hours R

Missisquoi Bay was ink. Even the stars seemed hesitant to show themselves above it. Marina De La Baie sat in silence on the northern extension of Lake Champlain.

Skipper leaned against the rusted rail of the abandoned marina pier, hands buried deep in a heavy wool coat, collar turned high. The air smelled of diesel, wet pine, and the faint mineral bite of cold iron. To anyone passing, he was just another night fisherman killing time—but no one passed this late. No one ever did.

A dim red light blinked in the horizon, a signal swallowed almost instantly by mist.

He exhaled slowly. They're on schedule.

Moments later, a shape emerged—a black GMC Yukon. When it pulled against the parking bumper, three figures stepped out as one.

No greetings. No names. Just efficient motion.

The first—tall, composed, movements deliberate—had to be Moroz, the field lead. He scanned the pier before even acknowledging Skipper.

The second, Vikhr, carried a sealed satchel strapped tight across his chest, eyes darting to the rooftops.

The third, Zmey, smaller and lean, stayed by the boat, watching the horizon with a predator's stillness.

"Border?" Moroz asked in Russian.

"Clear," Skipper answered in the same tongue, voice low. "Secondary checkpoint inactive since twenty-three hundred. Montréal sleeper handled your entry clean."

Moroz nodded once, not out of thanks but verification.

Skipper passed him a folded thermal envelope—keys, burner SIMs, a laminated map of the Champlain Valley, and a small metal tube the size of a pen. "Contact relay. Short range only. You'll transmit on channel twelve for exfil confirmation. No phones, no radio."

Moroz didn't open the envelope. He just tucked it into his inner coat pocket and said, "Where's the boat?"

Skipper gestured to the far end of the pier. The 28-foot speedboat bobbed against the dock fenders. Its hull wore a coat of black radar-absorbing paint designed to convert the electromagnetic energy to heat dissipated into its surface. So dull it refused to reflect light. Engine still warm, condensation faint on the windshield. Twin outboards, full tank, no trackers.

"Good," Moroz said, and turned to his men. "Six hours south. Button Bay. Then radio silence."

Vikhr and Zmey loaded their gear, wordless. Moroz climbed in last, pausing a moment to look back to make sure no one was in sight.

"You'll hear nothing," Skipper said.

Moroz gave a faint smile, the kind that never reached the eyes. "If I do, it means we failed."

A Canadian goose nearby lets loose a loud honk followed by hisses causing Vikhr and Zmey laugh.

Skipper crushed the burner in his hand, dropped it into the water, and whispered to himself:

"No names. No trail. Just shadows."

The lake swallowed the words whole.

——

Moscow – SVR Directorate "S" – 0654 Hours Charlie

The dawn light never really touched the sub-basement of Yasenevo.

The fluorescent panels buzzed faintly, turning the concrete walls into a colorless blur. Kir Smirnov sat alone at the console, sleeves rolled, collar unbuttoned, a half-finished mug of coffee gone cold beside a stack of encrypted dispatches.

On the wall, a secure link pulsed amber, not green. The operation was still in transit.

He keyed his headset.

"Confirm stage two. Montréal ingress."

A burst of static—then a male voice, flattened through multiple relays:

"Venise-en-Québec rendezvous complete. Transition to lake vector under way. Asset 'Skipper' dissolved contact."

Smirnov's pen stopped mid-stroke. "Dissolved?"

"Standard procedure, sir. He sank the line."

"Good," Smirnov said. "No residue."

He leaned back, rubbing at the scar above his temple—an old shrapnel line from a mission long classified. On the terminal, three call signs blinked alive: MOROZ, VIKHR, ZMEY. Each showing vital telemetry, heart rates, coordinates syncing southward toward the U.S. border.

Three ghosts in the fog, he thought. Exactly as planned.

A knock at the door.

A junior aide entered, voice tentative. "Director Volodin wants a status update. He's asking if this target warrants cross-border exposure."

Smirnov didn't look up.

"Tell him the window is closing. If we wait, the Americans move her again. If we strike now, it looks like accident, not execution."

The aide hesitated. "And if they fail?"

Smirnov's eyes stayed fixed on the screen—on the glowing dot marking Button Bay, Vermont.

"They won't."

He disconnected the link and opened a leather-bound notebook, the kind no one used anymore. One name written by hand, small but unmistakable: Сабля.

He underlined it once, then closed the book.

——

Montreal Russian Consulate

Morning drizzle. Timed to depart an hour after Moroz's departure from Venise—close enough to draw attention but timed so both tracks look independent.

Two mid-size SUVs eased from a consulate service lane, one with diplomatic placard (visible but not perfect), one unmarked. The driver showed a consular badge and a clipboard. Hotel receipts and a courier manifest sat on the passenger dash like props.

Four operatives (call-sign Aster) traveling openly from Montréal by highway toward the Burlington corridor. They were louder, less careful, designed to be seen.

The driver said, "We'll be in Burlington by noon. Hotel Champlain, third-floor conference room."

The convoy took the main highway toward the border, hugging visible routes. They stopped at a busy rest plaza, stretched, bought coffee, spoke loudly in Russian-accented English about "business and sightseeing"—exactly the chatter CSIS/RCMP loved to leak to their watchers.

As the waitress refiled their coffee, one operative flipped open a printed map and pointed to Burlington as if confirming plans.

Two hours after the uneventful trip, Aster checked into Hotel Champlain under business names; a local "contact" (planted by SVR) meets them briefly in the lobby for a five-minute exchange—too conspicuous to be normal clandestine trade, perfect for cameras.

"We must be seen. The package moves tomorrow. Call the number at 0800." The contact is photographed by a camera the team knows is watched.

Deliberate, traceable comms: one encrypted message that will be impossible to ignore but contains nothing real—just routing instructions designed to lead trackers along the highway corridor.

A planted "leak" (false intel sent to a monitored channel) hints at a warehouse pickup north of Burlington—immediate, easy to validate, and likely to draw uniformed attention.

——

Fort Meads Watchtower Ops

Sara checked with the Threat Detection Operations Team at Fort Devens. Local patrols had been repositioned, some watches positioned to highway checkpoints and shoreline teams given new taskings.

Will stood at the end of the long table in Watchtower's operations room, hands braced on the polished wood, eyes fixed on the shifting constellation of data points SYBIL was projecting across the wall.

A spike had appeared—sudden, clean, unmistakable.

Rick had flagged it first. "A burst of encrypted traffic through a relay node in western New York, followed by a short-range handset activation near the lake region. Almost theatrical in how unsubtle it was."

Exactly the sort of thing that made Will uneasy.

Sara stood beside him, arms folded, reading the same projection but seeing a different set of possibilities.

"It's the first clean signal we've had in forty-eight hours," she said. "If that's one of Kir's couriers checking in, we might not get another chance."

On the screen, the spike pulsed again. SYBIL highlighted it in amber, tracing the signal path through a cascade of anonymized relays.

Rick leaned back in his chair. "It's noisy," he said. "But sometimes noisy is just sloppy."

Will shook his head immediately.

"No," he said. "Kir is many things. Sloppy is not one of them."

Will didn't move. His gaze remained fixed on the amber flare.

He had spent years studying men like Kir Smirnov. The ones who survived long enough to matter. The ones who thought two moves ahead even when they appeared to be reacting. Men like that didn't make mistakes. They constructed them.

Sara glanced toward him. "You're thinking trap."

Will exhaled slowly. "I'm thinking Kir knows we're watching."

Rick frowned. "That assumes he knows we've identified the lake as a possible rendezvous."

Will tapped the table once. "Assume competence," he said. "Always."

The room went quiet.

SYBIL rotated the signal map, showing a secondary pattern—vehicle telemetry hits, license plate reads, a ferry terminal camera ping. The spike looked increasingly real the longer they studied it.

Too real.

Sara walked closer to the display.

"If we move a surveillance team now, we could have eyes on that relay zone within an hour."

"And if it's real," Rick added, "we roll up whoever's carrying the package before it ever gets near the lake."

Sara glanced at Will. "But if it's not real," she said, "we're pulling coverage off the lake."

That was the heart of it.

Operations like this rarely failed because someone made a mistake. They failed because someone made the wrong correct decision.

Will straightened slowly. "Kir likes misdirection," he said.

Sara gave a small nod. "He also likes certainty."

Will looked at her. "Exactly."

Sara understood immediately.

"If we chase that spike," she said, "we're telling him what we care about."

Rick rubbed his chin. "Or we catch him thinking we're predictable."

Will shook his head. "No."

He turned toward the display again, studying the flare as if trying to see the man behind it.

Kir Smirnov had once spent three months feeding NATO analysts a fabricated missile telemetry stream just to reposition one submarine. The operation had been beautiful in its patience.

Kir didn't use bait unless he was confident the prey would bite.

And Will knew Kir knew him.

Which meant the bait would be designed specifically for him.

"That signal," Will said, "is meant to look irresistible."

Sara watched him carefully. "You want to hold."

"I want to hold," Will said.

Rick sat up straighter. "We could lose it."

"Yes."

"We might lose the courier."

"Yes."

"We might lose the whole thread."

Will nodded once.

"Yes."

The room fell silent again.

Sara studied the map a moment longer, then looked back at him. "How long do you want to wait?"

Will didn't answer right away.

Instead he looked at the lake region highlighted in blue. Quiet. No spikes. No chatter. Just the patient emptiness of a place where something might—or might not—happen.

Kir would be watching the clock too.

Waiting to see if Watchtower blinked.

Will spoke. "Hold resources on the lake."

Rick exhaled. "And the spike?"

Will's voice was calm. "We watch it."

"Passive?"

"Passive."

Rick leaned back again. "You're gambling."

Will allowed himself a faint smile.

"No," he said.

"I'm refusing to play the hand he dealt."

Sara tilted her head slightly. "Last possible minute?"

Will nodded. "Last possible minute."

Sara studied him. "And if you're wrong?"

"Then we adjust," he said, voice even. "But we adjust once—when we know which direction the knife is coming from."

She didn't argue. She never did when he sounded like that—calm, sure, already weighing the next five moves ahead.

On the wall, SYBIL's map split in two—one thread glowing amber on the highway, the other faint, pulsing blue over the lake.

Will's eyes stayed on the blue.

——

Burlington VT - Hotel Champlain

The Aster decoy team left Hotel Champlain just after 1600 hours.

No words, no haste, just three men in civilian jackets slipping into a gray SUV that could've belonged to anyone.

They kept to the secondary roads, VT-15 East, Vermont Route 117, then I-89 South. Traffic was light, early autumn mist softening the edges of the trees. At

Route 100 South, the convoy turned inland, headlights cutting narrow ribbons through the mountain dark.

To anyone watching, it looked like a business trip—maybe engineers, maybe salesmen. The kind Vermont saw all the time.

At 1900 hours Romeo, they turned onto Tremblay Road in Waitsfield and rolled into Sugarbush Resort.

Check-in was quiet, routine. The clerk barely looked up as they signed the guest ledger under ordinary names and accepted keycards.

They unpacked nothing in their three bedroom condo.

The meeting they'd staged earlier at Hotel Champlain had done its job—chatter planted, watchers diverted.

Now the Aster team would stay visible, traceable, and meaningless... exactly as Kir Smirnov intended.

——

Fort Meade - Watchtower Ops Center

Staying at Watchtower. Running the operation from a screen instead of standing on the ground for the takedown. There was more than one threat in play, more than one possible target, and while the Russians were the most visible danger, visibility was never certainty.

Genevieve was already out of harm's way. Nemo was still at Nusquam. The board was set correctly.

He trusted his people completely.

But trust didn't quiet the instinct—the old, ingrained refusal to let others step into danger alone. He didn't like being absent when the moment came. He never had.

——

Fort Meade -ACIC Drone Command 0419 Hours R

On a wall of monitors, Cecil Brandon's operators watched the same stretch of road—but from ten thousand feet up.

Thermal signatures bloomed like tiny flares in the dark: four bodies, one vehicle, moving south.

Cecil stood with one hand in his pocket, the other gripping a tablet linked to SYBIL's live telemetry.

"Track delta," he said evenly. "Do not engage. Eyes only until we get confirmation from Morgan."

Rick's voice cut through on comms. "SYBIL's matching frequencies from their burst traffic to an old SVR pattern. Same used in Berlin in 2017."

Sara leaned over his shoulder. "Kir Smirnov's people?"

"Has to be," Rick said. "Nobody else uses quantum-modulated relays this clean."

On the far side of the room, SYBIL's voice carried, calm as glass.

"Signal now correlates to a secondary transponder hidden inside a vehicle chassis. Destination vector—Southern Vermont. Estimated arrival: 06:12 hours."

Sara exhaled slowly. "That's Nusquam."

——

Fort Meade -Secure Line 0423 Hours R

Will Morgan's voice came in low, controlled, the calm before a storm.

"SYBIL, patch me to Brandon."

"Link established."

"Cecil, I want the kill team under continuous track. No spotlight, no drone chatter, nothing to spook them. When they cross into Addison County, we move."

"Rules of engagement?"

"Observe. Record. But if they breach the perimeter—"

He hesitated. Then finished, "—they don't walk out."

Sara caught the tone. She knew that sound, that look. Will Morgan never rattled under fire. The greater the pressure, the calmer he became, narrowing to pure precision. He couldn't handle small bullshit like running out of coffee, but when it mattered, he was the one you wanted.

The shift was unmistakable. Will had moved from analysis to survival mode.

The air around them tightened. Colder.

Part of her admired it, that uncanny discipline that had saved them all more than once.

Part of her feared it too, the way he seemed to disappear behind it.

When Will locked in like this, there was no room for emotion, no hesitation, no softness.

And she knew—once he crossed that threshold, something was about to break.

The hunters were already being hunted.

Fort Meade – Watchtower Ops

The hum of servers was constant, a low, living pulse that matched the tempo in Derek Wilshire's head. Rows of monitors shimmered in the dim light, blue and green code crawling across glass. Highway telemetry, radar scatter, border feeds, civilian bandwidth bleed, weather clutter. Noise layered over noise until most people stopped seeing anything at all.

Major Nathan Harlan leaned on the back of Derek's chair. "I need a sanity check on something. Will Morgan says you're the best pattern man he's got. Says you're the only one he trusts when the chips get pushed in."

Derek didn't look up. "If it's sanity you're after, you came to the wrong place."

That got the small grin Harlan had been hoping for.

"CSIS and our side both flagged a convoy coming down from Montréal," he said. "Diplomatic plates. Straight line to Burlington. SYBIL tagged it as potential infiltration, but something about it feels too clean."

"Show me."

Harlan keyed the overlay live. Three monitors filled at once. The I-89 corridor blazed in orange with traffic signatures, radar reflections, cellular chatter, highway cameras, transponder spill. Loud. Convincing.

To the west, Lake Champlain sat in a broad dark sheet of near silence.

Derek stared without moving. He had been inside SIGNET's raw feed for the better part of an hour, parsing wide-spectrum intercept drift the way other men listened to music. Highway noise and digital scatter was predictable. Even false leads had their own kind of shape.

Then something pulsed.

He froze. Adjusted the filters. Narrowed the spectrum. The lake remained almost perfectly clean. Except for one faint rhythmic distortion buried so deep it barely existed at all.

"That's not nothing," he whispered.

Harlan bent closer. "What?"

"Too clean," Derek murmured. "Highway's all noise. The lake's... too symmetrical."

"Symmetrical?"

Derek pointed with two fingers toward a coordinate north of the border near Venise-en-Québec. "There. EM dropout. Two milliseconds of static fluctuation, then nothing."

"Could be cloud interference."

"Could be," Derek said absently. "Except it repeats every twenty-seven seconds. That's not weather. That's system-buried modulation. A timed beacon trying not to look like one."

His fingers moved fast now, almost impatient. SIGNET's spectral layers fanned across the displays in shifting color bands. A faint pulse appeared in the lake corridor like a heartbeat under skin.

"There," Derek said, voice flattening into the tone he used when the answer had become obvious to him and only him. "See the modulation shift? Someone's spoofing shoreline radar pings to cancel their own signature. You can't erase yourself perfectly. You always leave a fingerprint."

Harlan's expression changed. "So not the highway."

Derek shook his head slowly, eyes still on the feed. "The convoy's theater. Smirnov's feeding us noise. The real move is on the water."

Harlan let out a low breath. "You just found us the ghost."

"Ghosts leave echoes," Derek said. "You just have to listen to the silence long enough."

For the first time he leaned back, watching the faint blue track creep south along the map. "This one hums like an engine."

Harlan was already moving.

He called on the secure line.

Will Morgan looked up from the comms feed, one hand around a coffee mug gone untouched, the other resting beside a folder stamped ACIC // ULTRA. Sara Brandt was at the operations board. Grace stood near the wall display, reading the room the way she always quickly and too well.

The look on Harlan's face on the feed was enough to tighten the air.

"Talk to me," Will said.

Harlan pushed his tablet to Will's monitor. Lake Champlain glowed on-screen in layered blue, a faint line barely visible unless someone told you where to look.

"Wilshire cracked it," Harlan said. "The highway convoy is a diversion. The real team's coming down the lake."

Will straightened. "Confirmed?"

"SIGNET picked up a dampened propulsion pattern masked under civilian bandwidth. SYBIL backtraced it to Venise-en-Québec. Thirty-four, maybe thirty-five knots. Southbound. Likely Button Bay before dawn."

Sara leaned in, eyes moving across the spectral overlay. "So, the Montréal trail—"

"Dead air," Harlan said. "Staged to look perfect. Derek found the hole in the noise."

Will bent over the map. "What exactly am I seeing?"

"Low-band EM modulation at twenty-seven-second intervals," Harlan said. "Synthetic. Cloaked movement over water. Not meteorology, not shipping."

Will's jaw tightened. "How many?"

"Best estimate: three-man team."

Sara, said evenly, "I assume this disaster has a name already."

Direction, speed, terrain, access roads, shoreline approaches. Will's mind was already moving ahead of the facts.

Sara got there with him. "If they're that close, there's no time for an intercept mid-lake. Closest viable staging is onshore. Button Bay or south."

Will nodded once. He could already see the ground in his head: dark shoreline, scattered cottages, pine cover, too many civilian variables, too many ways for a small team to disappear after landing.

"Threat Detection Team Alpha spins up now," Harlan said. "Air Guard out of Burlington can be ready in twenty if you greenlight."

"Do it," Will said. "But hold visual contact only. No engagement until we confirm Sable's position."

Harlan nodded.

Will turned toward the operations board. "Sara, patch me through to the Devens field commander. I want a Quick Response Force on standby near Button Bay. Local law enforcement stays dark. We are not letting this leak."

Sara was already dialing.

Grace stepped closer, watching the red vector slide south across the lake. "You think it's the Russians."

Will didn't take his eyes off the screen. "I think Smirnov doesn't make mistakes. And if Derek heard an echo on that lake, it's not sonar. It's a heartbeat."

The wall display updated. Red vectors spread down the waterline.

"Retask drone assets from Fort Drum," Will said. "Infrared sweep. Low altitude. Tight cone. I want confirmation before they dock."

Harlan paused at the door. "You want Wilshire kept on the feed?"

"Keep him locked into SIGNET until I say otherwise. If they're out there, I want him listening when they breathe."

Harlan at once said, "On it." and hung up.

The room moved around Will in practiced silence. Sara on the secure line, Grace watching the map, SYBIL ingesting, correlating, updating.

Then the secure line chimed.

"Perry," came the voice.

"Sir, it's Morgan." Will's tone went clipped and level, The voice he used when the clock had already run out. "We've confirmed the SVR team. Not on the highway. On the lake. Southbound from Venise-en-Québec. Derek caught it in SIGNET drift."

A pause. Perry thinking.

"Verification level?"

"SYBIL cross-confirmed acoustic signatures. Three-man team, likely insertion at Button Bay. The decoy convoy is clean and deliberate."

"Your assessment?"

Will looked at the moving line on the lake. "They're targeting Sable. Timing matches chatter from Moscow Station. We still have Mansky's unilateral alert to DHS and FBI hanging in the air. That's a problem."

"Yeah," Perry said. "I know."

"If those agencies start spinning up blind response grids, they'll trip over us before the SVR does. They have no idea who they're protecting or what Nusquam is."

Perry's voice hardened. "Stratton authorized containment under Counterintelligence Directive Seven. You're in full control."

"I'll coordinate with Harlan's threat team," Will said. "We lock down Button Bay. Keep local law enforcement blind. Quiet and compartmented."

Perry's answer came back lower, rougher, more personal than bureaucratic. "You have operational authority, Will. Quiet. Surgical. They can never know she's gone."

Will held the silence for half a beat. Perry did not say things like that by accident.

"Understood."

The line clicked dead.

Will stood still after the connection closed, the weight of it settling into the room. Not just the threat, but the narrowing of the circle. Fewer hands. Less cover. No institutional cushion left between them and whatever was moving south through the dark.

When he looked up, Grace was watching him from across the room.

He gave her a short nod.

"We're on our own now."

——

Nusquam security command post

The security command post at Nusquam was a converted basement room lined with monitors. thermal feeds from the perimeter, acoustic sensors tuned to the forest floor, motion detectors wired through three separate systems. Karen Bolanowski stood in front of the primary display, arms folded, watching the feed cycle through the exterior cameras.

Will's voice came through the encrypted line, clipped and precise.

"Karen, we have confirmation of an inbound water vector. Fort Devens is mobilizing a QRF for the Button Bay intercept. Your priority is Nusquam. Elevated defensive posture, full alert. Assume the SVR has secondary contingencies."

Karen didn't hesitate. "Understood. How long until they reach Button Bay?"

"Forty-five minutes, maybe fifty. That's the intercept window. If they know about Nusquam, they might probe for backup options."

Karen's jaw tightened. "We'll be ready."

She terminated the call and turned to the security team—six personnel, three on-site, three augmented from the local contractor pool that Will had carefully vetted months ago. None of them were military. None of them had seen real threat response. But they were competent, and they knew the facility.

"Listen up," Karen said, her voice steady but not loud. No need to project panic. "We're moving to Amber status. That means all external doors lock. Thermal and acoustic monitoring stay live. No one enters or exits without my authorization. Understood?"

The team nodded. A woman named Torres, who managed the perimeter sensors, asked, "Are we expecting something specific?"

Karen considered the question. Will had been careful not to overstate it. But she'd worked security enough to read between the lines: the SVR team was being intercepted at Button Bay, but if they had backup assets, Nusquam was the logical target.

"We're expecting the possibility," Karen said. "So we prepare for it. Torres, I want thermal sensitivity cranked to maximum. Any warm body within two hundred meters of the perimeter, I want to know about it. Full audio monitoring on the lake approach—anything louder than wind, I want flagged."

She moved to the tactical map on the wall, pointing to the likely approach vectors. "If someone comes at us through the forest, they'll either come from the north treeline or the eastern slope. The western approach is too exposed, and the lake's the only soft point."

Another team member, a quiet man named Chen, asked, "What about the scientists inside? Do they shelter?"

Karen nodded once. "Sara's briefing them now. They move to the inner core—the quantum lab has reinforced walls and a secondary exit. Genevieve knows the protocols. If it gets to that point, she's in charge of evacuation while we handle perimeter security."

She looked at each of them in turn. "We don't fight unless we have to. We report, we observe, we maintain position. But we do maintain position. Nothing gets through Nusquam on my watch. Clear?"

"Clear," came the response, solid and without hesitation.

Karen returned to the primary display and pulled up the feed from the lakeside sensors. The water was black, featureless. Forest pressed in on three sides, dark and still. Everything looked quiet. Everything looked safe.

She knew better than to trust the quiet.

She keyed the internal comms. "All positions, this is Karen. We are now at elevated alert. Passive observation only. Report any anomalies immediately. No action without my authorization. Karen out."

The team settled into focused silence. Monitors flickered. Data scrolled. And Karen, standing in the center of it all, waited for the threat she now knew was coming.

Nusquam security command post and perimeter

Twenty-three minutes later, Torres's voice came across the comms, controlled but urgent.

"Karen, we have thermal bloom. Eastern slope, approximately one-eighty meters out. Could be wildlife, but the pattern's wrong. Two warm bodies, moving parallel to the treeline. Not approaching directly. Reconnaissance."

Karen's pulse didn't spike. Instead, it steadied. This was the moment she'd trained for, even if the training had been brief.

"Patch thermal to my display," she said.

The image bloomed across her primary monitor—two figures in the dense forest, outlined in false color. They weren't moving like hikers. They were moving like operatives: cautious, deliberate, scanning the facility.

"Chen," Karen said. "Cut external lights on the eastern perimeter. Full dark. I want them thinking we haven't spotted them."

"Cutting now," Chen responded.

The exterior lights flickered and died. The thermal figures paused—Karen could see them conferring, the heat signatures turning toward each other.

"Good," she murmured. "Now they think we're passive."

She keyed Will's direct line. "We have movement. Two warm bodies on the eastern approach, conducting reconnaissance. No hostile action yet. They're checking perimeter security."

Will's voice came back instantly. "Are they approaching the fence?"

"Negative. They're maintaining distance. Approximately one hundred and eighty meters. Looks like a pattern check—testing response time."

"Understood. Maintain observation. Do not engage. Do not let them know you've seen them."

"Copy that," Karen said.

She watched the thermal feed for another thirty seconds. The two figures conferred again, then began moving—not toward Nusquam, but northward, along the treeline.

"They're moving north," she reported. "Looks like they're repositioning."

Following a circuit," Will said. There was no question in his voice. He was thinking through the threat matrix. "They're testing all approaches. How's the lake?"

Karen checked the acoustic sensors. "Clean so far. No boat traffic, no disturbance. But that doesn't mean anything."

"No, it doesn't. Hold position, Karen. This is good discipline. You've got them boxed without them knowing it."

Karen ended the call and returned her attention to the monitors. The thermal figures had moved out of range, but the acoustic sensors were still active, still listening to the forest and the water beyond.

She pulled up the satellite feed from SYBIL's network—a live overhead view that showed Nusquam in context, the approach vectors rendered in real-time. The forest was a dark mass. The lake beyond was black glass. And the facility itself was a small island of illumination, hardened and prepared.

Torres looked over at her. "They testing us?"

"Yeah," Karen said. "Checking our response. Seeing if we blink."

"And if they don't find what they're looking for?"

Karen kept her eyes on the display. "Then they come at us. Or they decide we're too hardened and move on. Either way, we're ready."

But even as she said it, her hand moved to check the radio on her hip. Three channels open: direct to Will at Fort Meade, direct to the on-site security team, emergency line to the local law enforcement they were explicitly NOT supposed to call. Everything was in place. Everything was prepared.

The thermal sensors cycled again, picking up nothing but forest. The acoustic feed was silent except for the wind.

Karen waited.

——

Fort Meade - ACIC Ops Center

Will's phone buzzed before Harlan finished the sentence—an urgent, clipped tone that meant boots already moving. He glanced at the map one last time, then rose, the motion clean and decisive.

"We don't have time for politeness," he said. "Harlan, get me Fort Drum's IR sweep up now. Sara, patch me to Fort Devens—Major Hayes. Tell him we need a QRF inbound to the Button Bay area within forty-five minutes. Quiet approach. No sirens. No press. Use civilian transport vectors if you must."

Sara's fingers flew. "On it. One Quick Response Force coming up. Devens is awake. Hayes is patching."

Will watched the lake trace like a surgeon reading vitals. The rotor thrum Skipper had reported had changed the problem from search to interception. Whoever the rotors belonged to—friend or foe—was closing the window.

The screen lit with a secure link from Fort Devens. The feed showed a compact ops room; a short, tight-faced officer stepped forward when the call connected.

"Major Daniel Hayes," the man said. "ACIC, New England Field Office. We're prepped and can vector a six-man QRF with two tactical SUVs. How do you want to approach?"

"Light and fast," Will said. "No roadblocks. Two things: you hold back long enough for drone confirmation of the water vector, then move on a flank from the west—approach south of Button Bay along the tree line. Cecil Brandon will lead the first entry team; his guys—Rami and Talia—will cover extraction lanes. Keep it clean, keep it quiet."

Hayes's jaw tightened. "Understood. We'll coordinate with local sheriff for a permissive posture but no active response—stand-off only unless you give the order to engage."

"Good." Will flicked his gaze across the room. Grace and Rick were already pulling up imagery overlays; Derek's tag pulsed on the screen like a single, stubborn heartbeat.

"Harlan, get me that rotor signature through SIGINT—what frequency, altitude estimate, thermal profile," Will said. "If it's ours we need ID immediately. If it's not, we've got five minutes before they commit to shore."

Harlan tapped into the feed. "I've got a lock on a low-band rotor echo. Altitude's consistent with a utility helicopter pushing 800 to 1200 feet—fast enough to be reconnaissance, slow enough to be looking. Thermal bloom is small. Could be a civilian medevac or a private chopper, but it's on an intercept vector for Button Bay."

"Assume hostile until proven otherwise," Will said. "Fort Drum, you have authorization to run a tight Infared cone down the lake for positive ID keep it narrow and locked there. Derek, keep SIGNET on that twenty-seven-second modulation—if they try to mask comms, we'll hear it. Keep me live."

Derek's voice, flat and precise, came over Will's earpiece. "Locked. If the team is using low-band cloaking, they'll still radiate an engine harmonic. I'm listening for that harmonic against the rotor noise."

Will felt the old readiness settle in—calm, cold, focused. He moved through the checklist aloud so everyone heard the logic.

"Minimize footprint. No social media, no civilian chatter. Hayes, route your SUVs along County Road 7 from the North and then East on 17—tree line approach. Cecil will approach from the East on Basin Harbor Road. Prep non-lethal intercept first; lethal authority I retain. Rami, Talia—be ready to seal and search. Grace, stand by with the tech kit for hot-sample collection. Rick, lock comms and funnel all SIGINT through SYBIL channel three—no external sharing."

"Yes, Major," came the concise confirmations.

Outside, the sound of rotors threaded the air again—closer now, a distant drum beating time. On the screen the green dot ahead slowed, then held. Derek's cursor froze on the echo.

"There," Derek said. "Movement at the southern intake. They're about five miles out. Not yet on shore."

Will closed his mouth around the orders, the absolute clarity of them. "Then we move on their exit lanes, not the shore. Make the boat's path the trap; don't let them melt into the woods. Hayes—be invisible until you're visible. We'll hit the routes they'll use to leave the lake."

Hayes's face was a map of concentration. "We're wheels up inside thirty. Boat teams staging on the west shore. Local sheriff has been told there's an unusual vessel movement; they'll be three miles east, non-intervention. We'll be the ones who intervene."

Will let the plan hang for half a beat, then finished: "Remember: no leak. If this goes public early we lose the field and the asset. Move clean. Move dark. And if anyone on that boat moves like a combatant—stop them. Keep them alive if you can; if you can't, stop the mission and fall back to extraction. We find Sable intact."

He shut the file and felt the familiar, tempered weight of responsibility settle evenly on his shoulders. Outside the ops center a distant thrum rolled across the base—rotors, now unmistakable and inbound.

Button Bay - 2330 Hours R

The lake was black glass.

No moon. No sound but the hum of the boat's twin outboards throttled low.

Three shadows leaned into the wind — Skipper at the helm, Vikhr beside the gun crate, Zmey scanning the shoreline through night optics. Moroz checking his map. Their faces hidden under dark hoods, eyes reflecting faint starlight.

Ahead, the Vermont treeline loomed like the edge of the world.

A faint red beacon pulsed from the far shore — the prearranged marker from Button, their local contact.

"Time to landfall?" Moroz murmured.

"Six minutes," Skipper replied.

Vikhr checked his suppressed weapon, tone dry. "Six minutes to ghosts."

They throttled down to a whispering idle. The spray froze before it touched the deck.

Somewhere behind them, north up the lake, a faint blue spark blinked on the water's surface—unnoticed—a drone lens narrowing its infrared cone.

"Do we have confirmation from Smirnov?" Moroz asked.

Zmey tapped the encrypted receiver. A single light blinked green.

"Live order," he said.

Moroz's jaw flexed once, not from doubt—from discipline.

"Then we proceed."

They cut the engines and let the boat drift. The current carried them toward the marina dock shore, silent as the grave. It bumped the fenders and came to a gentle halt..

Button Bay, 2354 Hours

Cecil's convoy rolled in from the north access road—blacked-out SUVs gliding like shadows through the pines.

Overhead, two Air Guard Black Hawks swept low, rotor wash bending the trees. One settled on the strip at Basin Harbor Airport; the other hovered high above the marina, doors open, snipers poised.

Across the lake, three drones circled in perfect geometry, their sensor lights winking against the dark. Inside the ACIC ops feed, Will's voice was calm but surgical.

"Alpha Team, converge. Lock arcs. Keep them boxed."

At the docks, Moroz was already sliding a duffel into the waiting sedan. Zmey checked the trunk latch, while Vikhr scanned the waterline. Skipper paced nervously by the fuel pumps, breath fogging in the cold.

Then—a beam split the darkness.

A drone's searchlight burst alive, flooding the marina in white brilliance. Every shadow vanished.

"Move!" Moroz hissed, shielding his eyes. Vikhr reached for his weapon — too late.

"Не двигайся!" The voice boomed from the loudspeaker — Russian, commanding.

Then again, in English:

"Don't move!"

Skipper froze, hands rising. "Don't shoot! Don't shoot!" he yelled in accented English.

Vikhr spun, firing upward toward the glare—a fatal reflex.

Instantly, two lines of muzzle flash answered from opposite sides of the dock. Controlled. Triangulated.

Vikhr went down hard, rifle clattering into the lake. Zmey dropped seconds later, chest snapping backward in the crossfire. Moroz tried to dive for cover behind the car—one round, clean through the headrest, ended it.

Silence reclaimed the air, broken only by rotor thunder.

Cecil's voice over comms: "Three down. One alive. Hold fire."

The second helicopter flared in, floodlights pinning Skipper to the dock as he knelt, trembling, hands still raised.

"Target secured," Sara reported. "No civilian casualties."

Will exhaled through his teeth, watching the live feed.

"Tell them to bag the scene. Every weapon, every phone, every microdrive. And someone make sure that man lives long enough to talk."

Above the lake, the drone lights winked out one by one—darkness settling again, as if the night itself had just taken a deep breath.

Rick over comms, said, "I'll start the paperwork. Three suppressed rifles, one sedan, and what looks like an entire SVR career arc."

"That's not paperwork, that's an obituary."

The Aster Team – Waitsfield, Vermont

They waited. An hour. Then another. Eyes scanning tree lines, mirrors, rooftops—any shimmer, any motion that didn't belong.

Nothing.

No tail. No drone buzz. No thermal shimmer. Not even the telltale whisper of a long lens catching light.

"Either they're ghosts," the team leader muttered, "or no one's watching."

The team leader knew better. The quiet was too clean. The air too still. But nothing else to do. They packed up just before dusk, driving north without a word.

What they didn't know—what they couldn't know—was that ACIC had been watching the entire time.

Invisible optics buried in the hills. Pattern-tracking AI following every step, every pause, every heartbeat.

They were already ghosts—just not their own.

By the time they crossed back into Montreal, the file was closed.

CHAPTER FORTY-NINE

Wales

Cymru

Penrhyndeudraeth, Wales 0700 Hours Alpha

Penrhyn for short, pronounced pen-hreehn-DEY-draith village sat quiet beneath the morning mist—slate rooftops glistening with rain, the smell of earth and the taste of salt in the air.

From the window of a the secure safe house near the estuary, Gloria Jansson watched the River Dwyryd wind through the valley. The sound of distant church bells floated in from town.

She had arrived less than twelve hours ago.

Her new identification legend lay on the table: passport, driver's license, local utilities card. All in her new alias.

It felt strange, holding proof of a life she hadn't lived. Stranger still, knowing it was the only thing keeping her alive.

The burner phone beside the ID vibrated once. A secure call. American code.

She answered.

"Nemo?" she whispered.

His voice came through faintly, filtered through SYBIL's encrypted lattice.

"Connection established. Latitude confirmed. You're clear."

She exhaled, eyes softening at the sound of him. "I can see the water from here. It's... quiet."

Nemo's voice was calm, grounding. "Good. Quiet is what keeps you alive."

For a long moment, neither spoke. The link hummed softly between them—two voices bound by circuits and circumstance, both exiled in their own ways.

Finally, she said, "Tell Will thank you."

Nemo hesitated. "He already knows."

Penrhyndeudraeth, Wales

The Welsh countryside seemed to hum with its own quiet music—a soft, unhurried rhythm of rain against slate and the low murmur of voices shaped by centuries of song. The people were kind in that particular Welsh way: shy at first, then suddenly warm, their laughter lilting like melody. Even their small talk had cadence.

Gloria—still learning to answer to the name—found comfort in their company. The woman who ran the bakery down the lane taught her how to say the longest place name in the world,
Llanfair-pwllgwyngyll-gogery-chwyrn-drobwll-llan-tysilio-gogo-goch, syllable by patient syllable, both of them dissolving into laughter halfway through.

On weekends she jogged to Beddgelert, where the mountains pressed close and the air smelled of wet stone and pine.

There, beneath the trees, lay Gelert's grave—the faithful hound of Welsh legend.

She read the inscription twice, fingers brushing the carved letters, and found herself whispering the final line aloud:

"Faithful unto death."

It struck her more deeply than she expected.

In that still, green valley, she realized she was surrounded by a nation that remembered loyalty not as burden—but as love.

"For the first time in over a year, she smiled without caution."

Nusquam / Penrhyndeudraeth, Encrypted Link

Evening mist drifted down from the Vermont hills. Inside the sealed quiet of Nusquam's communications lab, Nemo sat before the SYBIL console, the glow of cascading encryption strings washing his face in pale light.

He keyed a narrowband link — the only one authorized for Gloria Jansson. The waveform pulsed once. Connection secured.

Across the Atlantic, in a small cottage overlooking the River Dwyryd, Verity's terminal chimed softly. She smiled, brushing away a strand of hair, and answered.

"Nemo?"

"I hear you've become fluent in Welsh folklore."

Genevieve chuckled. "Barely. But I can almost pronounce it now — Llanfair-pwllgwyngyll-gogery-chwyrn-drobwll-llan-tysilio-gogo-goch. Almost."

"That wasn't Welsh. That was packet loss."

She laughed again, the sound light and unguarded — the kind of laugh Nemo had only heard once before, in the lab after midnight.

"I visited Gelert's grave today. The faithful hound. Killed by mistake, mourned forever."

There was a pause on the line — long enough for the encryption buffer to cycle twice.

"Faithful unto death."

She nodded, even though he couldn't see her. "You know it?"

"Of course. They say it inspired Disney to make Lady and the Tramp. You think I don't read Welsh legends?"

"I think you read algorithms that become legends."

Another silence — softer this time, warm and electric across six time zones.

"Stay there as long as you need. Wales suits you."

"You sound like you've seen it."

"I don't have to. I can hear it in your voice."

The line shimmered for a heartbeat — static mingling with the rhythm of distant rain.

"Goodnight, Nemo."

"Nos da, Gloria."

The Welsh phrase caught her off guard — Goodnight. She smiled at the screen, whispering back the same words before closing the secure channel.

Fort Meade-Watchtower Ops 0312 Hours R

The operations floor was nearly silent. A few analysts still hovered over terminals, the low hum of servers the only constant sound. Will Morgan stood beside the SYBIL monitoring console, coffee cooling in his hand, eyes fixed on a single line of encrypted log data scrolling across the screen.

> *Transmission complete: NODE-ECHO (Nusquam) → NODE-VERITY (Wales)*
>
> *Duration:* 00:12:43
>
> *Content Integrity:* 100%
>
> *Flag: Non-operational length variance (personal exchange).*

He didn't need SYBIL to translate that last part.

Twelve minutes of clean, encrypted bandwidth. No red flags. No anomalies. Just... human.

He exhaled slowly through his nose, setting the cup down.

So much had been lost to secrecy, to the machinery of survival.

Maybe this one thing — two people who'd found something worth holding onto — didn't need to be dissected.

"Mark it logged and archived," he said.

SYBIL's voice, gentle as ever, responded:

"Confirmed. Do you wish to flag for supervisory review?"

Will shook his head. "No. Leave it clean."

The terminal light reflected faintly in his eyes as he added, almost to himself: "Let them have this."

He turned, the sound of his boots fading into the corridor's hush—leaving the console alive with a faint afterglow of the message already gone.

Penrhyndeudraeth, Dawn 0600 Hours Alpha

A thin mist rolled off the River Dwyryd, curling around the stone cottages as the first light pressed through the gray. Inside her small rented room, Genevieve stirred awake to the soft chime of the secure tablet on the desk.

A single message. She opened it, expecting a terse procedural note. Will's messages always were.

Sender: ACIC / FORT MEADE / W.M.

Timestamp: 05:41 GMT.

She sat up, pulling the blanket around her shoulders, and opened it. The note was short—typical Will: efficient, clean, no wasted words.

Status: Confirmed arrival.

All parameters stable.

Continue current cover.

End of transmission.

Then, at the bottom—one word not in any protocol.

Unshaken.

Her breath caught. A simple word, but she knew what it meant. Steady. Alive. Still with us.

Something only Will would say, echoing the phrase he'd once told her on a storm-tossed night in the lab: "Stay unshaken when everything else moves."

She smiled faintly, pressing her fingers against the screen as if she could feel the pulse of the message through the glass. Then she encrypted the reply.

Received. Still unshaken.

Outside, church bells began to ring from the village square—slow, clear, and full of life.

For the first time in weeks, she let herself believe she was safe.

CHAPTER FIFTY

She's burned

Fort Meade — Secure Conference Room. Three days after Button Bay.

Will Morgan sat across from Ed Perry. The folder marked EYES ONLY // PROTECTIVE RELOCATION lay closed between them. Neither man had reached for it.

"The hit team's gone," Perry said. "But the signal's out. Every Russian cutout in the hemisphere will be looking for her."

Will didn't look up. "She knew that when she signed it."

"She did. And she'll know what it means too. We can't bring her home. Not yet."

A long pause. The clock on the wall ticked once.

"How long?" Will asked.

"Until Smirnov stops looking."

"Smirnov doesn't stop."

"Then we wait until he can't."

Will closed the folder.

"She stays Gloria Jansson," he said. "For as long as it takes."

CHAPTER FIFTY-ONE

You held Nusquam

Nusquam-1040 Hours R

The sun was just breaking over the Vermont treeline when Will arrived at Nusquam in a black SUV, alone except for his driver. Karen was still in the security command post, but she heard him coming by the gravel crunching under the tires, the precise way the vehicle door closed.

She stepped out to meet him in the facility's main corridor.

Will looked exactly as he had when he'd left Fort Meade: composed, controlled, fresh. But there was something different in his eyes. The weight of having made a call that worked. Of having gambled and won.

"Karen," he said simply.

"Will. How bad was Button Bay?"

"Three Russian operatives, dead. One alive for questioning. The secondary asset in the forest is in custody. Clean sweep. No civilian casualties. No compromise of the facility."

Karen nodded. That was the best outcome possible.

"You held Nusquam," Will said. It wasn't a question. He was stating a fact.

"The eastern approach had a reconnaissance probe," Karen said. "Two operatives, testing response. They were communicating back to a secondary asset stationed in the forest northeast of the perimeter. We maintained position, observed without engaging, and reported to you. The Army swept the forest clean. No breach attempts. Facility remained secure."

Will's expression didn't change, but something in his posture eased. Just slightly.

"That's solid work," he said. "You kept them boxed without them knowing they were boxed. That's professional-level tradecraft."

Karen had been a lot of things in her life—a cop, a private contractor, an analyst—but professional-level tradecraft from Will Morgan meant something. It meant she'd passed a test she hadn't known she was taking.

"Thank you," she said.

Will looked at her for a few seconds longer. "You know what that was, right? That wasn't a game. That was a genuine threat response. You were the difference between a contained situation and a potential breach."

Karen met his gaze. "I know."

"Then you also know you belong here. On this team. Not in the background. In the decisions."

It wasn't effusive. It wasn't warm. It was just the truth, stated plainly. And somehow, that made it worth more than any amount of praise could have.

"I appreciate that," Karen said.

Will nodded once. "Get some sleep. Then report to Sara. We're going to need you for the international asset sweep. You've got the operational mindset for it."

He turned to leave, then paused.

"You held the line," he said. "That matters."

And then he was gone, back to the SUV, back to Fort Meade, back to the larger machinery of whatever came next.

Karen stood in the corridor a moment after Will left. Held the line. That was the kind of thing soldiers said about each other, not to each other, and not usually to people who'd been on the team eight months.

She walked back to the command post.

Torres looked up from the monitors. "How bad?"

"Not bad. We did what we were supposed to do."

Torres smiled and went back to her screens.

Karen took her seat at the primary display. The forest outside the perimeter cameras was starting to lighten. She let herself sit with it for a while — not the praise, exactly. Something underneath it.

Eight months ago she'd walked in here a probationary transfer Diane Watson had pushed for harder than she had any right to. Karen knew the file Diane had been working from. She knew her own file. Every other place she'd been, the file got there first — the story did, the legend did, whatever the current version of it was. It surfaced in sideways comments, in the recalculations people made when they thought they had her figured out.

Here, nobody had asked. She'd assumed at first they didn't know. Later she understood they did and it didn't matter to them. That had taken her longer to absorb than she wanted to admit.

She thought about the parking lot. Her body had moved before her mind had finished naming the threat. She'd known what to do. Tonight had been the same thing on a bigger scale, and Will had noticed, and Will had said so.

She wasn't going to let any of them down. She didn't make it dramatic about it. She just knew.

She settled in and started the stand-down checklist. Whatever came next, she'd be ready.

CHAPTER FIFTY-TWO

Quiet Hours

Fort Meade— Maryland

Will changed into a clean uniform shirt, the golden oak leaves gleaming on his shoulder boards. He slipped his pocket Constitution into its familiar place over his heart. Shoes polished, a rinse of mouthwash, the faintest mist of cologne.

Columbian Square sat halfway between Fort Meade and the UM campus. No staff function this time. No cover. He planned to be fifteen minutes early, the way he always was.

It had never dawned on him that whenever he offered to buy, the others were suddenly tied up, and Grace alone was always free.

He was seated when she arrived. Rising to greet her, he knocked over the water glass. The clatter made him flush.

Grace only smiled. The waiter appeared, mopped up the spill, set down fresh glasses. Will held her chair without thinking.

"Still early, aren't you?"

"Fifteen minutes. Old habit."

"It's not a bad one." She tilted her head. "Though I suppose it means you sit here overthinking what you're going to say before I arrive."

"Guilty as charged."

Grace ordered seafood. Will, a steak. The small talk came first—her classes, a book she was writing, the latest bureaucratic tangle at ACIC. Then it slipped into deeper currents.

"Do you ever stop carrying the weight?" Grace said. "Even for one night?"

Will's jaw tightened, then eased. "I don't know how. But being here. With you. It's as close as I come."

She reached across the table and brushed her fingers against his. His pulse quickened.

"You don't always have to be strong, Will."
He wanted to take her hand fully. The old instincts held him back.
Grace withdrew her hand slowly. "One day, you'll figure out I'm not going anywhere."
"You might be the most patient person I've ever met."
"And you might be the most stubborn."

Will walked Grace to her car. The block had gone quiet, streetlamps doing what streetlamps do at that hour.
She unlocked the door but didn't open it. Leaned against the frame instead.
"You know," she said, "for a man who can take apart a double agent without blinking, you're terrible at this."
"At what?"
"This." She gestured between them. "Us."
He'd had a hundred versions of an answer ready for a time like this. None of them came. "I don't want to rush it."
"Will."
"Or ruin it."
"You couldn't ruin this if you tried."
He almost stepped back. He wasn't sure why — habit, probably. She caught the back of his neck before he could finish the thought and kissed him.
His arms came around her on a delay he'd regret later.
When they parted, she didn't move far. "See? Not so difficult."
"I should've done that a long time ago."
"Maybe. But waiting made it sweeter."

He drove home the long way without deciding to.
Somewhere around the second mile he caught himself checking his reflection in the windshield, which was a thing he didn't do. He was smiling. He looked, for half a second, like someone he didn't quite know.
He pulled into his driveway still not having said a word out loud.
He didn't need to.

——

Fort Meade – Watchtower Conference Room – 1100 Hours

They had to get him out of the way first. That was the hard part.

Derek and Rick took point, pulling Will toward the annex with some half-baked excuse about a data inconsistency. Something just believable enough to buy a few minutes. Not more. Never more with him.

Gracie planted herself in the doorway between the annex and the main ops floor. Casual, but not really. No one was getting past her without a reason.

Cathy slipped in behind her, careful, quiet, carrying the cake like it was contraband.

Z moved fast. Grabbed Ed Perry. Then Carrone. No explanations, just that look that meant "trust me and move."

They all knew the clock was ticking.

Will didn't like waiting. His patience wasn't a slow burn. It was a fuse. Short. Predictable. Already hissing.

Sara handled the last piece. She dropped the package in the conference room, then called Will back to his office. Kept her body between him and the glass. The windows had already gone opaque, but still. With Will, you didn't take chances.

"Need a minute," she told him, like it was routine.

It never was.

By the time they got him moving again, everyone was in place.

Gussie sat between Cecil and Z, the two biggest men in the room, like they were anchoring her there. Not protective. Just... steady.

Ed Perry stepped into Will's office right on cue.

"Can we review some of these subcontractors in the conference room?" he said. Easy. Neutral. "I asked Rick to have SYBIL pull them up on the big screen."

That did it.

Will gave a short nod and headed into the conference room.

Inside, the lights were low. Screen glowing. Just like a normal briefing.

Rick stood at the console, deliberately slow, fumbling just enough to sell it.

"Hold on... SYBIL's still sorting the list..."

Will exhaled, already irritated. "We could sure use Gussie."

And that was it. That was the moment.

Sara hit the lights.

Bright. Sudden. Warm.

The room didn't move. No one spoke.

Will stood there, just inside the door, taking it in. The people. The setup. The silence.

Confusion flickered across his face, which almost never happened.

Then he saw her.

Gussie Brindisi.

Not in a hospital bed. Not in a report. Right there. On her feet. Looking... close enough to her old self that it caught you off guard.

For a second, everything in him just... stopped.

Gracie, watching from the side, could've sworn his eyes filled. Just for a beat. Gone as fast as it came.

Then Will did something no one in that room had ever really seen before.

He crossed the distance without a word.

Gussie stood, already smiling.

And he wrapped her up. Arms all the way around her. Not quick. Not restrained.

A full, unguarded, bear hug.

The kind that said more than he ever would out loud.

No one interrupted it. Not at first.

Then Sara, because it had to be Sara, cut through it with a grin.

"OK," she said, clapping once. "Cut the damn cake."

And just like that, the room exhaled.

Laughter broke loose. Shoulders dropped. Someone actually cheered.

And for a few minutes, just a few, Watchtower didn't feel like the center of a war.

It felt like a team.

——

Granville, VT

Marie-Claire could feel it before she could explain it. Something had shifted. Not loud. Not sudden. But deep.

The trucks had stopped coming and going at the Lavoie farm. Just... stopped. No dust on the road. No engines in the distance. It was the silence that made her notice.

And Gayle—well, Gayle had come back. After being gone long enough that people had started to talk, then stopped talking. She looked the same at first glance. But not really. There was something settled in her now. Or maybe guarded.

The Dufresne place was the strangest of all. Sold off just like that. Some company no one had heard of. And Marlene—sweet, scattered Marlene—was suddenly the caretaker. She called it a bed and breakfast, though it felt like more than that. She was so proud when she showed Marie-Claire around.

Giggly, almost glowing. The place looked beautiful. Too beautiful, maybe. And that motor home in the barn never seemed to move.

Then there was the airport.

Middlebury State had always been small. Quiet. A place you could forget about. But now? New control tower. Bright lights. A longer runway that could take planes no one in town had ever seen before. It didn't fit. Not really.

And the people.

They asked questions in that careful way. Polite, but not friendly. Strangers who said just enough but never too much. You didn't need a badge to know they were government. Maybe FBI. Maybe military. Something like that.

Granville had changed. There was money now. Real money. Things looked better. Cleaner. Fixed.

And yet...

It felt like something had passed through. Or maybe something had settled in.

The strange part was, after all of it, the town was quiet again.

Quieter than it had ever been.

CHAPTER FIFTY-THREE

Bring Her Home

Fort Meade - Watchtower Conference Room – 2015 Hours R

The overhead LEDs buzzed faintly against the hum of the servers beyond the glass wall. Three people in the war room. Ed Perry looked like he hadn't slept. Helena Quinn had — barely. Will stood between them, arms folded. The wall screen glowed with a map of northern Wales — a digital ghost of Gloria Jansson.

Perry broke the silence first.

"She's safe there, Will. Out of sight, off every grid we monitor. That's the point."

Will leaned forward, elbows on the table.

"Safety isn't purpose, sir. She's a scientist, not a fugitive. The work Nemo's doing at Nusquam can't move forward without her calibration expertise. Every day she's gone, we lose ground."

Helena's eyes flicked to Perry, then back to Will.

"He's right. Echo Reef's model is plateauing. Nemo needs a physicist who can see beyond code — someone who understands human error inside quantum architecture. Genev—"

She stopped herself, caught between names.

"—Gloria is that person."

Perry exhaled slowly. "And when the Russians realize she's alive? When they trace her out of Wales?"

Will's voice stayed even, but there was an edge beneath it.

"Then we handle it. We've already proven we can. She's been buried long enough. If she stays underground, they win."

Helena nodded. "And if she returns under ACIC custody, the optics are cleaner.

We can reclassify her as a technical consultant under OSP mandate. No public footprint, no formal citizenship disclosure."

"You're both assuming Stratton signs off on it."

Will didn't blink. "He will. He owes her that much."

For a long moment, the only sound was the soft tick of the secure clock on the wall.

Finally, Perry stood. "All right. Draft the reentry protocol. I'll brief the President myself."

Helena smiled faintly, already reaching for her tablet. "I'll handle the scientific cover story."

Will leaned back, the faintest trace of relief breaking through his restraint.

"Then let's bring her home."

——

Penrhyndeudraeth, Wales – 0930 Local

Rain brushed across the windowpane in soft, rhythmic lines — the kind of gentle Welsh drizzle that blurred time and thought.

Gloria Jansson sat opposite an unfamiliar man in a tweed jacket, his MI6 credentials folded discreetly beside his tea cup.

He had introduced himself simply as Mr. Llewellyn, though she doubted that was his real name.

The café was nearly empty. Two locals murmured in Welsh over toast and jam, oblivious to the quiet tension between the stranger and the woman in the corner booth.

He slid a sealed envelope across the table. "New orders, Miss Jansson. You'll want to read them carefully."

Gloria opened it. Inside was a single sheet marked with a pale watermark:

> US ACIC – CLASSIFIED/RETURN AUTHORIZATION

The message was brief.

> Subject: Immediate repatriation authorized.
>
> Cover: Civilian technical consultant, Project Echo Reef.
>
> Escort: MI6 transfer team via RAF Valley, then Andrews AFB.
>
> Effective: 0700 tomorrow.

Her pulse caught. She looked up, searching his face. "This has Ed Perry's authorization?"

"Personally signed," Llewellyn said. "President Stratton approved the coordination. You'll be under ACIC protection before nightfall tomorrow."

Gloria folded the letter carefully, feeling both the weight and the relief of the words.

"Eighteen months of living like a ghost—a scientist buried under layers of invented history, smiling at kind strangers and pretending the quiet hills were enough."

"Does Will know?" she asked softly.

Llewellyn allowed himself the smallest smile. "Aye love, he was the one who fought for it."

She looked out the window toward the slate roofs and mist-hung valley, where church bells rang faintly from down the hill.

A single tear slipped before she caught it.

"That's twice," she said to herself.

"Miss?"

"Nothing."

A quiet ache bloomed in her chest—part gratitude, part disbelief—as she wondered what made Will tick, this man who had saved her twice, and how ACIC managed to find people like him.

"Well," she said, steadying her voice, "then I suppose it's time to stop pretending I'm Welsh."

Llewellyn stood, placing his hat over his heart in a small, respectful gesture.

"Miss Jansson, Wales will miss you. But I suspect America needs you more."

He turned to leave. Gloria lingered, tracing the faint ring her cup had left on the table — then gathered her coat, tucked the letter close to her chest, and stepped out into the drizzle.

——

Penrhyndeudraeth Safe House – North Wales

Selyf "Sel" Morganwg and his wife, Ceinwen, ran the Penrhyndeudraeth safe house for MI5—a modest stone cottage tucked between heathered hills and the salt tang of the Dwyryd estuary.

Sel had been a Covert Human Intelligence Source for nearly three decades, one of those quiet pillars MI5 referred to only as "assets" in their ledgers but "agents" among themselves. Nearing retirement, London had granted him the post as a reward—a final assignment close to home, not far from his birthplace in Blaenau-Ffestiniog. He still spoke Welsh as easily as breathing, which made him invaluable when the Service needed local eyes and ears that didn't sound like London.

A cheerful, broad-shouldered man with an extraordinary bass voice that rolled like distant thunder through the chapel each Sunday, Sel was as much a fixture of the village as the church bell itself.

Gloria often wondered at the word he called her—"athrylith."

Ceinwen, his gentle and quick-witted wife, was amused that he wouldn't tell her what it meant. He would only grin and refuse to explain. Gloria wouldn't give him the satisfaction of constantly asking for translation.

It was Mary Grace, the baker, who finally leaned across the counter one morning, dusting flour from her hands, and whispered with a knowing smile, "It means genius, dear."

That afternoon, the wind shifted from the sea, bringing with it a cold drizzle that blurred the green slopes into muted watercolor. Ceinwen was at the stove stirring cawl in a cast-iron pot when she heard the gravel crunch of tires outside. Few people came up the narrow lane uninvited.

Sel set down his tea, cocked his head, and listened. "Not the postman," he murmured.

The engine cut off. Moments later, a knock sounded—two short, one long. The recognition pattern hadn't been used in years. Sel's expression changed; his usual warmth folded into professional composure. He motioned for Ceinwen to stay put and went to the door.

A man in his early thirties stood there, trench coat damp from the rain, a folder sealed in plastic tucked beneath one arm. His accent was London but softened by exhaustion.

"Mr. Morganwg?"

Sel's gaze flicked once to the man's shoes—muddy, expensive, London soles. "You're off the clock, son. Come in before the kettle cools."

The visitor hesitated, then stepped inside. Ceinwen, ever the hostess, placed another cup on the table without asking questions. The man removed his hat, revealing close-cropped hair and the eyes of someone who'd seen too much too soon.

"Courier detail," he said. "Directive from Thames House. Immediate hand-delivery." He placed the folder on the oilcloth table. A red stamp bled through the plastic:

CLASSIFIED / MI5 INTERNAL – EYES ONLY.

Sel wiped his hands on a towel, looked at Ceinwen, then back at the courier. "Don't often see you lot north of Llandudno," he said. "What's so pressing it couldn't come through the usual drop?"

The courier hesitated, glancing at the small window and the slow drip of rain beyond it.

"There's been... some sort of hush hush development Ma'am,"

Ceinwen froze, wooden spoon hovering over the pot.

"What kind of development?"

The courier met her eyes. "Extraction," he said. "Something important. They're not sure what yet."

The only sound was the slow simmer of the cawl and the rhythmic tick of the old wall clock. Then Sel exhaled, voice low and steady.

"Best fetch my book, love. Looks like retirement's been postponed."

Sel broke the seal on the folder with his thumb, unfolding the paper carefully, as if it might crumble in his hands. The courier stood motionless, rain still dripping from his coat. Ceinwen watched Sel's expression shift—first curiosity, then something deeper and harder to name.

He read the page twice before speaking.

"It's brief," he said finally. His voice carried that old field steadiness, the tone he used when things were about to turn serious. "Directive Seven-One from Thames House. 'Prepare for possible extraction. Athrylith is going home.'"

Ceinwen looked up sharply. "Gloria?"

Sel nodded once. "That's the name they're using. Same codename I gave her in the beginning—Athrylith."

The courier exhaled and clarified, "Directive says she's unaware. Plans are still being finalized. We're to stay on standby until confirmation arrives."

Ceinwen frowned. "Unaware? If she's to be extracted, wouldn't she need to know?"

The courier hesitated. "Not yet. London's worried about leaks. Until they have a secured route, she stays in the dark. You're to prepare in case the order comes through suddenly."

Sel refolded the message slowly, his thumb tracing the faint watermark. "And no transmissions?"

"None," the courier replied. "Full blackout until signal."

Sel nodded, opened the sideboard drawer, and tucked the message into the hollowed base of an old Bible—a relic from his field days, its pages carved out years ago for this kind of thing.

When the courier left, the cottage seemed to draw in on itself. Rain pressed against the windows, soft but insistent. Ceinwen turned from the sink, her voice low.

"I thought she was finished with all that," she said. "After that space thing. After what it cost her."

Sel sighed, rubbing the bridge of his nose. "So did I. But the quiet war is never really finished with anyone, is it? If they're saying Athrylith's going home, it means they're either bringing her in—or burying the trail she left behind."

Ceinwen looked at him, startled. "You think it's a cleanup?"

He didn't answer immediately. Instead, he stared out the window, where the rain blurred the view of the hills into a shifting watercolor of gray and green.

"I think," he said finally, "it means they can't replace her—and they don't really have a choice."

The old clock on the mantel ticked louder than usual. The smell of cawl filled the small room, warm and steady against the chill creeping in through the door.

Ceinwen folded her arms, voice barely above a whisper. "Then we'd best be ready, hadn't we?"

Sel gave a slow nod. "Aye, love. We'd best."

——

Andrews Air Force Base 2125 Hours R

The C-32 touched down under a thin winter haze, engines whispering to idle. The runway shimmered with floodlight glare and the faint mist rising from the tarmac. Two SUVs and a single black Suburban waited just beyond the security cordon — no markings, no fanfare.

Inside the cabin, Gloria Jansson sat buckled, her hands folded tight around the envelope that had delivered her fate.

The MI6 escort nodded once. "End of the line, miss."

She rose, heart quickening as the door hissed open. The stairs descended, gleaming in the landing lights. A gust of cold air rushed in—American air, sharp and familiar.

At the base of the stairs stood Will Morgan.

No uniform. Dark field jacket. Shoulders squared. Hands in pockets. The look of a man who had planned for every contingency—except the one that mattered most.

Their eyes met halfway down the steps.

For a heartbeat, neither moved. Then Gloria—Genevieve no longer—descended the last few steps and stopped before him.

He spoke first, quiet, and steady.

"Welcome home."

She almost smiled. "I wasn't sure I'd ever hear that again."

Will glanced toward the waiting vehicles, then back at her. "You're under full protection now. No leaks, no traces. From here on, you're cleared only as Echo Reef consultant. That's your cover, and your life—for as long as it takes."

She studied him—the exhaustion behind his composure, the weight he carried like part of his uniform.

"Does it ever stop?" she asked.

He shook his head once. "Not for people like us."

The faintest hint of warmth broke through the cold between them.

"Then I suppose," she said softly, "I'm back where I belong."

Will's mouth curved — not quite a smile, but close.

"Let's get you home, Dr Jansson."

The MI6 agent stepped aside. The Air Force security team turned their backs as the pair crossed the tarmac toward the Suburban, the roar of the jet fading behind them.

And somewhere above the runway lights, the night swallowed the sound—as if even the sky knew this reunion was meant to stay secret.

——

Nusquam Operations Bay 0830 Hours R

The morning light slanted through the narrow clerestory windows, sharp and cold across the reinforced glass walls. The hum of servers was softer now—a steady, satisfied rhythm. A low-level ozone smell persisted. Echo Reef had passed its final overnight test.

Grace Roberts was the first to notice.

She paused mid-sip of her coffee, watching through the observation window as Gloria and Nemo moved together at the central console—not touching, not even standing close, but in a rhythm too seamless to miss. A new gravity bound them.

Sara caught the look and followed Grace's gaze.

"Oh," she said under her breath.

Grace didn't turn. "You see it too."

"Hard not to. They're... synchronized."

"More than that," Grace said softly. "They're connected."

Across the room, Will Morgan entered—quiet, deliberate. He scanned the board, then the pair at the console. Nothing in his expression changed, but Sara had known him long enough to spot the flicker of understanding.

"Echo Reef stable?" he asked.

Nemo didn't look up. "Stable and self-correcting."

Gloria added, her tone perfectly neutral, "Final beta review ready for DARPA sign-off, Major."

Will nodded once. "Good work. Both of you."

He turned away, but Sara saw the faint, knowing smile ghost across his face. Will Morgan didn't pry. He didn't need to. In a place where secrets were currency, he respected the few that mattered.

Grace leaned close to Sara. "You think Will knows?"

Sara exhaled through her nose, a half-laugh. "Will always knows. He just decides what's worth mentioning."

The overhead intercom pinged—an alert from Fort Meade. Another layer of the world intruding.

But for the briefest moment, as the team moved back to their tasks.

The quantum array pulsed once—a perfect harmonic.

Echo Reef was alive. So, it seemed, were the two who built it.

— —

Granville, VT — Marie-Claire's store

A week later, Gloria drove into Granville for the first time as herself. Or as the version of herself the file said she now was.

Marie-Claire's bell rang the way it always did, two notes flat. Marie-Claire looked up from the register and her face went still in the particular way of someone deciding whether a memory matched a face.

"Gayle?"

"Hi, Marie-Claire."

"Oh my goodness. Look at you. Are you back?"

"For a while." Genevieve set a basket on the counter. Bread. Eggs. A jar of the local honey she remembered. "I should explain something while I'm thinking of it."

Marie-Claire waited the way she always waited. Hands folded on the counter. Patient.

"Gayle is my pen name. Persson, too. My given name is Gloria Jansson. I write romance under Gayle Persson — it's a long story, my grandmother's name on my mother's side, my agent thought it sounded warmer. When I was here last spring I didn't bother explaining the two names because no one had asked." She gave a small, embarrassed smile. "Then it felt strange to bring up later."

"You're a writer." Marie-Claire's face brightened. "I had no idea."

"Just the one book. A while ago now. Nothing anyone's heard of."

"What's it called?"

Genevieve hesitated, the way an author would hesitate before naming a book she had moved past. "The Long Way Home. It's on Amazon if you're curious. Don't be too curious."

Marie-Claire laughed.

"So which do I call you?"

"Gloria, if you don't mind. Gayle belongs to the book."

"Gloria, then." Marie-Claire began ringing up the basket, then paused with her hand over the eggs. "I knew there was something. You had that quiet about you. Writers have that."

Genevieve smiled and did not answer.

——

Fort Meade Nusquam Secure Link 2145 Hours R

The lights in Will Morgan's office were dimmed to protect the encrypted video relay.

Onscreen, Ed Perry, Commanding General of ACIC, leaned forward into the frame—jacket off, sleeves rolled, the fatigue behind his eyes tempered by authority.

"Congratulations, Major," Perry began, voice low but sincere. "Fort Meade got the full data push this morning. Echo Reef's stable resonance index is off the charts. DARPA's calling it the most promising defense tech since Radiant Sentry."

Will didn't smile. "That's not always good news."

Perry caught the tone immediately. "What's your read?"

Will hesitated — the kind of pause Perry knew meant the gears were already turning.

"SYBIL flagged increased chatter from multiple SIGINT nodes — Moscow Center, Chengdu, and a new relay in Prague. Nothing explicit yet, but the pattern is too deliberate to be coincidence."

Perry frowned. "Quantum intercept?"

"Maybe," Will said. "But I think they've linked the Vermont network activity to a protected program. Not Nemo by name — not yet — but they're circling it. Something's drawing them in."

Perry leaned back, rubbing a hand over his jaw. "We knew it was only a matter of time. Echo Reef crosses every red line in quantum defense. The moment they realize it's real, the hunt begins."

Will nodded. "I want to tighten the perimeter. Extend SIGINT coverage into Quebec and northern New York, coordinate with the Air Guard for low-altitude drone detection. And Ed..." He hesitated, choosing the words carefully. "Gloria's cover holds, but she's still a wildcard. The Russians won't stop after one failure."

Perry's eyes narrowed slightly. "You think Smirnov's still running his teams?"

"I'd bet my clearance on it."

The line hummed with encrypted static. Perry finally spoke. "All right. Keep her under full isolation protocol. No outside contact, no digital trace, nothing that leads back to Vermont. If they start moving again, I want to know before they cross the border."

Will gave a slow nod. "Understood."

Perry studied him and said. "You doing all right, Will? You sound... wound tight."

Will exhaled through his nose, the faintest ghost of a smile. "I'm fine, sir. Just—" he paused, glancing toward the observation glass where Gloria and Nemo were visible in the distance, shoulder to shoulder in quiet conversation—"—trying to keep everyone safe."

Perry's voice softened. "I know you are. Just remember — you can't protect everyone forever."

The screen dimmed, and the line cut.

Will sat in silence, staring at the faint reflection of Echo Reef's pulsing light on the wall.

Outside, the wind howled across the frozen hills of Vermont, carrying whispers that no encryption could silence.

——

Washington DC- Senate Select Committee on Intelligence 1000 Hours R

It was ten weeks after EIDOLON and room 216 in the Hart Senate Office Building had the particular stillness of places where careers end in silence.

Closed session which meant no cameras, no pesky press pool and no staff beyond the cleared aides seated against the walls with their notebooks and their careful expressions. The overhead lighting was the institutional kind—flat, without mercy—and it fell equally on the senators arranged in their curved arc and on the single witness seated at the table below them.

Helena Quinn had testified before this committee eleven times. She had learned, over those eleven appearances, that the most dangerous questions were never the aggressive ones. Aggression she could redirect. It was the quiet, genuinely confused questions that cut deepest — the ones asked by people who had finally done the math and couldn't make it balance.

Senator Carl Brethwaite of Maine was not an aggressive man. He was seventy-one, a former state attorney general, and he had served on this committee for nine years with the patient, methodical attention of someone who understood that most of what he was told was incomplete and that his job was to find the shape of what was missing.

He had found it this morning.

He looked down at the document in front of him — classified, eyes only, the summary assessment Helena's office had provided — and then looked up at her.

"Director Quinn," he said, in the tone of a man who had rehearsed the question and still wasn't sure he wanted the answer. "The committee has been informed that a significant body of intelligence assessments, produced between 2021 and 2024, contained corrupted source data. Specifically, data relating to the People's Republic of China's quantum computing capabilities."

"That is correct, Senator."

"And that these assessments informed budget recommendations to this committee during that same period."

"Also correct."

Brethwaite set the document down. Folded his hands. "I'm going to ask you something, and I want you to understand I'm not asking to assign blame. I'm asking because I need to understand what we're sitting with."

Helena held his gaze. "Of course."

"How many programs," he said, "did we reduce, restructure, or eliminate during those three years — because we believed the United States was already behind the curve on quantum development?"

The room went very still.

Helena had known this question was coming. She had known it since the morning SYBIL completed the decryption and the full scope of Zhengyi became clear. She had drafted three versions of an answer in the weeks since. None of them were adequate.

"Senator, I can provide the committee with a full classified accounting—"

"I'm asking you now," Brethwaite said, not unkindly. "Roughly. A number. A sense of scale."

Helena looked at him. Then she said, "Fourteen programs were restructured or had funding reduced during that window. Of those, four were paused entirely pending reassessment. Two of the four have since been restarted."

"And the other two?"

"The teams dispersed," Helena said. "Key personnel moved to the private sector or to allied nation programs. Reconstituting them would require—" she paused, choosing the word carefully— "significant effort."

Brethwaite nodded slowly. He wasn't surprised. That was somehow worse.

"So we made decisions," he said, "based on a picture of the world that was deliberately falsified. And some of those decisions can't be undone."

"That is an accurate summary, Senator."

The silence that followed was the kind the room was built for.

Senator Diane Okafor of Virginia, two seats down, leaned forward. She was younger than Brethwaite, sharper in her impatience. "Director Quinn, can you tell us who is responsible for identifying the corruption in these assessments?"

"I can tell you that the identification was the result of a classified counterintelligence operation. The personnel involved cannot be named in this setting."

"Can they be named in any setting?"

"Some of them," Helena said carefully, "cannot be named at all."

Okafor sat back, something moving across her face that wasn't quite frustration. It was the expression of someone confronting, not for the first time, the specific helplessness of oversight without access.

Brethwaite picked up his pen, turned it once in his fingers, set it back down.

"Director Quinn," he said finally, "I want the full accounting. Every program. Every decision point. Every dollar we moved because of assessments we now know were contaminated." He paused. "Not because I want to relegate it. But because if we don't understand what it cost us, we'll have no basis for understanding what we owe the people who fixed it."

Helena looked at him for a long moment.

"I'll have it to the committee within thirty days," she said.

She meant it. That was the part no one in the room could know, that somewhere in Vermont, in a facility that did not officially exist, the people who had fixed it were already back at work. That the debt Brethwaite was gesturing toward would never appear in any ledger he was cleared to read. That some costs were paid in currencies the committee would never see.

The gavel came down softly.

Helena gathered her materials and walked out into the corridor, where the light was slightly warmer and the air smelled of old carpet and coffee.

Fourteen programs. Two teams gone. She had known the number for ten weeks, and it had not gotten smaller in the saying of it aloud.

She put on her coat. Her hands were steady. Today that felt like its own kind of loss.

She walked toward the exit, already composing the accounting in her head — the one she could give them, and the one she never could.

CHAPTER FIFTY-FOUR

Standing Down

Moscow, Yasenevo Headquarters (SVR Directorate S)

The room smelled of ozone and cigarette smoke.

Kir Smirnov stood by the window, staring through the fogged glass toward the Moscow skyline, his reflection fractured by the frost. Behind him, a muted television looped a Western news broadcast—"U.S. intelligence sources confirm heightened security measures following the attempted assassination of a civilian scientist..."

Civilian. Scientist.

They were so careful with their lies.

His aide, a thin man with the hollow eyes of someone who never slept, placed a fresh report on the table.

"Comms from the Montréal cell, sir. The target's trail ends in Burlington. Local trackers report no confirmed visuals."

Smirnov didn't move.

"'No confirmed visuals' is a euphemism for failure."

"Yes, sir."

He turned, pacing slowly to the table, the faint echo of his boots on the marble floor underscoring each word.

"Satellite telemetry?"

"Interference near the border. We believe she may have been moved south."

"South?" Smirnov asked, almost to himself. "There's nothing south but trees, lakes... and Americans."

He stopped at the edge of the desk and leaned forward, scanning the report. A dozen pages of nothing.

"Sir," the aide ventured, "it's possible the Americans moved her under domestic intelligence.

There are indications of an ACIC operation in Vermont. NSA intercepts confirm spikes in Fort Meade traffic correlated to the same window."

Smirnov's eyes lifted. "ACIC..."

He said the acronym like an insult.

He reached for a pen and drew a thin line across the map pinned to the wall—from Montréal to Lake Champlain, then east, toward the Atlantic.

"Too neat," he murmured. "Too quick. She didn't vanish. She was erased."

The aide hesitated. "Sir, if we initiate another pursuit—"

"No." Smirnov's voice was sharp enough to cut air. "They want us to chase a ghost. They've already staged the kill. We'd be walking into their theater."

He tapped the map once with the pen.

"They think this buys them time. It doesn't. Not this time."

His hand lingered over the line tracing the river toward the sea.

"She's alive. And somewhere, she's still working for them."

The aide said nothing. He didn't need to.

Smirnov's reflection stared back at him in the glass—a man who'd spent too long playing chess with people who preferred poker. He'd underestimated Will Morgan once. He wouldn't do it again.

He turned away from the window.

"Recall Sunflower. Delete the trail. No more chatter through Montréal. We go quiet. Completely quiet."

"Yes, sir."

Smirnov adjusted his cufflinks, the movement almost meditative.

"Let them believe they've won. When they bring her back into the light... we'll be waiting."

He looked again at the television, where the news anchor's words were swallowed by static.

"A thin smile touched the corner of his mouth."

"Even ghosts," he said to himself, "cast shadows."

——

Nusquam VT 0400 Hours R

The convoy wound its way through the narrow, snow-dusted backroads, headlights cutting across frost and shadow.

By the time they reached Nusquam, dawn was a pale promise behind the mountains.

The compound slept—or pretended to. Only the LED security markers along the perimeter fence pulsed faintly in the cold.

Will led her through the access tunnel—the low hum of the biometric door and the soft hydraulic sighs of the airlock filling the silence.

It had been months since she last saw this place, yet nothing had changed: the scent of ozone and metal polish, the echo of distant systems breathing underground, the sterile beauty of isolation.

But something had changed.

Her place in it.

When the inner door slid open, Nemo was waiting. He stood beside a console, sleeves rolled, eyes shadowed from too many nights without rest. He didn't speak. Didn't move.

The silence between them stretched taut, charged with everything unspoken.

Gloria found her voice first. "You knew."

He nodded once, faintly. "Will told me when it was safe."

His tone was quiet—precise—but the edges softened by something almost human.

She took a step closer, searching his expression. "How much did you know?"

"Enough to miss you," he said simply.

The words stopped her cold.

In the sterile light, she saw the faint tremor of exhaustion at the corner of his mouth—or was it emotion? Nemo was a master of calm, of systems and logic, but this was something fragile.

She swallowed. "I didn't think I'd come back."

He tilted his head slightly, eyes holding hers. "You always come back. Equilibrium demands it."

It was the kind of answer only Nemo could give—half science, half faith. And somehow, it was enough.

She didn't move. Neither did he.

Somewhere down the corridor, Will's footsteps receded—the small mercy of a man who knew when to leave a room.

"Nemo." Her voice was barely above the hum of the airlock. "They had a rifle on the bridge in Burlington. Forty-eight hours ago I was a body they hadn't found yet."

"I know."

"Then say it." She didn't know where the words came from. "Say whatever you've been holding back. Because I spent the drive here counting the things I never told you, and I'm tired of running probabilities on my own."

He was quiet long enough that she thought she'd misread him. Then he stepped around the console.

"I've run every probability I can think of." His voice was lower now, stripped of the lab. "Every variable. Every outcome where you don't walk through that door again. I don't like the math."

"Then change it."

"I'm trying."

He closed the last of the distance. One hand came up, careful, like he was approaching something that might still vanish—the back of her fingers, her wrist, the line of her jaw. She felt the tremor in him and understood, finally, that the calm he wore in every room was a discipline, not a temperament.

"Gloria."

"Genevieve," she said. "When it's you, it's Genevieve."

He kissed her then. Not the reverent thing he might have imagined in some quieter version of this night—something rougher, more honest, "the kiss of a man who had spent every month of her absence rehearsing this and was done with rehearsals." Her hands found his collar. The hum of the facility fell away.

When they drew apart, his forehead rested against hers. He breathed out once, slowly.

"This one keeps repeating," he said.

"What does?"

"The probability. The one where you come back. It's the only outcome the math forgives."

She almost laughed—almost cried. "You always did know how to ruin a romantic moment with a footnote."

"I'll work on it."

Somewhere behind the glass, the cooling stacks shifted in their slow mechanical breathing. Nusquam slept on. And for the first time since Montréal, since the bridge, since the long careful death the agency had built around her, Genevieve let herself believe she had actually come home.

CHAPTER FIFTY-FIVE

Standing the Watch

Nusquam Core Lab-Six Weeks Later 0020 Hours R

The lab was almost silent except for the rhythmic hum of the cooling stacks and the low digital murmur of Echo Reef running its final diagnostics.

Rows of quantum servers blinked in a slow pulse, like some great machine breathing in its sleep.

Genevieve stood at the glass wall, watching the simulation bloom across the monitor, a cloud of color and light twisting in elegant symmetry. After weeks of calibration and sleepless nights, the lattice had finally settled into the shape they'd been chasing.

Nemo approached slowly, a steaming mug in each hand. He passed her one without ceremony.

"Two errors in twelve trillion cycles," he said. "The machine's practically singing."

"You sound almost proud."

"Almost." He studied the display. "But I think the system's learning faster than I am."

She leaned her shoulder lightly against his. He didn't move away.

The machine behind them chimed softly. Echo Reef had reached stability.

Nemo glanced down at her, the faintest lift at the corner of his mouth, the closest thing to peace either of them had known in years.

"It already has," he said.

-The End -

Thanks for reading

If you enjoyed The Loyal Traitor, consider leaving a review.

Even a few words help other readers discover the series—and allow the story to continue.

goodreads amazon books

Join the Watchtower Network

For updates on upcoming releases, exclusive previews, and intelligence briefings from the world of Watchtower:

Visit: spyscribe.com

Subscribe: https://spyscribe.com/newsletter-sign-up/

Stay informed.

FACEBOOK GROUP: WATCHTOWER COMMAND POST

https://spyscribe.substack.com/

Acknowledgments

This novel would not have been possible without the people who question assumptions, challenge conventional thinking, and insist on getting the details right.

To the professionals from the intelligence, military, law enforcement, and legal communities whose knowledge and perspective, shared through their writings, thank you. Your insights helped shape the decisions, constraints, and consequences that drive this story.

To the friends, colleagues, and early readers who offered thoughtful criticism and honest feedback, thank you for helping make this book better.

I also owe a special literary debt to the authors and researchers whose works are listed below. Their scholarship, historical analysis, and dedication to understanding the world informed much of the background that made this novel possible.

And finally, to those who understand that loyalty and betrayal are often separated by perspective, circumstance, and timing—this story is for you.

This version reads a bit more professional and literary while preserving the spirit of your original acknowledgment.

- Tradecraft, Tactics, and Dirty Tricks by Sean M. Wiswesser
- The CIA At War by Ronald Kessler
- A Spy's Guide To Thinking by John Braddock
- The CIA Book Club by Charlie English
- Spycraft for Thriller Writers by Edward Mickoll
- Key Figures In Espionage by Piper Bayard & Jay Holmes
- Spycraft Essentials by Piper Bayard & Jay Holmes
- Biohazard by Ken Albeck
- Spycraft Secrets by Nigel West
- Alan Turing: The Enigma by Andrew Hodge

WATCHTOWER SERIES

In Series Order

Radiant Sentry
The Loyal Traitor
Spy Legacy (July 2026)
Quid Pro Quo (September 2026)
VIRULENT (December 2026)
Q DAY (2027)
Obsidian Ledger (2027)
Borrowed Light (2027)
Private Treason (2027)

Short Stories

Will Morga: Quiet Leadership
Grace Roberts: Empath
Sara Brandt: Becoming Vesper
Cecil Brandon: Eyes in the Night
Cathy Wang: ECHO
Rick Huang: Expected Value
Claire Rourke: Obsidian Ledger
Morgan's Mustangs

About the Author

Charles M. Wayne draws on more than fifty years of experience in the global financial markets to craft high-stakes espionage thrillers.

His Watchtower Series centers on the Army Counterintelligence Command—newly empowered with full law enforcement authority where military or national defense is concerned—making it uniquely positioned to investigate threats both at home and abroad, with the power to act on what it finds.

His work blends the slow-burn precision of John le Carré with the scale and intensity of Tom Clancy

Chrysalis Architecture

The following schematic was developed by Dr. Adrian Keller (cryptonym: PYTHAGORAS) and deployed by Watchtower Operations during the events described herein. It is reproduced here in summary form. Operational details, target identifiers, and attribution data have been withheld.

Source: ACIC internal reference document, Watchtower Operations Division. Originally classified TOP SECRET // SCI // NOFORN. Approved for limited release.

OPERATIONAL OVERVIEW

Chrysalis is a ten-phase deception architecture designed to draw an adversarial intruder into a controlled environment, profile their behavior, capture their exfiltration attempt, and produce attributable evidence without exposing the targeted assets. The architecture is sequential but adaptive. Phases may overlap. SYBIL telemetry governs phase transitions.

PHASE SEQUENCE

#	Phase	Function	Method
1	BAIT	Seed credible content	Plausible dataset, draft document, or artifact. Believable over flashy. Provokes curiosity, not suspicion.
2	PATH	Open a visible entry point	Exposed development node or dormant account presented as operational oversight. Funnels entry without triggering caution.
3	MIRROR	Replicate familiar environment	Ticketing systems, share drives, colleague directories. Comfort encourages deeper engagement.
4	BREADCRUMB	Draw intruder inward	Each artifact references the next. Movement spirals toward the core rather than outward toward exit.
5	TELEMETRY	Build behavioral profile	Passive collection of timing, navigation patterns, and avoidance behaviors. Profile assembles without intruder awareness.
6	FORK	Force identifying choices	Decision points designed to expose tradecraft. Brute-force action versus lateral movement constitutes a fingerprint.
7	RECURSION PAIN	Induce stress response	Breadcrumb paths loop back. Intruder confronts evidence of own actions. Stress increases improvisation; improvisation exposes tooling.
8	FAÇADE	Capture exfiltration attempt	Synthetic outbound channel accepts transfer. Intruder believes operation succeeded. Architecture retains metadata and transfer trail.
9	ISOLATE	Contain and sustain	Trigger-based severance of paths to actual assets. Session snapshot preserved. Controlled illusions maintained to extend exposure.
10	REVEAL	Package for action	Session record, transfer headers, and behavioral profile compiled. Outputs routed to partner handoff, handler baiting, or legal action as directed.

OPERATING PRINCIPLES

Pride is the lever. The architecture assumes the intruder will interpret success as competence rather than permission. Comfort, recognition, and apparent achievement are the mechanisms by which voluntary cooperation is produced.

The trap is the environment. No single phase contains the operation. Removal of any one phase reduces yield but does not collapse the architecture.

SYBIL governs adaptation. Real-time telemetry permits phase compression, repetition, or skip based on intruder behavior. Static deployment is not recommended.

Pythagoras maintained that the architecture was not a trap but a conversation. "You let them ask the questions," he is recorded as saying. "You only choose which answers they find."

Acronyms

Due to the nature of the subject matter there are numerous acronyms used throughout.

ACIC	Army Counterintelligence Command	Established in 2021, the ACIC is the Army's primary counterintelligence organization, responsible for defending against foreign intelligence entities and protecting Army assets and personnel worldwide
DIA	Defense Intelligence Agency Counterintelligence	The DIA employs counterintelligence officers to safeguard the nation from foreign adversarial threats, conducting activities like insider threat investigations and technical operations.
CIA	Central Intelligence Agency	Civilian foreign intelligence service of the United States federal government tasked with advancing national security through collecting and analyzing intelligence from around the world and conducting covert operations.
CIMIC	Counterintelligence Mission Center	The CIMC protects CIA operations from compromise by foreign adversaries through analysis of their capabilities, intentions, and activities.
DARPA	Defense Advanced Research Projects Agency	U.S. Department of Defense agency, established in 1958, tasked with creating breakthrough technologies for national security and preventing technological surprise. It acts as a high-risk, high-reward, "idea factory" that funds research in AI, biotechnology, and robotics to maintain U.S. technological superiority
DHS	Department of Homeland Security	Includes the Office of Intelligence and Analysis and Coast Guard Intelligence.
DOJ	Department of Justice	Includes the Federal Bureau of Investigation (FBI) and the Drug Enforcement Administration (DEA).
DOS	Department of State	US Department of State
DOT	Department of Treasury	US Department of Treasury
FBICD or CD	FBI Counterintelligence Division	This division within the Federal Bureau of Investigation is responsible for protecting the United States from foreign intelligence operations and espionage within the country.
GEOINT	Geospatial Intelligence	The analysis and interpretation of imagery and geospatial information to describe and visualize physical features and activities on Earth
HUMINT	Human Intelligence	The collection of information from human sources through interpersonal contact, interviews, and espionage
IARPA	Intelligence Advanced Research Projects Activity	Organization, within the Office of the Director of National Intelligence, that is responsible for leading research to overcome difficult challenges facing the United States

		Intelligence Community.
INR	Bureau of Intelligence and Research	Primarily an analytical agency within the State Department,
INSCOM	U.S. Army Intelligence and GEU Security Command	Executes mission command of operational intelligence and security forces; conducts and synchronizes worldwide multidiscipline and all-source
NCSC	National Counterintelligence and Security Center	As part of the Office of the Director of National Intelligence (ODNI), the NCSC leads the integration of U.S. government counterintelligence and security activities aimed at countering threats to national security information and assets.
NOFORN	Not for release to foreign nationals	Prohibiting information from being shared with non-U.S. citizens, including foreign governments and organizations. It is applied to both classified and certain "Sensitive But Unclassified" (SBU) information, with strict restrictions on who can access it.
NGA	National Geospatial-Intelligence Agency	Provides geospatial intelligence (GEOINT)
NRO	National Reconnaissance Office	Designs, builds, and operates the nation's intelligence satellites
NSA	National Security Agency	Specializes in signals intelligence (SIGINT) and cybersecurity.
ODNI	Office of the Director of National Intelligence	U.S. agency that leads and integrates the country's Intelligence Community (IC). ODNI's mission is to integrate intelligence to protect the nation by focusing on areas like counterterrorism, counterintelligence, counterproliferation, and cyber integration. Role and function
ONI	Office of Naval Intelligence	Focuses on naval intelligence related to foreign scientific and technological research and foreign naval forces.
SIGINT	Signals Intelligence	The collection and analysis of signals to gain information on foreign targets for national security
TAO	Office of Tailored Access Operation	Cyber-warfare intelligence-gathering unit of the National Security Agency (NSA).

Five Eyes

Originated during World War II from a U.S.–U.K. signals-intelligence (SIGINT) sharing pact known as the UKUSA Agreement (1946). The alliance formalized deep cooperation in the collection, analysis, and exchange of intelligence—especially electronic and communications intelligence—among the five countries.

Core Characteristics

- Scope: Primarily signals intelligence (SIGINT), but extended to human intelligence (HUMINT), cyber defense, counterintelligence, and surveillance coordination.
- Integration: The member nations maintain joint databases, shared collection networks, and interoperable classification standards—allowing analysts to access and cross-correlate intercepted communications under shared protocols.

Agencies Involved

- United States: NSA (National Security Agency)
- United Kingdom: GCHQ (Government Communications Headquarters)
- Canada: CSE (Communications Security Establishment)
- Australia: ASD (Australian Signals Directorate)
- New Zealand: GCSB (Government Communications Security Bureau)

Function

Five Eyes countries divide global monitoring zones, exchanging raw intercepts and analytic outputs almost in real time. They also cooperate on cyber operations, encryption standards, and counter-espionage investigations. This alliance forms the foundation of the Western intelligence-sharing ecosystem, later expanded through partnerships such as:

- Nine Eyes (adds Denmark, France, Netherlands, Norway)
- Fourteen Eyes (adds Germany, Belgium, Italy, Spain, Sweden)

Foreign Intelligence Agencies

A foreign intelligence service is an agency tasked with gathering intelligence outside its own country's borders. Several countries have prominent foreign intelligence agencies, including the CIA (US), MI6 (UK), Mossad (Israel), and DGSE (France). These agencies play a crucial role in national security by collecting information on foreign governments, organizations, and individuals. Here's a list of some notable foreign intelligence services:

Acronym	Name	Country	Responsibilities
ASIS	Australian Secret Intelligence Service	Australia	Australia's foreign intelligence service
DGI	Dirección de Inteligencia	Cuba	State intelligence agency
BND	Bundesnachrichtendienst	Germany	Germany's foreign intelligence service
CSIS	Canadian Security Intelligence Service	Canada	Foreign intelligence service and security agency
DGSE	Directorate-General for External Security	France	France's primary foreign intelligence agency,
FSB	Federal'naya sluzhba bezopasnosti Rossiyskoy Federatsii	Russia	Federal Security Service
GRU	Glavnoye Razvedyvatel'noye Upravleniye	Russia	Military intelligence; counterpart and rival to SVR.
ISI	Inter-Services Intelligence	Pakistan	Pakistan's premier intelligence agency
MI6	Secret Intelligence Service	United Kingdom	Foreign intelligence agency
MOSSAD	Institute for Intelligence and Special Operations	Israel	intelligence gathering and covert operations,
MSS	Ministry of State Security	China	China's main intelligence agency
PLA	People' Liberation Army	China	The Military maintains its own intelligence service focusing on military collection, cyber warfare, and strategic reconnaissance
RAW	Research and Analysis Wing	India	India's external intelligence agency
SVR	Sluzhba Vneshney Razvedki Rossii	Russia	Russian foreign intelligence service
UFWD	United Front Work department	China	CCP organization that manages co-opts foreign elites, an monitors overseas diaspora Chinese communities to neutralize perceived threats.

Military Time Zones (NATO)

The U.S. military uses time zone letters from the NATO phonetic alphabet. Spelling: "Alpha" replaces Alfa; "Juliet" replaces Juliett.

The letter J is skipped in sequence.to prevent confusion with "I" and because some alphabets lacked it.

Special Designations: Z (Zulu): Greenwich Mean Time / Coordinated Universal Time (UTC ± 00:00). J (Juliet): Local time at the observer's position.

Usage Example: 0600 R = 6:00 a.m. in UTC – 5. Pronounced "zero six hundred Romeo."

Letter	Time Zone	UTC Offset	Location Example
A	Alpha	UTC+01:00	Berlin, Paris, Madrid, Rome
B	Bravo	UTC+02:00	Athens, Cairo, Helsinki, Kyiv
C	Charlie	UTC+0300	Moscow, Riyadh, Baghdad
D	Delta	UTC+04:00	Dubai, Baku, Yerevan
E	Echo	UTC+05:00	Islamabad, Karachi, Tashkent
F	Foxtrot	UTC+06:00	Almaty, Dhaka, Bishkek
G	Golf	UTC+-7:00	Bangkok, Hanoi, Jakarta
H	Hotel	UTC+08:00	Beijing, Singapore, Perth
I	India	UTC+09:00	Tokyo, Seoul, Pyongyang
J	Local	Local	Observer's Local Time
K	Kilo	UTC+10:00	Sydney, Vladivostok, Guam
L	Lima	UTC+11:00	Honiara, Nouméa, Magadan
M	Mike	UTC+12:00	Suva, Anadyr, Funafuti
N	November	UTC-01:00	Azores, Cape Verde
O	Oscar	UTC-02:00	South Georgia and South Sandwich Islands
P	Papa	UTC-03:00	Buenos Aires, Montevideo, Nuuk
Q	Quebec	UTC-04:00	Caracas, Halifax, Manaus
R	Romeo	UTC-05:00	New York, Bogotá, Lima, Miami
S	Sierra	UTC-06:00	Mexico City, Chicago, Guatemala City
T	Tango	UTC-0700	Denver, Phoenix, Calgary
U	Uniform	UTC-08:00	Los Angeles, Vancouver, Tijuana
V	Victor	UTC-9:00	Anchorage, Gambier Islands
W	Whiskey	UTC-10:00	Honolulu, Papeete
X	X-ray	UTC-11:00	Pago Pago, Niue
Y	Yankee	UTC-1200	Baker Island
Z	Zulu	UTC-00-00	London, Lisbon, Accra

U.S. Military Defense Conditions

Defense Condition (DEFCON) levels are a five-tier system used by the U.S. military to signal readiness for national security threats, ranging from DEFCON 5 (normal peacetime posture) to DEFCON 1 (maximum readiness for war). The scale runs in reverse—lower numbers indicate higher alert status. The U.S. military is currently at DEFCON 5.

Level	**Readiness**	**Exercise Term**
DEFCON 5	Normal readiness	Normal (Peace)
DEFCON 4	Increased readiness	Round House
DEFCON 3	Enhanced readiness (Air Force ready to mobilize in 15 minutes)	Fast Paced
DEFCON 2	High readiness (forces ready to deploy in under six hours)	Round House
DEFCON 1	Maximum readiness (war is imminent or underway)	Cocked Pistol

U.S. Security Classification Levels

Level	Potential Damage from Unauthorized Disclosure	**Examples of Damages**
Top Secret (TS)	Exceptionally grave damage to national security.	Armed hostilities against the U.S. or its allies, disruption of foreign relations, compromise of vital national defense plans or intelligence operations, or disclosure of critical technological developments.
Secret (S)	Serious damage to national security.	Disruption of foreign relations, significant impairment of a national security program or policy, or revelation of significant military plans or intelligence operations.
Confidential (C)	Damage to national security.	Revelation of strength of military forces, or disclosure of technical information on classified munitions of war.

Other Designations

- Special Access Programs (SAPs) and Sensitive Compartmented Information (SCI): These are additional controls that impose "need-to-know" restrictions beyond a standard clearance level, even for Top Secret information. This information is protected within specific, compartmented systems.

- Restricted Data (RD) and Formerly Restricted Data (FRD): These classifications are specific to atomic energy (nuclear) information and are used by the Department of Energy (DOE), often in conjunction with a Q or L clearance.

- Controlled Unclassified Information (CUI): This is a government-wide program for handling sensitive but unclassified information that requires protection based on law, federal policy, or government-wide agreement. This replaced older agency-specific designations like "For Official Use Only" (FOUO).

Security classifications can be assigned by officials with original classification authority (OCA), which includes the President, Vice President, and heads of executive agencies, or by officials to whom they have delegated this authority. For non-government organizations, the responsibility typically falls on the individual who created or owns the data, as they are best positioned to understand the information's sensitivity.

Foreign Space Weapons Capabilities

Chinese Space Weapons Capabilities	
Direct-Ascent ASATs	China's SC-19 missile successfully tested in 2007—destroying one of their own defunct satellites with a kinetic kill vehicle. Modified ballistic missile platforms provide the delivery systems.
Co-Orbital ASATs	Developing satellites capable of maneuvering close to targets—either for surveillance or direct engagement. Some may be equipped with robotic arms for physical manipulation or sabotage."
Electronic Warfare and DEWs	Systems to jam satellite communications and navigation signals. Directed-energy systems for sensor blinding and permanent damage to satellite optics.
Proximity Operations (RPO)	Chinese RPO-capable satellites have been conducting surveillance or probing defenses of U.S. and allied assets.
Cyber Capabilities	actively developing cyberattack strategies targeting satellite command-and-control systems, uplinks, and terrestrial support networks.
Other Capabilities	China's long-term objective is full-spectrum dominance of space."

Russian Space Weapons Capabilities	
Kinetic ASATs	Russia has launched satellites, such as Cosmos 2576, equipped with the ability to intercept and destroy targets in orbit.
Polyus Project	Legacy Soviet-era programs. Polyus was designed to house a laser weapon.
Almaz Project	Almaz, an orbital weapons platform equipped with a rapid-fire autocannon.
Cosmos 2543	"Demonstrated a non-destructive ASAT test—believed to be a precursor for more aggressive capabilities."
Nesting Doll "Matryoshka"	Inspired by traditional Russian nesting dolls, involves one satellite releasing a smaller satellite, which in turn releases another, and another. Demonstrated in 2019 by releasing a smaller satellite from a larger one, which then performed maneuvers near a US satellite.

Comparison of Title 10 vs Title 50 Authorities		
Aspect	Title 10 — Armed Forces	Title 50 — War & National Defense (Intelligence)
Primary Domain	Military operations	Intelligence & covert action
Who Operates	Department of Defense (Army, Navy, Air Force, Marine Corps, Space Force)	Intelligence Community (CIA, NSA, DIA, NRO, NGA + DoD intel elements)
Legal Purpose	Organize, train, equip, and employ U.S. armed forces in overt missions	Collect, analyze, and conduct covert or clandestine operations to protect national security
Chain of Command	President → Secretary of Defense → Combatant Commanders	President → Director of National Intelligence / CIA Director
Typical Oversight	Congressional Armed Services Committees	Congressional Intelligence Committees ("Gang of Eight" for covert findings)
Operational Character	Overt / acknowledged military activity under Law of Armed Conflict (LOAC)	Clandestine or covert activity where U.S. involvement may be deniable
Disclosure Requirements	Actions are publicly reportable to Congress and often acknowledged by DoD	Activities may remain classified; require Presidential Finding and briefing to Congressional leadership
Examples of Authority Use	Combat deployments, JSOC raids, cyber defense, force protection	Espionage, foreign HUMINT, SIGINT, covert action, psychological operations
Legal Basis for Force or Collection	Uses of armed force authorized by Congress (AUMF) or Commander-in-Chief powers	Covert action authorized by Presidential Finding under 50 U.S.C. § 3093
Public Acknowledgment	Uniformed service members acting under U.S. flag	Deniable actors or foreign assets under direction of U.S. intelligence officers
Inter-Title Coordination	DoD components may support intelligence under Title 50 if formally tasked	Intelligence agencies may request DoD support under Title 10 for operational cover or logistics
Common Gray Area	Special Operations conducted with CIA direction (e.g., bin Laden raid 2011)	Military intelligence units operating abroad with collection taskings that blur jurisdiction
Oversight Objective	Ensure proper use of military force and readiness	Ensure lawful conduct of intelligence and protection of civil liberties
Key Risk if Misapplied	Violation of Posse Comitatus or engagement without authorization	Unauthorized covert action or domestic surveillance without FISA authority

Espionage Crimes - 18 U.S. Codes 792-798

Title	Description	Penalty
18 U.S.C. § 793 (f)	mishandling of national-defense information through gross negligence or unauthorized transmission.	imprisonment for up to 10 years, or both
18 U.S.C. 792	Harboring or Concealing Individuals	fines, imprisonment for up to 10 years, or both.
18 U.S.C. 793	Gathering, Transmitting, or Losing Defense Information	fines, imprisonment for up to 10 years, or both.
18 U.S.C. 794	Delivering Defense Information to Foreign Governments	life imprisonment or even the death penalty in cases where espionage results in the death of any U.S. agent or affects critical defense systems like nuclear weaponry
18 U.S.C. 795	Photographing and Sketching Defense Installations	shall be fined under this title or imprisoned not more than one year, or both
18 U.S.C. 796	Use of Aircraft for Photographing Defense Installations	shall be fined or imprisoned not more than one year, or both
18 U.S.C. 797	Publishing or Selling Images of Defense Installations	shall be fined or imprisoned not more than one year, or both
18 U.S.C. 798	Disclosure of Classified Information	up to 10 years in prison, substantial fines, or both

"Pay-to-Play" Bribery Laws

The US "pay-to-play" bribery laws are primarily found in 18 U.S. Code § 201, which prohibits the corrupt giving, offering, or promising of "anything of value" to influence an official act. Other related laws include 18 U.S. Code § 666 for bribery in programs receiving federal funds. The term "pay-to-play" refers to a specific type of bribery where a political contribution or payment is made in exchange for preferential treatment, such as winning a government contract.

Key federal statutes

18 U.S. Code § 201: This is the primary statute for federal bribery. It criminalizes the corrupt giving of "anything of value" to a public official or a witness to influence an official act.

Definition of "thing of value": This is broadly defined to include not just money, but also gifts, meals, travel, entertainment, or anything else that has commercial or subjective value to the recipient.

Distinction between bribery and gratuity: Bribery requires proof of a direct, quid pro quo connection between the payment and the official act, and carries a higher penalty (up to 15 years in prison). A gratuity, which is a payment made "for or because of" an official act but not in direct exchange for it, is punishable by up to 2 years in prison.

18 U.S. Code § 666: This statute covers theft and bribery concerning programs receiving federal funds.

26 U.S. Code § 162(c)(1): This tax law prohibits the deduction of payments made as bribes or kickbacks.

Key concepts

"Pay-to-play": This refers to a practice where political contributions or other payments are made with the expectation of receiving a benefit, such as a government contract.

"Official act": This refers to any decision or action by a public official in their official capacity, or any matter coming before them in their official capacity.

"Corrupt intent": This is a critical element in bribery cases, meaning the person had a corrupt intent to influence the official act.

"Quid pro quo": This means "something for something" and is a key element in a bribery case, where a payment is made in direct exchange for an official act.

"Gratuity": This is a payment made "for or because of" an official act, but not in direct exchange for it. It is still illegal, but the penalties are less severe than for bribery.

www.ingramcontent.com/pod-product-compliance
Lightning Source LLC
LaVergne TN
LVHW090547110826
845146LV00001B/53

* 9 7 9 8 9 9 3 6 1 9 3 5 4 *